Hepburn's Necklace

"Second chances, twists of fate, and a glittering Lake Como backdrop combine to create Jan Moran's latest stunning read. Weaving back and forth through time, Moran creates an epic tale of love and loss that will make readers question what might have been. With lyrical prose and unforgettable characters, *Hepburn's Necklace* proves that Jan Moran is a writer at the top of her game." — Kristy Woodson Harvey, *USA Today* Bestselling Author of *Feels Like Falling*

"Jan Moran is the new queen of the epic romance." —Rebecca Forster, *USA Today* Bestselling Author

"A novel that gives fans of romantic sagas a compelling voice to follow." – *Booklist*

The Chocolatier

"A delicious novel, makes you long for chocolate." – *Ciao Tutti*

"A wonderful, smoothly written novel. Full of intrigue, love, secrets, and romance." – *Lekker Lezen*

The Winemakers

"Readers will devour this page-turner as the mystery and passions spin out." – *Library Journal*

"As she did in *Scent of Triumph*, Moran weaves knowledge of wine and winemaking into this intense family drama." – *Booklist*

The Perfumer: Scent of Triumph

"Heartbreaking, evocative, and inspiring, this book is a powerful journey." – Allison Pataki, *New York Times* Bestselling Author of *The Accidental Empress*

"A gripping World War II story of poignant love and devastating, heart-wrenching loss." — Gill Paul, *USA Today* and *Toronto Globe & Mail* Bestselling Author of *The Secret Wife*

"A sweeping saga of one woman's journey through World War II and her unwillingness to give up." — Anita Abriel, Author of *The Light After the War*

"A captivating tale of love, determination and reinvention." — Karen Marin, Givenchy Paris

"A stylish, compelling story of a family. What sets this apart is the backdrop of perfumery that suffuses the story with the delicious aromas – a remarkable feat!" — Liz Trenow, *New York Times* Bestselling Author of *The Forgotten Seamstress*

"Courageous heroine, star-crossed lovers, splendid sense of time and place capturing the unease and turmoil of the 1940s; HEA." — *Heroes and Heartbreakers*

"Jan rivals Danielle Steel at her romantic best." — Allegra Jordan, Author of *The End of Innocence*

Seabreeze Inn and Coral Cottage series

"*Seabreeze Inn* is truly an enjoyable, lovely read that will lift your spirits." — *Silver's Reviews*

"The women are intelligent and strong. At the core of Jan's books is a strong, close-knit family." — *Betty's Reviews*

BOOKS BY JAN MORAN

20th-Century Historical

Hepburn's Necklace

The Chocolatiers

The Winemakers: A Novel of Wine and Secrets

The Perfumer: Scent of Triumph

Contemporary

Coral Cottage

Coral Cafe

Seabreeze Inn

Seabreeze Summer

Seabreeze Sunset

Seabreeze Christmas

Seabreeze Wedding

Flawless

Beauty Mark

Runway

Essence

Style

Sparkle

Hepburn's Necklace

JAN MORAN

HEPBURN'S NECKLACE

JAN MORAN

SUNNY PALMS
PRESS

Library of Congress Cataloging-in-Publication Data

Moran, Jan.

/ by Jan Moran

ISBN (epub) 978-1-951314-16-3

ISBN (softcover) 978-1-64778-038-8

ISBN (hardcover) 978-1-64778-039-5

ISBN (large print) 978-1-64778-021-0

ISBN (audiobook) 978-1-64778-022-7

Cover design and images copyright ZeroMedia GmbH. Adapted by Sleepy Fox Studios

Sunny Palms Press

9663 Santa Monica Blvd STE 1158

Beverly Hills, CA 90210 USA

www.sunnypalmspress.com

www.JanMoran.com

To the memory of Audrey Hepburn…and for all who loved this sweet soul and cherished her work.

PROLOGUE

*R*uby stepped as close to the rocky point as she dared, taking quiet joy in overlooking the shimmering, deep blue water that filled the verdant fjord stretching before her. To the north soared snow-capped Italian and Swiss peaks. On either side of the lake, palms, firs, and mulberry trees clustered in villages tucked at the base of steeply sloping hillsides, where yellow daffodils and violet crocuses bloomed in abundance.

Ruby lifted her chin to the breeze the locals called *Breva*, Lake Como's afternoon winds from the south. She ran a hand over her dark red, shoulder-length coiffure. Though she had a top stylist who faithfully matched her trademark color, her hair was hardly the luxuriant, glossy mane that had earned her childhood nickname.

As a girl, her hair was so dark and shiny her mother called it ruby. The name stuck because Lucille Eunice was too long to call out. For her stage name, Ruby adopted her mother's maiden name of Raines. She'd thought it sounded so fancy and elegant —and her talent agent had thought her surname of Smith was too ordinary for an actress.

While the small, private tour group of retired film actors chattered on behind her, she folded an arm across her torso, recalling the feeling of Niccolò's arms twined around her as they'd stood on this very spot in Bellagio. His strong hands had spanned her narrow waist. At the memory, a fine, exquisite feeling filled her chest. Her love for him had never wavered, never dimmed.

This type of love was all that Ruby wished for her niece Ariana. Yet, Ruby feared Ariana might not have the chance.

My dearest, my Niccolò. They had met in the summer of 1952 on the set of *Roman Holiday*, which remained her favorite film. The story of an independent-thinking, runaway princess who scorns her duties for a magical escape in Rome and a taste of true love never grew old. That film had made Audrey Hepburn a star and, in a roundabout way, launched Ruby's career in film as well.

Placing her hand over the hollow of her neck, she caressed the worn silver pendant that Audrey had given her. Ruby had been moved by her generosity, though that wasn't the primary reason she'd cherished it.

That summer was imprinted on a movie reel in her brain— quite apart from the film shown in theaters.

IT WAS JUNE OF 1952...

Wearing a full, sky-blue skirt with a crisp white shirt and a jaunty scarf at her neck—compliments of the wardrobe supervisor—Ruby stretched out her legs on the Spanish Steps in Rome. The Hassler, a grand hotel where Audrey Hepburn, Gregory Peck, and Eddie Albert were staying, loomed above the steep stone steps.

In the summer heat, Ruby rolled her sleeves high on her arms as the wardrobe assistant had instructed and tried to focus on the script in her lap. She had to memorize the lines for her short scene.

Ruby rubbed her stomach, which was tied up in knots as tight as the bowlines her father had taught her to tie on the ranch back in Texas. Here she was, living the dream she'd imagined. *A real speaking part in a film in Italy!* She could hardly believe her good fortune. Ruby had her mother to thank for this adventure.

Just below her in the piazza, Mr. Wyler and his assistant director conferred. Miss Hepburn and Mr. Peck were relaxing between takes while their hair and makeup were being refreshed. Grips and gaffers adjusted equipment and lighting. Above them, people watched from railings, and smoke from their cigarettes curled into the warm air. Their chatter would be silenced when filming began again.

A shadow crossed her script.

"Buongiorno, Signorina."

Ruby shielded her eyes and looked up into a pair of incredible blue eyes rimmed with thick, dark lashes and a slash of eyebrows. With sculpted cheekbones and shiny dark hair that framed a strong face, he was the most breathtakingly beautiful man she'd ever seen.

"Hi," she managed to say as her throat constricted.

"Americana?"

"I'm a Texan. The state used to be a republic. For ten years." Silently, she chastised herself. *Why did I say that?* She'd been as nervous as a cottontail rabbit ever since she'd arrived in Rome.

A smile played on his full lips. "I'm Niccolò. Do you mind if I sit with you? We can rehearse together," he added, opening a copy of the script.

"Ruby. Pleased to meet you." His melodic voice made her toes curl with pleasure. "Where did you learn English so well?" she asked.

"I learned a little from my parents, but mostly at the cinema, American films, English films. I love the magical way they make you feel. I've wanted to act—and maybe write—for as long as I can remember. Maybe we're alike that way." He touched her shoulder as he spoke. "And now, here we are, part of that magic, too."

She nodded, barely able to speak. What Niccolò said was exactly what she felt in the depths of her soul, too. "So much alike."

. . .

RUBY BLINKED IN THE BREEZE. THAT SUMMER HAD PROFOUNDLY changed her life. Had it really been that many years ago? Time passed so quickly. She had an urgent matter to address this summer, too—one she'd been dreading for years.

The young Italian tour guide touched her arm. "Signora Raines," he said in a soft, respectful voice, his left eye twitching slightly. "Will you step back from the edge? We would hate to lose you."

"I've lived on the edge all my life, Matteo. Wouldn't this be a stunning place to die?" Sensing the young man's nervousness, Ruby stepped back, her ivory silk palazzo pants rippling in the breeze. "Though not today, I promise."

Matteo was visibly relieved. If he let a famous American film star plunge to her death, he'd probably lose his job, but what a magnificent, dramatic headline that would make. *The Great Ruby Raines Flings Herself from Alpine Precipice.*

Though it was actually a rolling Lombardy hill. Lovely, but not nearly as memorable.

The tour guide turned back to the small gathering. "If Lake Como looks familiar, it's because the films *Casino Royale* and *Ocean's Twelve* were shot here."

Ruby tapped her custom-designed cane—a twisted, aromatic cedarwood design topped with a ruby-eyed silver eagle that she'd commissioned on a return trip to Texas. The press had once dubbed her the Fiery Texan and compared her to Maureen O'Hara and Katharine Hepburn. That was after she'd completed her first western film, *Diary of a Pioneer Woman*, with a famous cowboy movie star.

Actually, that actor made so many passes at her that she'd relished the scripted slaps across his face. He'd earned every one of them, but none of them wiped that self-satisfied smirk off his face. Even after she won awards for Best Actress around the world for that film. At least she had that satisfaction.

Ruby still remembered everything.

She shrugged off the memories and planted her cane on a rock. *Though walking stick sounds more elegant.* While that wasn't quite correct, it was certainly more palatable. All because of an ill-timed step from a curb at home in Palm Springs that left her with a sprained ankle.

Really, she was hardly old enough to depend on a cane.

Ariana had insisted that she take it. "At least take a cane to help your balance, Auntie."

"There's nothing wrong with my balance," Ruby had retorted, though she secretly loved hearing Ariana dote on her. Her sweet, strawberry blond-haired niece had the heart of an angel, though she was often too accommodating.

Ruby nestled the tip of her walking stick into the rocky ground. *Here, right here, is where Niccolò and I planned our future.* Dreams as big as the canopy of sky overhead, pinned in place by snow-capped peaks.

But we were so young, so naïve.

Acting had been her dream ever since she'd seen her first film, *The Yearling*, at the old movie theater. Her mother drove them more than an hour over rutted dirt roads in the rusty Ford pick-up they used on the ranch. They wore their Sunday best, too. Her mother made a new red-gingham dress with navy-blue piping for her.

From the first flicker on the screen, Ruby was immersed in the celluloid saga, identifying with the little boy on screen. A few years later, on a whim, her mother sent photos of Ruby to her sister, Vivienne, who lived in Hollywood and knew a talent agent. Her mother begged her father to let Ruby have a little adventure before she settled down with a husband and children. Before long, Ruby was on a train bound for Hollywood.

On the hillside, Ruby swayed a little, then righted herself with the walking stick. The past often seemed more vibrant than today. Lately, she'd found herself forgetting little things that hardly mattered, a date, or the name of an acquaintance. *Not too bad for a youthful-looking woman of a certain age*, she told herself. She wouldn't admit to a day over sixty-five, at least not to the media. What difference did a few more years make? She didn't feel old, except in her joints on rainy days.

But Ruby remembered everything that had happened in Italy. Reveling in her memories, she lifted her face to the sunshine. A moment later, she felt a tug on her sleeve and turned around.

"*Scusi, Signora.*" Matteo was by her side again.

Ruby lifted a brow. "I promise I'm not contemplating offing myself."

The guide chuckled. "Honestly, I needed a moment myself. Sometimes I forget what a beautiful home we have here." After gazing over the windswept lake, he turned to her. "Did you enjoy yourself in Rome?"

Another guide had led the tour there. "I did. I had a chance to relive an important chapter of my life. My first film, even though my part was cut in final editing. It starred Audrey Hepburn and Gregory Peck, but you're probably too young to know it."

"*Vacanze Romane,* or as you say in America, *Roman Holiday.*" Matteo grinned, tenting his hand against the sun. "It's still very popular here. That must have been an enchanting time."

Ruby smiled. *But not in the way you think.* Securing her emerald-green, print silk scarf that was fluttering in the breeze, she said, "It certainly was. That was the first Hollywood film shot entirely on location in Italy. During those magical weeks, it seemed all of Rome buzzed with excitement. And we had a wonderful group of talented actors and technicians. Everyone knew Gregory Peck, of course. He was already a big star. In fact, he was in the first movie I'd ever seen, *The Yearling.*"

"Who directed the film?" Matteo touched her elbow to steady her.

"William Wyler—Willie to his friends, but Mr. Wyler on the set," Ruby said. "He risked casting a relatively unknown actress who'd been working in England. *Roman Holiday* had been Audrey Hepburn's big break. Mr. Wyler knew she had the potential to be a huge star." Ruby paused. "I miss her so much. I really looked up to her on the set. Aside from being a brilliant actress, Audrey was such a fine woman with a huge heart."

Matteo smiled at her comment. "If you don't mind my saying, you seem awfully young to have been in that film."

"You flatter me." Ruby laughed. "I was barely seventeen, but that film paved my path to success. And after *Roman Holiday* came out in theaters, I went home to Texas and took my family to see it." Amused, she shook her head. "I was in a few scenes as an extra, and you've never heard so much whooping and hollering about that."

Her mother had been ecstatic, though her father didn't approve of her acting. Her mother, Mercy Raines Smith, had spent weeks cajoling her husband to let Ruby go.

"In Rome, did you see any of the places where the movie was filmed?" Matteo asked.

"Oh, yes," Ruby replied, tucking her hand through the crook of his elbow for balance. "We visited the Palazzo Colonna, the grand palace in the last scene of *Roman Holiday*. I strolled the cobblestone streets of Via Margutta, where all the bohemian artist studios were located and found the flat used as Joe's apartment in the film. And then I had lunch at a café with a view of Castel Sant'Angelo and the Tiber River, or the *Tevere*. You might remember that setting. It was the scene of the melee on the barge, where Audrey smashed a guitar over a policeman's head."

"It must have been fun to be there for that."

Ruby chuckled. "We'd had a long night of filming. I was in the scene as an extra, just one of the people dancing. We were all hot and tired, and after Audrey and the other actors crashed into the water at the end of the final take, we all jumped in for a late-night swim in the Tiber. What fun we had."

"Sounds more like a magical summer holiday than work," Matteo said, joining her in laughter.

"Indeed, it was."

In Rome, Ruby had also left the tour group to find the pensione where she had stayed during filming. Outside, she'd gazed up at the second floor, locating the sunny room that had been hers. The building had been renovated, but the narrow staircase where she and Niccolò had chased each other up the stairs was still there. As she'd rubbed her hand over the worn railing, she could almost hear their peals of youthful laughter.

Matteo's phone buzzed, and he silenced it. "I wish I could hear more of your stories, but that's our signal to move on. Maybe you'll share some over dinner tonight?"

"I'd be happy to," she said, smiling.

"It will take me a few minutes to gather everyone," Matteo said.

"I'll wait here, if that's okay." She tapped her cane on the ground. "Don't worry. I'm on stable ground."

As much as Ruby loved Rome, the highlight of this trip was Lago di Como—Lake Como—or Lario, as the Latin poet *Vergilius* or Virgil referred to the magnificent Y-shaped lake. Its beauty had endured through the centuries.

To Ruby, the romance of the region was palpable. Bellagio was perched at the tip of the Larian Triangle. As she recalled, the evening lights glinted like diamonds in the moonlight dusting the surrounding slopes. On either side, the lake's graceful arms cradled the village while orioles trilled their songs.

Ruby lifted her nose to the breeze as it swept across the lake, carrying the scents of a thousand gardens.

Glancing across the lake, she saw villas from centuries past hugging the shoreline. To one side was the village of Tremezzo with the lovely Villa Carlotta. Farther south on the lake, she recalled the stories of Cernobbio with the exquisite Villa d'Este. Yet the other shore and the sweet *comune* of Varenna, where a modest bell tower marked the location of a small church, drew her attention.

So many memories.

Ruby rubbed her arms and turned away, unable to look too long.

Surely a goddess had smiled on Lago di Como, long before humans had discovered its stunning beauty. A memory flitted across Ruby's mind as she recalled Niccolò's description of Lago di Como.

It's a culture of beauty. La cultura del bello.

Ruby had left her heart here long ago. Instead, she had devoted her life to acting, theatre, films, television. When talent agent Joseph Applebaum had gambled on her, he'd guided her into a rapid succession of films. Besides movies, Ruby had also lent her image to cosmetic and fashion advertising campaigns and starred in a long-running television series, racking up awards as she went. Even her signature perfume campaign won a Clio award. Now, she still welcomed occasional roles.

"If only Ariana could experience this," Ruby whispered into the soft breeze. Ariana was her grandniece or great-niece, although Ruby seldom made that distinction because it made her sound ancient. Appearances counted in her industry.

As a child, Ariana had played in Ruby's closets and developed a superb eye for fashion and costume detail. Ariana's mother hadn't condoned her daughter's education in fashion. To tough-minded Mari, only a degree in science or business or engineering was worthy of investment.

When Mari refused to pay for Ariana's study in fashion design, Ruby stepped in, despite Mari's protests. Ruby paid for Ariana's attendance at the Fashion Institute of Design and Merchandising in Los Angeles, where the young woman had blossomed.

Now, Ariana worked long hours at a studio as a costume designer for an ungrateful, emotionally abusive boss. And her boyfriend wasn't much better.

There was nothing Ruby wouldn't do for Ariana, the child of her heart whom she loved more than life. If only Ariana knew, or could accept, how truly gifted and loved she was. To Ruby, it was critical that she intervene in Ariana's off-track life. She wanted her final gift to Ariana to be happiness.

But how?

Ruby was desperate to set things right with those she loved. Her sister Patricia's death last year—and the instructions she left —made it imperative that Ruby address lingering issues. She owed that to Mari—and sweet Ariana, who loved her for who she really was, not the Technicolor characters she'd played. Patricia had left the most difficult task to Ruby.

Placing a hand at her neck, Ruby recalled the letter she'd read so often that she had memorized it like a script.

My dear Ruby,

By the time you read this, I will be resting peacefully. As I write, I am still grappling with my diagnosis but thought I should take measures while I can. You have my gratitude for whatever decisions you've had to make on my behalf. But I have one more private request that I cannot bring myself to face.

I have left a letter and personal items in a safety-deposit box for dear Mari. Please understand that these are only for Mari's eyes. I'll leave it up to you to decide the details, Ruby, as to when, or even if, you want to share this with her. Be gentle; her will is as fierce as yours and her heart just as soft.

My dear sister, we have lived through the most heartrending times together. My deepest gratitude to you for the gifts you shared—not only with me but our entire family. You have all my love forever. Now, as to my instructions—

Matteo was motioning toward Ruby. Herd-like, the group had shifted toward the van. It was time to leave. Flinging her scarf across her shoulder, she strode toward the van.

"Signora Raines, if I may." Matteo offered his hand to help her slide into her seat.

"*Grazie*, Matteo. Such exquisite manners." Bestowing a radiant smile upon him, she slid her hand into his as she lifted her skirt, extended a long leg, and made her entrance into the touring van.

As Matteo smiled, Ruby lowered her eyes and inclined her head as Mr. Wyler had once suggested she do, making her entrance like a queen. The great director wasn't known for giving much direction, so that guidance had made an impact. Usually, his instructions had been simple. *Again, again.* Or, *Do better.* Still, she adored him, and they'd grown close over the years.

Matteo held her hand and beamed.

Ruby smiled. She still had it.

After Matteo took the wheel, they started off. Ruby gazed from the window, delighting in the scenery. Oleanders, roses, and bougainvillea blossomed in profusion. On a small lane close to the lake, Matteo eased the van to a stop. Outside, a low stone wall covered in a jumble of jasmine and pink climbing roses partly obscured a tile-roofed villa from another era. Chiseled into the stone arch above the gate were the words, *Villa Fiori.*

Fiori. Flowers.

A villa of flowers. What could be more romantic?

A small, bright yellow sign tacked to the wooden gate caught her eye. *Vendesi.* Scribbled numbers beckoned to her.

Ruby's skin tingled foresight, just as when that first spotlight had warmed her face. She leaned forward. "My dear Matteo, would you write down that telephone number for me?"

"That one needs a lot of work, Signora, but I'll take a photo for you." He gestured toward the phone in a sleek leopard case she carried. "*Posso?*"

"*Grazie.*"

Matteo pulled to the curb, and she handed him her phone. While he took photos, she craned her neck, trying to see more of the property. *Stone walls. Tall windows. An overgrown garden.* It was intriguing. But at her age, she reminded herself, it was only a dream.

Or was it?

The guide climbed into the van and handed her the phone. "*Bellissima,*" he said, touching his fingers to his lips. "Now you have beautiful photos to remember it by."

Through the window, the sun shone warm on Ruby's face. The van wound along the hillside, with the rhythm of the switchbacks lulling her to sleep.

1952...

Seated on the wide Spanish Steps near pots of purple bougainvillea, Ruby and Niccolò took turns practicing lines in their small scenes. Ruby was intrigued by how many different ways Niccolò could deliver his lines. He used voice inflections, facial expressions, and gestures to alter the tenor of his scene, often making her laugh.

After trying a few different approaches for her part, Ruby stopped and fanned herself with her script. She rolled up the sleeves of her white shirt another notch and loosened the scarf knotted at her neck.

"Hotter today than usual," Niccolò said. "How about we get some gelato?"

"Sounds perfect." Ruby pushed off the stone steps. Other people on set were taking a break, too.

Taking her hand, Niccolò led her along a busy cobblestone sidewalk. His grip was sure and confident. Holding hands seemed like the most natural thing to do, and his touch sent thrills through her.

As they passed small restaurants, a flurry of aromas jostled in the air—the scent of fresh bread, Italian herbs, and baked cheese. Ruby inhaled, savoring the intensity.

"How were you hired for *Roman Holiday?*" Ruby asked while they walked. She'd discovered that many cast members had worked together on other films.

"I answered a casting call," Niccolò replied. "I acted in school, and my old teacher encouraged me to try out. She told me this was a big opportunity. How about you?"

"It was kind of a lark," Ruby said. "My aunt lives in Los Angeles, and she knows a talent agent. On a whim, my mother sent some of my photographs. The agent liked them, so I took a train from Texas to meet him. Do you know, he sent me out for an audition the very next day?"

She shook her head, still surprised at her luck. "I don't think I was any better than others, but the casting director told me I had the right look. My agent arranged a few acting classes for me, and the next thing I knew, I was boarding a ship for Italy. It's all been so exciting."

Ruby had been thrilled and amazed—especially that her father let her go to Italy. Her mother had begged him to let Ruby have a little adventure before she married and settled down. If only her mother could have come, but the fare to Italy was too costly. Her mother emptied her secret pin money earned from selling eggs that she kept in a boot in the back of the closet. Mercy Smith bought her daughter a camera and film to capture what she would never experience. Ruby promised to return with pictures.

Niccolò stopped at a narrow shop open to the street with a sign that proclaimed, *Gelato fatto in casa.*

"It's as good as homemade," Niccolò said as they ducked under an awning. "*Salve, come va?*" Niccolò said to the gelato vendor, an older teenager.

"*Bene,*" the boy replied.

While the two spoke in rapid Italian that Ruby couldn't

follow, she gazed over bins of the most luscious swirls of a frozen treat she'd ever seen.

Niccolò turned to her. "What would you like? *Limone, fragola, cioccolato, pistacchio?*"

"What's *fragola?*" she asked.

Niccolò grinned and pointed to a rosy pink bin. "Strawberry. And that's pistachio."

"I can't decide," she said. "I like them all, but I definitely want to try pistachio."

Niccolò said something to the other boy, who began to scoop out several flavors onto wafer cones. "You can try several," he said. "We can share if you don't mind."

Balancing cones, they strolled along the *strada* until they reached a fountain, where they stopped to sit. The water cooled the air.

After Ruby had tried every flavor on their cones, Niccolò asked, "Which one is your favorite?"

She wanted to say, *you,* but instead, she said, "Pistachio. I love it."

"Better than American ice cream?"

"Different," she said. "But absolutely delicious." Her cone began dripping in the heat, and she quickly licked every delectable drip.

Niccolò laughed. "Come here."

Ruby felt a cold spot on the tip of her nose.

"*Mi permetta,*" he said, kissing the tip of her nose. "Like a puppy, no?"

Ruby dissolved into gales of laughter, and then, taking her finger, she swiped strawberry gelato across his nose. Making funny faces and crossing his eyes, he tried to reach it with his tongue. Finally, she swiped the gelato off with a napkin, giggling as she did.

THE ROLLING MOTION OF THE VAN CEASED, AND RUBY SHIFTED IN her seat.

"*Scusi, Signora,*" Matteo said. "We have arrived at the hotel."

"I guess I dozed a little." Ruby blinked and sat up.

"*Signora, per favore.*" Matteo stood by the open door, ready to assist her down the little stone steps to the entry. Bellagio was primarily a walking village—or *comune*—with narrow lanes that led down the hillside to the lake.

Ruby stepped from the van. She wasn't ready to return to her room. A cool drink at the terrace bar would be perfect, she thought, straightening her shoulders to make her entrance. She'd grown a head taller than her mother, but Mercy Smith had always insisted that Ruby hold her head high. Even now, her mother's words rang in her mind. Her mother was named Mercy —Mercy Raines—at birth, because of the torrential downpour that had broken a drought on the day she was born. No matter how dark the day, her mother always looked on the positive side.

Ruby walked through the marbled entryway.

Years ago, paparazzi might have lurked near the entry, but not today. Tossing the long edge of her scarf over her shoulder, she strolled through the hotel to a table outside overlooking the lake. The view was so exquisite that it made her heart ache with memories. Though she'd had her share of romantic partners along the way, none had ever compared to Niccolò.

A waiter appeared by her table, and Ruby ordered a Bellini with prosecco.

"*Pane e olio?*" The waiter asked.

"*Grazie.*"

As Ruby sipped the refreshing concoction of sparkling wine and peach puree, she studied the photos that Matteo had taken on her phone. One was of the for-sale sign, while others were of the villa and its gardens. Maybe this wasn't such a far-fetched thought.

She tore a small piece of fragrant rosemary bread the waiter had brought and dipped it into the olive oil, reveling in the taste. Gazing at images, she wondered how her life might have turned out. She might have lived with Niccolò in that very villa overlooking the lake. Sipping her cocktail, she let the story play out in her mind, imagining their children, boating on the lake, leisurely dinners spent gazing at the Alps. Making love under clear, starry skies or rainy nights.

A story. Only a story. One that was never destined to come to life.

Sighing, Ruby took another drink. If she hadn't been an actress, she might have become a writer. Still, she was proud of her work and her ability to provide for those she loved and others.

While her parents' property in the Texas Hill Country wasn't anywhere near as large as the nearby Hillingdon ranch, Ruby had eventually erected a new house for her parents. She'd also built a new barn, invested in the ranch, and supported her older sister and her husband when they needed it. That was only right, all things considered.

Ruby blinked back tears that lined her lashes at the memories. They were all gone now. She'd done the best she could for her family. In her heart, she'd made the only decision she could at the time, although it hadn't been easy.

She'd promised her parents she'd never sell the ranch. After their deaths, she hadn't visited as often as she thought she would, so she converted the ranch into a nonprofit organization for underprivileged kids from the city to have a break and learn outdoor life skills. She'd taken Ariana there when her niece was younger to ride horses, appreciate authentic, melt-off-the-bone barbecue, and sleep under stars that crowded the night sky.

Suddenly, Ruby's phone chirped a tune, surprising her. She assumed it was Stefano, her Palm Springs houseman, though it was still early in California. He'd be having coffee, or maybe working out at the local gym. She checked the number that appeared on the screen and smiled. *Ariana.*

"Hi, sweetheart."

"I'm glad you picked up, Aunt Ruby." Ariana let out a little squeal. "I'm so excited I've hardly slept. You'll never believe it, but Phillip and I are finally getting married."

Should Ruby try to be happy for her niece? Ariana knew how she felt about Phillip.

"He proposed?" Ruby asked, stalling. *Obviously.*

"Yes, and we're getting married right away. At that little church in Studio City you used to go to."

"It's quite charming," Ruby said.

"They had a cancellation. How soon can you return?"

"Tell me your date, and I'll be there." The tour could continue to Venice without her.

Ariana did and then hesitated on the line. "And I'd really like for you to give me away."

"I'd be delighted, but why not ask your mother?"

"I tried," Ariana spat out, sounding hurt and angry. "Mom went off on her marriage rant again, saying that marriage is an antiquated system. Just because she got divorced doesn't mean every marriage is destined for that. She refuses to take off work."

"Wall Street is demanding, darling, especially at your mother's level," Ruby said, trying to diffuse the situation. Mari was still bitter over her divorce, but Ruby was dismayed that she refused Ariana's need for her. "Sweetheart, I'll be honored to give you away."

As Ruby hung up the phone, she shook her head. Ariana's mother had erected a brick wall around her heart after she'd divorced. Ruby's elder sister Patricia, Mari's mother, had started exhibiting symptoms of early-onset Alzheimer's that same year. And Ariana was just a little girl in grammar school. By then, Patricia couldn't be trusted to look after Ariana. Bitter and determined to start over, Mari took a job in New York.

Unable to break through to Mari, Ruby had committed herself to being there for Ariana. The poor girl had lost her father when he left her mother for another woman. In turn, her mother had slammed the door to her heart. At least Mari allowed Ruby to dote on Ariana.

As if compensating for her failed marriage, Mari Ricci threw herself into her work, earning her way through the ranks to become a successful investment banker on Wall Street. Ruby had to admire her commitment and drive, but success and the long hours required grated on her relationship with her daughter.

At first, Mari's housekeeper looked after little Ariana. But soon, Mari began to travel extensively for work, so she put her daughter in a boarding school. On Ruby's request—and offer to pay in full—Mari acquiesced and sent her to a boarding school in California on the relatively quiet outskirts of Los Angeles.

When Ariana tired of returning to New York to see her

mother, Ruby organized her schedule around Ariana's breaks. Her niece had a room at Ruby's house in Palm Springs, just an hour's drive from the school.

As for Ariana, perhaps Ruby had overcompensated, but it was what Patricia would have wanted, too. Besides her hyper-focused, business-minded mother, who else did Ariana have? Ruby certainly wasn't counting Ariana's boyfriend, that self-centered man-child Phillip, even if they were getting married. Phillip was an overambitious filmmaker whose primary focus was his career—not the relationships in his life. Ruby feared that might include Ariana, too.

Had Ruby been ambitious when she was young? Naturally, she hadn't had much choice, but she'd always valued her relationships. Even when forced to make the ultimate choice, she had chosen her family over herself.

Despite Phillip's shortcomings, Patricia would have wanted Mari to go to Ariana's wedding, too.

Ruby sipped her cool drink. Had it been almost a year since Patricia's death? She blinked against the emotion welling in her eyes. Her sister was the only one who knew the price Ruby had paid for her success.

Ruby dabbed her eyes with a linen napkin. Although Patricia had lingered for years, her illness had stolen her from them long ago.

Almost a year. Patricia had left one crucial task to her—if she chose to do it. The safety deposit key was still tucked in Ruby's purse. Although Ruby didn't know the exact contents of the box, she could guess. This year, the days had slipped by, none of them quite the right one to share the story that had happened so long ago.

Ruby took another sip of her Bellini. She picked up her phone again and found the number in New York she wanted. After tapping it, she waited.

A young woman answered. "Mari Ricci's office."

"May I speak with Mari, please?"

"Who's calling?"

"Ruby Raines."

Sputtering erupted on the other end of the line. "I'm sorry, it sounded like you said…well, never mind. Your name again?"

"You heard correctly," Ruby said pleasantly. "Mari is my niece." *Who clearly hasn't briefed her new assistant very well.*

"I'm sure she's available for you, Ms. Raines. She's not taking calls, but I'll tell her it's you."

"Oh, let's surprise her. It will be fun."

"Great idea. Hold, please, Ms. Raines."

A few moments later, her niece answered, her voice crisp and efficient. "Mari Ricci. Who's calling?"

"Mari, it's Ruby. Ariana just gave me the news."

Mari let out an exasperated sigh. "Let's talk about this later."

"Later seldom comes," Ruby said, trying to be conciliatory. "Won't you please come to her wedding? She'd love for you to give her away."

"If she'd been more organized and planned farther ahead, I could have," Mari said. "I won't reward her for selfish behavior."

"Mari, it's her wedding." Ruby was trying to be patient. *Where is Mari's heart?* She tried again. "It won't be complete without you there. And Ariana will remember this for the rest of her life. You don't want to regret your decision."

"There's a lot I regret," Mari shot back. "Like her father. This won't be one of them. Besides, marriages have what, a fifty-percent chance, if that? I like better odds. And no, I don't feel the emotional need to attend. She's a grown woman; she'll be fine. Besides, she has you."

"Mari, dear, I wish you weren't still so angry." Ruby held her breath.

"I'm not angry. I'm realistic. Ariana doesn't need me there to do anything, and I have prior commitments with clients who do. Now, I have to return to work. You have no concept of what's going on here."

"But Mari—" *Click.* With a sigh, Ruby placed her phone on the table. At least she'd tried. She wouldn't tell Ariana she'd spoken to her mother. Why wound the poor girl twice?

Ruby took another sip of her chilled cocktail. *Dear Ariana.* If only she could bring her great-niece here for a break before it was too late.

For all of them.

But maybe there was another way. Villa Fiori loomed in her mind. She raised her hand to the waiter, who hurried to her.

"Would you ask the concierge to join me?" Ruby asked. "I have an urgent request."

1

BEVERLY HILLS, 2010 - TWO WEEKS LATER

*I*n the Rodeo Drive jeweler's private viewing room, sunshine poured through a clerestory window above, illuminating the filigreed canary diamond necklace in Ariana's hands. Of all the jewelry that Ariana had chosen for her casts and clients, this piece exuded the greatest warmth. The shimmering golden hues would beautifully reflect her client's expressive amber eyes.

After studying the impressive necklace, Ariana raised her gaze to Yasmin, the jewelry executive seated across from her at the polished, antique desk.

"Solani Marie would wear this for the Palme d'Or at the Cannes Film Festival," Ariana said. "Would there be any trouble transferring it to France?" The studio had mounted a major campaign for Solani Marie's latest film. While these yellow diamonds certainly couldn't compare to the astounding 128-carat Tiffany diamond that Audrey Hepburn had worn for the jeweler's advertising campaign years ago, they were dazzling, nevertheless.

"We can ship it to our office there," Yasmin said. "They'll handle security for it."

Ariana held the necklace up to the natural light, examining it. The stars would walk the red carpet in the afternoon hours, so she was concerned that the color might wash out in the sun. But the stones blazed brighter than ever.

"This is a stunning piece." What excited Ariana was not the value of the stones nor mingling with celebrities, but the sheer joy of creation and respect for artistry. She loved envisioning a look for a character—or a real person—and bringing that vision to life. The glow of gems, the drape of fabric, the brilliance or subtlety of color. These elements and myriad details infused actors with the confidence and power to convey emotional stories.

While some—like her mother—had called fashion design frivolous, Ariana knew the power behind it. She loved helping women blossom with the right clothes. That edge was often enough to help them conquer their corner of the world.

Ariana lowered the necklace, satisfied with how the sunlight illuminated the stones and brought out the color. She held the necklace against the black matte jersey of her dress—one she'd designed and made. The yellow diamonds popped against the black fabric.

"This is one of the most stunning necklaces we have," Yasmin said, leaning forward.

Ariana had worked with Yasmin for several events. The company that Yasmin worked for—one of the oldest jewelers on Rodeo Drive—often lent jewelry to stars. This consideration of jewelry worth millions was business as usual for them.

Ariana detected the jewelry store's signature orange blossom perfume wafting from a nearby candle. The scent might have made some women in her condition queasy, but not her. Not yet, anyway. She breathed in, appreciating the aroma. Underfoot was an antique Persian rug probably worth six figures. Opulence was evident in the French antiques surrounding them. And behind them, a uniformed security guard with a wired earpiece stood by the office door.

Presumably, if Ariana were to bolt for the high windows, she wouldn't get far.

Yasmin's eyes shifted to Ariana's left hand and bare ring finger. It was subtle, but Ariana caught it. She noted the look of concern in Yasmin's eyes and shifted in her chair under the scrutiny. Before Yasmin could say anything, Ariana asked, "Has anyone ever worn this on the red carpet? Or for other events?"

Yasmin clasped her hands. "It's a brand new piece."

"You'll have excellent media coverage for it," Ariana said, pulling a swatch of fabric from her purse for comparison.

This morning, Phillip had been in a mood. Upset over budget pushbacks on a film he was set to direct, he'd snapped at her when she'd asked him to look at flowers for the wedding over the weekend. *Why can't you make a decision without me?* She was quite capable of that, she assured him, but her defense only fueled his anger. She'd merely wanted his involvement. He'd finally apologized—sort of—by telling her that he understood her hormonal changes were probably at fault. Just thinking about their argument made her head throb again.

"That's why we're offering your client this opportunity," Yasmin said, discreetly checking her slender platinum and diamond watch.

"This piece works quite well with the fabric I'm using," Ariana said. "And to be the first to wear significant pieces of jewelry matters to my client." As a multi-award-winning actress, Solani Marie was exacting in every aspect of her clothing and accessories. Having fired a succession of stylists, the star asked Ariana for help after she'd designed costumes on Solani Marie's last film.

"Even though Solani Marie is young, she's hot on social media," Ariana said. "You'll have extensive media exposure and a good chance of selling this necklace soon after the awards show." That was the business value of lending jewelry worth staggering amounts of money.

Ariana recalled the old days of Hollywood when actresses wore their personal jewelry or borrowed from the costume departments. Elizabeth Taylor had incredible jewelry, as did Ginger Rogers, who'd been the highest-paid actor of her time.

One of the most talented costume designers had been Edith Head, who'd dressed stars onscreen and off for decades—and won more Oscars for costume design than days of the week. Edith Head had dressed Audrey Hepburn, Greta Garbo, Mae West, and hundreds of others.

Ariana loved photos of Grace Kelly in Edith Head's understated, ice-blue elegance for the 1955 Academy Awards. The costume designer had explained, saying, *Some people need sequins, others don't.* Ruby once told her that when Edith Head dressed her, she felt a magical transformation—as if she could inhabit the character she needed to play almost without effort.

Yasmin's eyes darted to Ariana's hand again.

"This is a classic Hollywood piece," Ariana said, musing over the necklace. Ruby had a closet full of such clothes and jewelry that Ariana had often raided as a teenager for parties. She'd grown up understanding how people could transform themselves through clothing and costumes. Ruby was a prime example. From a dusty Texas ranch on the Edwards Plateau in the hill country to the pinnacle of Hollywood—her aunt could play any part with aplomb.

Ariana let the necklace spill through her fingers, imagining how the drape would mirror the neckline of the dress she'd designed for Solani Marie. Ariana designed the young star's costumes for her breakout television series, then for her hit movies, and now, for the red carpet. From costume designer to red carpet stylist, Solani Marie trusted few others for her look.

"Our security will accompany this piece," Yasmin said. "We'd prefer it returned right after the show."

"So would I." After the last event in which Ariana had styled a celebrity, the actress had slipped out to a party, losing the guards in the process. Ariana had received a blistering call from the head of the studio. Thankfully, the jewelry had turned up, but it was nerve-wracking.

Not a scene Ariana wanted to reenact.

Thanks to her Aunt Ruby, who had taught her to sew and introduced her to the head costume designer at the studio, Ariana had been working there since she'd been in college. She began working as an intern in the costume department while she completed her studies in downtown Los Angeles. The Fashion Institute of Design and Merchandising had a long relationship with the studios, often mounting Hollywood costume exhibits in conjunction with the awards season. Ultimately, Ariana progressed to a senior role, and just last year, she'd receive her first award nomination.

Yasmin's gaze rested on Ariana's left hand. "I don't mean to pry," Yasmin said. "I noticed you're not wearing your ring. If there's a problem with the fit, we can resize it."

"It fits perfectly, thanks."

Yasmin frowned. "Are you happy with it?"

"It's beautiful." Ariana shifted in the burgundy velvet wingback chair. After the initial shock of the pregnancy test had worn off, Phillip proposed by saying somewhat begrudgingly, *I suppose we might as well get married.*

Under pressure from his ultra-competitive friends, Phillip had made a big deal about buying a ring from Yasmin. The ring he chose was showy and ostentatious. Ariana would have preferred a more delicate design. But Phillip, as always, had to outdo his friends.

Realizing Yasmin was still waiting for an answer, Ariana hastily added, "I forgot it this morning." That much was true. Phillip's temper tantrum had frazzled her nerves. Her chest grew tight at the thought.

"I hear that a lot," Yasmin said. "It's only been a week. You'll get used to wearing a ring that size."

Will I? Ariana wondered.

Now in her early thirties, Ariana knew she should be overjoyed at her engagement. Maybe only younger brides experienced giddy happiness. She and Phillip had been dating off and on for years. As many of their friends married, he'd become more serious about their relationship.

I'm ready for a family now, he'd told her one morning as if an alarm on his cell phone had gone off. Although she'd wanted a family, too, she'd remained noncommittal. Until her pregnancy test came back positive.

Phillip often talked about how she could provide costumes for his films. Working together, they'd be a Hollywood power couple. This is what she wanted, right?

"Are you free for lunch today?" Yasmin asked. "I've love to hear all about your wedding plans. A friend of mine married at an incredible castle in France, but she'd considered a lot of venues. I can put you in touch with her."

"I can't today. I have another meeting." Ariana returned the necklace to the velvet-lined tray on the French desk before her. She couldn't face another deluge of questions.

Yasmin's eyes widened. "You have to do something amazing. That enormous ring just screams big wedding plans."

"We're planning something small and intimate." *And fast.* Not that being pregnant on your wedding day was the issue it would have been in her grandmother's day. Still, Ariana was old-fashioned. Her pulse raced, just thinking about the wedding. Without her mother there, the event was already fraying at the seams.

"You'll reserve this necklace for me?" Ariana asked, needing to exit this conversation.

"Will do."

"Thanks. I'll see myself out." Ariana hurried past the security guard.

As Ariana emerged into the bright California sunshine and the sound of traffic, the reality of her future gnawed at her. Los Angeles—or most any city where she could make her living—was a busy metropolis.

After her parents divorced, Ariana shuttled between boarding school and her great-aunt Ruby's home in Palm Springs. While her friends flew home to extended families, Ariana often felt lonely without her mother. If not for Ruby, and Stefano, her aunt's devoted houseman, she would have had a miserable childhood.

Phillip allayed that loneliness with his presence. And when they had children, she'd finally have the family she craved.

On the sidewalk outside the jewelry store, Ariana started for the garage where she'd parked. Cutting through the crowded walkway, Ariana recalled how she used to spend a few weeks in the summer in New York with her mother. Even then, she felt like a burden. Mari told her that to make it on Wall Street meant working harder than every man around her. As a result, Ariana often had dinner with the housekeeper.

As Ariana grew older, her visits to New York grew shorter. She spent the long hot summers in Palm Springs with Ruby—or wherever Ruby was. Sometimes her aunt was filming a series in Los Angeles or performing on the dinner theatre circuit across the country. They'd have pajama parties at the Drake Hotel or tea parties at The Huntington. Aunt Ruby loved to work, but she always made time for fun with Ariana.

While Ariana waited on a corner to cross a busy street, she thought about her parents. Her father had a second family and hadn't contacted her in years. And when Ariana had called her mother with the news about the wedding, Mari's reaction disappointed her.

"Two weeks? Oh no, you'll have to postpone it if you want me there," Mari had said in her brittle, business-like voice. "You should have planned farther ahead."

Ariana heard no excitement or apology in her mother's voice. "That's the only date available at the church until next year." It was a small church, but perfect for the intimate ceremony Ariana wanted.

"Then find another venue," Mari retorted. "I'll have my new assistant check my calendar and give you some dates. Six months out, at least, I should say."

Once again, Ariana's time with her mother was dictated by someone else. "Mom, Phillip wants to get married now." She didn't mention why.

"Come back east," Mari said. "If you're determined to do this, maybe I can fit in a weekend. I'll have to cancel an event, of course. My assistant can—"

"Check your schedule. I know."

Her mother's brittle voice crackled over the line. "You can't expect me to shift my schedule due to your lack of planning. And you know how I feel about marriage. I honestly don't know why you feel the need to possibly destroy your life."

"Maybe you're right." Ariana tried not to let on how hurt she was. Still, she felt like screaming, even though she knew from experience that would be futile.

Would her mother have come if she'd told her she was pregnant? No, that wouldn't have made a difference. Likely, that news would have generated another lecture on Ariana's failure to protect herself.

Now, as Ariana wove through the throng of tourists on Rodeo Drive, she felt her chest constrict, and her pulse quicken. With her heart pounding, she hurried up a flight of concrete stairs to her car. A flush of heat blazed on her neck, and she pushed back her hair. By the time she reached her car, she'd broken out in a cold sweat.

She attributed this sudden attack to fluctuating hormones. However, she'd had intermittent episodes for at least a couple of months before her pregnancy.

Ariana slid into her vintage MGB convertible—which she'd probably have to trade for a practical mom-car—and fumbled open the thermos bottle she kept there. After taking a long swig of water, she drew measured breaths until she felt her heartbeat slowing. She rested her head against the steering wheel and kept breathing. *In, two, three. Out, two, three.*

In her purse, her phone rang, and she dug it out. "Hi, Phillip." She tried to keep the distress from her voice.

"Babe, glad I caught you. There's this thing—big producer in town from New York with his wife. They want to meet us. You'll have to leave right now."

She caught her breath. "Phillip, I'm working."

"You sound like you've been running," he said. "Take the rest of the day off. Kingsley will understand."

She'd never thought to put those two words together. Her boss wasn't a man known for being understanding about anything. Kingsley once berated a woman for missing work to take her little boy to the hospital for an emergency appendectomy. *Wasn't there anyone else you could get to do that?*

"Phillip, I've already taken time off to select Solani Marie's jewelry. And I still have to fix the sleeves on her outfit."

"Don't you have an assistant to do that?"

She did, but that was beside the point. Phillip didn't *ask* her to drop everything for him. He expected it. And her boss, Kingsley Powers—what kind of parents strapped a kid with a name like that?—wasn't understanding. Quite the opposite. She'd come under increasing pressure from him. What Ariana had always found relaxing—designing, sketching, draping, and even sewing fine stitches by hand—was now a source of anxiety.

"Just meet us for a cocktail."

"Phillip—"

On the other end of the phone, Phillip erupted. "Don't you know how important this is to me?"

"Like my work isn't?"

"Come on, babe. How much longer are you going to stay at the studio? You said yourself you wished you could do something else."

Something else. Yes, she had. Ariana closed her eyes.

A horn blared in back of her, jolting her. A man in an expensive, growling sportscar waved his hand. "Hey lady, are you coming out of that space or what? I don't have all day."

"What's going on?" Phillip demanded.

Ariana turned the ignition and shifted her phone to hands-free. "I'm in a parking garage. Some guy is getting anxious."

"You always let people get to you. Tell him to—"

"Stop telling me what to do, Phillip." Her heartbeat sped up again. Reversing, she pulled out of the space. Another horn blared.

"Phillip, I have to go." She tapped the phone off while he was still in mid-reply.

An angry voice rang out. "Look first, why don't you?"

As Ariana slammed on the brakes, another wave of heat coursed through her. *This is too much,* she thought.

I. Can't. Do. This.

Ariana escaped the garage and pulled to the side of the road. Panting through another attack, she sent a message to Kingsley that she wasn't feeling well and another one to her assistant. Undoubtedly, Solani Marie would pout because Ariana wasn't there for the star's umpteenth fitting, but a fingerbreadth off the sleeves was certainly something Ariana's assistant could handle.

I have to get away.

Kingsley and Solani Marie could manage their tantrums without her. Ariana turned her car toward the highway.

And so could Phillip.

As if on autopilot, she set her course toward the distant mountains to the east of Los Angeles.

Two hours later, Ariana cleared the mountain pass into the Coachella Valley, where the temperature rose several degrees. Passing the windmill farms that blanketed the desert, she veered from the highway toward Palm Springs.

Her aunt lived in a quiet, historic section known as the Movie Colony, where film stars had sought refuge from the glare of stardom. The area had been home to Marilyn Monroe, Cary Grant, Jack Benny, and Dinah Shore. Most of the houses were built between the 1930s and the 1960s, including her aunt's sprawling mid-century compound, which she'd bought after one of her early big movie deals.

Ariana tapped her entry code on the keypad, and the gates swung open to reveal a shady desert-scape under softly rustling stands of palm trees. Ruby's vintage Cadillac convertible was parked in front under the porte-cochère. Ariana pulled in behind it.

Moments later, Ruby's houseman Stefano opened the door. A smile lit his face. "What a surprise. Is Ruby expecting you?"

Ariana flung her arms around the solid man who'd looked after Ruby and her home for years. Now in his fifties, Stefano had once been a serious bodybuilder and still had the muscles to prove it. With Stefano around, Ariana never worried about her aunt's safety. He was Ruby's houseman, chef, and confidante.

"Is that who I think it is?" Ruby's voice rang out, and she appeared behind Stefano. "Didn't expect you, darling, but always delighted."

"I took the rest of the day off." Ariana hugged her aunt, noticing how vital she seemed, even at her age.

"Come on in and kick your shoes off," Ruby said, a slight Texan drawl still evident. She cast an appraising eye over Ariana but did not comment on her obvious distress. "Up for a cool Bellini? I had the most magnificent one in Bellagio. Stefano has everything we need to make them."

"Sounds perfect." Ariana stepped inside the high-ceilinged house. "Would you make mine without alcohol? A little early for me to start drinking."

Ariana hadn't told Ruby she was pregnant. A part of her was still in disbelief. She couldn't be more than six weeks right now, and she wanted to make sure she didn't have an early miscarriage. The sort of queasiness her friends experienced hadn't hit her yet. But she was definitely pregnant. The doctor had confirmed the home test.

A thought taunted the frayed edges of her consciousness. *Would I be getting married if I weren't pregnant?*

That was a question Ariana didn't want to think about.

Opposite the entry was a wall of glass that framed the nearby San Jacinto mountains. The pool glimmered in the sun, looking inviting. Ariana's chic black dress and heels—perfect for the city —now felt restrictive and overdone.

"I'm going to change," Ariana said. "And Aunt Ruby— thanks for coming back from Italy so quickly."

"Sweetheart, you couldn't keep me away from this wedding if you tried," Ruby said.

After kissing her aunt on the cheeks, Ariana slipped off her heels and padded across the cool tile floor toward her old bedroom. When she reached the room, she slid open a glass door, drinking in the clear desert air. Inside, the décor was classic Palm Springs. Pale pink walls with white furnishings and a turquoise duvet with shell-shaped pillows. Her aunt's home was stylish, yet frozen in time. Still, Ariana loved it. It was home.

Ariana shimmied out of her dress and into an orange one-piece swimsuit she preferred for lap swimming. Glancing in the mirror, she placed a hand on her abdomen.

Not much sign yet.

After scooping up a fluffy white towel, she made her way toward the pool and draped the towel over a chaise lounge. She stepped to the edge of the pool, raised her arms overhead, and dove into the cool water.

Instantly, the world around her fell away. Focusing on her rhythm, she swam the length of the pool with a vengeance, flipped with a kick against the tile, and raced toward the other end. After several fast laps, her muscles had awakened, and she'd regained control of her breathing, though she was winded. She felt good, cleansed of the turmoil she'd left behind in L.A.

Ariana swept back her wet hair and pulled herself from the pool before toweling off.

Ruby sat at a table in the shade watching her. "You sure attacked that water."

Stefano served a pair of chilled cocktails in champagne glasses. "And your virgin cocktail," he said to Ariana.

"Thanks, Stefano." Ariana slid into a comfortable stuffed lounge chair and took a long sip, feeling grateful that she had a place to run away to—not that she was proud of what she'd done. As Ariana sipped her drink, she noticed Ruby's unusual pendant. It was a curved, filigree design accented with a small ruby. "I've never seen you wear that necklace. Did you get it in Italy?"

Ruby touched it with reverence. "Years ago."

"It's not your usual style," Ariana said, detecting a deeper meaning in her aunt's voice, though Ruby did not elaborate.

After Stefano left, Ruby leaned forward and changed the subject. "What's bothering you, honey?"

"I just got overwhelmed. Between my work, the city…" Ariana hesitated. She didn't want to tell her she was pregnant. Not yet. She wanted it to be special. *After the wedding*, she decided. Yet, after she and Phillip were married, she couldn't just flee on a whim and hide out here.

Ariana fidgeted with the edge of her towel. Ruby was waiting. "It's Phillip."

"Ah, yes. The great director," Ruby said.

Her aunt had once told her that Phillip put on airs he hadn't earned. Ariana gazed toward the mountains. "He's been after me to design and manage costumes for his new film. He put an extravagant amount into the budget for it."

"Would that mean leaving the studio?"

"Probably."

"You always wanted to be independent."

"Then I would be." Ariana knew she should be pleased about this plan.

"No. You'd be dependent on Phillip."

For everything. Ariana leaned over, putting her elbows on her knees. The constriction around her ribcage started again, and she tried to breathe against it.

"Darling, are you okay?" Ruby lowered her sunglasses to peer at her.

"Just a flush of some sort." Ariana straightened in her chair, trying to alleviate the pressure. Next came the racing heartbeat, then the heat that began in her torso. She wrapped her towel around her.

"Indigestion?"

"Maybe," Ariana said, although she hadn't had anything to eat. She sipped the icy mocktail.

Ruby leaned forward and placed a smooth hand over Ariana's. "I have a lot to tell you about my trip to Lake Como."

Heat ripped up Ariana's neck and face, and her pulse throbbed in her temples. She passed a hand over her forehead. "Can we talk about it later?"

Staring at her, Ruby drew her finely arched eyebrows together. "You don't look well."

Ariana jerked her hand back. "I'm fine. Just stressed over...*everything*," she said, finishing with a wave of her hand.

Ruby stared at her, which elevated Ariana's heart rate even more. "You don't have to do this," Ruby said evenly.

"No? Then what else could I possibly do? This *is* my life." Ariana pushed back from the table and lurched toward the pool. Feeling light-headed, she stumbled on a step. Flailing, she felt herself falling. From the corner of her eye, she saw Ruby racing toward her.

When Ariana came to, Stefano was kneeling beside her. His fingers were pressed on her wrist, monitoring her pulse, while Ruby was adjusting a cushion from a chair beneath her head.

"You fainted, and you nearly had a hard fall," Ruby said. "Have you seen a doctor for this?" When Ariana shook her head, her aunt pressed on. "Could you be pregnant?"

Ariana squeezed her eyes shut, though hot tears slipped from her eyes. "I hadn't meant to tell you like this."

Ruby's face lit with joy. "A baby! Oh, my stars, think of that.

We'll have a little one toddling around here in no time. Come, let's sit in the lanai." Ruby helped Ariana to a covered area open to the breeze, where fans in the shape of palm fronds spun lazily overhead.

Stefano brought her a thick, terry cloth robe and a fresh towel for her hair.

Feeling cared for, Ariana managed a wan smile.

Ruby tucked the robe around Ariana. "That explains why you didn't want any alcohol. No wonder you fainted."

"It's not that." Though Ariana's first inclination was to minimize her symptoms, Ruby was the only one she could talk to without reservation.

"This began before I found out I was pregnant," Ariana said, bringing her hands to her torso. "It begins with this vise-like grip around my ribcage, and then I get extremely hot. Dizziness sets in, and I feel like I might faint." Twisting her lips to one side, she added, "This time I actually did. Anyway, the feeling passes in a few minutes, but I feel weak afterward."

Ruby nodded. "Stress can cause panic attacks. I had something similar years ago during my first live Broadway show run. Stage fright, which hit me off-stage, too. Still, you should be examined. Dr. Espinoza—Lettie—is still practicing in Palm Springs. Stefano can make an appointment with her right away."

"I should return to work. And Phillip..." Ariana sighed. "He wouldn't be happy."

"It's almost the weekend," Ruby said. "Take Friday off. A break from Phillip won't hurt." Ruby hesitated. "Is he pleased about the baby?"

"That's why he proposed."

Ruby pursed her lips and nodded.

"I'll stay." While Ariana hated missing work, she dreaded the morning drive back to Los Angeles. As for Phillip, Ariana needed this time with Ruby more.

On a table beside her in the lanai sat an open box of vintage photo albums and mementos. Ariana peered inside, anxious to avoid further comments Ruby might have about Phillip. "What are all these photos?"

"Those are from early in my career," Ruby said. "I haven't

looked at them in ages. Stefano found that box when he was cleaning out the storage room. Now, about Phillip. Are you sure this is what you want? Today, you don't have to get married."

"I'm thirty-two."

"So?"

Deflecting Ruby's interest in her relationship, Ariana rifled through the box. "These are really old." She pulled out a faded cigar box. "Why are you looking through all this stuff now?"

Ruby didn't answer her, but Ariana heard her aunt suck in a breath. The brand name of King Edward the Seventh was emblazoned across the gold printed top, with the word, *Invincible*. Ariana lifted the lid. A portrait and miniature crowns graced the interior lid, which proclaimed, *A Distinctive Blend of Fine Tobaccos*. "What's all this?"

"Souvenirs," Ruby said.

Stefano appeared beside them with a tray. "Herbal tea for Ariana, and the rest of your Bellini."

Ruby beamed at him. "Stefano, you're a dream. Thank you, darling."

"Look at this," Ariana said. "*Aida* at Terme di Caracalla, 1952." She lifted out an old opera program. "You must have enjoyed it. You drew hearts on the program." She handed it to her aunt, who held it in her hands as if it were a rare artifact.

Ruby pressed the program to her chest. "In the summer, the world-renowned opera company, Teatro dell'Opera, performs at Terme di Caracalla, the ancient Roman baths in the middle of Rome. I remember this performance so well." Her hands sketched out the scene in mid-air. "Maria Pedrini's magical voice soaring through the balmy night air, the stage set between the enormous *propylaea* of the *calidarium*. Utterly colossal. An enchanting evening…" Her voice trailed off.

"Sounds memorable."

"I'll never forget it," Ruby said softly.

Her aunt's voice held a note of melancholy that Ariana seldom heard, aside from Ruby's onscreen performances. Studying her aunt, she saw her blink back raw emotion. This was real, not manufactured for directors or cameras. Ariana reached out to her, smoothing her hand over Ruby's shoulder. "Did something happen there, Auntie?"

Ruby sniffed in annoyance. "Reminiscing doesn't accomplish anything. Live in the present, that's what you must always do." She returned the program to the cigar box and brushed her palms together as if she were finished with the conversation.

Now Ariana's interest was piqued. She picked up the program. "1952. Aunt Ruby, I didn't know you made any films in Italy back then. That would have made you about—"

"Seventeen." A look passed between Ruby and Stefano. "My performance didn't make the cut, but I managed to gain a part in another film as soon as I returned to Los Angeles. That was *Moonlight Dance.*"

"And what a film that was," Stefano said with a smile.

Ruby chuckled. "Had to learn how to dance for that one."

"You sure did," Stefano said.

"And then I made *Diary of a Pioneer Woman.*"

Ariana was used to her aunt's rambling train of thought jumping the tracks. "Back to 1952."

Ruby's eyes sparkled. "That was the most amazing year of my life." She blinked rapidly and seemed to slip into a memory of a faraway time.

Stefano cleared his throat. "Since Ariana is here, I could make a nice dinner for us."

Ariana felt a sudden urge to get out. She glanced at her aunt. "I know you've been dying to try that new restaurant in Rancho Mirage. We could go there. You, too, Stefano."

Ruby smiled, shaking herself from her memories. "Only if you're up for it."

Ariana shifted. "I'm feeling better just thinking about it." Ruby loved to dress and go out. "Then you can tell me all about your trip to Italy. Phillip has talked about going. Maybe you can tell me where to go." Ariana noticed Ruby's smile dissipated at the mention of Phillip's name.

"I love all of Italy, but my heart lies in Lago di Como and the villages that line its banks. I saw such a sweet old villa in Bellagio, and I thought it would be so lovely to have—"

"But having a second home there would be difficult at your age," Ariana said.

Ruby pressed her lips together in a thin, perturbed line. "Not you, too, Ariana."

"I mean—"

"I know very well what you mean. Dr. Lettie uses the same words." Ruby huffed. "My ankle is nearly healed now. Anyone could step off a curb the wrong way. You forget that my grandmother lived to one-hundred-and-two, and that was before the advent of fancy antibiotics and such. She swore by a shot of tequila after supper. And I have every intention of outliving her." She picked up her cocktail for a sip.

"Point taken," Ariana said sheepishly.

Ruby stood. "If we're going to dinner, we'll have to bathe and change." She peered at Ariana. "You're sure you're feeling better?"

"Absolutely certain."

Ruby hesitated and motioned to the box of photos and mementos. "You're welcome to go through those albums, but please keep everything together. I haven't been through that in years."

Ariana promised, and Ruby sashayed from the lanai bent on a new mission, giving Stefano instructions along the way. Shaking her head, Ariana opened an old album and sipped her drink. As she'd told her aunt, she was feeling better, but she was still concerned. If these episodes were stress-induced, what could she possibly change in her life? She'd worked hard to create the life she'd dreamed of living.

And with a baby on the way...

As Ariana sorted through the mementos in the cigar box, she couldn't help smiling at the assortment Ruby had saved.

Coins imprinted with *Repubblica Italiana,* paper *lire,* train tokens, curled black-and-white snapshots of people she didn't recognize. She unfolded a few pieces of paper.

"A script." Ariana smiled at the notes pertaining to movement and inflection scribbled on the side. "Must have been Ruby's scene."

A red-and-blue corner of a thin envelope marked *Per Via*

Aerea peeked from the stack. It was addressed to Miss Ruby Raines at a Hollywood address. The faded red stamp read *Poste Italiane* with the postmark, *Roma*. Ariana ran her fingers over the faint writing.

She opened the envelopes, but they were empty, long ago robbed of their contents. Ariana sighed, thinking about the lost art of letter writing. She had little to cherish from Phillip. Texts and emails were often deleted, though she had plenty of photos on her phone.

Ariana thought about the necklace Ruby had on. It was clearly old and cherished, yet she'd never seen her wear it. Her aunt usually favored more extravagant jewelry. Maybe it had some significance, like the scattered tokens and opera pamphlet Ruby had saved. Ariana decided to ask her aunt about these things later.

2

Rome, 1952

*N*iccolò held out his hand to her. Tentatively, Ruby rested her fingers in the fold of his palm, setting off the sizzle that coursed through her every time she touched him. Instead of giving their *lire* to street vendors for hot paninis made from the finest thin-sliced prosciutto, the freshest tomatoes and basil, and the creamiest mozzarella and then nursing small, strong espressos at a café where they could sit for hours and watch people, he'd suggested a surprise.

"Do you trust me?" Niccolò's vivid blue eyes sparkled with mischief, and his subtle, melodic accent mesmerized her.

For some reason she couldn't fathom, Ruby nodded. "Where are you taking me?"

Shifting the cloth bag he had thrown over his shoulder, Niccolò grinned. "I want to show you the very best performance in all of Rome. Maybe the best you'll ever see."

Ruby glanced down at her clothes. She wore a simple cotton seersucker dress she'd made before she left Texas. "I hope it's nothing fancy."

"It's very fancy," he said, guiding her in the direction of

trailers that were being used for various filming needs. "But I have a plan. Come on."

They'd finished the first week of filming, which had commenced with the opening reception scene shot at the baroque Palazzo Brancaccio filled with Italian nobles in their gowns and jewels who'd answered a casting call. They were just as intrigued by the Hollywood film as the ordinary people who lined the streets during filming.

Now, much of the cast had dispersed to explore the city on their day off. She'd heard Audrey Hepburn mention that her mother, Baroness Ella, had made reservations for high tea at Babington's, an English tea house near the exclusive Hassler hotel where Miss Hepburn was staying. Others, including the director, might be watching dailies or sipping a Bellini or Negroni on Via Veneto, a fashionable street filled with cafés.

Ruby had heard about the Italian cocktails and wondered what they tasted like, but she'd promised her parents not to drink alcohol and to watch herself around boys. Once this week, she'd settled for a chilled latte macchiato and had felt very grown-up, indeed.

Wine didn't count, she'd decided after a few days in Rome. Even kids her age sipped red wine as they ate lasagna or ravioli or other pasta she could hardly pronounce. And she was supposed to be eighteen, so she had to act the part. *A part within a part*, she mused, making herself laugh.

Holding his fingers to his lips, Niccolò led her into the costume trailer. He tapped on the door. "David, it's me. Niccolò."

The door swung open, and the sound of jazz music wafted out. Niccolò handed his bag to a young male assistant to the wardrobe supervisor.

"Amaretto and limoncello," Niccolò said. "Very fine."

"Excellent. You surprise me," David said in a Midwestern drawl. He looked inside the bag and then motioned them in. "You can borrow most anything but items reserved for Miss Hepburn, Mr. Peck, or Mr. Arnold. And don't spill anything on the clothes. Niccolò, I have your suit ready over there."

"I don't know where to start," Ruby said, gazing at the racks of costumes.

David swung his attention toward Ruby and stroked his chin. " You're about the same size as Miss Hepburn. I know just what will suit you."

Niccolò laughed. "David wants to be a fashion designer like Coco Chanel."

"More like Elsa Schiaparelli," David said, smirking with glee as he flipped a silver high heel and balanced it on his head like a hat. "Elsa created a shoe *chapeau* in collaboration with Salvador Dali in 1937. Darling, it was all the rage in the pages of *Vogue*."

Ruby giggled. She'd never met anyone quite like David, but he was fun. Another assistant had fitted her costume when she'd reported to work, but David had retied her scarf just so.

He pointed Niccolò toward the rear of the trailer. "Now, off with you while I work with your girlfriend."

"Oh, no," Ruby said, feeling herself blush. "I'm not his girlfriend." Although, as she said the word, she felt flutters in her chest. Ruby had never had a proper boyfriend, but if Niccolò asked her, she would consider being his girlfriend.

David smiled. "The night's still young, my dear. I'll be right back."

Ruby stopped in front of the costumes reserved for Miss Hepburn, whose cotton shirts and full skirts were similar to Ruby's. But the regal outfits for the Princess Ann character were extraordinary. Hanging before Ruby was a lace dress with full sleeves that looked as sweet and delicate as the spun sugar she'd once had at a fair.

Ruby caught her breath at the ballgown displayed on a dressmaker's form. The dress was spectacular, which wasn't a word she'd used much on the farm. The off-the-shoulder gown of silver brocade had a narrow bodice and an impossibly full skirt. Even without accessories, it was regal and awe-inspiring.

"Magical," she whispered, daring to touch the fabric. Ruby could sew, but she'd never seen such beautiful material. The craftsmanship was exquisite. She inspected tiny stitches rendered as her mother had shown her, though her work would never be that fine. As long as she could sew, she wouldn't starve in Los Angeles, but neither would she ever have what she craved.

David returned, carrying a sleeveless aquamarine dress with a boatneck neckline and a full skirt. "How about this?"

"Oh, I couldn't," she replied, although it was a stunning dress. She ran her fingers down the fabric, which was so fine it was almost iridescent. A petticoat filled out the skirt, emphasizing the tiny waist.

"Pure Italian silk, made in Como," David said. "Try it on. For me."

Ruby twirled her finger. "Turn around, please." She unbuttoned her shirt and slid the dress over her head before taking off her skirt. She eased the dress over her slip. "Okay, you can look."

When David turned around, his mouth opened in surprise. "Oh, mercy me. You're an absolute star!" He finished zipping the dress. "We'll add pearls, *faux*, of course, and flat silver sandals. Mind if I style your hair, my pet? I've never seen that exquisite shade before." He lowered his voice to a whisper. "Is it natural?"

"Since I was a little girl." Ruby giggled. "Where are you from?"

"Omaha," David replied with a drawl.

"You're funny," she said. She'd never met anyone like David, who was so fashionable and fun. "Is everyone from Omaha like you?" She had no idea where that was, but it sounded exotic.

"Darling, no one from Omaha is like me. That's why I high-tailed it to California. Even so, I was nervous about showing my costume portfolio to Miss Head, but she hired me right away after seeing it."

"Aren't you nervous that you could be fired for this?" Ruby whispered. Edith Head had designed costumes for all the stars, and she'd won more awards than any other costume designer. She wouldn't stand for a transgression like this.

"She's far away in Hollywood. If you ain't telling, neither am I." David winked at her. "What drove you to Tinseltown?"

"I love the movies," Ruby said, smiling at the glittering term for the film industry. "You get to pretend you're someone else. And get paid for it." She dropped her voice to a whisper. "A lot, if you're good. My family could sure use the money, so I'm going to learn everything there is to know about acting."

She caught a glimpse of her transformation in the mirror. The icy blue color contrasted beautifully with her dark red hair.

"Stay right there," David said. After turning up the dial on a record player in the corner that was spinning a black-and-gold 78-rpm record, he scooped up a hairbrush and a makeup bag. "Mmm, that's my desire," he sang along. "Can you believe I found a Louis Armstrong record in a shop here?"

"I've heard him on the radio," Ruby said, excited. Although her father seldom let her tune the dial to anything but country and western stations.

David snapped his fingers to the music. "That's jazz, baby. Satchmo—that's his nickname—tours often in Italy, so folks here know his music." David's eyes brightened. "He made a film right here in Rome, *Botta e Risposta*, which means, 'I'm in the revue.' It's a screwball comedy, and this song is from that. It's called *You're My Desire*. And you should hear the Italian jazz. Wow." He fanned his face.

Ruby laughed, but soon she was tapping her toe to the music. As she stood still, David brushed her hair from her face and secured it with a pair of rhinestone combs. Using a fine cosmetic brush, he dabbed red lipstick on her lips, and then he stepped back, admiring his work.

"I need to record this for my portfolio," he said. "Hold still."

David angled a bright light toward her, which threw a long shadow. He adjusted the lens on a complicated looking camera. "Don't smile," he said. "Look just over my shoulder."

As she did, Niccolò sauntered out, snapping his fingers to the music. He wore a dark, slim-cut suit that made him look much older. Her heart quickened, and her lips parted in awe.

"That's it," David exclaimed.

A flash popped in her eyes, momentarily blinding her.

Niccolò knelt beside her and clasped her hand. "Do you know how beautiful you are?" His voice was thick with emotion.

"And you, too," Ruby managed to say.

"Dress-up time is over," David said, clapping his hands.

"Bring these clothes back by tomorrow afternoon. Four o'clock sharp. No earlier. I have a date with a hangover."

Ruby and Niccolò raced out the door, laughing and hugging each other.

On the way, Niccolò bought a snack from a street vendor of *arancini*, delicious little fried balls of rice, cheese, and peas that Ruby ate with care so as not to smudge her lipstick. As they sat in a square with napkins draped over their finery, the setting sun cast its gossamer glow over them. So far, the evening had been magical. One that Ruby knew she would hold tight and remember.

Afterward, they took a taxi past the Pantheon, the Roman Forum, and the Colosseum. Niccolò pointed out his favorite places. He'd lived here in Rome with his family, but he also spoke of Lago di Como in the north where his mother's family lived.

"How did your parents meet?" Ruby asked as they sat with their legs touching in the back of the cab. The warmth of his body next to hers was enthralling.

"My mother's father has vineyards in the north, and my other grandfather had an art gallery in Rome. One day my mother traveled with her father to deliver wine to a gallery, where my father was working. Wine and art—a good match, they always say."

She lifted her face to the warm breeze through the open window. "And is it, do you think?"

Niccolò laughed. "What a funny thing to ask. We have so much love in our family." He kissed her on the cheek.

Niccolò's simple kiss sent tingles clear down to Ruby's toes. Giggling, she returned the kiss on his cheek. The driver smiled at them in the rearview mirror as he slowed in front of their destination.

"This is Terme di Caracalla," Niccolò said, gesturing toward towering ruins. "That means Caracalla's bathhouse," he added, chuckling. "My mother loves opera."

Ruby stared out the window. "Opera?"

"You've seen opera, yes?"

"No, but I can't wait." Beautifully dressed people milled

about, laughing and kissing each other on the cheeks. *Ciao! Come stai?* She frowned. "Is it expensive to get in?"

Niccolò laughed. "I have a cousin." He paid the driver and took her hand, helping her slide across the bench seat in her dress.

As she slid from the car, she noticed a few people looking at her. Frowning, she pressed a hand to her chest and asked Niccolò, "Do I look okay? People are staring."

"That's because you are mesmerizing," he said, sliding his arm protectively around her.

Relieved, she raised her face to his. Niccolò pressed his cheek against hers, kissing her cheek and neck. Her heart was bursting with such emotion she'd never felt. *This is passion.* A warm feeling flooded her. The passion she'd seen portrayed on the screen was actually real.

Niccolò pulled away and cradled her face in his hands. "*Anima mia,*" he said in a husky voice. "My soul."

"*Anima mia,*" she repeated.

He laughed. "Not bad. I'll teach you Italian if you want to learn."

"Oh yes," she cried, completely lost in his embrace. And yet, she was found—by another soul so much like her's. She'd never dared hope he might exist, but here he was in her arms. She felt like the luckiest girl in the world and a million miles away from Texas.

He motioned toward the front of the crowd. "*Andiamo.*"

Clasping her hand, he led her through the crowd. "*Teatro dell'-Opera* performs here in the summer. This year, they are performing *Aida*. You know *Aida*, yes?"

Ruby shook her head. She was hardly paying attention to anything but him, and the passion she saw in his eyes, too.

"Wait until you see it and hear it." Niccolò touched his fingers to his lips. "*L'opera è magnifica.* Sensational. Maria Pedrini is performing, and she has the voice of an angel. If I ever have a daughter, I would name her Mariangela. It even sounds musical." He grinned. "Say it for me."

"Mariangela." Ruby laughed with him, but she loved what he was saying. And the name did flow off the tongue.

When they reached Niccolò's cousin, the man, who was a little older than Niccolò, nodded and waved them in with a smile.

"Now, we have to look for empty seats, but don't be too obvious about it," Niccolò said in a low, conspiratorial voice. "Act like we're looking for friends."

"I can do that," Ruby said, grinning.

They waited with nonchalance near a row that had open seats until the lights went down. Quickly, they scurried into the empty seats, stifling their laughter. But as soon as lights illuminated the stage, which was positioned between massive stone pillars, Ruby and Niccolò watched in rapturous awe.

Ruby loved everything about the opera—the music, the story, the performers, the costumes. The soaring passion of the performance reflected what she felt in her heart. Niccolò whispered a little about the story, but even without understanding a word, she comprehended the meaning deep within her being.

If given a chance, she vowed silently, she would bring these emotions to the stage and to film—in her way, of course, but she would be just as strong and memorable.

After the opera ended, the crowd erupted in applause and cheers. Ruby and Niccolò stood with everyone else, and Ruby was amazed at the outpouring of love.

As they made their way out, Niccolò snatched a program from a chair for her. *Aida, Giuseppe Verdi, 1870*. Taking a pen from his jacket, he drew hearts on a page before giving it to her. "For you to remember tonight."

"How could I ever forget it?"

They splurged again and took a taxi.

"*Scalinata di Trinità dei Monti*," Niccolò told the driver.

The Spanish Steps were near where Ruby was staying with the rest of the cast. Her pensione wasn't as fancy as the Hotel Hassler where the stars were staying, but she loved simply being in Rome and having a chance to be a part of the production.

At the base of the broad steps, they lingered in the Piazza di Spagna, perching on a low wall near a large sculpted fountain. The sound of rippling water muted nearby conversations and the breeze off the water cooled Ruby's bare arms.

Gazing at the fountain, Ruby recalled something she'd heard from a fellow cast member. "Baroque style, right?"

"You know art?" Niccolò smiled. "This is the Fontana della Barcaccia. Fountain of the boat."

Ruby regarded it with a finger to her chin. "Aptly named, seeing as how someone left their boat in the middle of the fountain."

Niccolò chuckled and drew close to her, lifting his arm around her shoulder. "You make me smile so much inside." He'd removed his jacket in the balmy night air.

Ruby shivered in his embrace with anticipation.

Sliding his fingers under her chin, he tilted her face and grazed her lips with his in question.

Responding, she kissed him back, softly, but surely. This was her first kiss, here in Rome with a boy whose heart beat in rhythm with hers and whose eyes saw into her very soul. She would never forget this night.

"*Anima mia,*" she whispered.

3

Los Angeles, 2010

*H*er heart thumping, Ariana flung open the door of the small church and raced outside. Gripping her flowing, hand-beaded silk skirt in her fists, she wedged herself and her bridal finery into her vintage MGB convertible.

"Ariana!" Phillip called out, but she dared not turn around.

Although she hadn't planned to wear her dress in the car, going with a slim silhouette of a wedding dress over a billowing, crinoline-enhanced style was the right choice for a fast getaway. Even with the top down, a full-skirted dress simply wouldn't have fit into the sportscar.

"Stop," he called again.

No way was she taking time to change.

After the wedding, she and Phillip had planned to put the top down and drive up the coast of California. Phillip wanted to see the towering redwood trees and play golf with friends from school at Pebble Beach. Since she didn't play golf, she'd be on her own for much of the time. As much as she'd looked forward to their honeymoon, that was his dream trip. Her aunt's trip to Italy sounded more romantic.

"He can go there by himself for all I care," she muttered.

With a glance in the mirror, she confirmed what she thought. Her cheeks were blazing through her carefully applied makeup with the crimson heat of anger and embarrassment. How could Phillip have done this to her?

Her veil tangled in the leather-bound steering wheel. She struggled to free it without damaging the delicate vintage *Dentelle de Calais* lace and tulle that she'd carefully sewn onto Ruby's pearl and diamond hair comb.

Through the church's open door, Ariana could hear the organ player dutifully playing wedding music for a ceremony that would never happen. She rolled her eyes over the irony.

"Ariana, I can explain," Phillip yelled. "Please, I need you."

The only things Ariana needed were to feel the warm sun on her shoulders and a cold iced tea on her lips.

She turned the key in the ignition and stomped the clutch with her handcrafted high heels. She'd taken such care with her bridal outfit and accessories, but now she couldn't wait to take it all off. How could she have missed all the signs in her relationship with Phillip?

Swiftly reversing out of the parking space, Ariana spotted their friends and Phillip's parents gathering outside the modest church on Coldwater Canyon in Studio City. Many celebrities and regular folks had married at the Little Brown Church, a knotty-pine paneled church that predated most of the development in the area. *An intimate wedding*, she'd insisted.

Thank goodness.

Shock lined familiar faces outside the chapel. Phillip's parents wore expressions of apology and embarrassment, which is what Phillip should have been feeling. Her great-aunt Ruby stood away from the others by the doorway, imperious as always in an extravagantly plumed hat that she'd probably worn in some film decades ago. Raising her manicured red nails to her matching lips, Ruby blew a kiss toward Ariana and smiled.

Only Aunt Ruby understands. In retrospect, Ariana should have listened to her. She could have saved herself this embarrassment.

Ariana slid the stick shift into gear and gunned the engine. At once, Phillip loomed before her, his arms outstretched. She slammed on the brakes. Her nearly-husband-to-be bounced off the hood.

"Ariana, for heaven's sake, *stop*." He pushed himself off the hood. "I'm here now. Let's do this."

Lifting herself in the seat, she jabbed her finger over the windshield. "*You* were late. *You* had second thoughts. *You* stayed out all night with some woman you met in a bar. *Now* you're sure?"

"Come on, nothing happened." Looking infuriatingly handsome in the tux she'd designed for him, Phillip spread his hands. "Lots of guys get cold feet at the last minute. It happens, babe."

"Not to me, it doesn't. You're either in this relationship, or you're not. And you gave me just enough time to think."

Everything Phillip had to do was more important than anything in her life. A cocktail party he suddenly had to attend trumped an awards dinner where she was nominated for a prestigious costume design award. A romantic weekend she'd planned was canceled because he'd promised to play basketball with the guys on Saturday morning at Beverly Hills High School. She could go on, but what was the point?

He'd kept her waiting at the church for more than an hour because *he* couldn't decide if he was ready to get married. No call, no text, nothing. His best man had admitted that Phillip hadn't returned to the hotel before they left for the church.

"When did you last see him?" Ariana had demanded.

His best friend, who was so hungover his face was green, admitted Phillip had left with another woman.

Last night, as Ariana watched the clock for hours and repeatedly punched the redial button to his mobile phone, the truth had dawned on her.

And as she'd waited for Phillip today, she decided she didn't want to be a bit player in his life. She wanted a real partner. Despite everyone else's supposedly better judgment—her matron of honor, Phillip's parents—Ariana was taking charge of her life.

Now, with one foot on the brake, Ariana slid the stick shift into neutral and revved the engine.

"Alright, alright." Phillip held his hand. "Kid's probably not even mine. I was doing you a favor, you know."

"That's it," Ariana cried. She tugged off his gaudy ring and heaved it toward him. The weighty diamond tumbled across the hot asphalt, and Phillip dove after his investment.

He grabbed it and stood up, holding it up like a trophy before turning toward their guests and waving a finger beside his temple. *Crazy woman.*

Now he was going to spin this his way.

With her heart pounding, Ariana lurched forward in the car. As she wheeled from the lot, a gust of wind caught the veil she'd tossed into the vacant seat behind her. Billowing in the breeze, the veil took flight.

Cursing under her breath, Ariana whipped the car around to retrieve the veil. If it weren't attached to a treasured piece of Ruby's jewelry, she'd be careening down Coldwater Canyon right now.

Before Ariana could get to the veil, Ruby stepped forward and opened her arms. The tulle and lace tumbled into her arms.

Ariana pulled the car beside her aunt, who was wrangling the exquisite fabric and fluffing it like cotton candy. The plum feathers on her hat rustled in the breeze, and Ariana couldn't help thinking that this looked like a scene from one of her aunt's comedies.

"Don't stare. Open the door." Ruby inclined her head. "Or I can drive."

Ariana dared not look back at the small crowd chattering behind her. "I wish you could. But it's a stick shift."

Ruby smirked. "What do you think I learned on, sweetheart? Let's get you away from here."

"But your ankle...and Stefano."

"Relax, it's not my clutch foot. And Stefano knows the way home. *Andiamo*, darling."

"You're on." Ariana flung open the door to change places with her aunt.

After shoving the armful of bridal finery into Ariana's arms, Ruby whipped off her plumed hat. "Here, put these in the boot."

"Boot?"

"It's an English car, so that's only proper." Ruby sighed. "The trunk, dear. And get on with it. That photographer you hired is trying to earn his wages. You don't want to see this day immortalized, do you?"

Ariana opened the small trunk, which contained two small travel bags. Tossing Phillip's designer luggage to the ground, she tucked in the veil and Ruby's hat before sweeping herself into the passenger seat. As soon as Ariana slammed the door, Ruby squealed into traffic, leaving a trail of tire smoke and gaping guests.

Ariana slid down in the seat and covered her face with her hands. "I don't know whether to cry or scream or laugh."

"Celebrate," Ruby said, deftly changing lanes with a finesse that belied her age. "You're free, and he definitely wasn't worth it."

"I know. But the baby…" Ariana breathed through the panic curling in her chest.

"We'll figure it out." Ruby set her jaw and shifted gears.

Ariana knew her aunt had performed driving stunts in a film years ago, but seeing her whip them away from the church was impressive—even for someone half her age. "How'd you know Phillip was wrong for me, Aunt Ruby?"

Ruby shot her an incredulous look. "Experience. Count yourself lucky. Men, unlike wine, don't necessarily improve with age."

She might wish he'd be out of her life forever, but with a child on the way, it was unlikely. Second thoughts nipped at her mind. "What have I done?" Ariana flung her head against the seat.

Ruby shot her a triumphant look. "You've done what a million other women wish they'd had the guts to do—leave that old goat who mistreats them at the altar. Just imagine them cheering you on." She raised a fist in the air and let out a whoop.

Ariana matched her and immediately felt a little better. "Whoa, whoa, whoa!" With her fist in the air, she noticed the wide-eyed stares from cars they were passing. "I can't believe I did that," she said, dissolving into hysterical laughter.

She'd been dating Phillip so long that she'd forgotten why she'd been attracted to him in the first place. Well, almost. He was the best-looking man who'd ever asked her out, and he had confidence enough for both of them. But she'd excused his selfishness long enough. Ariana wiped tears of hysteria from her eyes.

"That took guts," Ruby said, extracting a delicate handkerchief from the pocket of her nubby suit and handing it to her. "Proud of you, sweetheart. Now, come back to Palm Springs with me," Ruby said. "No sense going back to your apartment."

"Which is packed and ready for movers anyway." Ariana made a face and tilted her head against the seat, still feeling overwhelmed. "The movers are coming tomorrow." Phillip had paid a company to move and unpack everything in their absence, and his personal assistant was managing the effort. Ariana had already donated her post-college furniture.

"I just realized I'm homeless and pregnant." Ariana gave a wry laugh. "New tenants are moving in next week, and they're paying considerably more than I was."

"Too small for the baby." Ruby dismissed this with a wave of her hand. "The movers can put your belongings in storage until you find something else."

"You make it sound so easy," Ariana said, slipping her feet from her shoes.

"Sure beats the alternative." Ruby shot her a wry grin. "Since you're blocked out of work for a month, why not use that vacation time? Dr. Lettie would certainly approve."

The physician that Ariana had seen in Palm Springs at Ruby's urging had given her a physical. While Ariana was healthy, the doctor had told her that she had classic stress-related symptoms. Dr. Lettie had suggested exercise, yoga, and a therapist. *You have to find methods of dealing with the stressors in your life.* Fortunately, the baby was fine.

Stressors. That would be Phillip and her work. *Well, one down.* Ariana unhooked the top eye on her strapless wedding gown so she could breathe easier.

"I should probably save my vacation time for the baby." Ariana thought of all the plans she'd have to cancel or change right away.

She had been looking forward to taking a break. Her boss, Kingsley, had a perpetual scowl on his face, and little Ariana did could make him happy. When she paid attention to period details in clothing for a film, he dismissed her as too picky and insisted she was running up costs, even when she found vintage store bargains. There was no making him happy.

Ruby shifted through the gears with ease. "I think you need a vacation now more than ever. I'll have Stefano book a couple of tickets for us. I'd been planning to surprise you soon with a trip anyway."

"Just us?" Ariana sat up, intrigued by the idea. She hadn't traveled with her aunt in years, not since her college breaks, but they'd always had such fun. "Where?"

Ruby lifted her chin. "Lago di Como."

Ariana frowned. "Isn't that where you just went?"

A smile bloomed on Ruby's lightly lined face, a testament to decades of diligent skincare. "I've been dying to take you to Lake Como. And I have a surprise for you."

"What's that?"

Ruby laughed and wagged a jeweled finger. "Oh no, my darling. Not until we get there."

4

Lago di Como, 2010

"What would I do without you and Stefano?" Ruby rested her hand in the crook of Ariana's arm as they exited the airport in Milan after a long flight from Los Angeles through New York to Milan.

Not that Ruby needed the support—her ankle was practically healed. Still, she enjoyed being close to Ariana, and not having to hurry to keep up with her niece's lovely, long-legged stride. Now she preferred to enjoy the time she had left with intention.

Besides, taking one's time was so much more elegant.

As they walked, Ruby noticed that several men turned to watch them. "You're attracting admirers, Ariana. Oh, I just love Italian men." *One in particular, of course.*

"I think they recognize you," Ariana whispered.

Ruby patted her niece's arm. "Don't minimize your considerable charms, dear."

While Ruby hadn't expected to return to Italy so soon, she was thrilled to have a month here with Ariana. Dear Stefano had arranged the entire trip for them. Why, just two days ago, Ruby had spirited Ariana away from the little chapel, never looking back at the poor girl's gaping groom who didn't deserve a treasure like her. Or the child she was carrying.

As soon as they had reached Palm Springs, Ruby had told Ariana to pack her swimwear and a couple of casual outfits. They'd buy whatever else she might need when they arrived. Ruby wanted to take her niece shopping in the villages that lined Lake Como and spoil her as much as she could, especially after what Phillip had put her through. Ruby was sure that Ariana had made the right decision.

"Signora Raines, it's a pleasure to see you again so soon." A driver in a slim-cut dark suit greeted them and took their carry-on items. "Your assistant, Signore Stefano, retained me for anything you might need while you're here."

"Why, Matteo," Ruby exclaimed. "How lovely to see you again." She turned to introduce Ariana. "This lovely man was my tour guide on my last visit here."

Because they had flown upper class, their suitcases were among the first on the baggage carousel. Matteo collected their luggage, and minutes later, Ruby and Ariana stepped out into the sunshine and followed the driver to a sleek black car.

Ariana grinned. "I'd forgotten how nice it is to travel with you. First-class all the way."

"I earned every penny, so I might as well spend it as I wish," Ruby said. "And I want this to be a trip to remember. For both of us. I told Stefano to make it extra special for you."

"All these years, Stefano has been your substitute husband," Ariana said. "Maybe I should follow your lead." A frown creased her smooth complexion. "But I worry about handling a baby on my own."

"Today, you have plenty of options." Ruby squeezed Ariana's arm, emphasizing her words. "And if that's the biggest disappointment over Phillip, then you made the right choice."

"Maybe you should have married Stefano." Ariana laughed. "There's still time, Aunt Ruby."

"Stefano has his own life, dear," Ruby said, tilting her head. "He doesn't want mine. We're close, but I would never cross that line. We respect each other. Sometimes we go to the movies or share a glass of wine and laugh about the past, but that's it.

Good help is hard to find, and so is the position he holds. The situation is ideal for both of us."

Ruby loved Stefano, but it was a love borne of mutual respect and friendship. He had no remaining family, and she had little, except for Ariana and her mother. She'd made sure to include Stefano in her will and provide for his retirement.

Besides, there had always been someone else in her heart.

Matteo held the rear door open for Ruby, and she slid into the cushy seat, gracefully lifting her legs together and swinging them into the car as her acting coach had taught her so many years ago. One simply didn't forget those lessons.

While Matteo loaded their luggage in the trunk, Ruby stretched out her legs.

"But you enjoy Stefano's company," Ariana said. "That's a big plus in a marriage."

Ruby patted Ariana's hand. "After the passion wanes in a marriage, what remains are companionship, common goals, and family. Or so I'm told." Ruby opened her purse and slipped on a pair of dark designer sunglasses to shield against the sun and painful memories.

"Do you regret never marrying, Auntie?"

Ruby gazed at Ariana for a long moment. "I had my opportunities."

Ariana went on. "Like who?"

Ruby sighed. "The son of a rancher who owned an adjoining property in Texas who wouldn't tolerate my desire for a career of any kind," she said, ticking off her fingers. "A handsome costar with a hidden alcohol addiction. A younger screenwriter who only wanted me to produce his work."

"That sounds dismal. Wasn't there anyone special?"

Oh, yes, Ruby thought, though she shook her head. "There was the sweet physician who looked after me when I got a parasite from a mosquito while filming in a jungle near New Orleans —the same location where the Tarzan movies were filmed. Though he fearlessly nursed me through malaria, Hollywood intimidated him. He opted for a small practice in Mammoth Lakes, California, where he immediately fell in love with his nurse, and they skied the slopes happily ever after."

None of them compared to what Ruby had felt for Niccolò. But she couldn't talk about him. Not yet, anyway.

"I wonder if my parents were ever in love." Ariana opened her purse and withdrew a little pot of lip gloss. "In Mom's case, it's just work, work, and more work. I couldn't believe she wouldn't arrange time off for my wedding." She dabbed a glossy sheen onto her lips and pressed them together.

Ruby heard the hurt, anger, and disappointment in Ariana's voice. Once again, when Ariana needed her mother, Mari wasn't there. Ruby had hurried to place another call to her before they left Palm Springs, but Mari hadn't returned her call.

As a child, Mari had been abrupt and unyielding, too. Even Patricia, her sainted sister, had hardly been able to handle the unruly child, yet she took the challenge in stride.

Ruby smiled at Ariana. "Someday, your mother might get another chance to attend your wedding."

Ariana shook her head. "Not for a long time, if ever. Honestly, I've had it with men."

"There's a difference between closing your heart and being selective," Ruby said.

"I'm going to be awfully busy for the next seven months." Ariana ran a hand over her forehead. "How will I manage everything?"

"Plenty of people do."

"You never had to."

Contemplating this, Ruby smoothed a finger over a vein in her hand. "Each of us has a different journey." She felt Ariana's quizzical gaze on her. "You're stronger than you know."

Matteo shut the trunk and took his place behind the wheel. "Are you in a hurry, Signora?"

"Let's take the scenic route," Ruby said, eager to change the subject. "This is my niece's first visit." Ruby could feel the energy pulsating in the air. She loved Milan, but the airport was north-west of the city, and her beloved Lake Como awaited them. Another day, she thought.

Ruby eased back in the seat. Once Ariana saw Lake Como and Bellagio—and especially Varenna—she would be in a better frame of mind to receive what Ruby had to share with her. Not right away, of course. Ariana needed a little time to relax and process the twin shocks to her world, although in Ruby's mind, both were positive.

Phillip gone, check. Baby on the way, double-check.

Ruby rubbed her temple. If only she could figure out a way to bring Mari here, too. It wouldn't be easy, but it was imperative that Ariana and Mari heal their rift before the baby arrived. Ruby understood the pain of a fragmented family.

"I'd like to visit Milan, too," Ariana said, peering from the window. "It's one of the fashion capitals of the world. When a film budget allows, I often order fabric for costumes from a supplier in Milan. They have such beautiful silks."

"*Scusi, Signorina,*" Matteo said, glancing in the review mirror. "You'll find beautiful silk and clothes around Lago di Como, too. Silk production has been a Como specialty for centuries—ever since the Duca de Milano established the silk industry there."

"Really?" Ariana asked, leaning forward, her expression brightening.

Matteo's voice rose with pride and passion. "Today, Ratti, Frey, Mantero, and Clerici produce exquisite silk—scarves, clothing, tapestries. Our companies supply the finest silk to the couture trade." He gestured with pride. "All over the world, there is none better than Como silk."

"How are you so knowledgeable about fashion?" Ariana asked, looking interested.

"In Como, beauty is part of our heritage. My wife is a talented textile designer," he said as he pulled away from the curb and into the airport traffic. "And we have a boutique in Bellagio."

"Then we must visit your shop," Ruby said. Glancing at her niece, pride swelled in her chest. "Ariana, I still get so many compliments on that black silk cape you designed for me."

"If you're a designer, you must visit the production facilities," Matteo said. "All the best design houses come here. Versace, Missoni, Armani, Prada, and Ferragamo."

"I've been designing costumes for years," Ariana said, taking in the city as they left the airport. "I work at one of the studios in Hollywood."

"Like your famous aunt," Matteo said, navigating through traffic. "I am twice privileged to serve you ladies."

"I don't work much anymore," Ruby said. The rigors of a starring role—and the subsequent promotions and appearance— had become tiring to her. Though she still relished cameo roles and unique opportunities. She'd invested her earnings well; now, she worked for pleasure. She patted Ariana's knee. "But Ariana could be anything she wanted to be."

"Aunt Ruby, don't be silly," Ariana said, bristling at the comment. "I'm not ten years old anymore."

"My advice hasn't changed. Your job will be awfully demanding with a little one." Ruby quickly changed her tone. "Not that you couldn't manage, of course. Your mother certainly did. But maybe there is a more pleasant way of living."

Matteo's phone rang. "*Scusi,*" he said, and he tapped his earpiece. He spoke softly into his headset. "*Prego?*"

Ariana gazed out the window. "It's not like I could change my world overnight."

"Of course not." Ruby smiled. "We have a whole month."

When Ariana started to protest, Ruby held up her hand. "If you tell me how terribly old you are again, or how your options are limited, I'll have Matteo turn this car around, and I'll send you back to the States. Time is relative. We might have a day, a year, or decades left. The beauty of not knowing means anything is open to us—if we have courage and creativity. Live and do what you want right now, at this very moment in time. Because it will never, ever come again." She choked a little on her last words as she thought of Niccolò.

Ruby pulled a handkerchief from her purse. Even as she had cherished her time with Niccolò, she hadn't dreamed it would prove so fleeting. The tragedy of their union shaded her outlook on love for the rest of her life. No one had ever compared with Niccolò.

Instantly, Ariana looked stricken. "I'm so sorry. I didn't mean to upset you." She reached out to clasp her aunt's hand. "Aunt Ruby, are you feeling well?"

Ruby dabbed the corners of her eyes, studiously ignoring her question. "It hurts me when you sound so defeated." If only she could make Ariana understand. Gazing into Ariana's bright green eyes, she spoke again, more forcefully this time. "Life can change in a moment. *You* can change it. You must grasp the tremendous power your decisions have in your life." Realizing the tight grip she had on Ariana's hand, she released it.

When Ruby had left Italy so many years ago, she had been sure she would see the man she loved again. Ever since then, she'd thought of everything she wished she'd said. If only she could have seen Niccolò just once more. How different her life would have been. Everyone's life, for that matter.

In ways known only to her, Ruby had made a mess of her life. Her most fervent desire was to make sure Ariana didn't. She let out a soft sigh. So many important life decisions were flung at people when they were young and inexperienced—and far too trusting. At least Ariana wasn't as young as Ruby had been.

Ruby was determined to set things right now.

As the countryside slipped past, Ruby reached out to Ariana. "I'm proud of your decision about Phillip."

"I might not like to hear it, but I can always count on you to tell me the truth." Ariana shook her head. "Imagine what Mom is going to say."

"You still haven't spoken to her?"

Ariana shook her head. "I wasn't in the mood to hear her gloat or remind me how the trip would've been a waste of her time."

"It's never a waste of time to support those we love when they need us," Ruby said. Even when they don't realize it, she thought.

They grew quiet, taking in the views. As they climbed into lush, verdant hills, Ruby waited for the first view of the lake.

"There it is," Ruby cried. "Matteo, please pull over when you can. I want Ariana to take this all in."

"*Sì, Signora.*"

A few moments later, Matteo pulled off the road, and Ruby and Ariana stepped from the car.

"Here she is," Ruby said, filling her lungs with fresh air and linking arms with Ariana. "Just imagine...for centuries this view and this region have captured the hearts of artists, writers, and musicians."

From their position high above the lake, the view was breathtaking. Deep, sapphire-blue water lapped the hillside footings. Lush green mountains soared behind sherbet-colored villages and stately villas tucked against the shoreline. Boats skimmed across the surface, parting the water and leaving streamers in their wake.

Ruby watched Ariana's reaction.

Her niece pressed her hand to her chest and sighed. "Now I understand why you wanted me to come here. Photos can't capture all of this."

Ariana didn't really understand yet, but in time she would. Ruby opened her arms to the broad vista as if to bring it all into her heart. There were few afflictions worse than broken hearts that had never healed.

If anything could heal her, she would find it here.

For now, Ruby smiled to herself in anticipation. She couldn't wait to tell Ariana about her surprise.

5

Rome, 1952

"*P*laces, everyone," an assistant director called out, and Ruby hurried to her designated spot. Hundreds of people had gathered around the avenue in Rome, where the filming of a brief café scene would take place. Despite the pervasive heat, happy chatter and laughter floated across the crowd.

Ruby sat at a table outside the café, surreptitiously dabbing perspiration from her upper lip. For the actors and crew from California, the summer heat in Rome was stifling, but having grown up in Texas, she was more acclimated.

Niccolò slid into the chair across from her. "*Buongiorno.*"

Ruby suppressed a laugh. "Aren't you supposed to be at the other table?"

"I switched." He took her hand. "I don't trust that Vespa scooter. I need to protect you."

"They've choreographed that part. We'll be fine."

"No, no, no." He shook his head, then tapped his temple. "You see, I know things."

"Excuse me?" Ruby extricated her hand from his. "That's spooky. Don't kid with me."

He dropped his voice to whisper. "No, really. I know I can trust you. Sometimes, before things happen, you know?"

"Oh, for Pete's sake, stop. Now you're acting creepy. The good Lord will strike you down for saying that." She shrugged and flipped the scarf that David, the wardrobe assistant, had tied around her neck.

Niccolò's eyebrows drew up like her old hound dog's when she threatened to put him outside on a rainy night. He looked genuinely hurt. "You're teasing me now," she said. "Or you're a better actor than I thought."

"I'm an excellent actor. But I'm not acting." He reached for her hand again.

The couple stationed at the table next to them frowned at them. "Shh. Mr. Wyler is watching you. We're about to begin."

"Oh, swell." Ruby flicked his hand away. "Don't get me in trouble. I need this job." The director, William Wyler, liked people who were prompt and prepared, like Audrey Hepburn, who was always on time and knew her lines. Ruby was trying to emulate her.

Niccolò pulled his hand back, but he continued to stare at her. A smile touched his lips, and his eyes were as blue and bright as the sky.

Ruby couldn't look at him for fear her heart would burst through the thin cotton shift she wore.

Since the evening Niccolò had taken her to see Aida, they'd spent most of their free time together. On set, it was often a hurry-up-and-wait proposition, so they'd had a lot of time to talk and play cards.

Many of the cast passed the time playing gin rummy, including Gregory Peck, Audrey Hepburn, and her fiancée James. They often gathered around the outdoor, marble-topped tables at Caffè Greco on the Via Condotti. Crowds collected just to watch them. And Audrey clearly loved her fans. She joked with them, signed autographs, and even turned cartwheels for fun.

Most of all, Ruby loved talking to Niccolò and sharing their plans for the future. And then, when the cameras were rolling, it was magical to think that they were being captured on film that would someday be shown around the world.

"Ready on the set," the assistant director called out. "This take is to confirm the route the Vespa will take."

Mr. Wyler called out, "Action."

Niccolò and Ruby bent their heads together, murmuring silly things to look like they were having a real conversation over coffee.

Ruby heard the whine of the Vespa behind them. They weren't to look at it until it reached them, and then they were to leap from their chairs. Some extras would be shocked, while others would yell or gesture. Ruby thought it would be so much fun to ride the scooter around the city like Princess Ann in the story, played by Audrey, was supposed to do. Only she'd want Niccolò with her.

Niccolò had positioned himself across from her instead of beside her. He looked up from under his dark eyebrows.

"Don't look into the camera," Ruby whispered. "Act natural."

At once, the whirring engine noise was upon them. The Vespa, driven by a stuntman, accelerated and jumped the curb.

Niccolò's eyes grew large, and his lips parted in shock. Before Ruby could say a word, he'd leapt across the table and pulled her toward him. They tumbled onto the ground, where they landed in a heap.

Screams erupted behind them as the scooter slid out of control. "Watch out," people yelled, diving out of the way of the careening scooter.

Ruby glanced back. The chair she'd been sitting in was on its side. One leg was broken.

"Oh, my stars," she said shakily.

Niccolò held her in his arms. "Are you hurt?"

"I don't think so." Other extras helped her to her feet and brushed dirt from her skirt and blouse.

Mr. Wyler hurried to her. "How are you, my dear?"

"Just shaken," Ruby said to the director. Mr. Wyler had never spoken directly to her before.

He took her hand and held it. "If you need a doctor, I can call one."

"I don't think that's necessary."

Inclining his head, he said, "You're playing the part of an American reporter, aren't you?"

Ruby was impressed that with all the people on the set, the director knew her little part. "Yes, sir. And I'm so excited to be here."

"Where are you from, miss…?"

"Ruby. Ruby Raines," she replied, offering her hand. "I'm from Texas."

Shaking her hand, Mr. Wyler seemed to take in every feature on her face as if cataloging her for future reference. "I can hear a slight accent in your voice now. And you're quite tall. Very interesting."

Ruby gave him a gracious smile. She'd been trading elocution lessons for horseback riding lessons with a fine, top-drawer lady from Connecticut who'd married one of their neighbors a couple of ranches over. Carol Clarkson had been afraid of horses but was determined to learn to ride, while Ruby had nearly swooned at the woman's elegant manner of speaking. All rounded vowels and full endings on words, just like a movie star.

And it's paying off, Ruby thought, thrilled to be speaking with Mr. Wyler, the director of *Mrs. Miniver* and *The Best Years of Our Lives*, some of her favorite dramas.

Mr. Wyler's gaze fell on Niccolò. "This young man certainly acted quickly on your behalf. What's your name, son?"

Niccolò introduced himself, and the director nodded. "You play the part of the ice cream vendor."

"That's right." Niccolò beamed.

"Quick reactions. I appreciate that. But we'll make sure this won't happen again." Mr. Wyler paused. "Miss Raines, do you want to sit out this scene?"

"I'm okay," she said. "Like my mother always says, 'chin up, on we go.'"

Mr. Wyler chuckled. "Chin up. I like that." He motioned to the prop master, and then he turned to the crowd. "We'll take a ten-minute break while we inspect the scooter and set up the scene again—safely, to be sure."

As the director left to tend to business, Ruby gazed after him in awe. Many actors loved to work with him, and she could understand why. He seemed to bring out the best in people. Whispers were already circulating that Audrey Hepburn would be a star after this film, and she might even win an Academy Award.

Ruby sighed. She could hardly imagine how exciting a life like that would be. Why, an actress like that would have her pick of any fella—fellow, she thought, mentally correcting herself. Not just the rancher her father had picked out for her. Oh, Granger Johnston was all right. He could break a horse like nobody's business, and he was a church-going man, but Ruby wanted more. She wanted all of this. Exploring the world, meeting new people, wearing fancy costumes—but most of all, she yearned to breathe life into characters and whisk people away with a story. Folks needed that.

Niccolò caught her hand. "Mr. Wyler liked you."

She felt her cheeks color. "He liked you, too."

"Maybe he'll use both of us in his next film. He sure knows who you are now." Niccolò held his thumb and pinkie to his ear like a telephone receiver and spoke in a girlish voice. "Hello, Mr. Wyler? It's me, Ruby, the girl who almost got run over by a Vespa on your set in Rome."

Ruby playfully punched his arm. "Cut it out. He might see you."

Laughing, Niccolò pecked her on the cheek. "I hope so. I do a lot of imitations, too."

"A man of so many talents. Let's see," she said, placing a finger to her temple. "Clairvoyant—"

"And aren't you glad?" he said, adopting a Cary Grant demeanor.

"Does a dreadful Italian Cary Grant impression."

"Aww." He clapped a hand over his heart as if wounded.

"Can you at least cook?"

A slow grin spread across his face. "Ah, *sì, sì.*"

"Then prove it," she teased.

"This Friday. You'll come for supper."

"To your place? I don't know…" Though she thought she could trust Niccolò, her mother had specially told her not to be alone with any man. They didn't have the money for her mother to chaperone her in Italy as Audrey's mother had. *As I should have,* her mother had said. *You have to behave yourself.*

"I shouldn't," Ruby said regretfully.

"No, no, no, no," Niccolò said, instantly understanding her hesitation." I live with my parents. How old do you think I am?"

Ruby nearly burst out laughing. "How old do you think *I* am?"

Niccolò lowered his voice. "Just between us, I'm seventeen, but everyone says, 'Niccolò, you look much older,' so I tell them what they want to hear. *Capisci?*" He waggled his eyebrows. "But, I'll be eighteen next week."

As if locking in his secret, Ruby twisted her fingers at her lips, though she took care not to damage her lipstick. "I always liked older boys," she said softly. She cupped a hand to his ear and whispered.

Niccolò's eyes grew wide, and then he threw his head back and laughed. "I could kiss you for that," he said.

"Don't you dare," she said, shielding her makeup with her hands. She'd whispered that she'd told a fib about her age, too.

"Heads up everyone," the assistant director called out.

Ruby and Niccolò were still laughing when the scooter zoomed past. This time, the path between tables was wider, and the speed was a little slower.

Ruby saw Mr. Wyler nod his approval after conferring with his camera operator. "Excellent. Places, everyone. Again."

"Hurry," Niccolò said, taking her hand. "Now we're being watched." They took their seats at the table. With a wink, Niccolò whispered, "Chin up."

Mr. Wyler sat down in his canvas director's chair and tapped his fingertips together. "And, action!"

Ruby caught her breath, yet tried to act nonchalantly. They weren't supposed to look at Audrey and Gregory on the Vespa— or the camera—but it was hard not to. Audrey was driving, and she executed the scene perfectly, driving right through the middle of the tables and chairs on the sidewalk café.

Right on cue, Ruby and Niccolò jumped up, waving their arms.

The camera followed the action for a while, then Ruby heard, "And cut."

Everyone cheered and clapped at the success of the scene without incident, but the director looked unfazed. Mr. Wyler nodded and said, "Again."

Once more, Ruby and Niccolò took their seats, and the scene was repeated. Over and over, they performed the scene, even though Ruby couldn't see much difference. She thought all the acting was superb, and she was particularly impressed with how well the lead actors executed their parts. Watching them, she made mental notes.

"Someday that will be us," Ruby said, nodding toward the leading pair.

Niccolò stared at her. "For you, I have no doubt." He took her hand and cupped it to his lips, kissing the palm of her hand.

Ruby's chest fluttered. Her mother had warned her against Italian men. Niccolò was only a year older, but he was a world apart from the boys she knew in Texas. They knew about horses and cattle and how to fix their pick-ups. Those boys could two-step in their best boots on a Saturday night at the local veterans' hall, where the country & western music blared with Hank Williams and Kitty Wells. She closed her eyes for a moment, trying to imagine Niccolò there.

It was impossible.

But Ruby was discovering a lot of new things she liked. She adored the songs that Doris Day and Patti Page and Ella Fitzgerald sang. She'd also discovered Nat King Cole and Frank Sinatra, although her father wasn't keen on them.

Here in Italy, she'd experienced opera and Verdi and *Aida*. The grandeur had sucked her in and left her in awe. She hadn't even known what she'd been starving for. Discovering the delights of a new world was like eating ice cream so fast it made your chest hurt.

Niccolò called it *la dolce vita*—the sweet life—and he was

right. Everything appealed to her romantic sense, from the flavorful focaccia and fresh mozzarella to Roman art, architecture, and history that she drank in like her morning cappuccino or rich espresso. She'd never known so many types of olive oils and cheeses and bread. Even the fresh violets in her hotel room had a heady, sweet scent she'd never imagined.

The fashions sent her creativity spinning as well. Women wore full skirts in a rainbow of colors and silk scarves rendered in the most vibrant colors and intricate designs she'd ever seen. Ruby longed to bring home a dress or a real silk scarf.

And at the center of it all was Niccolò. She adored how he looked at her, touched her, and made her feel like she was the most beautiful girl on earth. His words sounded like music, soaring into the depths of her heart. He was so expressive and warm—nothing like any other boy she'd ever had a crush on.

But this feeling wasn't a crush; it was so much more. What Ruby felt for Niccolò was new and exciting, more heartfelt than any feelings she'd ever known. She now understood the literature of Shelly and Keats that her neighbor Carol Clarkson often asked her to read aloud. Ruby loved the prose, but now she understood the source of the emotion.

Ruby knew, beyond a doubt, that she was falling in love.

6

LAGO DI COMO, 2010

"*Y*ou've actually bought this place?" Ariana wrinkled her nose at the musty smell as she followed Ruby and Matteo into the dilapidated villa in Bellagio.

A chiseled stone marker read, *Villa Fiori*. Sure, the view on the drive was spectacular, Ariana thought. Yet, the grounds and interior were filthy and neglected—even with richly veined marble floors and ornate columns that looked like they belonged on a film set. It seemed more like a hotel than a residence.

Was her aunt losing her mind? Or at least, her judgment? Ariana couldn't imagine why Ruby had acted so impulsively in buying this property. She could've stayed at the best hotel here for the rest of her life with what she'd probably spent on this monstrosity.

What was it about Lake Como that was drawing her aunt back?

"I wanted to surprise you," Ruby said, clapping her hands with glee. "This is a genuine, historic villa. Although Villa Fiori is a fairly small villa by Como standards—many villas here are like palaces—this sweet place is special. It has witnessed a parade of heads of state, writers, and artists. You see, it once belonged to the legendary Francesca Sofia Vitelli, who rivaled actresses Sarah Bernhardt and Eleonora Duse in their day."

"And exactly what day was that?" Ariana asked, furrowing her brow at an elaborate labyrinth of cobwebs.

"Late 1800s and early 1900s. The age of grand theater." Ruby made an equally grand gesture. "This villa was an important gathering place, an intersection of art and commerce. Francesca's husband was a wealthy silk manufacturer, and there's even a museum in Como that has an entire wing dedicated to Alfredo and his work." She pressed her hands together as a blissful expression lit her face. "Just imagine the splendid wardrobe she must have had."

Frankly, the clothes would interest Ariana more than the house, which needed a deep cleaning, paint, landscaping, and who-knew-what in the kitchen and baths. "Please tell me it has indoor plumbing."

"Darling, I'm surprised at you. This house was renovated in the 1950s. And even the ancient Romans had indoor plumbing."

"That is true," Matteo said, nodding. He looked vaguely insulted.

Ariana didn't care. She was not looking forward to staying here. The musty smell was making her slightly nauseated, too.

As she looked up, her interest was drawn to the frescoes on the ceiling of cherubs and cascading vines and flowers, which she grudgingly admitted were beautiful. But something was amiss.

From the moment they'd stepped inside the house, her aunt had bloomed with a new, higher level of exuberance and enthusiasm—even for Ruby. Ariana had never seen her aunt like this. Ruby was swirling around the room like Rosalind Russell in *Auntie Mame.*

Her aunt pushed open wide French-paned doors that led to the terrace and stepped outside. "Isn't this incredible? Imagine the parties we could have here. And there," she added, pointing to a shady corner. "That's a perfect nook for relaxing and reading."

Tenting her hand above her eyes against the sun's reflection off the shimmering lake, Ariana surveyed the vista stretching before her. Homes dotted the shoreline, and ferries and pleasure craft crossed the water. "We're right on the lake," Ariana said, struck by its beauty. As she stared, tension eased from her shoulders.

I could stare at this forever, Ariana thought, surprising herself. Glancing at Ruby, she saw her aunt was looking at her with smug triumph.

"You win," Ariana said. "This is stunning. And the house has potential, I suppose."

"And just look at these gardens," Ruby said.

An untrimmed citrus grove flanked one side of the wide terrace, and a weedy flower garden lined the other. Climbing pink and white roses tangled together on a broken trellis while a voluptuous magenta bougainvillea with arching floral bracts encroached on a quaint gazebo.

"And here's where yachts can pull alongside the steps," Ruby said, gesturing to a wide stone staircase that led directly to the lake. Water lazily lapped the stone steps. "Imagine, door-to-door water taxi service." She framed majestic, snow-capped peaks in the distance with her hands. "It looks like a painting. Isn't this one of the most gorgeous views you've ever seen?"

"This is an incredible location." And it must have cost her aunt quite a lot, despite the condition of the property. "Aunt Ruby, can you really afford this?"

Ruby waved her hand. "Years ago, I had an excellent agent who negotiated many of my film contracts with gross percentages. With videos, DVDs, streaming services, and all sorts of other distribution and remake deals, royalties have been flowing in and adding up for years."

"But it's another mortgage. And the repair costs..."

"Honestly, Ariana," Ruby said, jabbing her hands on her hips. "Give me some credit. I paid cash for my Palm Springs house. Plus, I've invested well." She raised her shoulders in an elaborate shrug. "What else will I do with it all?"

Ariana couldn't begrudge Ruby her pleasure, though she couldn't help wondering just how much her aunt was worth—not that it mattered much to her. All these years, Ruby seldom talked about money. "I suppose you have a point."

"More important, I have an offer for you." Ruby put an arm around Ariana. "Help me restore this home, and it's yours when I pass on to that great theater in the sky."

"Aunt Ruby, I can't accept this."

"Why not? Who else is there to leave it to? You and your daughter."

Ariana made a face. "It might be a boy. Leave it to charity," Ariana said. The thought of this much responsibility was overwhelming.

Ruby tapped Ariana on the chest. "If you want, you can give it to charity. But believe me, my favorite charities will be plenty happy with what I've already planned. Why shouldn't I enjoy my last days in style?"

Ariana didn't want to argue with her aunt over such a morbid thought. "You'll live a long life. You've said so yourself."

Again, Ariana wondered about her aunt's motivation for buying a home here. Ruby was shrewd. She'd surrounded herself with equally smart agents and managers. One didn't reach the top of the entertainment industry and stay there by accident. Yet, Ruby's generosity was legendary as well. Several young female directors owed their career breaks to her, as she'd funded their initial projects.

Ruby twirled around the terrace, her long, turquoise silk skirt fluttering in the breeze. Her aunt lived for self-expression and connection. Throwing parties and introducing friends made her happy. She loved connecting people, and many had benefitted from her introductions.

Chuckling at the absurdity of it all, Ariana went back inside. Matteo followed her.

"I want you to know that I didn't influence your aunt," Matteo said earnestly. "Signora Ruby has a strong will. She asked me to take photos, but I had no idea she would buy the villa. Most tourists look at property and dream about living here, but few people act. I just thought she was a nice middle-aged woman on a sightseeing trip."

Even though *middle-aged* was a compliment, Ruby would still bristle at that term because it sounded so pedestrian, and she was perennially young at heart. "You didn't recognize her?"

"Not until she mentioned she had been in films." He looked sheepish. "I read a lot."

"Nothing wrong with that." Ariana could understand. Even working in the industry, she couldn't keep up with all the stars on every streaming series. But because of that explosion in television series, there was more work than ever for actors, writers, and behind-the-scenes workers like herself.

Ariana glanced at the dirty floors. She had less than a month now. Feeling frustrated, Ariana shook her head. "I have a job to go back to in Los Angeles, and a boss who wouldn't understand if I'm even a day late." And a doctor to check in with. She chewed the side of her mouth.

Kingsley probably thought she was on her honeymoon since she hadn't been in touch with the studio. Nor had she invited anyone from the studio to her wedding, preferring to keep her private life private. Only a few of her closest friends from school were at the little chapel. But would Phillip broadcast the news?

The last thing she wanted was for her boss to insist she return to work. She could just hear Kingsley now. *No marriage, no honeymoon? No vacation. We need you here. Come back.*

No, this was the only way she could take a break that she desperately needed. Ariana seldom took her vacation time, and she had more weeks accrued than anyone else. She'd need them soon. *For the baby.*

Ruby whisked through the door, her turquoise and coral silk scarf billowing around her. "Ariana, darling, would you take notes as we go through the house?"

"Notes?"

"Well, of course. If we're moving in at the end of the week, we have a lot to do."

"Excuse me," Ariana said as she followed Ruby through an elaborate hall. "We're not staying at the hotel?"

"No longer than needed. Why would we stay there when we have this gorgeous place?"

As Ruby twirled her hand in the air, her silver bracelets jingled. "Formal dining room here—just look at that chandelier.

A music room there—with a piano, aren't we lucky?" She stopped and swung open a door. "And the kitchen, *voila*."

"Oh, wow…" Ariana stepped inside the cavernous space, a 1950s professional kitchen with vivid, hand-painted Italian tiles covering the backsplashes and counters. In the center of the room, a stainless-steel cooking station stretched out. Cooktops, griddles, grills, and prep stations topped a bank of ovens. She ran her hand along the surface. The medallion on the tomato-red porcelain read *Bertazzoni*.

"Imagine the banquets that have been served from this kitchen," Ruby said, her eyes sparkling.

Ariana shook her head. "Kind of wasted on me. All I need is a coffee pot and a microwave."

Behind them, Matteo coughed. "But this is Italy."

"And that means…?" Ariana was nonplussed.

"Food and wine are like making love here," Ruby said as Matteo looked slightly embarrassed, though he nodded in agreement. "The freshest ingredients, the finest wine. Slow cooking, slow living. We'll take our time making meals—*osso buco* or *risotto alla Milanese* with saffron, lake trout or perch. We'll watch the sun set, share wine from Montevecchia, Brianza, and Valtellina. Oh, darling, we'll make many new, wonderful friends."

"But you don't cook, Aunt Ruby. And unless there's a microwave…"

Matteo spread his hands. "You can take lessons. Many chefs here offer classes."

"Better send for Stefano," Ariana said.

"Don't and can't are two different things." Ruby put a hand on her hip. "I never said I didn't know how to cook."

"You're kidding," Ariana said, shocked at this revelation. "All these years, and I've never seen you turn on a stovetop."

"I didn't want Stefano to feel like he wasn't needed, and the kitchen is his domain." Ruby waved her manicured hands. "But yes, I learned how to cook as a girl in Texas. Grits, brisket, enchiladas, peach marmalade. And I learned more here in Italy." She shrugged. "It's been a while, but cooking is like tap dancing. It's something you never forget." A dreamy glow softened her face like a soft-focus filter.

"This I have to see," Ariana said. "I still think we should send for Stefano."

"Wouldn't he love it here?" Ruby's eyes brightened.

"And let's take cooking classes. We'll have a cooking fest and invite all the neighbors." She turned to face an attached room with a stone fireplace so large a person could stand in it, and a long rustic table that could comfortably seat a crowd. "What fun we're going to have."

"We don't know anyone here," Ariana said.

"We know Matteo," Ruby said as the slender young driver inclined his head. "And that wonderful hotel concierge, Vera Orsini, who helped me find a real estate attorney to handle the purchase. And the attorney. Look, that's four, and their spouses or plus-ones. They can each bring another interesting person or two, and there you have a party of sixteen or twenty. See how that happens?"

"I'm not helping you cook for that many people. I can't imagine how exhausting that would be. We'll get take-out."

Ruby dismissed her comment. "Darling, you've been cooped up in an office far too long. Insular, that's what your life has been. Let me show you the other side."

Ariana opened her mouth to protest, but Ruby clapped her hands and sashayed from the kitchen, clearly bent on a mission. "On we go. Bedrooms on the second floor."

Lightly touching the dusty railing on the grand, curved staircase, Ariana followed Ruby up the stone steps. Halfway up, Ruby paused on a landing.

"Wouldn't this make a marvelous atelier?" Ruby said, turning to the spacious hall below them. "I can just see models swooping down this staircase, with rows of beautiful clients on either side of the catwalk. Why, this could almost be Paris, in dear Hubert's atelier—that's Givenchy, darling. Rest his dear soul."

"First, a hotel, now an atelier."

"Did you leave your imagination at home?" Ruby turned again and climbed the rest of the stairs with the nimbleness of a dancer. "Oh, and make another note. We'll need plants inside and out. Palm trees, ferns, and bushels of flowers."

Just watching Ruby was making Ariana tired. A thought

struck her. Just when had they reversed roles? Then another thought occurred to her. "Aunt Ruby, did your doctor change your medication recently? Because you're acting awfully euphoric."

A wave of disappointment crossed Ruby's face. "How dare you suggest my enthusiasm for life is medically enhanced."

Immediately, Ariana felt guilty. Especially since, at Ruby's age, she might not have another chance to live her dream. Maybe that's what this was.

"All my life, I've traveled the world at a moment's notice," Ruby said, standing imperiously at the top of the stairway. "Location filming, film festivals, commercials, photoshoots, runway shows. This is my life, darling. And I'm going to live it. You can join me—or get a flight home. But I won't stand for any more complaining." Ruby lifted her chin. "I will excuse you on account of your condition."

Ariana winced with remorse over her hasty words. How and when had she become so narrowly focused and judgmental? Perhaps her aunt was right about her insularity.

"I'm sorry. I shouldn't have questioned you like that." Ariana reached the top of the stairs and wrapped her arms around her aunt. Aside from her mother, Ruby was the only family she had. So what if her aunt was a little flamboyant, a little adventurous? At her age, Ruby could do whatever she wanted.

Ruby hugged her back with surprising strength. "Leave the old you in L.A. Here, you can be a brand new you." Ruby smoothed her hands over Ariana's cheeks. "Like those little silk-worms that feast on mulberry leaves, you've been trapped in a cocoon, but now you're ready to fly."

"But I'm worried about the baby," Ariana whispered, even though Matteo was waiting outside.

"All the more reason to have fun right now."

Ariana blinked back a surge of emotion. Between work and Phillip, Ariana had spent a decade of her life worrying about making other people happy. "I hardly know how to do that ."

Ruby smiled and kissed her cheek. "You'll have a month to figure it out. Who knows what could happen?" She took Ariana's hand, and they walked on.

To Ariana's surprise, the bedrooms were large and airy, with windows that opened over the lake with the most spectacular views. Each room had parquet floors, fireplaces, high overhead beams, and antique wood furniture that only needed bedding. And maybe a rug and a pot of fresh flowers. Ariana caught herself imagining how she'd decorate each room.

"Choose any bedroom," Ruby said. "The rest we'll set up as guest rooms or whatever you'd like. One could be a nursery."

"Maybe," Ariana said, still overwhelmed. She couldn't take much time off as long as she worked for Kingsley. What if the baby became ill? Kingsley had fired people for less.

Ariana walked into the largest of the high-ceilinged rooms that featured a fireplace, bookshelves, a sitting area, and a private balcony. Connected to the main bedroom was an adjoining room. The bathroom was not one but two, each with an enormous tub or shower, chandeliers, gilded mirrors, and space for furnishings.

Although the fixtures were circa the 1950s, Ariana wouldn't have changed much. Everything had been immaculately cared for. She glanced into another room, which she took for a dressing room.

"I've never seen a closet like this, Aunt Ruby."

A long, trifold mirror stood at one end beside a raised step and upholstered stools. Walls of closets and drawers would have held several times her wardrobe. "It's an entire dressing room," Ariana added. "And it's even larger than your closet in Palm Springs. I didn't think that was possible. This should be your retreat, Aunt Ruby."

"I don't need this much. Why don't you take it?"

"I'd be lost in here."

Ruby smiled. "Not if you weren't alone."

"I'm in no hurry to audition replacements." Ariana found herself vacillating between never wanting to date again and longing for a soulmate.

"You never know where you'll find talent," Ruby said.

Ariana chuckled and ran a hand over her abdomen. "I'm on the cusp of a major life change."

As Ariana peered from a wide picture window overlooking

the serene lake, she smiled. Waking to this view would be blissful. "Villa Fiori is rather magical, isn't it?"

"Oh, we're just beginning," Ruby said, arching an eyebrow before gliding from the room, her skirt billowing behind her.

Ariana stared after her, wondering what Ruby was planning.

7

Rome, 1952

"I'm worried they won't like me," Ruby said, biting her lip. They were just outside the door to the building that Niccolò and his family lived in. He'd invited her for dinner, and they were to help cook.

"They're going to love you. You're an American *principessa*," Niccolò added, kissing the tip of her nose.

Ruby followed him up a staircase that opened into a second level flat, where a delicious aroma wafted through the door when he opened it. Opera music from a record player filled the air.

Niccolò called out to his parents while Ruby took in her surroundings. Late afternoon sunlight poured through tall windows draped with burgundy velvet and caught with gold-threaded ropes and tassels that reached the wooden floors. Low-slung sofas and upholstered chairs gathered around a large fire-place, and a staircase led to an upper level. But the most striking element in the room was the artwork that lined the walls. Ruby took a step toward a pastoral lake scene painting as tall as she was.

"This is a stunning work," Ruby said. Once, her mother had

taken her to Dallas, where they'd stayed with one of her mother's childhood friends who'd married and moved to the city. Her mother had taken her to a museum. *You need some culture in your life*, she'd told her. This oil painting could have been on display alongside those she'd seen in Dallas.

"You have so many paintings," she said, glancing around the room.

"My father is an art dealer," Niccolò said. "My grandfather founded the business when he was a young man, so most of the paintings in this room have been in the family for a long time. They're all from Italian artists, but this one is my favorite. That's Lago di Como, a beautiful lake in the northern part of Italy. I'd paint it if I could, but I didn't get the gift. Instead, Papa plans for me to run the business with him someday." He gazed at the painting. "The scenery is even more stunning than you see here; it's truly a magical place."

She peered closer. "What a sweet little village on the tip of that point."

"That's Bellagio. And my mother's family has a home right about there in Varenna," he said, pointing to a stand of palm trees close to the lake's edge. "We often spend holidays there."

Ruby was utterly enchanted. The artist had depicted clusters of tile-roofed houses surrounding a deep blue lake. Flowers and trees grew in abundance on green hillsides, and snow-capped mountains rose into cloudless blue skies. "It's hard to believe a place like this truly exists."

"It's even more beautiful than that." He grinned at her. "You should visit before you leave Italy."

"I don't think I can." She needed to bring home as much of her salary as she could.

"Do you have to go back so soon?"

"It's not that." She shrugged, feeling a little embarrassed over her situation. Her parents hadn't said anything, but she'd overheard them talking. Money was tight this year. "I can't afford to travel very much."

"What if you could?"

She gazed into his brilliant blue eyes and then at the painting on the wall. "I'd love to see this."

Niccolò folded her into his arms and kissed her cheek. "Let's go meet my parents."

She nodded, swallowing hard against the jittery feeling in the pit of her stomach. What would they think of her? Compared to them, she was an uncouth Texan who had more experience on dusty ranches than in the cultured world of Rome. In her home, the record player would be playing Johnny Cash or Jimmy Dean, not Italian opera. Niccolò couldn't possibly understand how she felt.

He took her hand, and she followed him past a dining room with gilded mirrors. *Baroque?* She was trying to learn new terms, but there was so much she didn't know. Her head was stuffed full of new words that swirled in her mind. Every time she heard a new word, she'd write it down in a little spiral notebook she carried and look it up later. Only by promising she'd study Roman history and architecture and visit historical sites had her parents allowed her to come.

Niccolò's mother stood by the stove in the kitchen, wearing an apron over a pretty cotton dress. She greeted her son in Italian with a hug and cheek kisses. "Mamma, as I told you, I've brought my friend Ruby for dinner tonight."

His mother turned to them, and her youthful face broke into a welcoming smile. "*Ciao*, Ruby. What a lovely name. *Come stai?*"

"*Molto bene, grazie*, Signora Mancini." Ruby was surprised at the warm welcome.

"No, no, no," Niccolò's mother said, waving her finger. "Call me Carolina. We're modern here. Signora Mancini is my mother-in-law. My husband will be home soon, and I know he will be happy to meet you."

"Carolina," Ruby said. Niccolò had mentioned that his mother had spent part of the war years in England, so her English was excellent. A large pot simmered on the cooktop, and sliced carrots and potatoes sat to one side, along with sprigs of rosemary and thyme and other fresh herbs. "Whatever you're making smells delicious."

"*Grazie*," Carolina said. "*Osso buco* is one of Niccolò's favorites."

"Ruby doesn't believe I can cook," Niccolò said. "To prove it, I want to make the Caprese salad and risotto."

His mother's eyes lit, and she patted his cheek. "*Assolutamente, grazie.*" Nodding upward, Carolina added, "The tomatoes are ripe. Would you bring down a few?" She handed him a basket.

Niccolò led Ruby upstairs and onto a terrace with a spectacular view overlooking Rome. "We'll probably eat here tonight," he said, gesturing toward a table and chairs. An umbrella stood nearby, and all around were planters and raised beds of vegetables, herbs, and flowers. "My mother loves to garden, so she's taken over the terrace."

"So many types of tomatoes," Ruby said. Niccolò pointed out several, though she knew them by different names. Plump cherry tomatoes, fat beefsteaks, and ripe Roma tomatoes. A lacy grapevine and a lemon tree were also heavy with fruit.

At the ranch, her parents grew as much as they could before winter set in. She'd often helped her mother make strawberry preserves and peach marmalade. They pickled okra and cucumbers, canned fruit and vegetables, and bagged pecans and walnuts.

Working together on the terrace, Ruby and Niccolò picked the ripest, juiciest tomatoes and pinched off basil leaves, which smelled zesty and sweet.

"We use basil in the Caprese salad and as a garnish," he explained, showing her where to pluck the best leaves before moving on to the oregano.

"You sound like you know what you're doing."

He looked surprised. "Of course. Why wouldn't I?"

"Not many men cook where I'm from." But then, her father worked hard on the ranch, and her mother took care of the cooking and housework. *Women's work*, her father called it. However, Ruby liked helping her father. She preferred feeding chickens over making beds because she could be outside. She'd often take eggs to town and trade for flour and sugar.

Now that she was away, Ruby realized her work fell to her mother and father, though her mother had supported her. *I want you to have the adventure I didn't.* Her mother had barely finished school when she'd gotten married. Ruby's sister was born soon after.

Ruby lingered by a stone railing, gazing over the rooftops. From this vantage point, she had a clear view of the center of Rome. Church domes and spires dotted the urban landscape, and the Parthenon rose before them. "I can hardly believe I'm here," she said.

Niccolò came up behind her and wrapped his arms around her. "I feel the same way. You're like a magical *principessa* who fell into my arms." He gazed into her eyes. "After the filming is over, I hope you'll stay. There is so much of Italy that I would like to show you."

She started to tell him that she had to leave right away, but then she thought, *Why not?* When would she ever have the chance to come to Italy again? This might be the only time in her life that she would have this chance. She hated the thought of leaving Niccolò.

"I'll send a telegram to my agent," she said, lifting her face to the breeze. "If he doesn't have another part for me, maybe I can stay a little longer."

Niccolò tickled her neck with light kisses, and she turned in his arms, needing to feel his lips on hers. For a few blissful moments, they shared a kiss that sent a thrilling new sensation through Ruby.

"We should go," Niccolò said, regret heavy in his voice.

"Yes," Ruby agreed, although neither of them moved. She rested her head against his chest. *This is love*, she thought.

Finally, with a last kiss, they parted. Before they left the terrace, Ruby helped Niccolò pick lemons and tangerines.

Downstairs, his mother glanced up with a smile, as if she knew why they'd taken so long to pick a few fruits and vegetables. Ruby felt her cheeks flush.

Signora Mancini slipped off her apron and hung it on a hook. "I'm going to check on your sister. The kitchen is yours."

As soon as his mother was gone, Niccolò hugged Ruby and swung her around, laughing. "Ready to start cooking?"

"I thought I was watching," she said.

"No, no, no, no. I'll teach you. It's so easy." He put her down and handed her another apron. "First, you put this on to protect that beautiful blouse. Then, we start with the Caprese salad. When the risotto is ready, it cannot wait to be served."

While Ruby rinsed the tomatoes and basil, Niccolò brought out a hunk of white cheese and drained its liquid. "Mozzarella," he explained. "Easy peasy, as you say. We slice it, then add sliced tomatoes and basil. Like this." Niccolò sliced the mozzarella and tomatoes, then arranged them in an overlapping pattern around a serving plate.

Ruby followed his directions.

Next, Niccolò drizzled olive oil and twisted a pepper mill over the dish. "Then we add the basil." Niccolò fed a chunk of mozzarella to her, followed by a slice of tomato and a basil leaf. "Good?"

"I love the flavors together," Ruby said. It was delicious, and like nothing she'd ever tasted before. "So fresh and so simple."

"See? It's not hard to cook well."

"That's not really cooking. That's slicing and arranging," Ruby said, teasing him.

Niccolò laughed. "Wait until we start the risotto."

His mother returned and prepared a tray of olives, nuts, and cheese. Carolina put this out with olive bread and offered them a glass of wine, which Ruby accepted. Going out after a day on the set with the rest of the crew, she'd learned to sip wine ever so slowly with food, and it made her feel warm and relaxed. But she never drank more than half a glass, or she'd feel light-headed. She had to keep her wits about her.

A tall, elegant man in a tailored suit came into the kitchen. "My papà," Niccolò said, introducing him.

Ruby said hello, and Niccolò's father instructed her to address him as Dante.

"My parents are very progressive," Niccolò whispered. "That's the art world influence."

His parents left them alone in the kitchen, and Niccolò wagged his eyebrows. Laughing, Ruby mussed his hair and kissed him on the cheek.

"Now for *risotto alla Milanese*." Niccolò brought out a bag of rice and a bottle of white wine from the pantry, along with olive oil, butter, onion, and a wedge of cheese. "*Parmigiano-Reggiano,*" he said, holding the fragrant cheese to his nose and inhaling the aroma. "The best."

"We'll use *Carnaroli* rice tonight," Niccolò said, motioning to a pan of beef broth on the cooktop. "Sometimes, we use *Arborio.* And how we prepare it is *molto importante.* You must watch and learn. No playing around or kissing the chef," he said sternly, and then stole a kiss from Ruby.

"If you think you're such hot stuff, then show me," Ruby said.

"Hot stuff. Is this good?"

Ruby laughed. "It's very good. It means you do something well."

"Hot stuff. I like that. I'm hot stuff, yes?"

"You don't usually say that about yourself."

His eyes sparkled with mischief. "I see. So, I have to show you." He adjusted the flame under the rich beef marrow broth his mother had left in a pan. "The broth must be hot."

Niccolò explained the steps as he worked. "The secret is the *zafferano.* The saffron. But we'll get to that later. Now we chop the onion until the pieces are the size of the rice."

Ruby watched as he sliced an onion on a cutting board. He began to dice the onion the way her mother often did. "I can do that," Ruby said.

Grinning, Niccolò handed her the knife.

Ruby diced the onion finely, and when she finished, tears were streaming down her face.

Niccolò laughed and kissed her tears away. "That's one way to get an actor to cry."

She raised her gaze to his. "Besides breaking her heart?"

"Never," he said solemnly. "Now, we cook the onion in olive oil and butter. Gently, like so."

When the onion touched the oil and butter, it sizzled and released a delicious aroma. While that cooked, Niccolò ladled broth over thin strands of orange saffron.

"We let that steep," he said. When the onion had turned golden, he measured the rice and added it to the sautéed onions, along with a healthy splash of white wine. "The alcohol from the wine cooks away, and we add the rind of the *Parmigiano-Reggiano* cheese. That part has the best flavor. Next, the most critical step of the risotto. Are you ready?"

"You sound like a surgeon ready to operate," Ruby said, smiling. His delivery reminded her of the radio dramas she listened to with her parents. Even without trying, he would make a superb actor.

Niccolò adjusted the heat. "The risotto should never boil. Now we add the hot broth, *il brodo, poco per volta*. Little by little." He poured a ladle of broth over the rice mixture. "We stir, wait for it to cook, then add more."

Ruby watched the gently simmering concoction. Just as the broth cooked down and the rice absorbed the liquid, he added another ladle. "Only one ladle at a time?"

"*Sì, sì*. No more than one centimeter over the rice at any time. Now the saffron." He sprinkled the vibrant strands into the mixture and stirred. "While I add the broth, you can grate the cheese."

Ruby picked up the wedge of *Parmigiano-Reggiano* cheese and began to grate it over a bowl. She was enjoying herself. Cooking with Niccolò made her a little homesick for her family. But she was so happy to be here with him. Glancing at him from the corner of her eye, she thought, *What if I'd never come here? So much I would have missed.* Right then, she resolved that she would never pass up an opportunity. Already she was wondering how they might stay together.

Niccolò continued to monitor the rice and absorption like a scientist conducting a delicate experiment. Finally, after the rice reached a glossy, lightly thickened consistency, he scooped a little into a spoon and tasted it. He smacked his fingers against his lips in approval and held a spoonful to her lips. "Tell me what you think."

"Oh, that's delicious," Ruby said, turning the taste over in her mouth.

"Almost ready." He worked quickly now, removing the softened *Parmigiano-Reggiano* rinds and stirring in the cheese she had grated, along with a lump of butter.

His mother looked into the kitchen. "How is your risotto?"

"*Perfetto*," he exclaimed. He lifted another spoonful of risotto. After blowing on it, he slid it into Ruby's mouth. "This is perfect, the best I've ever made."

Signora Mancini laughed. "He makes it better than anyone else in the family because he is patient. Some woman will be lucky to have him."

After Niccolò scooped the risotto into a serving bowl, Ruby removed her apron. They all pitched in to carry food upstairs onto the terrace where his parents had set the long table.

His mother poured a small splash of wine into Ruby's glass, although Ruby felt she couldn't risk another drop. Most of the Italian kids her age, including Niccolò and his older siblings, sipped wine with their parents.

But then, back in Texas, her father sometimes gave her a cold longneck beer after a day of hard labor in the unrelenting summer sun. *You've earned it*, he'd say with a wink. *Just don't tell your mother*.

The sky turned a dusty shade of pink before flinging ribbons of brilliant orange and gold into the twilight sky. Niccolò's brothers and sisters joined them at the table, and soon laughter and good-natured arguments and a mixture of Italian and English rang out in the balmy night air. As the night sky encroached, the lights of Rome twinkled before her. Ruby couldn't recall when she'd had such a good time.

When Niccolò's father tasted the risotto, he held up his glass to his son. "To our chef," Dante said. "*Delizioso!*"

Niccolò beamed with pride. He leaned toward Ruby. "Now you admit I'm hot stuff, yes?"

"Okay, you win," Ruby said, laughing. "You're definitely hot stuff. This is delicious. I can't believe you can really cook." Everything on the table was new to her, and she loved each dish she tasted. The Caprese salad was fresh, the risotto moist, and the *osso buco* rich and flavorful.

Ruby felt like most of Niccolò's family accepted her, except for one sister, Valeria, who stared at her and hardly said a word. Ruby guessed that Valeria was a year or two older and tried to engage her, even trying a few words in Italian, but Valeria would only blink and shrug. Ruby felt like a bumbling American.

Niccolò noticed his sister's actions and took Ruby's hand under the table. "Don't worry about her," he said softly.

"Did I say something wrong?" Ruby worried about making a poor impression. "Did I accidentally insult her in my terrible Italian?"

"No, it's not that."

"What is it then?"

Niccolò started to reply, but he stopped and shook his head. "It's complicated. I'll explain later." He raised her hand to his lips and kissed her fingers.

Ruby fought to return a brave smile as if Valeria didn't bother her. While Niccolò kissed her fingertips, she thought about how demonstrative he was—his entire family, in fact. If her father saw Niccolò kissing her hand at their supper table, he would tell the young man to rein in his behavior in no uncertain terms.

And that would be the end of Niccolò.

Sadly, she couldn't imagine bringing Niccolò home to Texas. *Live for the moment,* she reprimanded herself, determined to enjoy a spectacular evening. She pressed her glass of red wine to her lips. Nevertheless, feelings of doubt gnawed at her.

After filming finished in Rome, the cast, which had grown so close, would disperse. This summer had changed Ruby. How could she return to the girl she was before?

As she gazed into Niccolò's eyes, she realized it was impossible. She would never be that naïve girl again. She'd fallen in love, and her life would be forever changed. From now on, Niccolò would be beside her, and all would be right with the world.

If only she could figure out how to make that happen.

8

Lago di Como, 2010

"*W*hile you rest, I'm going to speak to the concierge," Ruby said to Ariana after they left the villa and returned to the hotel. Ariana was nodding off due to jet lag, but Ruby's mind was whirring with ideas. And with the right help, it wouldn't take long. Ruby made her way downstairs.

"You've been such a love," Ruby said to Vera, the concierge who'd been instrumental in helping her acquire Villa Fiori. As much as Ruby loved the luxurious hotel, she was excited over moving into the villa. She slid a cream-colored envelope containing an engraved thank-you note and crisp euros across the antique desk.

"I'm so happy Villa Fiori found a new owner," Vera said. "It was once a lovely home, but the heirs couldn't be bothered about upkeep until the community forced them. After that, a manager oversaw it, but that's not the same as having an owner in residence." She smiled. "Welcome to Bellagio. We're so glad to have you."

Ruby told her about the condition of the house. "I'd like the house cleaned and furnished as quickly as possible. Bedding, linens, sofas, and lamps. Who can you recommend for that?"

Vera brightened. "My sister is an interior designer. She can provide whatever you need. Even the silverware."

"Fortunately, the kitchen is fairly well equipped," Ruby said. "How about a housekeeper? We have plenty of room for someone, or a couple, to live in."

Vera tapped her chin. "I'll make a few calls. Will you be here today?"

"I have an appointment at the hair salon and spa. I'm available after that."

Ruby checked in at the spa for a massage treatment, which was a key part of her method to overcome jet lag and time zone changes. Later, she emerged from her massage feeling refreshed. After relaxing by the pool and having a swim, she visited the salon for hairstyling.

Before she left, she made a spa and hair appointment for Ariana, whose strawberry blond locks could use a fresh cut. Although she'd had a lovely hairstyle style for the wedding, Ruby knew Ariana had been too busy before the wedding to get a haircut. She wanted Ariana to feel pampered.

What a dreadful affair the poor girl's wedding had been, Ruby thought, reflecting on their getaway in the MGB. She chuckled. Why, she hadn't driven a stick shift in years, but fortunately, she hadn't forgotten how. She would've done anything to get her niece away from that Phillip character.

Thank heavens that disaster was averted. She was proud of Ariana for having the courage and self-determination to walk out. The girl had spunk.

In this world, she'd need it.

Ruby thought of her young adulthood. How different societal norms were in the 1950s and early 1960s. At the time, she'd listened to people who thought they knew what was best for her life and career.

As Ruby strolled through the hotel, enjoying the luxe décor in sunny silks and tapestries, she looked back on her life. Not to dwell on the past but merely to consider it. She thought about the choices she had made so long ago and how those decisions impacted her life.

One choice, in particular, had been critical in advancing her career—and benefitting those she loved—but she'd had deep regrets. She'd hurt the people she loved the most. Worse, they didn't even know the extent of her transgressions. She couldn't change the past, but was it too late to make amends now?

She stepped onto the hotel terrace to bask in the sunshine and enjoy the view. Knowing how to act had been her salvation, in more ways than one. If she'd exhibited her complete devastation, her life would have been ruined long ago.

How Ruby envied others their truthfulness. Was it too late for her to share her truth? Or would she die a lonely old woman as a result of it? She'd often wondered about people who'd taken secrets to their grave, only for their family to discover them later. She understood those tortured souls, but she felt the need to correct the past.

Was that selfish on her part? At the time, nothing she'd done had been selfish—quite the opposite.

Vera hurried toward her. "Signora Raines, I've made great progress on your request. My sister is near the hotel. If you're available, she can meet with you shortly. She's arriving on the ferry."

"That's marvelous," Ruby said. "Do ask her to join me on the terrace for lunch. And you as well." Ruby loved dining with others. While some performers recharged alone, she drew energy from people.

A *maître'd* led Ruby to a table at the edge of the terrace, where stone balustrades rimmed the patio and the lake lapped beneath it. A waiter brought her sparkling water with lime, and a few minutes later, a ferry boat docked close to the hotel. All manner of people disembarked, from young mothers with children to business people in suits and tourists on holiday.

An attractive woman of about thirty-five stepped from the ferry, and Ruby thought how stylish she looked with a vibrant magenta silk scarf draped over her teal-blue shift and kitten-heeled sandals. Perhaps she was Vera's sister.

Sisters shared a special bond, Ruby mused, thinking of how

much she missed her sister. As organized as Patricia had been, she had left unfinished business. It was Ruby's responsibility to tend to her final wishes.

The waiter brought a menu, and Ruby perused it while she waited. Presently, Vera and the fashionable woman from the ferry approached her table, and Vera introduced her sister.

"I'm so happy to meet you," Gia said. "I love your films. And I read that you appeared in *Roman Holiday*, too."

"Uncredited, but yes," Ruby said, rising to greet the woman with the traditional kiss to each cheek. "The filming was done in Rome, although I also visited here."

"And now you're a resident," Gia said. "My sister tells me you bought Villa Fiori."

While the two women spoke, Vera excused herself to attend to other guests.

As they chatted, they ordered a light lunch of *antipasti di lago* with marinated trout, smoked whitefish, and Bilacus trout fresh from the lake. Following that, they had *zuppa di farro*, or soup made with borlotti beans, pancetta, tomatoes, and olive oil.

"Will Villa Fiori be a part-time home for you, or do you plan to make it your year-round residence?" Gia asked.

"I have another home in Palms Springs," Ruby said as she sipped her sparkling water. "But I'd like to spend as much time as I can here. Palm Springs is quite warm in the summer."

Gia nodded. "Would you like to see some of my work?"

"Very much so."

Gia brought out her design portfolio and opened it. "This is a villa with a modern Scandinavian design." Turning a page, she said, "And here is a classic Lago di Como design."

"I like that," Ruby said, resting her chin on her hand. "A relaxed style appeals to me, though I also love Italian antiques and artwork. I once saw a grand painting of the lake that was as tall as I was," she said, transported to that dinner with Niccolò and his family so long ago. "The sky and the lake were dazzling blue, and the hillsides were covered with palms and pine trees and flowers. That was the day I fell in love with the lake."

Gia leaned forward with interest. "Do you recall the artist?"

"I don't," Ruby said. "The art dealer's name was Mancini. In Rome. But that was long before you were born."

"I could look for similar local paintings."

"That would be lovely," Ruby said quietly.

Gia turned another page in her portfolio. "How about this? The lake and flowers and villas inspired these serene colors. As I recall, Villa Fiori has wonderful parquet floors and frescoes."

"We can visit this afternoon if you have time," Ruby said. Looking up, she saw Ariana strolling across the terrace toward them.

"Hello, Auntie," Ariana said, smiling. "Leaving me out of all the fun?"

Ruby was pleased Ariana had joined them. Her niece looked well-rested. After introducing Ariana and Gia, she said, "My niece is a costume designer. What do you think about this interior scheme, Ariana?"

Ariana studied the photos. "I like the soft, rich shades. Rose, blue, lavender. Colors that reflect nature. That would be so restful against ivory draperies."

"As long as you like it," Ruby said. Ariana would have longer to enjoy it than she would.

"It's casually elegant," Gia said. "We create beautiful silk in this region."

"Oh, yes. I know," Ruby said.

"I have your list, Aunt Ruby." Ariana accessed it on her phone and showed Gia. "This is what we need."

"I'd like to have the basics delivered as soon as possible," Ruby said. "Bedding, linens, towels. The house needs a good cleaning. And I'd like flowers everywhere. Could you take over all that?"

"My sister will help me with the shopping, and I have a housekeeping couple I think you would like," Gia said. "We can begin tomorrow. In a week, you'll have a clean home and a new bed to sleep in."

"That sounds wonderful." Ruby smoothed her hand over her niece's. "And Ariana, would you work with Gia? Feel free to choose whatever you like. I'm happy to be in the hands of two extraordinarily capable artists. Surprise me. I'd like that."

Ruby smiled at the two women, who both looked pleased to start the project. They were about the same age as well. Maybe they'd become friends in the process; Ariana could use a friend here.

As Ariana and Gia chatted, Ruby relaxed. Life was good, and she'd been through enough to appreciate it now.

When Ruby was a girl on the ranch, a life like this had existed only in her dreams. As she took inventory of her life, she thought not of what she'd accumulated, but of the people whose lives she had touched and improved. The promising young directors and writers who'd simply needed the right introduction or a check to start filming a great script. Her life as an actress had been a hard climb, but in retrospect, what mattered most were the people she could bring together. They were the pillars of her success.

All she wanted now was one more try. And this time, it was personal.

Later that day at the villa, as Ariana and Gia made their way from room to room, envisioning each one, a knock sounded on the door. Ruby excused herself to answer it.

A woman stood at the door. "Gia called and asked me to come. I am Livia."

"Do come in," Ruby said, opening the door wide. At first, with Livia's dark-blue uniform and sensible shoes, Ruby thought the woman looked like she'd been sent from Central Casting. But when Livia took off her broad sun hat, she revealed a short crop of purple hair.

Ruby smiled. "I love your hair."

"I'm also an artist," Livia said shyly.

Ruby liked her better already.

Since Ariana and Gia were busy determining bedding and other necessities, Ruby showed Livia through the house before leading her to an attached caretaker's cottage. The woman asked few questions, but she seemed efficient and ready to work. Ruby liked that. Gia had told her that the older man Livia worked for had passed away, and the home was up for sale.

"I can live here," Livia said, glancing around. "And my

husband. He will take care of the garden and bring fish from the lake, too."

This arrangement might work out even better than Ruby had hoped. "Do you have children?""

"All grown and married. We have a cat. It's okay?"

"Yes, of course."

"I'll start now," Livia said, patting her bag. "I have some supplies, and tomorrow I will bring more."

Ruby discussed terms and rate of pay, and when they'd both agreed, Ruby handed her an extra key. "Welcome to Villa Fiori."

Leaving Livia to her work, Ruby found a chair on the terrace to catch her breath. Taking in the view of the lake, she made a mental list of what she needed to do here, which had little to do with cleaning or furnishing the house.

A pair of small passerines—golden orioles marked with sunny yellow and inky black feathers—sang to her from a nearby tree while she relaxed. The little birds reminded her of when she and her sister would lay under the shade of a tree on a hot summer day on the ranch, watching the sparrows.

If only Patricia were here with her now. Although the two sisters hadn't always agreed, Ruby had always known that she could count on Patricia.

Ruby sighed. She had been living a lie for most of her life now. If only her sister hadn't left the final decision to her. The safety deposit key nestled in her purse could be a key to disaster.

The closer Ruby drew to her decision, the more nervous she became. As the orioles twittered their song against the rustling palm trees overhead, she considered her dilemma.

It wasn't too late to change her mind. But could she live with that?

9

Lago di Como, 2010

When Ariana stepped inside Villa Fiori, she was amazed at the transformation that had taken place over just a few days. As she walked through the house, she saw that the cobwebs and dust were gone, banished by the industrious Livia and her husband, Emilio.

She made her way into the kitchen. The musty smell that made Ariana feel so nauseated had been scrubbed away with a lemony scent, which was fresh and appealing. Ruby was arranging colorful, handmade ceramics decorated with fanciful swirls, lemons, and grapevines.

Since they'd arrived, Ruby seemed revived, as if she'd discovered an untapped reservoir of energy. Even the well-earned lines on her face seemed to have softened,

"Good morning," Ariana said. "What beautiful pottery. Did you find that here?"

"Livia did." Ruby pointed to an open door. "In the china closet. I can't imagine how long all this was locked up. Decades perhaps." She arranged a grouping of platters and jugs, which bore vibrant lemons and green leaves, in the center of a rustic wooden table worn smooth from years of use.

"This is *majolica* pottery," Ruby said. "Regions produced different motifs. This lemon design is probably from Amalfi, which is known for growing the finest lemons." She stepped back to admire her handiwork. Brushing her hands, she asked, "How are you and Gia doing?"

"Very well," Ariana said, easing onto a stool. "I couldn't have done this without her. It would have taken months to do what she did in a few days. She should be here soon because she said an early delivery is arriving today. I think she wants to take me to a factory of some sort, too." She glanced around the kitchen.

"Livia wasted no time in stocking the refrigerator with fresh fruits and vegetables," Ruby said. "What a treasure she is."

Ariana opened the refrigerator and discovered a bunch of grapes. Bringing out the bowl, she placed it on the table to share with her aunt. She popped a grape in her mouth, marveling at the flavor. "I can hardly believe I'm here. I was supposed to be on my honeymoon right now."

"Life is full of interesting twists," Ruby said. "Are you happy with your decision now?"

"So happy that I feel guilty. Was I misleading Phillip?"

"I don't think so," Ruby said. "You were just caught up in his plan rather than having your own."

Ariana plucked another grape and thought about that. "Our relationship was convenient." She'd never liked change. It had seemed more trouble to break up and date new people than to carry on with their relationship. "As I sat waiting for him at the church, I finally realized that my happiness would always be secondary to his."

"Time to start fresh," Ruby said, touching Ariana's hand. "In many ways. Decide what you want to do and approach it with purpose."

"You mean, as in my work?"

Ruby nodded. "Just because you loved it once, doesn't mean you have to keep on with it. Maybe you've outgrown your position."

"I've definitely outgrown my boss. Kingsley would go ballistic if he knew I'd called off the wedding and took a vacation instead."

Ruby gave her an enigmatic smile. "You're welcome to stay here and explore your options."

The thought of that was intriguing, though far-fetched. "I can't imagine that I won't be on a plane back to L.A. at the end of the month." Besides, she had to support herself. And soon, a new baby.

After landing her first job after college, Ariana had never asked for money from her mother or Ruby. Her mother would have lectured her on the importance of responsibility and self-reliance. As if self-reliance hadn't been forced upon her when her mother had shipped her off to boarding school as a child.

Most people thought of boarding school students as privi-leged—and she was the first to agree that most were—but she'd been on a strict budget from her mother. Ariana had resorted to proofreading term papers and tutoring to earn extra money.

"You're very talented, my dear," Ruby said, plucking grapes from the bowl between them. "Maybe inspiration will strike here."

Just then, Livia appeared at the doorway to the kitchen with Gia. "*La signora* to see you," Livia said.

"*Grazie*, Livia," Ariana said, sliding off the stool to greet her new friend. Gia was married with a little girl, but other than that, the two of them had much in common. And Gia's sister Vera was a little older with three children of her own.

They chatted about the deliveries that were due today, and Ariana told Ruby that she'd briefed Livia the day before. Outside, Emilio was busy tilling the soil to plant.

"The first delivery truck was pulling in behind me," Gia said. "I have to make sure everything is placed where we discussed. And my car is full of sheets and towels."

"I'm excited to see how everything looks," Ariana said, following Gia from the kitchen.

Two men had already unloaded a rug for the main living area and were bringing in the sofas that Gia had suggested. The creamy colors were cool against the exterior view of the lake, and

Ariana imagined how the cushions would look with pops of brightly colored pillows.

Next off the truck were lamps, and Ariana helped Gia place those throughout the house. Livia took the linens to wash, and soon everything was done.

"It's still sparsely furnished," Ariana said, looking around.

"It won't seem like that once the plants arrive," Gia said.

Ruby pushed open the doors to let the morning breeze in. "I like the airy spaciousness."

Gia turned to Ruby. "Would you like to go to the silk factory with us? Vera reminded me of our connection and arranged a special visit for us. I thought Ariana would find it interesting."

Ruby perked up. "What's the name of it, dear?"

"Bellarosa. The company has been here for years. They supplied silk for one of the first homes I designed. I'd almost forgotten, but Vera remembered."

"Ah, yes. You'll find some beautiful pieces there," Ruby said. "I have a little shopping to do, but you two go and have a wonderful time."

Soon, Ariana and Gia were on their way, winding around the steep hillside on narrow roads that took Ariana's breath away. She let out a little yelp as an oncoming car passed close on a curve.

"You'll get used to the roads," Gia said, expertly whipping the car around the bends in narrow lanes. "That wasn't as close as it looked. I hope I'm not scaring you."

"It's okay," Ariana said, hoping she wouldn't become nauseous. "Ruby drives just like this."

When they arrived at the silk factory, Ariana sighed with relief, glad that Gia was a good driver. She was a little queasy, but the feeling soon passed.

After they arrived, they walked toward the building, which to Ariana looked more like a villa with its tall windows and fragrant gardens. Gia spoke to a receptionist at the front, but Ariana's high school Italian only allowed her to catch a few words. The woman directed them to a group of chairs and sofas, where they sat down to wait.

"If I were going to be here longer, I'd like to work on my Italian," Ariana said.

"With your last name, I thought you might speak the language."

"Ricci was my father's name, and he didn't stay around long enough to pass on anything."

"I'm sorry to hear that," Gia said. "Did your mother remarry?"

"She was too busy working even to date," Ariana replied. "She's an investment banker in New York."

"I can't imagine how difficult raising a child would be without my husband. He's amazing with our little one." Gia paused. "Your mother must be an incredible woman. That's a demanding position, especially being on her own."

Ariana hadn't thought about it that way. "She's…unique. As I grew older, I spent more time with Ruby, so I'm closer to her. My mom didn't even plan to come to my wedding."

"You're married?"

Ariana sighed. "I left him at the altar. Actually, I'm relieved." *Even though I'm facing single motherhood,* she thought.

Gia's eyes widened. "You have courage. Like your mother and aunt." She looked up. "Here's Alessandro."

Ariana followed her gaze. What struck her was not the man's good looks, although, with his commanding height and hair that curled just beneath his ears, he certainly was attractive. Rather, it was the way he moved. Self-possessed, yet graceful—and in a thoroughly masculine way. He would have caught her eye anywhere.

The cut of his clothing was immaculate, too. A silk shirt—it had to be silk with that drape—was fitted trim to his torso, but not too tight, and his trousers sat just right on his hips. A thousand actors would kill for his physique, and she caught herself wondering what it would be like to design clothes for that body.

He greeted Gia by pressing his cheeks to hers as they exchanged a few words. He turned to Ariana, clasping her hand. "*Ciao. Come stai?*"

"*Benissimo,*" Ariana remembered to say. She'd understood a few words that Gia had said to him—she'd asked about his children. A glance at his ring finger confirmed it.

As Gia introduced them, Ariana pushed her thoughts aside. Undoubtedly, many women found him attractive, but he was married. *Full stop.*

When Gia told him that this was her first visit to Lake Como, Alessandro looked surprised. "Then I must give you a tour of our factory."

Ariana started to protest, but the factory looked more like an artist's haven than a place of commerce, and she was intrigued. People were chatting outside in the garden or walking around the property—devoid of the tension she saw on employees' faces where she worked.

While she was sure that they had their share of concerns, the atmosphere was different. It seemed more conducive to creativity and work—unlike the constant stress and anxiety that circulated at the studio. Maybe it was the surroundings. Perhaps the serene waters of Lake Como—broken by the occasional water taxi or ferry—had a calming effect on people.

"My father's family has been in silk production for almost three-hundred years," Alessandro said. "In the 1500s, the Duke of Milan, Ludovico Sforza—Il Moro—had mulberry trees planted and bred silkworms. Did you know that silkworms are hungry little creatures that will eat almost anything, but they only produce silk cocoons when they eat the leaves of the mulberry tree?"

Although Alessandro must have given this lecture countless times, an expression of marvel and delight lit his face, and he pressed a hand to his heart. "This is a true miracle of nature. We are so privileged to carry on this tradition."

While Ariana found the history interesting, it was Alessandro's passionate delivery that intrigued her. She blurted out, "Do you really enjoy what you do?"

"But of course," he replied, seemingly perplexed by her question. "We create beauty with natural materials. As with wine or perfume, a person can tell the moment they encounter authentic, high-quality silk. We're proud of our heritage. Although Como no longer breeds or spins as much silk as before, we are experts in silk weaving and design."

Looking into Alessandro's eyes, Ariana could tell he was

devoted to his craft. As he led them through the factory, where a brilliant array of silk yarn in every imaginable color on spools filled pegs, he explained that China now provided most of the raw material due to the labor-intensive process.

"We perform all the processes of warping and weaving in-house," Alessandro said, pausing by an intricate loom. "This is one of our recently restored looms. My grandfather once used it."

Gia cut in. "Ariana would like to see your designs. As I mentioned when I called, her aunt purchased Villa Fiori."

"An exquisite jewel box with a superb location," he said, nodding thoughtfully. "If anyone has the style to resurrect Villa Fiori, it is Signora Raines. She has great personal style."

Ariana smiled. Fans loved her aunt. "You've seen her films?"

"Oh, yes. And we had tea at the hotel a few weeks ago. Your aunt is a beautiful woman."

Ariana and Gia traded looks. Her aunt had never mentioned having met Alessandro, and from the look on Gia's face, she was fairly certain that Gia hadn't known either. So how had they ended up here?

Vera. Gia's sister had suggested it, Ariana recalled.

Alessandro was looking at her with interest. "We can make whatever you can imagine. We have about 100,000 designs in our archives. Would you like to see our design department?"

As Ariana followed him, she noted how people's faces lit up when he approached. "*Ciao, ciao,*" he said to employees. He paused to praise one woman on her work and to answer a question from another man. She was struck by how familial they all seemed, and she couldn't imagine anyone at the studio treating Kingsley with such affection. Or anyone else in management.

Her work environment hadn't always been that way, though. When she'd first started working at the company, creativity was the *lingua franca*, but since being acquired by a private equity firm, the entire management had shifted. Kingsley was one of the private-equity hires whose job was to focus on the bottom line and squeeze every ounce of profit from his departments.

Alessandro paused by one large room filled with hi-tech equipment. "Besides our designs, we can also take hand-drawn designs and digitize them for printing. We also print by hand for our most high-end clients. After printing, steaming fixes the ink to the fabric and enhances the color. Then, the fabric is washed, dried, and finished."

The scent of dye permeated the air. As Ariana watched, bolts of white silk fabric were fed through machines that printed intricate designs. "The intensity of color after steaming is impressive," she said.

Alessandro turned to her with a look of interest. "Your aunt told me about your costume work. Did you always want to do that?"

"No," she blurted out. What was it about this man that made her speak without thinking? Yet that was the truth. "I studied fashion design because I love to create. I like to see people transformed by clothes they love to wear. Likewise, the right costume helps actors get into character. It's been a lot of fun, but I miss designing for real people."

Alessandro's smile broadened. "Spoken like a true artist. We are alike in that way," he said, his deep voice reverberating in his chest. "Come, I'll show you more."

His words and phrasing caressed her like the softest silk Ariana could imagine. She shot Gia a look, but Gia seemed unfazed. Was Ariana imagining things, or were all Italian men as smooth as Alessandro? Maybe this is why her aunt loved Italy. If anyone was addicted to adoration, it was her aunt. Or perhaps that's the image she wanted to portray. After all these years, her aunt was still an enigma, often surprising her.

They continued to another room that was full of samples and archived designs. "We have digitized our designs," Alessandro said, pulling out a chair for her at a long table where swatch books were stacked.

Gia joined her and began to peruse the samples. "There are many good options here."

Whether it was Alessandro's attention or the dizzying array of choices before her, Ariana felt overwhelmed. Looking between Gia and Alessandro, she said, "Since you two know my aunt and Villa Fiori, what do you recommend?"

"May I?" Alessandro glanced at Gia, who nodded her assent.

"Permit me," he said, flipping through samples with a practiced hand. "One moment."

In a flash, Alessandro left, but then he returned a moment later carrying several magnificent rolls of silk. With great showmanship, he unfurled them across the table. "What do you think?"

Ariana ran her hand across silk as soft as an angel's breath. Magenta, fuchsia, violet—hot floral colors strewn across a shimmering turquoise background. "Oh, yes," she murmured, not even stopping to consider all the details she usually would have.

Instinctively, she knew these were perfect. The dusty colors she'd once considered would wash out against the vibrant backdrop of the lake and mountains. And she knew Ruby would love the vivid colors.

"And this." Alessandro draped another choice over the table, the fabric flowing like a waterfall of aquamarine hues.

Ariana held an edge to her cheek, reveling in the cool, whisper-soft texture. She could see these fabrics in luxurious throws and pillows of all shapes and sizes, or draping from a window, puddling to the floor. Looking up, she was surprised to see Alessandro staring at her. A small smile tugged his lips.

"You like it?" he asked, holding her gaze.

"It's perfect," she said, losing herself in the moment. Catching herself, she blinked. Was she being too hasty? She let go of the fabric. "But of course, I'd like to see some others, too." At her comment, she registered a brief flash of disappointment in his hazel eyes.

He gave a slight nod. "But of course," he said, echoing her words in a deep baritone.

Ariana turned to Gia. "What do you think?"

Gia seemed as transfixed as she was. "These are excellent choices, but let's see what else we can find."

They spent the next half hour sorting through some of the most beautiful silks Ariana had ever seen. In the end, they only added a few other designs to Alessandro's recommendations, though Ariana loved his choices the most.

Gia folded her hands and smiled. "Alessandro is a renowned silk savant."

A woman appeared at the door. "*Scusa*, Alessandro?" She tapped her wrist to indicate the time.

"*Sì, sì.* I must go," Alessandro said. After introducing Paolina, he excused himself, promising to return soon.

Paolina slid into the chair Alessandro vacated and took up where he left off, helping them calculate the amount of fabric they would need. At one point, Paolina asked for coffee, and Ariana was grateful for the little cup of strong espresso.

After finishing the details, Ariana and Gia started back to the car. Just then, Alessandro pulled up beside them in the parking area. He stepped from a four-door Maserati and waved at them.

"*Momento*," he called out, just as two children tumbled from the back seat. Laughing, they raced toward the front door to the factory. "*Scusi*, Ariana, may I ask a question?"

Just then, Gia's phone buzzed. "It's my husband. Go ahead. I'll take this in the car."

Ariana slid on her sunglasses and waited. Behind her, Paolina met the children at the door with hugs and led them inside. The children clung to her as if she were their mother, which made Ariana wonder if she was. Plenty of married couples worked together. She couldn't recall if Paolina wore a wedding ring, but now she realized she probably was the children's mother.

And Alessandro's wife.

Alessandro strode toward her. "I'm sorry I had to rush out, but you can see why. I'm afraid I lost track of time. And then the kids...it's always something with them."

Striving to be cordial, she said, "They're adorable. How old are they?"

"Sandro is seven, and Carmela is five. They're so inquisitive and rambunctious. Do you have children?"

"No, no." Ariana stumbled over the word, but she wasn't about to divulge her secret to a stranger.

"Not married?"

Nor was Ariana going to share her disastrous attempt at marriage. "Absolutely not."

Alessandro rocked back and forth in his loafers and chuckled, though his laughter had a strangled, nervous edge. "Then, may I ask you out for coffee sometime? Or dinner? I don't know—whatever it is that you do in America. Drinks?"

Did I hear him correctly? Ariana's lips parted, and she swung her gaze from Alessandro to the children, who were chattering away with Paolina in the doorway. Something wasn't right here. But she was not going to be the American fling for a month.

Whipping off her sunglasses, Ariana lashed out at him. "I can't believe you would ask such a thing—and in front of your children?"

"*Che cosa?*" He spread his hands and stared at her. "What?"

Ariana snapped on her sunglasses. "I appreciate your help today, but I shouldn't have to explain." She whirled around and opened the passenger door to Gia's car.

Gia hung up the phone, looking a little frazzled.

"Let's go," Ariana said, disgusted and angry that Alessandro ruined what had been a perfectly lovely day.

"My little girl is sick," Gia said. "She has a fever, so I have to pick her up and get medicine for her."

Before Ariana could tell her about Alessandro, the conversation shifted to Gia's daughter.

"That's okay," Ariana said. "I just remembered I have to talk to my aunt about something." Like trying to set her up with unsuitable replacements for Phillip—which was even crazier than buying a villa in Italy.

A sudden thought seized her. This behavior was unusual, even for Ruby, who could be impulsive about little things, like new shoes or hairstyles. Or surprising her with a weekend trip to a spa. But extravagant purchases like a villa in Italy?

Ariana slid her hand over the back of her neck in thought. Maybe there was another explanation, although it was one that Ariana hated to address. Could Ruby's lapse in judgment be attributed to mental decline?

Ariana sighed, recalling her own Nana Pat, who'd had Alzheimer's disease for almost as long as Ariana could remember. Patricia and Ruby were sisters. Could Ruby's behavior be an early signal that the disease was attacking her, too?

10

Rome, 1952

A messenger boy clad in baggy, faded trousers held up by suspenders raced toward the fountain where Ruby was sitting while writing postcards to her family back home.

On this muggy morning, she'd discovered that sitting down-wind of the fountain was the coolest—and she used that term relatively—spot to watch the hub-bub of life before filming began.

Being on set was thrilling, and Ruby soaked up everything she could. She never grew tired of watching Audrey Hepburn, who acted so naturally that she hardly seemed to be acting at all.

The boy skidded to stop in front of her. With perspiration beading on his face, he panted, "Ruby Raines?"

"That's right." He was probably one of the crew's children, making himself useful on set while his parent or parents worked. Many of the cast had brought their families along for an extended holiday. Even Mr. Wyler's children, Judy and Cathy, had been in the school scene as schoolchildren.

"You have to report to David in Costumes right away. Mr. Wyler's order."

Ruby tucked her postcards into the pocket of her skirt. *At Mr. Wyler's request!* Could this be her lucky break? She hurried on her way.

When she arrived, David gave her a quick hug. The assistant wardrobe supervisor was a wiry whirl of energy this morning.

"The stand-in for Miss Hepburn is sick today," David said as he pulled clothes for her. "Even though Mr. Wyler is shooting in black-and-white—thanks to budget constraints—we still need to approximate Miss Hepburn's wardrobe for lighting. We needed a fill-in, so I suggested you. You're the same size as Miss Hepburn, and Mr. Wyler approved. The camera and lighting supervisors agreed. Same height, same skin and bones. Are you a dancer, too?"

Ruby nearly burst out laughing with one of those awful hee-haw honks that her mother always shushed. She was in Rome now, a professional actress on a set—well, almost—and she was supposed to be acting not just her age, but older.

"Oh, yes, I dance, too," she said with what she hoped was an air of calm and sophistication.

Never say you can't do anything. Her agent's words rang in her ears. *You can learn how. Say anything to get the job.*

David tossed a scarf over a hanger. "Thought so. Muscular calves, strong arms." He flipped open a book that contained sketches and swatches. Frowning with concentration, he ran his finger down a list.

She'd earned her long, lean muscles not from ballet as Miss Hepburn had, but from herding cattle on horseback with her father. And the only dancing she knew was the Texas kind. The two-step with its quick-quick steps, the *schottische* with its funny little hops, and the traditional polka that she danced with her grandpa at Gruene Hall in New Braunfels and parties in Fredericksburg. She knew how to waltz Texas-style, but that looked little like the grand, sweeping waltz she'd seen in the movies.

"What's that?" Ruby asked, peering over David's shoulder at the thick binder he was consulting.

"Our costume bible," he said, tapping a page. "This has Edith Head's sketches, fabric swatches, measurements, and a complete list of every accessory and detail for each scene. For continuity purposes, not a hairpin or a sock will be out of place from one day of filming to the next. And heaven help the actor who gains weight. Or loses it."

"Why?"

"Alterations take time and damage continuity." He put his hands on his hips. "Gregory Peck is losing too much weight, but he's a star," he muttered. "With all this fabulous food around, who loses weight in Italy?" A frown knitted his brow. "Pity we can hardly partake of the feast."

Ruby laughed. The unionized craft services provided American-style food on the set, which included tasteless white bread with American cheese, pressed bologna, and canned peas. She'd always had crisp peas fresh from the garden; these strange, gray-green pretenders were salty and mushy. And the bread was nothing like they made at home.

"Don't you eat the craft services food?" Ruby asked.

"Not if I can help it." David grinned. "I pay a kid to sneak in paninis and Italian sodas for me." He held up a hangar full of clothes. "Now, take your clothes off."

"I beg your pardon? Here?"

David rolled his eyes. "Honey, I'm the last person on this set a girl like you needs to worry about."

"I'm not sure what you mean…"

A smile spread across David's face, and he chuckled. "Oh, sweetie, you *are* green. How old did you say you were?"

She tilted her chin up. "Old enough."

"Uh-huh." David arched an eyebrow in obvious doubt. Harried, he shoved the clothes toward her. "Go change, but don't go out without my checking you. I don't care if it is just a lighting check; you will be perfect. You reflect on me. Now go." He flung his hand toward a small changing room.

Once inside, Ruby wriggled out of her clothes and into the skirt and blouse. Emerging from the dressing room, she asked, "How's this?"

"Oh, darling, no, no, no," David said. "Valentina, we need some help here."

An older woman hurried to help Ruby untuck the shirt and tuck it in again. She gathered the fullness to the sides and back with crisp folds, which gave the blouse clean lines in front. Then she added a wide belt to cinch Ruby's waist and tied the striped scarf around her neck.

David stood back, apprising her look. "You should have been in makeup first. Go now, and have it applied very carefully. Tell the makeup artist not to get a speck on my costume. The lighting supervisor will need to check the lighting on your face." He whisked a hand toward the door. "What are you waiting for?"

"Thank you, David," Ruby said.

"Thank that boyfriend of yours for the limoncello," David said with a grin. "Now, go!"

"He's not my boyfriend," Ruby called out as she raced to the door and stumbled on her shoe.

David flung up his hands. "And don't run. You can't scuff those shoes."

Ruby slowed her pace, yet still managed a brisk walk to the next trailer, where makeup stations were set up similar to the beauty shop where her aunt Vivienne worked in Hollywood. Several people were languishing in chairs chatting and reading fan magazines.

Ruby cleared her throat. "I'm here for makeup."

An older man nudged the woman in the chair who was talking the loudest. "Marge, you're up."

Marge pushed herself from a chair. "You should have come here first."

"I'm filling in for a stand-in who is out sick," Ruby said. "They're going to adjust lighting and places, so David in wardrobe told me to come over. And asked that you be careful with the costume."

"I'll bet," Marge said, chuckling to herself. She yanked a makeup cape from a hook. "Come on, sweetie. Let's get that shine off your face and add color to those lips." She motioned to a chair.

Ruby eased in, and Marge unfurled the cape over her costume. The woman snapped it snugly around Ruby's neck. After matching the tint to the skin on Ruby's face, Marge applied it liberally to Ruby's cheeks and forehead, blending as she went.

"The lights are hot, so this is sweatproof," Marge said.

"Might be difficult to wipe off afterward. Do you have any cold cream?"

"Ivory soap and water?" Ruby fidgeted under the cape.

Marge clucked her tongue and nodded toward a white ceramic jar on the counter. "Take a jar of that Pond's cream with you. You should be using it anyway, at night. Not that you have any wrinkles, but if you're going to be in pictures, you can't start taking care of your skin too soon. Look at Garbo. Now that's a face."

"Do you know why she retired?" Ruby asked.

"Seeing as how Garbo retired in forty-one, I wouldn't likely know her." Marge brushed color onto Ruby's face as she talked. "That was before my time, so I only know what's in the fan mags. Garbo is one of the greats, though, that's for sure. Fans still adore her."

Ruby sat as still as she could while Marge penciled in thick eyebrows like Miss Hepburn's. Taking another, narrow brush, the makeup artist dabbed on lip color. After pressing powder onto her skin with a sponge, Marge stepped back. "See what you think."

Ruby gazed into the mirror, amazed at the transformation. Now she really did look eighteen, even twenty or older. "Thank you," she murmured, awestruck at her image.

"You're ready." Marge grinned and whisked off the cape.

Ruby pushed herself from the chair and stood. "I'm not sure where to go."

Just then, a young man rushed in the door fanning his face with a newspaper. "Are you the stand-in for Miss Hepburn today?"

"I am."

"They need you on set right now. I can drive you."

"See you around," Marge said. "And don't forget the Pond's."

Ruby tucked it into her purse and set off with the young man in a little Fiat automobile. As they careened through the streets, Ruby asked, "Where are we going?"

"They didn't tell you?" the young man asked, steering through a roundabout that had Ruby clutching the dashboard. Without waiting for an answer, he went on, "The Santa Maria.

It's an old church at the Piazza della Bocca della Verità, or Mouth of Truth. As the old legend goes, if you're not telling the truth, it bites off your hand." He paused for dramatic effect. "You're going to have to put your hand in there."

Ruby angled her chin. "I'm not afraid."

Chuckling, he eased to a stop in a piazza crowded with onlookers. "And here we are."

Ruby had been fine up until now. As soon as they arrived at the designated filming location, she began fidgeting.

It was one thing to watch movies and dream of being in them, but now, here she was in the middle of the chaos, in the stifling heat of a city teeming with crowds that followed them wherever they went. She'd have to learn to block it all out if she were to become a great actress.

Heads turned as they hurried to the side of the church, where the film crew milled about. Ruby was quickly folded into the crowd and rushed to the set.

"Where should I go?" Ruby asked, her heart quickening.

"Right over there," the driver said, pointing to a spot beside a large round piece of stone.

The disk had a frightening-looking face carved into it, with hollow eyes and a gaping mouth. Ruby cut through the crowd.

"Here she is," another man called out.

Ruby recognized him as the assistant director. Beside him in a folding chair sat Mr. Wyler, calmly watching everything around him. He brightened and nodded toward Ruby.

"You're the young lady who was almost run over by the Vespa, right?" Mr. Wyler put out his hand.

Ruby shook his hand, pleased that he remembered. "Yes, sir." His calm demeanor and the way he smiled at her put her at ease. He reminded her of her father, who remained unruffled, even when faced with adversity. She'd watched her steely-eyed dad manage dangerous situations ranging from rattlesnakes and wild boars to rabid dogs. *Stay still,* he'd say. But she wondered if the director also had a fierce temper like her father. She blinked, forcing her thoughts back to the present.

Mr. Wyler was staring at her. "David was right. Remarkable

likeness in size. Now, if you'll stand there, very still, we'll set up the scene and adjust the lighting."

Ruby stood next to the mammoth, carved marble disk, which was slightly unnerving, but she smiled and turned this way and that way as directed while the crew tested different lights and made adjustments. Another man dressed in a suit as the stand-in for Gregory Peck soon joined her. Together they marked the scene as directed.

Even though Ruby wasn't acting, she was still excited to be on the set. She absorbed everything. The crowd surrounding them was chattering away, and people were snapping photos as if she were a star. It was all so fascinating. She vowed to do whatever it took to make a career of this, despite her father's admonition. After all, she was nearly an adult.

Ruby smiled to herself. *Imagine getting paid to do this.* Her agent, Joseph Applebaum, had negotiated a reasonable sum for her work, plus her trip to Italy. Joseph said it could be a big break for her because William Wyler was one of Hollywood's best directors.

"Now, Ruby," Mr. Wyler was saying, pulling her back from her thoughts. "Turn to the side and put your hand in the mouth of that disk. The Mouth of Truth. This is an important moment."

Her fellow actor laughed nervously. "Better you than me," he chuckled. "No telling what's in there."

Ruby gritted her teeth and eased her hand into the gaping mouth. "Nothing to it." She wouldn't be intimidated by an old artifact, although she took care not to let her hand touch the sides. Texas was full of scorpions and rattlesnakes, and she wasn't afraid to shoot a rabid varmint.

"Just like that," Mr. Wyler said. "Good. Now hold it, and turn this way." He asked his crew to check the lighting and angles.

After the scene was blocked out, the director declared a break, and Ruby and her fellow stand-in were released. They were told not to venture too far, so Ruby stayed near the set while Mr. Wyler called in Miss Hepburn and Mr. Peck.

As Ruby made her way from the church and the frightening

disk, she came face to face with Miss Hepburn, who looked at her and laughed. Ruby introduced herself.

"I feel like I'm looking in a mirror," Audrey said, touching Ruby's identical skirt.

"Me, too," Ruby said. "Only I think I have the better view."

"Nonsense," Audrey said, her voice lilting with laughter. "You're so beautiful. Do you dance, too?"

"A little, but not like you," Ruby said, feeling her cheeks color.

"Thank you for blocking out the scene, Ruby. You made it look so easy. But I don't like the idea of putting my hand in the mouth of that monstrous stone." Audrey shivered.

"It wasn't so bad," Ruby said.

"Well, I think you're very, very brave."

Mr. Wyler clapped his hands and called out, "Places everyone."

Audrey's hand flew up to her neck. "Will you help me take off this necklace? I slipped away for gelato and stopped at a little shop along the way. I thought this was so sweet. But I can't wear it in the scene."

"Continuity, right?" Ruby was proud to use one of her new terms.

"That's right," Audrey said. "It's such a dear piece of jewelry, too." She glanced at Niccolò and smiled back at Ruby. "Is that your young man?" she whispered, indicating Niccolò, who was standing with a group of people watching. "I've seen you two together a lot."

Ruby nodded. "I think so." Maybe everyone could see it in her eyes. Audrey was engaged, so she knew what it was like to be in love.

"He's terribly handsome." Audrey fiddled with the clasp of the silver, heart-shaped necklace. Two small red stones crowned the top of the heart.

"I can do that for you," Ruby said. She unclasped it and handed it to Audrey.

"You're too kind." Audrey smiled. "Why don't you keep the necklace? It's a heart that can be divided, see? Although I hope you are never separated from your loved one." She pressed the necklace into Ruby's hands. "This will be so pretty on you. I love the little rubies, and since your name is Ruby, I think it's meant for you. I want you to have something lovely to remember Rome."

"But this is such a treasure."

"So are you, dear Ruby," Audrey said, breaking into a broad smile. "Oh, there's Mr. Peck. I should hurry. I hope to see you again soon."

The two women hugged each other carefully, being mindful of their makeup. With a little wave, Audrey hurried to her place.

Mr. Wyler was talking to Gregory Peck, who then took his place next to Audrey in the scene.

Niccolò sauntered toward her. "Hey, Tex. You looked like a real star in that scene."

"Shh," Ruby said, holding her finger to her lips. "They're about to begin."

The assistant director called out, "Quiet on the set!"

As the crowd hushed, Niccolò put his arm around her, and Ruby felt her heart flutter. She pressed her fingers against the silver necklace that, until moments ago, had graced Audrey's slender neck. Ruby knew she would cherish this forever.

The lights flared, and the camera operators focused on the actors. Ruby got the chills thinking that she had been standing there just like that only a few minutes ago. She was becoming a real actress. Just the thought of that made her breathless with joy.

A clapperboard operator carefully wrote the scene and take-number with chalk on a slate board. He stepped before the camera and called out the identifiers before clapping the top of the board.

A hush swept across the crowd.

"Action," Mr. Wyler called out.

The two actors slid into their characters, transfixing the audience surrounding them. Ruby was impressed with how naturally Audrey acted opposite her experienced co-star. They two actors ran their lines, and Ruby was drawn into the story. Sure enough, Audrey—as Princess Ann—hesitated when putting her hand into the Mouth of Truth, but she did it, just as Ruby had.

Now it was Gregory's turn. He slid his hand in, and then, when he pulled it out, his hand was missing.

Audrey shrieked, and Ruby saw the director smile and motion to keep the camera rolling. Gregory had tricked her by pulling his coat sleeve down over his hand. It was a silly joke, but Ruby probably would have screamed, too.

Finally, Mr. Wyler called out. "Cut."

Audrey and Gregory dissolved into laughter at the trick he'd played on her.

"That's a wrap," Mr. Wyler said.

"Just one take?" Audrey asked incredulously.

"It was perfect," the director replied. On his motion, the crew began breaking down equipment for the day.

Elated, Audrey turned to Ruby. "One take! That's because you set up the scene so beautifully. Will you join us on Via Veneto? We're all meeting at Café de Paris, or maybe Harry's Bar. Look for us, will you?"

Ruby promised she would and touched the silver pendant around her neck. "And thank you for the necklace."

"It was truly meant for you, Ruby." Audrey waved and hurried off.

"I'm impressed," Niccolò said, admiring the necklace.

"Audrey couldn't wear it in the scene. Did you see me standing in as they were setting up the scene?"

"Saw it all," Niccolò said, jerking his thumb back toward the crowd. "Some of my friends are here, too. They want to meet you. They think you're a star."

Ruby shook her head. "I'm a stand-in with a bit part."

Niccolò shook his head. "I told them you're an American actress from Texas who's going to be a big star." He paused to glance toward them, signaling that they'd join them in a moment. "They said you hold yourself like a princess, too. Like Miss Hepburn with her ballet training."

Ruby laughed. More likely, her posture was from barrel racing at livestock shows. "I was once crowned a cattle princess. Even had a tiara fitted over the brim of a cowboy hat."

Now Niccolò burst out with a hearty laugh. "Did you know this is the *Foro Boario*, the ancient cattle market?"

"No wonder I feel at home here," Ruby remarked, thinking about her family's ranch. Although she missed saddling up with her father and rounding up the cattle on horseback—when times were better—this life was exciting.

Niccolò crooked his elbow, and Ruby hooked her arm through his. "Introduce me to your friends. I'll tell them I rode a horse to school." Although she acted as if this were a joke, it was the truth.

"You're so funny," Niccolò said, his eyes roaming over her face. "I've never met anyone like you."

His gaze enveloped her in a virtual caress that left her hungering for more.

"*Anima mia,*" Niccolò whispered to her as he kissed her on the cheek. "You are my soul. How will I ever let you go?"

"Don't," Ruby said simply. She gazed around, reminding herself that this was her life now. *Rome, films, Hollywood.* And Niccolò. As much as she missed her family, how could she ever return to the ranch or the life she'd known before? As long as she made money and was generous with her folks, maybe she wouldn't have to. And yet, Hollywood was sprawling and impersonal. "Come back with me," she blurted out.

"You mean it?"

Suddenly, the idea took hold of her, and it seemed entirely plausible. "Let's figure it out."

Niccolò grinned. "I know how."

"How?"

"Just say 'yes.'" Niccolò's bright blue eyes sparkled with passion.

Ruby giggled. "How could I ever say 'no' to a boy with such dreamy eyes?"

As she and Niccolò chatted with his friends, who seemed a little starstruck even though she wasn't famous, the messenger boy who'd brought her to the set earlier charged toward her.

"Miss Raines, telegram for you," the messenger boy called out. He waved an envelope in his hand.

"For me?" Only important people received telegrams. Unless… With a trembling hand, Ruby tore the envelope open, nervous about what news it might contain.

Niccolò slipped his arm around her shoulder, understanding her trepidation.

The message was from her sister, Patricia. Ruby pressed a hand to her mouth as she read it.

No rain, drought worse. Mama and Daddy need help. Can you wire money?

She knew what that meant. The crops had failed again.

Last year, the drought had been relentless. After the crops withered and dried, Ruby burned off the thorns of prickly pear cactus to feed their cattle. Thankfully, the rain had come early this spring, so her parents hoped this year would be better. Yet, by the time Ruby left Los Angeles for Italy, Patricia warned her that the crops and pastures were becoming parched.

If the vegetation had died, Patricia's telegram meant her parents needed money for food for the livestock—and themselves. For Patricia to reach out to Ruby was a last resort.

Worried, Ruby looked up at Niccolò. "I have to send a wire transfer and a telegram right now." She would wire the paycheck she'd just received. Her parents had wanted her to save that money for her marriage, but she had to help.

"*Andiamo.*" Niccolò took her by hand, and they hurried through the crowds.

Ruby gritted her teeth. Acting was no longer just an adventure. She would also send a message to her talent agent and have him arrange more auditions as soon as she returned from Italy. That was the only way she knew to help her parents, along with Patricia and her husband. Her sister didn't mention their need, but Ruby was sure they were in trouble, too.

Unless Ruby kept earning money, her family would lose their ranches and livelihoods. Now, it was up to her to save them if she could.

11

LAGO DI COMO, 2010

*R*uby opened the old address book that she'd carried for decades and ran her finger over blue fountain pen ink that had faded over the years. A piece of paper slipped out, and she bent over to pick it up off the bedroom floor. Pages crisscrossed with yellowed cellophane tape barely held together now.

She unfolded the paper, but it wasn't what she was looking for. Ruby turned a page with care. In her hands, she held the private telephone numbers of family and friends and fellow stars. Names and numbers were crossed out, written over, added. She didn't like the electronic gizmos Mari used, or the digital addresses Ariana kept in her phone. This worn book that had traveled the world with her was a reliable friend filled with memories and notes.

"Where is it?" Ruby thumbed through the address book, but the letter was missing. "How can this be?" She drew a hand over her forehead in distress. *Of all things to have been lost.*

"What are you looking for, Aunt Ruby?"

Ruby looked up. "Oh, I didn't hear you come in." Although it was tempting to share her concerns with Ariana, the girl wouldn't understand. *Not yet.* She closed the worn address book and arranged a smile on her face.

"Come sit with me." Ruby sat, patting a place beside her on the new duvet cover that Livia had placed on the bed.

How could she have lost that letter she'd carried all these years? Is this how Patricia's condition began?

"I'm concerned about you," Ariana said, scrutinizing her with a look reserved for older people who were losing their mental faculties.

Ruby straightened her shoulders. *Not Ruby Raines.* Not like her sister, for heaven's sake. She took Ariana's hand. "I will not have dementia. I'm fighting against it like an old dog with a thorn in its paw."

That thorn was the constant reminder of what her sister had gone through. Ruby had made sure that Patricia had the best care possible and spent her last days in a beautiful facility. Mari had been too busy to visit much, saying, *Mom doesn't recognize me, so what does it matter?* Ruby understood that Mari's pain kept her away. Beneath the younger woman's crusty veneer Ruby believed was a wounded heart, so she'd visited Patricia every chance she could. She owed that to Patricia as well as Mari.

As if to make her feel better, Ariana rubbed her hand. "You're older than Nana Pat was when she was diagnosed."

"Good Lord, don't remind me," Ruby said. "I take all the supplements, get regular physical and brain exercise. I read and write every day. Lately, I've been brushing up on my Italian." She tapped her temple. "I'm as sharp as I ever was."

Ariana smiled with relief. "I'm so glad. It was hard seeing Nana Pat slip away like that."

"My childhood went with her," Ruby said. Patricia had always been the memory keeper of the family. Though Ruby remembered everything, her sister was the collector. Articles, photos, mementos.

Ruby thought about the safety deposit key in her purse. *Please understand that this is only for Mari's eyes. I'll leave it up to you to decide the details, Ruby.* And handle the inevitable fallout. Though Patricia's instruction was specific, it was Ruby's story to tell, wasn't it?

Why had Patricia left this unfinished business? For so many

years, her sister had thought it unnecessary—Mari was difficult enough. But now the letter that the executor had given Ruby raised more questions. Should Ruby be there when Mari opened the box, even though the instructions expressly forbade it?

Maybe her sister hadn't been in her right mind at the time.

Ariana bent to the floor. "Is this what you were looking for?" She held an old, folded letter in her hand.

"Why, thank you, dear child," Ruby said with relief. She tucked the brittle paper into her address book. For years, she had read that letter every evening. Now, just knowing it was with her was enough.

Ruby squeezed Ariana's hand. "I think the house has come together rather well. Livia and Emilio have done a remarkable job. We can check out of the hotel in the morning. And how was your day?"

"Gia and I found some beautiful silks," Ariana said.

"I'm so glad." The moment she had met Alessandro on her previous visit, she'd thought of Ariana. Alessandro had just finished a meeting with the hotel manager, and Vera had introduced them. Ruby invited him for tea and told him about her desire to purchase Villa Fiori. Alessandro was handsome; he also had style, intelligence, and empathy.

"And did you meet anyone interesting?" Ruby asked mildly.

Ariana pursed her lips. "If you're referring to Alessandro, yes."

"And?" He'd been so charming. Ruby had mentioned Ariana, too. How could she not?

"No, Aunt Ruby." Ariana rose abruptly. "I don't need that kind of help."

Ruby wondered what could have happened between them. Vera had confided in her that Alessandro was lonely. Maybe Ariana and Alessandro should have met under different circumstances.

"Let's have a house welcoming party this weekend," Ruby said. "Invite whoever you'd like."

Ariana sighed. "I don't know anyone here."

"Let's ask Gia and Vera and their families. Matteo, of course, and his family. And the attorney who handled the purchase," Ruby added, tapping her address book. "We'll have such fun."

For the rest of the week, Ruby concentrated on filling Villa Fiori with new linens, plants, and artwork. Between Gia, Vera, Ariana, Livia, and Emilio, Ruby had a veritable army at her disposal, and she was pleased with how quickly the old villa transformed into a comfortable home.

It wasn't perfect, of course. Dishes had a few chips, the cutlery and glassware were mismatched, and the pipes and paint had seen better days, but Ruby loved it. It reminded her of another villa on the lake she'd visited so many years ago, which was the last time she'd experienced pure bliss.

Now, on this sunny Saturday morning, Ruby was organizing last-minute essentials. Livia had done a marvelous job of putting together a menu for the party.

"I'm off to buy wine for tomorrow," Ruby said as she finished her light breakfast of cappuccino and a slice of rosemary bread slathered with local butter that melted into the fragrant bread. They'd planned the party for Sunday afternoon. Adopting a nonchalant attitude, she glanced at Ariana. "Would you like to come along?"

Ariana peered over the rim of her coffee cup. "Is Matteo taking you?"

"Alessandro is picking me up. Do come with us." As soon as she mentioned his name, she saw Ariana bristle. She still wondered what had happened between them. Alessandro hadn't said a word, and Ariana refused to talk about him. "We're going to visit his friend, a wine distributor in Lecco, and have lunch along the way."

As if on cue, a motorboat sounded outside. Alessandro cut the engine and moored the boat. He stepped off the craft.

Ruby rose and opened the door to the terrace. "Come in for a coffee," she called out, feeling Ariana's glare on her back.

"*Buongiorno*." Alessandro walked in, looking quite smart in linen trousers, deck shoes, and a blue twill shirt.

Ariana abruptly stood to leave the kitchen.

Ruby cleared her throat. "Aren't you going to say hello to Alessandro?"

Ariana threw him a begrudging look. "Fine. Hello again."

"I hope your design work is going well," he said, his face lighting at the sight of Ariana.

"It's fine," Ariana shot back. "And how are Paolina and the children?"

Ruby noted that Ariana's voice had a sarcastic edge that took Alessandro by surprise, *What's wrong with her?* Ruby wondered.

"My sister is doing well; thank you for asking. She's looking after the children today."

Ariana's eyes widened. "Paolina is your sister?"

"Our father left the business to us, so we co-manage the silk factory."

"I thought..." Ariana's face reddened, and she turned away.

At once, Ruby realized what had happened. "Paolina is such a lovely woman, and she's so good with the children. I would think some people might mistake her for your wife."

Alessandro chuckled and glanced at Ariana. "Maybe they do."

"I think I have work to do," Ariana mumbled, sloshing coffee into her cup.

Ruby ignored her. "And I can only imagine how difficult it must be raising children on your own." Why was Ariana continuing to be so rude to him?

Ariana paused with the ceramic creamer in mid-air.

"These last two years have been tough, but life goes on." Alessandro spread his hands. "They're good kids, thanks to Serafina."

Ariana put the creamer down with a thud on the tile counter. "So you're divorced," she spat out in an accusatory tone.

Ruby saw Alessandro's forehead crinkle. "Forgive my niece," she said, appalled at Ariana's behavior. "As Americans, we can be frightfully direct. And sometimes we forget our manners." She sent a piercing glance toward Ariana, who should have known better. What on earth was wrong with her today? This behavior was beyond hormones. Ruby knew the difference.

"My wife, Serafina, died two years ago last week," Alessandro said quietly. "It was a painful shock, but our little children, Sandro and Carmela, were hurt the worst."

"It's hard to lose the people we love," Ruby said gently. "Perhaps we should go now. The fresh air on the lake will do us good." She glanced back at Ariana. "And I will see you for dinner." Without giving her niece the chance to change her mind, Ruby swept off with Alessandro.

As Alessandro helped her into his boat, she said, "What a beautiful craft. I remember these."

"It's a vintage Riva yacht," he said. "This beauty is from 1951. Took me several years to restore it."

The polished wood gleamed in the sunshine. Once she was comfortable on a cushioned bench, he fired the engine. "How long has it been since you've been on the lake?" he asked.

"Far too long," Ruby replied. "I last visited during the filming of *Roman Holiday*. And I think I rode in a yacht just like this." She smiled. "That was the best time of my life."

"Then you must have been in love," Alessandro said.

"What makes you say that?"

"Life is sweeter when you're in love."

Ruby nodded thoughtfully. "You're a young man to be so wise."

The breeze swept his dark, glossy hair from his forehead, and he chuckled. "Not that young."

Ruby slid on a pair of sunglasses. "Yes, I was in love then." She liked the way he spoke so openly about love—and his love for his children.

"And what happened?" he asked quietly. "Did you marry?"

Ruby hesitated. Alessandro was so easy to talk to. Finally, she said, "I haven't been lucky in love."

"So, no children?"

Ruby gazed out at the lake. Today the water was a brilliant shade of shimmering blue and nearly blinding in the sunlight. "This is why Ariana and I are so close. She's like my granddaughter. If only her mother weren't so stubborn. Even on the best days, she's tough on Ariana."

Nodding thoughtfully, Alessandro adjusted his sunglasses. "Is that why Ariana was upset today?"

He was perceptive, but his guess was off the mark. "A week ago, Ariana was preparing for her wedding and honeymoon. Instead, she left her fiancé at the altar—which I must say, showed tremendously good judgment." She didn't think it necessary to mention the baby.

"And how did her mother and father take her decision to call off her wedding?"

"Her father is out of the picture, and her mother didn't have time to attend."

At that, Alessandro shook his head. "That's terrible. I feel so bad for her, but it certainly explains Ariana's attitude. Is she angry at all men?"

"I hadn't thought so, but maybe she is. She's not usually so sharp-tongued."

Alessandro steered the yacht through the open waters toward another shore. "When I asked her out, she, how do you say—I think the term is, she *chewed me up*. I bungled the invitation. I haven't asked a woman out since Serafina died."

"At least you tried." Ruby thought about the look of disappointment on Ariana's face when they left. "Maybe you'll have another chance."

Alessandro shook his head and shrugged. "No disrespect to you, but I have to protect my heart, too."

He raised his hand in greeting to another boat owner who was pulling away from a dock. Alessandro pulled alongside it and moored the yacht. Before them stretched the *comune* of Lecco.

After helping Ruby disembark, Alessandro told her about the area. "Some of the best wine in this region of Lombardia come from Montevecchia. If you don't mind walking, we can have lunch and then visit the wine shop."

They strolled on the lakeside promenade under the watchful bell tower of Basilica di San Niccolò, which made Ruby smile. Everything reminded her of Niccolò. Alessandro went on to tell her about the secret tunnels and caves under the tower.

The cobblestone streets were narrow, and a mountain rose behind the bell tower. They had lunch overlooking the lake, and afterward, Alessandro introduced her to his cousin, who helped them select an assortment of local wines for the afternoon party.

Ruby also arranged a large delivery to stock her wine room. She chose wines from Montevecchia and across Lombardia, as well as the neighboring Piemonte region.

"I've enjoyed this day so much," Ruby said to Alessandro on the way back.

If only Ariana hadn't been in such a mood, because Ruby would have liked her to join them. Alessandro was such a joy to be around.

Ruby smiled to herself. Maybe tomorrow at the party she'd have another chance to bring them together.

12

Lago di Como, 1952

*B*y mid-August, the heat in Rome was growing increasingly insufferable for the cast. Filming was done early in the morning and later in the evening with a long break for lunch during the hottest part of the day. One day, Mr. Wyler told the cast that filming would halt for the Ferragosto holiday. The director and his family went to the beach resort of Fregene to enjoy the ocean breezes.

"Let's go north," Niccolò said, his eyes glowing with excitement. "I want to show you Lago di Como, one of the most beautiful lakes in the world."

"How far is it?" Ruby asked, remembering the painting she'd admired.

"We can take an overnight train and be there by morning. We can stay with my aunt and uncle. You're up for an adventure, aren't you?"

"Only if you're paying," she said. She'd sent most of her pay home to her family.

Yet the timing was perfect. Ruby's brief scene had already

been filmed, so she could relax a little. She was still on the schedule for the general crowd scenes.

An hour later, Ruby tucked a couple of cotton shirts with a skirt and cropped pants into a small bag, slid her feet into the espadrilles she'd bought at the Olvera Street market in Los Angeles, and hurried from her room at the pensione.

She and Niccolò raced to the train station, which Ruby found overwhelming with so many trains and platforms and names of cities she didn't recognize. High overhead, destinations rotated and clicked into place. Everything was new and thrilling to her; she felt like they were in a film of their own.

"*Due biglietti per Milano, per favore.*" Niccolò slid *lire* across the counter.

Ruby furrowed her brow. "Milano? I thought we were going to Lago di Como."

"We'll change trains in Milano for Lago di Como," Niccolò said. "Don't worry. I'll take care of you."

She smiled and slipped her hand into his. She could trust him.

"Hurry, we can't miss the train. *Andiamo.*" He took her hand, and they raced through the crowd with Niccolò shouting out, "*Scusi, scusi.*"

She laughed as the crowd parted for them, with people cheering for them as they jumped onto the train, barely making it. They hung on, waving at the crowd as if he were Gregory Peck and she were Audrey Hepburn. And when Niccolò kissed her, shouts of *bravo* reverberated through the station.

Ruby felt adrenaline surge through her; every nerve in her body was tingling with exhilaration. *This is living. This is love.* She never wanted any other life than this one.

"Come on, let's have some *antipasti* in the dining car," Niccolò said.

They wedged inside the crowded car, where they drank bubbly prosecco and ate prosciutto and cheese with crusty bread and olives. Ruby thought it was one of the finest meals she'd ever had.

Against the setting sun, Ruby watched the countryside hurtle by, entranced by the ever-changing landscape of rolling vineyards and postcard-perfect villages.

She was so excited to be exploring Italy with Niccolò that she could hardly sleep on the train. Instead, they stayed awake, whispering and sharing stories of their lives and families and aspirations. Niccolò had such a good heart, and he told her of his plans to help his family, such as helping his siblings go to university. His father earned a decent living, but with four children, they still had to economize.

As Ruby listened, her heart filled with admiration and love for him. Surely her father would agree that Niccolò was a young man of the highest character.

More than that, Ruby was convinced that Niccolò was her soulmate.

They changed trains in Milano, and by the time they arrived in Varenna, the sun had crested the alpine ridge. Ruby was in awe. She stepped off the train at the small station and drank in the scent of honeysuckle that tumbled along a stone wall. Niccolò led her down narrow cobblestone streets to the edge of the lake.

"And there it is," Niccolò said, speaking in a reverent tone. "Isn't this a marvelous view?"

Ruby leaned her head on his shoulder. "I'm so glad you brought me here."

She had never seen terrain like this—except in the pages of *National Geographic* magazines in the mobile library van that visited the county once a month.

Spinning around to take in the view, she felt dizzy with sensory overload. Tall cypress trees, swaying palms, and leafy mulberry trees lined the banks. Standing here with a vast, crystalline lake lapping at her toes and snow-capped peaks rising majestically from the water's edge to kiss the sky was a dream come true.

"I want to show you everything I love here," Niccolò said, pointing across the lake. "There's Bellagio on that triangular tip —we'll go there—and there's the ferry we'll take, and we'll have the finest food you've ever tasted." He spun her around. "And up there, that castle, Castello di Vezio. We'll explore that, too."

"Does anyone live there?"

Niccolò shook his head. "It was built a thousand years ago for Teodolinda, the queen of Lombardia. Some say she still walks the grounds."

Ruby slapped his shoulder and laughed. "I'm not going to a haunted castle."

"It's only a little bit haunted," he said with a chuckle. "The villa that belongs to my aunt and uncle is not far from here. It's an easy walk, and you can meet them and my cousins."

He slung her bag over his shoulder, and they set off along a narrow lane. Stone walls rose steeply from the road, and mountains soared behind hillside homes. Golden butterflies flitted among azaleas and ferns as they walked, and Niccolò told her about how his mother's family shared the small villa. Her elder brother inherited it, but it was for the entire family to enjoy when they visited.

Soon they turned onto a lane lined with oleander trees festooned with blazing pink flowers. The road led to a stone villa perched on a hill that sloped to the lake. All around them, roses bloomed in profusion, spilling over stone walls and climbing a sun-bleached pergola in wild abandon.

"Here, you can step outside the villa and enjoy a feast," Niccolò said. He pointed out a variety of trees surrounding the house. "We have pomegranate, fig, chestnut, and olive trees. And over there is the citrus orchard with lemon, mandarin orange, citron, and grapefruit."

"I love the thought of that," Ruby said. Although it was too cold in the Texas hill country to grow much citrus, she loved the ruby red grapefruit shipped from McAllen near the Mexican border. All around her, the sweet scent of citrus blossoms perfumed the air. As they passed under an archway laden with purple wisteria, Niccolò slipped his arm around her waist, and Ruby thought this was the most romantic place she'd ever visited.

"Italy is such a beautiful country," Niccolò said. "We're spoiled. Long stretches of beaches, the rolling hills of Tuscany, the islands off our coastline, and this…a deep, clear lake filled with fish, and mountains topped with snow. Does Texas have anything like this?"

Ruby shook her head. "It's a different, rugged sort of beauty. We're in the hill country in the middle of the state. We have lakes, but we also have plains that stretch on forever. We have ancient oak trees, the sweetest pecans, and the meanest rattlesnakes. Rivers and streams that you can fish in and swimming holes where you can strip down on a hot day to cool off. It gets blistering hot in the summer, so we move the beds onto the screened-in porch where we sleep in the night breezes."

"We have many types of winds here, too," Niccolò said. "The gentle *Tivano* early in the morning from the north, and the stronger *Breva* just before noon from the south, among others. I'd like to see Texas sometime. I want to meet your parents and ride horses with you. It sounds like a John Wayne western film. Do you wear holsters and carry guns?"

"My grandpa did, but it's not what you think now," she said, laughing. "Still, we set up tin cans on the wooden fence for target practice. Out there, sometimes your life depends on your ability to shoot. You can't sweet-talk a hungry mountain lion."

Niccolò looked impressed. "Hollywood must be pretty different. Playground of the stars, right?"

"You've been reading too many fan magazines." Ruby thought about the mild climate, palm trees that rustled in the breeze, and kids her age who spent weekends at the beach. "But I'm there to work, not play."

"Do you go to the beach and surf?"

She laughed. "I've been once, but I didn't surf. I work as much as I can."

"And what are the guys like there?"

"Nothing like you."

Niccolò grinned. "I saw Marlon Brando in *Streetcar Named Desire*." He gave her a brooding frown and tucked a thumb into a belt loop, mimicking Brando. "And Gene Kelly in *An American in Paris*. Wow, the way he dances." He did a fancy step and twirled her around. "People say Paris isn't like that, but I haven't been there. Have you ever met Frank Sinatra? His family is from Italy, you know. Liguria and Sicily. Oh man, what a voice."

Just as he began to sing, *I'm a Fool to Want You*, Ruby burst out laughing. "I think you're going to be a great actor."

"I want to travel the world with you. We'll see everything there is to see." He took her in his arms. "Will you do that with me?"

"I'd love to," she murmured. Niccolò's enthusiasm was infectious.

Bending toward her, he teased her lips with his, brushing against her cheeks, smoothing a hand over her hair. Every nerve in her body tingled with delight at his touch. Compared to the clumsy pawing efforts of the boys she'd met at dances, Niccolò's touch was gentle and respectful. They came together naturally— two halves of a perfect union.

"*Cuore mio,*" he murmured, dragging his lips along her neck.

Here, under the wisteria, the sun dappling their shoulders, Ruby yearned to tell Niccolò she loved him. Surely he already knew; surely he felt as she did.

She'd never dreamed she would fall in love in Italy. Closing her eyes, she knew her life would never be the same again. Niccolò was her destiny; she knew that as certainly as she knew her heart would beat from one moment to the next.

"Let's go inside," he said, his voice sounding thick.

Niccolò knocked, but there was no answer. His mother had given him a key, which he slipped into the old lock. Pushing open the door, he called out, but his voice only echoed in response.

Niccolò dropped their bags and led her into the kitchen, where propped against a wine bottle was a note. He read it. "They've gone to Como, but we're welcome to use the villa." He turned to her. "We have the place to ourselves."

"Oh," Ruby said, unsure if it was proper that she should be alone with Niccolò.

Niccolò kissed her forehead. "Don't worry, *amore mio*. You're safe with me. Come, I'll show you around."

He led her through the villa graced with hand-painted tiles, antique furniture, and fresco ceilings. Pausing, he swung open the door to a bedroom. "And this is where you can sleep."

Ruby peered in. A snow-white cotton duvet and fluffy pillows covered the bed, and antique furniture lined the walls. "It's perfect," she said.

"And I'll be in the room next door," he said with a silly grin. "Hey, are you hungry?"

"Famished." They'd had some coffee and bread on the train, but it wasn't the kind of breakfast she was used to in Texas with over-easy eggs, venison sausage, and a short stack of flapjacks. In Hollywood, her aunt served freshly squeezed orange juice with homemade yogurt and buttered toast, but Ruby was always hungry before lunch. At least they fed the cast and crew well on the movie set.

"Let's make *paninis*," Niccolò said, guiding her outside. "We'll pick tomatoes and basil and peppers."

Niccolò led her to the garden, where she almost cried when she saw the abundance. Ruby told him about the crops on her family's ranch that had been lost this year in the drought. Corn, okra, squash, green beans, tomatoes.

"In comparison, this area is like paradise," Ruby said, filling a corner of her skirt with plump tomatoes and peppers. She raised her hand to the sun, which was warm, but not as brutal as the Texas sun that scorched the soil until it cracked. "Last year, the rains didn't come, and our shallow well might still run dry this summer." Ruby had wired money from her last paycheck, and she'd keep sending as much as she could.

"How are they doing now?" Niccolò asked. He'd been with her when she'd received the telegram from Patricia.

"The crops are a total loss. My parents bought food, and they're rationing the water they have left." Without rain, the cattle were close to starvation, too. Her parents needed to drill a deeper well, but they didn't have the money. Still, even a well couldn't water all the pasture land the livestock required.

When Ruby thought about how desperate the situation was on the ranch, she felt guilty about being in this lush environment. Acting in movies was even more critical for her now to support her family.

"I feel bad that there isn't more I can do for my family," Ruby said, her throat constricting at the thought of what they were going through.

"You're doing what you can." Compassion shone in Niccolò's eyes. "The recovery after the war has been hard for people in

Italy, too, especially in the south. Films made in Rome create a lot of jobs for people. This is our future. We have our whole lives ahead of us; imagine what we can do together, Ruby. And with your talent, you can give your family a palace someday."

Ruby laughed at that thought, but some actors in Hollywood did live in splendor. Douglas Fairbanks and Mary Pickford lived in a lavish Beverly Hills estate called *Pickfair*. Anything was possible if she was willing to work for it.

And she was. Ruby folded her skirt around the vegetables.

They made their way back into the kitchen, where Ruby helped Niccolò wash and slice the vegetables. Niccolò roasted the peppers and piled them onto rustic slices of bread, adding provolone cheese and thin prosciutto. He pressed the sandwiches onto a hot grill. While he watched the paninis, Ruby sliced soft mozzarella cheese, stacked it on top of thick slices of tomatoes, and sprinkled sprigs of basil over it all.

"*Mangiamo*," Niccolò said with a flourish. "Time to eat this masterpiece."

He poured a splash of wine into glass tumblers, and they carried their meal outdoors to eat under the shade of the rose-covered pergola. They enjoyed a leisurely lunch, watching yachts and ferries cross the lake and clouds drift across the sky.

After they finished eating their paninis, Niccolò brought out a plate of purple grapes. Ruby plucked a handful. "Open wide," she said, aiming for his mouth. He did, and she tossed a plump grape toward him that bounced off his nose.

"Try again," he said, laughing. The next one, he caught.

They took turns with their silly antics, dissolving into a fit of laughter. Between the delicious food, the mild sun on her shoulders, and the beauty surrounding them, Ruby thought she'd never had such a beautiful afternoon. The wine was making her a little giddy, but she liked the feeling. She pushed her glass toward him. "More, please."

"Oh, no, no, no. I think you've had enough." Niccolò moved the bottle away.

Ruby stifled a yawn. "Maybe I need a nap instead." She hadn't slept much on the train. Now, after a good meal and maybe a little too much wine, she was growing drowsy.

"That's a great idea," Niccolò said. He took her hand and led her inside, up the stairs, and to her room. Niccolò flung open the windows, and a gentle breeze lifted the white cotton curtains.

As Ruby collapsed onto the bed, she reached out for Niccolò and pulled him down with her.

"Hey," he said as he turned to face her. Brushing her hair from her face, he peppered her forehead and cheeks with soft kisses.

Ruby raised her lips to his. A moment later, she was lost in the warmth of his mouth. Swept away on waves of pleasure, Ruby succumbed to his embrace. She slid her fingers beneath his shirt, feeling the strength of his heartbeat, which matched hers.

Niccolò caught her hand in his. "I should go," he whispered. "You stay here and sleep. Alone."

"Please stay." Ruby often felt alone, and she hated it. Away from her family and those she loved, she now bore a huge responsibility of providing for her family—and doing it alone. Here with Niccolò, she could be herself, and she knew she had his support.

"Are you sure?" Niccolò smoothed her hair from her cheek.

Ruby sighed and turned into his palm. His simple touch caused an avalanche of feelings in her that she'd never felt before.

She flicked the top button of his shirt. Niccolò gripped her hand, but she fumbled open another button. Moments later, his shirt slid to the wooden floor beneath them.

"*Quanto ti amo,*" Niccolò murmured, and she answered him in kind.

His kisses filled her with the sweetest desire, and she brought herself to him, calling his name, unwilling to resist. Whatever separate paths they might have been on before, they joined together as one now. One heart, one destiny, one life.

This was the man she would love for the rest of her life.

RUBY OPENED HER EYES AND LIFTED HER HEAD FROM Niccolò's chest. Outside, the sun was setting, and the breeze had grown stronger. Niccolò snored softly, but as she rustled, he tightened his arms around her.

This togetherness felt so right to her. Yet instantly, a thought gripped her. *What have we done?*

Her hot tears trickled onto Niccolò's chest, and she turned away from him.

"Hey," he said, lifting himself onto one elbow and wiping the tears from her cheeks. "Don't cry, *mio tesoro*. You are so beautiful. You're my heart, my soul."

He murmured the loveliest words in her ear, and although Ruby didn't understand all of what he said, she felt her fears melting away.

"I love you," he said. "I have loved you from the moment I first saw you on the set. I knew we would be together for the rest of our lives."

Ruby turned back to him. "Do you mean that?"

Niccolò's eyes warmed her with love. "With every drop of my blood," he said, kissing her neck.

"But what we've done…"

"*Non sono dispiaciuto.*" He kissed the tears from her eyes. "*Quanto ti amo.* Why should we apologize for love?"

A thousand questions raced through her mind.

Niccolò wrapped his arms around her. "I want to marry you."

"What?"

"We are meant to be together," he said. "Can you deny this?"

Ruby gazed into his eyes, which were clear and bright with certainty. "This is a serious step."

"Not if we truly love each other."

"How can you be so sure?" Ruby drew her teeth over her swollen lips. Hearing words of love on Niccolò's lips filled her with feelings of warmth and security.

"Because it's time we lived our lives together." Niccolò folded his hand over hers and pressed it to his chest. "I know this for certain. Trust me, and we'll have the most wonderful life you can imagine. Here, Rome, Hollywood, Texas. Where you go, I'll go." He raised her hand to his lips and kissed her fingers. "From now on, we'll never be apart."

On hearing those words, joy bloomed in Ruby's heart, and she smothered him with kisses before pulling back from him. "How will we do this?"

"There's a priest I know here. He's a friend of my uncle. For a few *lire*, he'll do it."

"This weekend?" She frowned up at him. "But, my parents..."

"We can have another wedding in Texas next month. The film will be finished soon. But we are as one now. We should be married as soon as possible."

Ruby nodded and smiled up at him. He understood her worry. If her father knew what they had done, he would demand that Niccolò make an honest woman of her. At the thought, a twinge pinched her neck. She'd always hated that phrase. What was so dishonest about love like this?

"I think my parents will be happy when they meet you."

"Do you want to call them and tell them?"

She did, but as thrilled as she was at the thought of getting married, she knew her father would be far less so. Not because he was against marriage for her, but because for years he'd been planning for her to marry a neighboring rancher's son—just as her sister Patricia had at seventeen. Her mother had made a deal with her father to let Ruby go to Hollywood. In two years, Ruby would return to settle down. Ruby knew what that meant, and she didn't want to be trapped on a ranch for the rest of her life, scratching out a living on dry land. What she wanted was to experience life.

This life. And she wanted Niccolò. *Why destroy the bliss we have right now?*

Ruby slid her arms around Niccolò's neck and kissed him lightly. "Let's surprise them later."

13

Lago di Como, 2010

*H*igh on a bedroom balcony of Villa Fiori overlooking the lake, Ariana watched as Alessandro arrived and moored his bobbing craft beside their dock. He'd brought Paolina and the children, and another man that Ariana assumed was his sister's husband.

Laughter floated upstairs from the gathering below. Ariana had been helping Livia in the kitchen, but as soon as Ariana had seen Alessandro's yacht pulling alongside, she'd raced upstairs like a teenager to avoid him.

Yesterday, she'd made a fool of herself. Not only a fool but a rude, inconsiderate, obnoxious fool. Those were Ruby's scathing words, and Ariana knew she deserved every one of them. Had her relationship with Phillip ruined how she looked at men?

Not that she was in the market to replace Phillip so quickly. A little more than a week ago, she was getting married. And now she was going to be a mother in about seven-ish months.

She gazed out at Alessandro. With the sun glinting off his aviator sunglasses and a sweater tossed over his shoulders, he looked like he'd just stepped from a glossy tourist ad for Lake

Como. If she were interested in a rebound fling before she blossomed with child, he could be a perfect candidate—except that he had two small children to occupy his time.

Ariana pressed her fingers against her throbbing temples. Life was getting complicated in her thirties. All she had to think about before was school and work. Why had she been so stressed over things that now seemed mundane and unimportant in comparison?

In retrospect, Ariana thought her best years were probably behind her. Though she hated to admit it, she was beginning to understand her mother, who'd thrown herself into a new career after Ariana's father walked out. Mari Ricci had been too proud to take her daughter home to Nana Pat's and admit defeat. Too proud to accept assistance, except for Ariana's education.

At some point, Ariana would have to tell her mother about the baby. The thought filled her with dread. She couldn't expect any help from her mother, who had been against her relationship with Phillip from the beginning.

As Ariana thought of what she was going to need for her child, she panicked. She didn't know the first thing about babies. How would she manage? A gust of wind blew in from the lake, and Ariana sneezed.

Suddenly, Alessandro looked up. Ariana gasped and jumped back. Stumbling on the rug, she cried out, furtively waving her arms like a slow-motion clown trying to keep her balance. In the end, she didn't.

Fortunately, she fell into the plush duvet on the bed. Staring at the high ceiling, she moaned at her predicament. Alessandro was sure to have seen her spying on him. How could she have made yet another *faux pas*?

She was still on the bed when footsteps sounded outside her open door.

"Ariana, are you up here?" Ruby's voice echoed through the hall until she stopped in the doorway. "Goodness sakes, are you not feeling well?"

Ariana pushed herself up. "I'm okay."

"No tummy issues?"

Ariana shook her head. Too late, she realized that would have been a good excuse.

"Well, then, come downstairs. Livia said you ran upstairs when you saw Alessandro's yacht." Ruby put a hand on her hip. "Hiding is not going to help."

"I'm so embarrassed."

"You should be. But I think Alessandro understands—and he's concerned. He told me he heard a strange yelp from upstairs and asked me to check on you."

Ariana groaned and sank her face into her hand. Just when she thought the situation couldn't get any worse.

"I could send him up, and you two could talk."

"Absolutely not." Ariana clambered from the bed and smoothed the wrinkled sundress Ruby had bought for her on her trip with Alessandro yesterday. Her aunt had insisted she wear it today, saying that the pink and yellow print illuminated Ariana's strawberry blond hair. Not that she had anything else to wear. She hadn't been shopping yet to augment the few clothes she'd packed.

Glancing in the mirror, Ariana saw that her aunt was right. The cheerful print also masked the turmoil Ariana felt inside. "I'll be down in a moment."

"I'll wait," Ruby said. "We can walk down together."

Ariana blew out a breath. Disagreeing with her aunt was useless. "Let's go then."

"Like that?" Ruby arched her eyebrow. "You look like you've been rolling around in bed. We have company downstairs. So brush your hair, put on a little lip gloss. Now is not the time to seclude yourself."

Ariana groaned. "Isn't that what women used to do? Hide their pregnancies? Sounds like a good idea to me."

"Stop it." Ruby's vivid green eyes flashed with annoyance. "Having a baby is nothing to be ashamed of. That was an archaic attitude. Think of your child. Your growing baby needs good food, fresh air, and a positive attitude from you. Now let's go."

Ariana couldn't argue with that. She ran a brush through her hair and touched gloss to her lips before following Ruby downstairs. Her aunt's silk print caftan flowed behind her on the stairs as she tossed her fiery red hair over her shoulder. Pure elegance.

Pausing on the landing, Ariana surveyed the crowd in the salon below. Villa Fiori was full of laughter. Gia and Vera were there with their husbands and four children between them. Alessandro and Paolina and her husband were chatting with them, while little Sandro and Carmela were playing with the other children. Matteo and his wife were there, and a few other people that Ariana didn't recognize.

"Ariana, I'd like you to meet a few people." Ruby steered her to a new group and began the introductions to two couples. "Our neighbors, the Colombos and Vernates."

Feeling Alessandro's eyes on her, Ariana greeted their guests, who were actually quite interesting. In a few days, Ruby had managed to meet the neighbors—an artist and a writer—as well as local officials and an opera singer. People were naturally drawn to her aunt, even if they didn't recognize her or weren't familiar with her films. Ruby's charisma and exuberance for life were irresistible.

The children soon raced outside to play tag in the garden. Ariana strolled out to watch them as they skipped through the orchard and played under the pergola. As much as she had wanted children, it was nearly inconceivable that she was about to take such an important step by herself. She leaned against a stone balustrade and ran a hand over her abdomen. This certainly wasn't how she'd once imagined her family would unfold.

Had she made a mistake by leaving Phillip at the altar? Yet, his harsh words still rang in her ears. *No*, she thought, setting her jaw. Marrying him was no longer an option. She wanted a husband who was all in, not someone who would grudgingly throw money at her little problem.

This was her *child*.

As the magnitude of this dawned on her, Ariana blinked into the breeze. The children's laughter wound around her, sounding sweeter than the wind chimes that tinkled in the gusts off the water. Her world would have to change, but maybe that wasn't the disaster she'd imagined.

"May I join you?" Alessandro stepped beside her, casting a shadow across the terrace in front of her.

Ariana felt a flush spread across her chest, and she shifted against the stone railing. "I owe you an apology."

His lips quirked to one side. "You made your position known. I can't fault a woman who has strong values."

"But, I was wrong." She slid a glance toward him.

"*Sì*, that you were." Alessandro nodded toward his children. "Now you know my story."

Ariana turned toward him. "Is this where I'm expected to share mine?"

"Not at all. You don't owe me anything."

"Other than an apology."

He grinned. "You already did that. And I thank you." With a quick little bow, he turned to walk away.

"Wait." Ariana tucked her windblown hair behind her ears. *Why does he have to be so attractive?*

"Yes?"

"I, uh, appreciate your fabric suggestions." Ariana stumbled over her words. "You know, we could start over."

He shrugged. "Not if you're uncomfortable."

"I'm okay. Really. It's just that, well, it's been a week from hell." When he didn't reply, she went on. "I'm supposed to be on my honeymoon right now, but I didn't go through with the wedding."

"I'm very sorry for you."

"No, don't be. It was my decision. And I'm fine with it." She blinked into the breeze, feeling more confident of her choice now that she spoke it aloud.

Alessandro nodded. "It takes a strong will to know when a relationship isn't right."

"A marriage is forever, right?"

"Ideally, yes, but..." Alessandro coughed and cleared his throat.

At once, Ariana realized her mistake, and another apology tumbled out. "Please forgive me. I'm so sorry. I wasn't thinking." How could she have been so thoughtless?

Swallowing hard, he shook his head. "If it weren't for Serafina, I wouldn't have Sandro and Carmela now. That is how I have to look at the situation. People come into our lives for different reasons. What we want and what God has planned for us...well, it's often different. What good would it do to question that?" He gazed after his children. "Especially when I am so blessed. Serafina would not have wanted me to suffer."

Ariana grew quiet, watching the children. She wondered how his wife had died, but now was not the time to ask.

Moments later, Sandro and Carmela raced to their father and flung their arms around him, chattering with excitement. She tried to follow along, and although it had been quite a long time since she'd take Italian in school, she discovered that she understood some of what they were saying. Maybe she could practice her Italian while she was here.

"They're hungry," Alessandro said, grinning. "Kids are always hungry."

Carmela tugged on Ariana's skirt and turned her sweet little face up to her. "*Ho fame e sete.*"

Fame. Hungry. *Sete.* Thirsty. Ariana took the little girl's hand. "If you don't mind, I'll get them something to drink and make a plate for them. Is there anything they can't eat? Because of allergies, I mean."

"No, and they like almost everything. I'll help you." Alessandro guided his young son toward the kitchen.

As Ariana led the children into the house, she caught Ruby's eye. Seemingly satisfied, her aunt turned back to the conversation. Ariana had to admit that Ruby was right. Hiding in her room wasn't a solution.

Ariana arranged sliced tomatoes, sweet peppers, cucumbers, cheese, and bread onto plates for the children. Within minutes, they were happily eating at the kitchen table, swinging their little legs.

"They seem like such sweet children," Ariana said.

Alessandro smiled. "I'm lucky. They're good kids."

Before long, Livia began to put out the main meal. An assortment of *antipasti*, several types of salad and soup, pasta, fresh fish, and meatballs. Everyone gathered around the tables that Emilio and Livia had organized outside on the terrace.

Ruby pulled out a chair for Ariana across from Alessandro, so she could hardly escape him, but after they'd talked on the terrace, she no longer minded. Once everyone began eating and toasting, Ariana relaxed and enjoyed herself.

"Will you visit Lago di Como often?" Alessandro asked.

"She might never leave," Ruby interjected. "Who would want to leave this gorgeous place?"

Ariana shook her head. "I have to return to work, Aunt Ruby. While I still can."

"Do you love your work?" Alessandro asked.

Lacing her fingers, Ariana thought about that. "I like the idea of what I do. But the person I work for isn't very nice. And it's not that he's tough, though he's that, too. He's petty and vindictive."

Ariana thought about the time Kingsley had fired a pregnant colleague because he thought her pregnancy would interfere with her work. He decided to give the job to a friend of his. When Human Resources told him it was an illegal termination and insisted that he hire the woman again, he did, but he proceeded to make her life as miserable as he could. He demeaned her, told her that she was no longer attractive, and required longer hours of her than others. Ariana often stayed, and after Kingsley left, she sent her colleague home and finished her work. Ariana shuddered as she imagined what Kingsley would do to her once she told him she was pregnant.

Thinking about returning to work for Kingsley lessened Ariana's appetite. She put down her fork. "Allowing for flight time, I have to return in less than three weeks."

"Are you sure you can't stay longer?" Alessandro asked.

Ariana glanced around the lively scene full of excellent food and fascinating people. The wine was flowing, though she was drinking water, and she'd laughed more today than she could recall in months. And surprisingly—or not—the attacks she'd been having for so long hadn't seemed to bother her here.

"I wish I could," Ariana said.

Ruby smiled. "We still have a lot to do here."

Alessandro picked up a bottle of wine on the table and

offered Ruby more. After she nodded, he poured a little and then turned to Ariana and the empty wine glass before her.

Ariana swiftly covered the glass with her hand. "None for me."

"You don't like the wine?" Alessandro asked.

"I didn't feel like drinking today," Ariana said, which was partly true. The thought of drinking alcohol wasn't at all appealing to her, even though she loved wine. She'd lost her taste for it, although she'd noticed she was craving other foods.

After they finished eating, the adults sat and talked while the children played in the garden. Everyone seemed so at ease enjoying the day and each other's company.

Glancing at his watch, Alessandro said, "I lost track of time. I'm sorry to break up a good party, but we should go while it's still daylight." He motioned to Paolina and her husband.

After thanking Ruby and saying goodbye to everyone, Alessandro led his children onto the vintage wooden yacht. Paolina and her husband were getting them settled on the craft when Alessandro stepped back onto the dock. He gestured to Ariana and hurried toward her.

"I'll be meeting a client nearby tomorrow," Alessandro said. "When I'm free, would you have time to have coffee?" He named a time.

Although starting a relationship with Alessandro was definitely against her better judgment, she'd enjoyed talking with him today. And it was just coffee. "I'd like that," she said, feeling Ruby's eyes on her.

His eyes lit with delight. "I'll call you," he said, touching her hand before he left.

Ariana gazed after Alessandro. Once he was underway, she lifted her hand, waving at him and his children. Little Carmela waved the longest, and Ariana blew kisses to the little girl, who joyfully returned them. Ariana waved until they were out of sight.

As she walked into the house, she wondered why she'd been so quick to accept Alessandro's invitation. It was a waste of time —hers and his. At the thought of that, a sense of disappointment rippled through her. Perhaps she should tell him about her pregnancy, but she didn't want his pity. What was the harm in having a friendship with him?

Ruby caught up with her. "You're seeing Alessandro again?"

"It's just one cup of coffee," Ariana said firmly. "I know what you're doing, but it won't work. I'll soon be back in Los Angeles." She had to be practical now. Still, as she glanced back at the wake Alessandro's boat left in the lake, she felt a twinge of sadness. Why couldn't she have found someone like him instead of Phillip?

14

Lago di Como, 2010

*R*uby glanced at the calendar on the desk in front of the window in her bedroom. "Less than three weeks," she said, catching the scent of the creamy white roses she loved that Livia had placed on the desk. Ruby didn't have much time left with Ariana here. Her niece was still determined to return to Los Angeles.

Ruby took a sheet of stationery from the drawer and picked up her pen. *Mari.* What could she say to bring her here?

Gazing across the lake, Ruby thought about her sister. Watching Patricia's memory and essence slip away had been so painful that it was almost a relief when she'd finally died. Yet Ruby still missed her. Throughout life, her big sister had always been there, one step ahead of her.

Ruby couldn't blame Mari for distancing herself from her mother. They'd had a tempestuous relationship as it was. Once Patricia was diagnosed, Ruby suspected that Mari's guilt was more than she could bear.

Fearing that she wouldn't have the capacity to put her affairs in order if she waited, the ever pragmatic Patricia had tended to almost all the details of her life. She'd asked Ruby to find a care home for her when she could no longer live on her own. Ruby had done so, covering all her sister's expenses and sparing nothing. She wanted Patricia to be as comfortable as she could be.

Yet Patricia had left the most important task to Ruby. The first anniversary of Patricia's death was almost upon them, and Ruby decided she could wait no longer.

Ruby put down her pen and picked up the safety deposit key she'd been carrying. The executor of Patricia's will had given it to her months ago. Turning it over in her hand, she thought of what the box might contain. Patricia had been very clear about her instructions. Ruby glanced at the letter the executor sent her, though she knew it well.

1. *Ruby is to decide when—and if—Mari is to receive the contents.*
2. *Only Mari can access the contents.*
3. *Mari must access the box alone.*
4. *What Mari decides to do after that is her decision.*

Ruby had to swear—in writing to Patricia and the attorney who was acting as the executor—not to question Mari. While Ruby didn't agree with this approach, she had promised her sister. In many ways, Ruby owed her success to Patricia. And so much more.

The only thing Patricia would say is that she was leaving a letter for Mari.

She would abide by Patricia's wishes. If Mari wanted to talk about the letter or whatever else was in the safety deposit box, it would be her choice. Not Ruby's.

However, that didn't mean that Ruby couldn't provide the opportunity for Mari to unburden herself.

Ruby lifted the silver key to her lips and kissed it. It was time to send it to Mari. Ruby couldn't bear the thought of Ariana and Mari becoming estranged, not with a new baby on the way. And given how Patricia had died, Ruby feared a similar diagnosis. If that happened, their history would be lost.

Some might argue it would be better that way.

Ruby wrapped the key in tissue paper and tucked it into an international express envelope. Mari would receive it the next day.

Picking up her pen, Ruby thought about the letter she wanted to enclose. Mari was not one for emotional appeals. That would be counterproductive. She touched the pen to paper and began to write.

DEAR MARI,

Your mother asked that I make sure you received this safety deposit key. The first anniversary of your mother's death is almost upon us, so this is an appropriate time to complete the details of her final bequest.

The banker's card is enclosed, and her office is a short distance from yours. Please call her at your earliest convenience.

I also have a business proposition for you. I would like for you to take over the sole management of my charitable foundation and my not inconsequential estate, including stocks and bonds, real estate, and intellectual property. I am not asking this as a favor; you will be very well compensated. As my most direct living heir, you should begin to understand the estate. I am not getting any younger and am concerned about my health.

I am at my villa in Lake Como and am making preparations to finalize my estate. This may be the last time we have to visit, so I ask that you plan to arrive within two weeks. While it is short notice, you will understand the urgency when you arrive. Stefano will contact you with travel options. Upon your arrival, I will review the estate with you and address any questions you might have.

With love,
Your Aunt Ruby

RUBY FOLDED THE NOTE. THE TONE WAS TOO BUSINESSLIKE FOR Ruby's taste, but that was the approach most likely to appeal to Mari.

And she needed Mari here in Lake Como. For Mari's sake, and for Ariana and the next generation. Ruby sealed the envelope and addressed it.

Making her way down the stairs, she called out to Livia. "I'm off to the *poste*. Is there anything we need from the grocer?"

"No, no, no," Livia said, wiping her hands on a dishtowel. "That is *my* job, Signora."

"*Grazie*, Livia." Ruby smiled to herself. Livia was just as proud as Stefano.

Ruby stepped outside and threaded through the narrow cobblestone streets until she reached the *Poste Italiane*. She chatted with people in line before posting her express mail. As she watched the envelope change hands, she thought how that letter would change everything. As soon as tomorrow.

She drew a breath, mentally bracing herself.

On her way back to the Villa Fiori, Ruby took a detour, searching for a particular café. On her last trip here, she had looked for it, but she'd been unable to find it. *If it's still here.* So much had changed over the years.

Presently, she came to a stop before a café on a corner that was so popular people were waiting for tables. A sign read: *Lorenzo's*. She turned around, considering the view from the tables. Her heartbeat quickened.

This is the one. She was sure of it.

Ruby closed her eyes, rewinding the memory reel of her mind. *An afternoon of celebration, so many years ago. The music, the food, the faces. And Niccolò. Always Niccolò.*

She opened her eyes, glancing at the people seated at tables outside—especially the men of a certain age—as if she might find him among the patrons. But no, that was too painful even to imagine.

Ruby glanced at the line of people waiting for a table. Another day, perhaps. As she turned to leave, she noticed a vacant shop space next to the café. She paused outside to peer through the large windows.

A man wearing a casual sport coat approached her. "*Scusi, posso aiutarla con qualcosa?*"

"*Forse.*" Ruby understood enough.

He quickly switched to English. "Ah, American?"

Ruby nodded. "I would like to know if this space is available."

"I think it is," he said. "A boutique was here, but it never had the right styles. My landlord also owns this space, so I can take your name and give it to him."

Ruby pushed her sunglasses over her hair to look in her purse for a card. "Is this your café?"

"For ten years," the man said with pride, and then he exclaimed. "Signora Raines, what a pleasure. I am Lorenzo Pagani. I heard you bought Villa Fiori. Welcome to Bellagio."

Only ten years. He's too young to remember anyway. "It's a pleasure to be here. And, please, call me Ruby."

"Signora Ruby." Lorenzo pressed a hand to his heart and dipped his head. "Will you be my guest for lunch today?"

"What a lovely invitation, but tomorrow would be better. May I bring my niece, too?"

"Yes, of course," Lorenzo said. "I will reserve my best table for you. And don't worry, you will have complete privacy. No paparazzi."

She smiled. The photographers didn't follow her anymore. They only wanted those who were young and photogenic, and whose photos could command a price worthy of the effort.

Ruby thanked Lorenzo before he hurried back to the café.

Ruby sighed. *Oh, Niccolò. If only you were still here.* It was silly, but she liked to think of it as *their* café. She recalled telling Patricia about that day in great detail so many years ago. And that was the last time she'd ever spoken of it.

Gazing at the vacant shop, Ruby pressed a finger to her chin in thought. Perhaps her memories had beckoned her for a reason.

Ruby strolled back to the villa, an idea forming in her mind.

15

Lago di Como, 1952

*U*nder the rose-covered pergola, Ruby leaned against Niccolò and cupped her hands around a mug of cappuccino he'd made for her that morning. She was still a little bleary-eyed from the wine and limoncello they'd had, and her feet ached from hours of dancing, but she was so happy being here with him.

Last night, they had gone out in Varenna for the celebration of Ferragosto. They'd eaten and danced and watched fireworks bursting over the lake. Ruby couldn't recall when she'd had so much fun. The holiday reminded her of the Fourth of July in America, and when she told Niccolò that he'd laughed, saying that everyone liked an excuse for fireworks and dancing.

"After mass, we can speak to the priest," Niccolò said. "He's young, and I think he'll help us. Varenna is in the Diocese of Milan, and they are not so strict about paperwork. Do you have your passport with you?"

"I do." Since she was born at home on the ranch, Ruby had never had an official birth certificate. Her aunt Vivienne had told the talent agent, Joseph Applebaum, that Ruby was eighteen.

When she was chosen for *Roman Holiday*, Joseph told her she would need a passport and suggested it would be easier for the studio if she weren't a minor. Her parents quickly applied for Ruby's birth certificate and added a year to her birth date. Then, they used the birth certificate to obtain her passport. According to that document, she was eighteen and could legally sign contracts, open bank accounts, rent an apartment—and get married.

Ruby looked up at Niccolò. "Do you think we'll be able to get married here?"

"We'll find a way," Niccolò replied, kissing her cheek. "This will be a private ceremony just for us. That way, we will know in our hearts that we are bound together. Then we can tell our parents."

"How do you think your parents will react?" Ruby liked his mother, but she feared this might not be a welcome surprise. As for her parents...she couldn't even think of that now. Frowning, she took another sip of coffee.

"My parents adore you. They will be so happy for us. My older brother and sister are already married, and my parents love their spouses."

Ruby considered this. "I'm not so sure they'll welcome an American girl who plans to steal their son away to Hollywood."

Niccolò put her coffee cup down and took her in his arms. "My ambition is to act. They accept this, so I know they'll support me going to Hollywood. Especially with you, the woman I love."

Ruby had to trust him. She didn't have any choice. What they'd done was so beautiful, but she knew it was against all her teachings from her parents and her church.

Niccolò stroked her back. "Are you worried about your parents?"

"My father had another idea for me." She wanted to be truthful with him. "My sister married a rancher whose land adjoins ours. My father said that when I'm through making movies, I must return to the ranch." She blew out a sigh. "He wants me to marry the son of another rancher." She clutched Niccolò in her arms. "I can't do that. I *won't* do that."

Niccolò gazed at her with a solemn expression. "Then it's even more important that we get married." He took her hand and stood up. "We should get ready for mass."

Ruby went inside with him. She didn't ask Niccolò about how mass was conducted, because everything in Italy was new to her. She would simply follow along.

After she dressed, Niccolò gave her one of his aunt's shawls to cover her hair and shoulders. They walked to the church hand in hand. Ruby loved the feeling of being so connected to Niccolò. All around them, everything seemed sunny and bright. They were together, and that was all that mattered. She touched the little silver necklace she wore that Audrey had given her and thought about how it had brought her such luck.

Daisies grew on the steps leading up to the church beside it, a bell tower with a clock soared above them. The tall, wooden doors of Chiesa di San Giorgio were open, and Ruby and Niccolò stepped inside the cool, dark sanctuary. Ruby's heels tapped on the black marble tiles, and she gazed in awe at the old paintings of saints who lined the walls and columns.

"This church is about a thousand years old," Niccolò whispered.

Ruby wasn't sure what to do, but since she didn't understand most of what the priest said, she simply followed Niccolò's lead.

After the mass, Niccolò spoke to the young priest.

As Niccolò translated to Ruby, he added, "You are Catholic, yes? Otherwise, I don't know if he will marry us."

"My family is Catholic," Ruby said, nodding. Technically, that was correct. Her mother's family, the Raines, had originated in England, but her father's family, the Smiths, were practicing Catholics in Ireland before arriving in the United States. She'd been baptized, and her father kept the traditions, but they lived far from any church. Ruby often went with her mother to a small nondenominational gathering. But Ruby couldn't wait to get married. Surely it would be okay, she told herself.

"Where do I get these documents?" Niccolò asked.

The young priest gave him some instructions, including the address of another person who could expedite the process and provide witnesses for a small fee. After leaving the church, they went directly to the person the priest had suggested. The man told them the amount of donation they would need to give him, and then he would arrange it all.

"Are you sure this is the way it's done?" Ruby asked as they walked back to the villa. "What if this man can't provide the documents we need? We've already paid him." They'd been told to wait for someone to contact them.

"My uncle is well known here," Niccolò said. "I don't think this man would risk making him upset."

Ruby didn't understand the way things were done here. All she wanted was to get married to Niccolò. After their mistake, they had to marry soon. Even though she didn't like to think of their beautiful connection as a mistake, or a sin, she'd been taught that it was. Her parents had been strict with Ruby and Patricia. In their eyes, the only way to make herself whole was to marry Niccolò.

However, Ruby certainly didn't feel like she had sinned. Did that mean she was a heathen? She didn't feel like that either. Instead, she felt like she'd had a wondrous awakening. She was more in love with Niccolò than ever, and she couldn't imagine living without him. She was sure they would have married anyway, regardless. The only feeling she had was one of pure happiness.

"What should I wear?" Ruby asked. She was feeling so excited about the ceremony now.

"Let's look in my aunt's closet," Niccolò said. "She's about your height."

Once they returned to the villa, Niccolò led her into his aunt's room. Ruby was thrilled to find a blush-pink dress and an ivory lace shawl. When she put it on, she felt like it was the most beautiful dress she'd ever worn.

Niccolò rapped on her door. "Can I see how it fits?"

"Go away," Ruby cried out. "It's bad luck for you to see my dress." She couldn't remember if it was the dress or the bride, but she wanted him to be surprised.

The next morning as Ruby was making an American-style breakfast for Niccolò with sunny-side-up eggs and thick buttered toast, a knock sounded on the door.

When Niccolò opened the door, a breathless young boy told them they were wanted at the church soon. *"Per il matrimonio,"* he said before racing back toward the village.

"It's time." Niccolò wrapped his arms around Ruby.

She was so happy and excited that she could hardly eat the food she'd prepared, but Niccolò wolfed it down and proclaimed it the best breakfast he'd ever had.

Ruby changed clothes into the blush-pink dress and draped the lace shawl over her hair. She wished her family were here, but it was better this way, she told herself. When she emerged from the room to meet Niccolò downstairs, he was waiting for her in the front salon.

Niccolò appeared freshly shaven and dressed in one of his uncle's suits, which was only a little large. He was so handsome that she almost cried with joy.

"And this is for you," he said, picking up a bouquet of delicate white roses and glossy green ferns. He'd wrapped the flowers in a white handkerchief. Dropping to one knee, he held them out to her. "I don't have a ring of gold for you today, but I chose the best roses from the garden. Whenever you see white roses, I want you to think of this day."

Ruby blinked back tears and accepted the flowers. Closing her eyes, she breathed in their heavenly sweet scent. She wanted to remember everything about this day.

Ruby slid her hand over Niccolò's arm, and they walked to the church. Golden orioles chirped overhead, and the sun was warm on her face. All signs pointed to the happy promise of a sweet future ahead.

When they arrived at Chiesa di San Giorgio, Ruby saw that the man Niccolò had spoken with was there with an elderly couple who would serve as witnesses. The woman was agitated, shaking her head.

"What's the matter?" Ruby asked.

"Agosto," Niccolò said. "She thinks it's bad luck to be married in August."

"That's ridiculous," Ruby said, although the woman was making her nervous.

The man with her pressed an object into Niccolò's hand, motioning for him to put it in his pocket.

Niccolò looked at it and chuckled. "It's a broken piece of a tool. But it's made of iron, so that's good luck."

"Hope that offsets the curse of August," Ruby said.

The priest motioned for them to join him. Ruby could hardly believe this was happening, and she wished she could understand the priest. Yet the Italian language was an exquisite melody to her, and she loved the romance of it. She understood the essence of the priest's words and the solemnity with which he spoke.

Most of all, she understood that this commitment was for life, forever and ever, until the day they died.

When the priest motioned for a ring, Niccolò blushed and shook his head. Seeing that he was embarrassed, Ruby whispered, "Unfasten my necklace."

"Why?"

"I'll show you," she said, smiling. "And take off yours, too."

Niccolò did as she asked. With trembling fingers, she divided the heart. Taking the thin, silver chain he wore, she threaded one side of the heart onto it. After clasping the chain around his neck, he did the same for her. Each of them wore one-half of the heart crowned with a small ruby.

"*Ti amerò per sempre.*" Niccolò kissed her hand. "Always, I'll always love you, *amore mio.*" He slid a finger under her chin and kissed her with a tenderness that brought tears to her eyes.

"And I will always love you," she murmured.

As the priest joined them together in matrimony and blessed their union, Ruby felt transformed by the love Niccolò had for her, and the love she had for him. What they felt for each other was rare and beautiful, and Ruby was sure that they would celebrate their love every day of their lives.

"We're really married," Ruby cried with glee as they left the church.

"*Evviva gli sposi,*" called out the older couple who had acted as witnesses in congratulations.

Ruby and Niccolò turned and waved.

After the ceremony, Ruby and Niccolò were famished. Still

wearing their wedding finery, they boarded the ferry to Bellagio to go to one of Niccolò's favorite restaurants. Once they arrived, they strolled to the café arm in arm. When other patrons realized Ruby and Niccolò had just married, people surrounded them, wishing them well and showering them with champagne and food. Strangers became friends, and Ruby fixed every joyful face in her mind.

Although they were celebrating their vows without their family, Ruby cherished their wedding day. She promised herself she would remember every detail forever.

Yet, even as they kissed and toasted to their future, she couldn't help but wonder how their parents would react to their news. Would they be as happy for her as these strangers were? Would they see the love in their hearts—or only the impediments to their union?

16

Lago di Como, 2010

*A*riana tipped her face to the sun, feeling the warmth on her cheeks as Alessandro steered the yacht across the lake. It was such a glorious, sunny day, and when Alessandro had suggested a ride on the lake, she thought, *why not?*

After all, she had been scheduled to be on vacation. Without the intended husband, but still, she deserved to enjoy herself.

As her aunt had told her this morning, *You can stay in your room and cry, or you get on with life and enjoy yourself.* Despite Ariana's complaints, Ruby had then pushed open the curtains in her bedroom to let in the morning rays.

When Alessandro turned up just after lunch, she had been properly nourished by the purple-haired Livia, who was an extraordinary cook and kept insisting that Ariana was too thin.

Here on Lake Como, Ariana was starting to feel better than she had in years.

"Have you heard of Villa d'Este in Cernobbio?" Alessandro eased off the throttle and guided the vintage Riva yacht toward the dock.

"I once saw it featured on a travel channel." Ariana ran her hand along the restored wood trim, which glimmered in the sun. "What a beautiful boat this is." There was another row of cushioned seats behind them, as well as an area where people could sun themselves.

"We call these yachts here," Alessandro said, smiling. "This one is almost sixty years old. Restoring it helped me keep my sanity after Serafina died." With a practiced hand, Alessandro guided the yacht toward the dock. "So, do you and your aunt holiday together often?"

Ariana had to think about it. "It's been a couple of years." *Four, actually, since any kind of vacation.* "I went with my aunt to London so that she could accept a lifetime award." She laughed. "She told them she wasn't through yet and gave out her agent's number from the podium."

"And did that work?" Alessandro asked.

Ariana chuckled. "That's how she got her last movie role. And she won another award for that one."

"Maybe she's not ready to retire."

"Ruby loves to work. But she also likes to enjoy life." As they neared the shoreline, Ariana could hear laughter rippling from the outdoor restaurants and the nearby swimming pool that stretched out into the lake.

Alessandro tilted his head. "That's the Italian way. My work is important, but my family is more so."

Ariana grew quiet, thinking about that. Ruby often asked her to travel with her to different events, but Ariana seldom took time away from work. Phillip had expected her to make time for him after they married, and she'd thought he was unreasonable. While she didn't regret leaving him at the altar, perhaps the scales had tipped too far in favor of her grueling job.

Not unlike her mother.

Ariana turned to Alessandro. "You left the factory to pick up your children from school the other day."

"Every day," he said, smiling. "I love to meet them after school and hear how their day went. It's a special time for each of us."

"Do you have an *au pair*?"

Alessandro shook his head. "I want to spend as much time with them as I can. Seems like yesterday that they were babies."

Ariana thought of an executive woman she worked with who hired an *au pair* to pick up her children from school, make dinner, bathe them, and tuck them into bed. If she were lucky, she made it home to read a story to her children before kissing them good-night. Most nights, she wasn't. Which left the weekends. Sunday, at least, because she often had to work on Saturday, or go to the gym, or have her hair done.

Thinking of all that was exhausting.

Other women she knew did what her mother Mari had done, which was simply to send their children to boarding schools and summer camps. That way, parents could turn out well-educated children with remarkably little effort. Sort of like delegating a project at work, Ariana imagined.

That wasn't what she wanted.

Ariana clasped her hands around her knees. She'd worn one of the bright print sundresses that Ruby had bought for her. And it was roomy enough to allow for her pending midsection expansion.

"I enjoy being creative and productive," she said. "But, I'm beginning to think I want a different sort of life."

"You'd leave the daily grind?"

"Maybe not right away. A job offers security." She needed stability for her child.

"Does it?" Alessandro steered the yacht into position along-side the dock. "Aren't you talented enough to create a path of your own?"

Ariana made a face. "Ouch, that hurt. Are you questioning my talent or my confidence?"

"I meant that as a compliment," he said, tying the lines to the dock. "You're smart and talented. Many people would pay you well for what you could create."

Ariana hadn't let herself think about that in years. In fashion school in Los Angeles, she'd dreamed of creating a fashion line. *Small and exclusive.* She wouldn't want an empire the size that Ralph Lauren or Giorgio Armani had built. Producing seasonal fashion shows and managing armies of employees would make her head hurt. But on a smaller scale, she would love it.

"Maybe I could start a line, or have a shop," she said, the ideas seeded in her mind.

"I'm sure you could." Alessandro held out his hand to her to help her from the yacht.

She hesitated for a moment, then slid her hand into his. His touch was firm, yet accommodating. Not like the men who yanked you from your seat, or those whose grip was so limp you couldn't depend on them.

Not that she was looking for anyone to depend on. Her mother had hammered the concept of self-reliance into her. As she'd had to, Ariana conceded. Her father hadn't contacted her since she'd been a little girl.

Once, being curious, Ariana had found photos he'd posted online with his new young family. That had been painful, and she'd quickly closed the images. Someday, maybe she would meet her half-siblings. If they even knew she existed.

Alessandro stepped from the yacht and helped her out.

She held onto his hand, enjoying his touch. Alessandro's dark hair ruffled in the breeze, and the sun kissed his nose and cheeks with color. With his lean, muscular build, he looked healthy, as if he spent a lot of time outdoors. She liked that. Not that it mattered, of course.

"And here is the magnificent Villa d'Este," Alessandro said. He released her hand and motioned toward an expansive, lakeside villa of gleaming white with beige accents. People were lounging on rows of balconies covered with apricot awnings. To one side, a long pool stretched out from the shoreline as if suspended in the lake.

Ariana gazed at the hotel and its manicured grounds in awe. "The hotel is one of our clients," he said. "Sometimes I come here for a respite."

Ariana fell in step beside him as they strolled the grounds.

"Villa d'Este is one of the most beautiful, historic villas on the lake," Alessandro said. "It's known for its beautiful gardens and interior, as well as impeccable service. You couldn't come here and not visit Villa d'Este."

"It's gorgeous," Ariana said. Numerous trees shaded walkways, fountains bubbled, and flowers bloomed in profusion.

"Do you like history?" Alessandro asked.

"I do," she said.

"Villa d'Este dates to 1568," Alessandro said. "Pellegrino Pellegrini, a famous architect of the day, designed it as a summer home for the Cardinal of Como. It was originally named Villa Garrovo, after a stream that flows into the lake. Then, Caroline of Brunswick, the Princess of Wales, bought it in the early 1800s. Finally, it was converted into a hotel in 1873. It's only open part of the year and closes in the winter."

"Does it get cold here?"

"We get the chill from the Alps, but it's not too cold. I like it because it's quiet then."

In the distance, Ariana could see an intimate wedding taking place. The couple was holding hands, and the bride's dress was a simple, beautifully fitted, strappy white silk sheath that fell to the woman's ankles. Judging from the couple's body language, they were unquestionably in love. When was the last time she'd gazed at Phillip like that? She glanced away.

"This is a popular venue for weddings," Alessandro said.

"Where did you get married?" As soon as the words left her mouth, Ariana wished she could take them back. "I'm sorry, I didn't mean to bring up difficult memories."

"Not at all. That was one of the happiest days of my life."

"Did you meet her here?"

"You would think, no?" He shook his head. "We knew many of the same people. But we met when we were both attending university in Roma." A wistful look crossed his face. "It's interesting to recall the first day you met someone, not realizing the role they would play in your life. Or you in theirs."

Ariana enjoyed listening to him. "You sound like a philosopher."

He grinned. "I studied philosophy and literature."

"And yet, you manufacture silk. How do you reconcile being a merchant with philosophy?"

"I love what I do," he said. "First, we employ people. Second, what we do is a beautiful, highly creative craft. We produce the most sumptuous textiles that people will cherish, often for generations. Every day I'm privileged to share excellence, joy, and happiness with the world." He paused. "How do you share your unique talents?"

Ariana was taken aback by that question. "I haven't really thought about it. I suppose the costumes I design for movies and television are part of the pleasure that people experience when they watch the production."

"And does that give you joy, too?"

"It did in the beginning," Ariana said thoughtfully. "But I have a boss who has created such a toxic environment that I dread going to work every day. If it weren't for my creative work, I'd shrivel and die from it."

Alessandro looked at her with alarm. "Ariana, forgive me. I hardly know you, but you must leave that job. I can see the hurt it causes you in your eyes. Stay here with your aunt for a while. Decide how you will change your life. Believe me, life is shorter than we realize."

Alessandro gripped her hand, which sent another thrill through her. Was it merely hormones that were causing this strange effect?

Still, Ariana let her hand remain in his. "You've never been in a position where you had to work at a demanding job for a living."

"Ah, you don't know me very well," Alessandro said. "After university, I worked as a management consultant in Rome and Milan. I traveled all the time. Hardly ever saw my wife, who was also working and looking after our first child." He shook his head. "We made money, but it was no way to live."

"What brought you back here?"

"My father passed away. It was time for my sister Paolina and me to make a decision. We could sell the silk factory, or hire a manager, or move home and run it ourselves. We did the latter."

"Are you happy with that choice?"

"I wish I'd returned here long ago. Those were harried, wasted years." He shook his head. "Seize the opportunity to change your life. You're a beautiful woman who should be living the life you want."

Ariana was taken aback by his words. He was so direct and spoke with such passion. "Are you flirting with me?"

"Flirting?" For a moment, he looked confused. "I see beauty in your soul but sadness in your eyes. You must live a life that is true to your heart. An authentic life." He brought her hand to his lips and kissed it. "And if I were to flirt with you, you would not have to ask."

"Wow." Ariana laughed lightly. She hardly knew how to respond. She'd never met a man like Alessandro.

He paused by a garden of fanciful topiaries. Stepping closer to Ariana, he draped an arm over her shoulder. "Relax. I will make no demands on you. I only want to see your broken heart healed." He smiled down at her. "I know what that is like."

Ariana gulped back a sudden cry. Was she that transparent? She shook her head. "Phillip—my fiancé—didn't break my heart. I broke my heart over him. Since I've been here, I realized I wanted him to be something he wasn't capable of being." She tilted her head. "Ruby once told me an adage about teaching a pig to sing. You'll only waste your time and frustrate the pig."

Alessandro threw his head back and laughed. "That's funny. But, so true." He smiled and held her for a moment, and then, he took her hand.

Ariana still felt the warmth of his arm around her. His embrace had been comforting—there was nothing overtly sexual about it. Yet her body had responded as if she'd found water in an arid desert.

It had to be the hormones.

They moved on through aromatic gardens brimming with roses and lilies and hydrangeas. Ariana walked hand-in-hand beside him as if that were the most natural thing to do. She'd only just met him, yet she felt comfortable with him. And so much more that she couldn't quite name yet.

They paused, taking in the view of Villa d'Este that stretched before them.

"I'm truly impressed," she said, referring not only to the villa and the gardens but also the man beside her.

After winding through the gardens, they arrived at the entry to the grand hotel. Alessandro led her through the entryway, nodding in greeting to those who recognized him.

Ariana took in everything, from the soaring ceilings and glittering chandeliers overhead to the blue-and-yellow patterned carpet underfoot. She gazed through expansive windows to the lake and the villages beyond that hugged the shore.

"To work and live among such beauty is such a privilege," Ariana said. "Do you ever take it for granted?"

"Never," he said. "While I was consulting, I was often sent to industrial areas to work with clients. It was then that I realized how fortunate I was to have been born here, and how ingrained the appreciation of natural beauty and preservation of culture was in me." He gestured around him. "This is my heritage, and I want my children to be able to enjoy it as I have, and my ancestors before me." He grinned at her. "How about that coffee I promised you?"

"Sounds good now," Ariana answered with a smile.

Alessandro led her to a terrace restaurant that overlooked the lake, and soon they were seated at a table covered with white linen, polished silver, and sparkling crystal. Pink geraniums and snowy alyssum spilled from flower boxes mounted on the railing.

Ariana thought it was one of the most romantic settings she'd ever seen. Not that this was a romantic interlude. It was just coffee, after all.

As they sipped tiny cups of strong coffee, Alessandro asked about her family, and Ariana told him about her mother and Nana Pat. She shared stories about Ruby and how important her great-aunt had been in her life. For some odd reason, she felt herself opening up to him, trusting him with thoughts she rarely voiced. Or even acknowledged.

"You're awfully easy to talk to," she said after telling Alessandro a story about Ruby.

"I like to listen." He grinned. "And you have a beautiful voice. A strange American accent, but—"

"Hey," she said, playfully batting him on the shoulder. "I'll have you know that I'm practicing my Italian. I studied the language in school."

"Then you must stay here longer to practice," he said, his eyes dancing.

Ariana rested her chin on her hand. "Maybe I will," she said. Between urging from both Alessandro and Ruby—and the relaxing beauty of the area—the idea was becoming more appealing. If only she could act on it. She frowned, remembering the vulnerable life forming within her. "On second thought, it's probably impossible."

Alessandro leaned across the table and took her hands in his. "Few things are truly impossible. Maybe you just haven't thought of a way yet."

As she gazed into Alessandro's gold-flecked hazel eyes, she realized he had a point. What if there was a way she hadn't thought of yet? She smiled. "Are you flirting with me again?"

He grinned and shook his head. "I promise that you'll know when I do."

Ariana arched an eyebrow. "Ah…*when* and not *if?*"

Now it was Alessandro's turn to laugh. "I think you're flirting with me."

Ariana opened her mouth to deny it, and then she realized that once again, he was correct. Heat rose in her cheeks, and she lowered her eyes, embarrassed.

"And I like it," he added.

They laughed and continued to talk until Alessandro told her it was time they left. "Paolina took the children to their music lesson after school today, but I don't want to miss them for supper. And the *Breza*, the afternoon winds from the south, will probably increase later, making the water quite rough."

"I understand," Ariana said, pleased that he was such an attentive father. After the experience with her father—and Phillip's harsh words—that was critically important to her.

They held hands as they walked back to Alessandro's yacht. As they sped across the lake toward Villa Fiori, Ariana welcomed the fresh mist on her face and the breeze in her hair. She felt lighter than she had in ages.

To think that this was the beginning of a new relationship was a sweet thought, but it was unrealistic. She was pregnant with Phillip's child. Although her ex-fiancé wasn't willing to accept responsibility, she would be holding that child in her arms in just a few months. At her age, this might be her only chance to be a mother. She didn't want to make any mistakes.

Ariana understood the challenges ahead. She recalled that when she was thirteen, she'd accused her mother of driving away her father and rendering her fatherless. She'd never forgotten the profound hurt on her mother's usually stern face. Now that her family history was repeating itself, Ariana regretted her actions.

Ariana let her gaze rest on Alessandro, whose strong profile nearly took her breath away. Yet, he had his responsibilities, and she had hers. And even if she found a way to stay, he didn't need the responsibility of another's man's child.

Smiling wistfully, Ariana thought of how they might help each other mend their broken hearts through the occasional coffee and easy banter. She would wait to tell him she was pregnant because it would be no concern of his. They could enjoy each other's company, but that was all.

Though the thought saddened her, that was her reality.

17

Rome, 1952

The cast and crew had just returned from the mid-August break for the Ferragosto holiday. When Ruby finished her stand-in tasks for the director for lighting and camera angles, she left the set. Nearby, she saw Audrey shuffling cards, waiting for her call. Her dark eyes lit with delight when she saw Ruby.

"You looked so lovely up there, and I appreciate your patience," Audrey said. Today, they wore the same costume—a light-weight blouse and skirt.

"I'm learning so much," Ruby said. "It's exciting."

"I know you're going to be a famous star someday," Audrey said, setting the playing cards aside. She picked up a fan to alleviate the blistering heat. "And how was your holiday?"

Ruby perched in a canvas chair next to her. "We went to Lake Como."

"We?" Audrey's voice dropped to a whisper. "You mean, you and Niccolò?"

"We had such a wonderful time," Ruby said, nodding. She would love to tell Audrey that she and Niccolò had married, but she'd promised her new husband that they would inform his parents first.

This weekend.

In the meantime, Niccolò was staying with her in her room at the pensione. He'd told his mother he was staying with a friend near the filming locations.

Audrey's gaze slid to Ruby's neck. "The necklace," she exclaimed. "Did it break?"

"It comes apart, remember?" Ruby touched the silver pendant. She'd tucked it beneath her costume for the scene, but it had slipped out now. She smiled. "Niccolò is wearing the other half." She was bursting to tell Audrey about their wedding, but she couldn't.

Audrey's eyes widened. "You're going steady. That's what they call it in America, right?"

"Actually, it's more than that," Ruby said, tempted to confide in her.

Audrey took her by the shoulders. "You're engaged!"

Laughing, Ruby could only shrug off her guesses. She'd promised Niccolò.

"I knew that necklace would bring you luck," Audrey said, hugging her.

"You have no idea how much luck," Ruby replied.

Audrey's eyes flashed with delight. "Oh, don't tell me that you…"

"I can't, not yet. I promised Niccolò."

"I want to hear all about it as soon as possible," Audrey said, her eyes sparkling with delight. "And I want to come to your wedding."

At that moment, Mr. Wyler called for Audrey, who scooted off the canvas chair with her name on it and hurried to her spot.

Ruby stayed to watch the principal actors go through the scene several times. She studied how Mr. Wyler orchestrated each scene, the way the actors delivered their lines, and what the director asked from them. Ruby rested her chin in her hand, analyzing everything on the set.

Her life was perfect. She was doing what she adored with the man she loved. Ruby felt like the luckiest woman in the world.

The week of filming flew by, and Niccolò promised his parents that they would join them for supper on Friday.

After the end of filming on Friday, Niccolò walked with Ruby to her pensione. He squeezed her hand. "I can't wait to tell my parents about us tonight. They're going to be so happy."

Not wanting to jinx the evening, Ruby smiled. But inside, a whirl of anxiety churned. She couldn't help but feel that his parents might not be as thrilled as Niccolò thought.

LATER THAT EVENING, RUBY SAT BESIDE NICCOLÒ AT A TABLE IN his parent's kitchen, clutching his hand.

"Niccolò, would you hand me a knife for the parsley?" Carolina asked as she adjusted a flame on the stove. The sweet aroma of sautéed garlic filled the air.

Niccolò sprang to help. Niccolò had also chopped garlic, and Ruby had grated *Parmigiano-Reggiano* cheese. "Here you are, Mamma."

Carolina was preparing artichokes for *carciofi alla Romana* and *pancetta* for *spaghetti alla carbonara*. She quickly chopped a handful of parsley.

Glancing back at Ruby, Carolina smiled. "I love having you two in the kitchen. You're welcome here anytime, Ruby."

"I'd like that," Ruby said. She loved being part of this family. Carolina was already treating her like a daughter, fussing over her and telling her she should eat more.

Niccolò whispered to Ruby and took her hand. He couldn't keep their secret a moment longer. They had planned to tell his parents after supper, but Niccolò was too excited to wait.

"Mamma, Papà, please sit down for a moment," Niccolò began, smiling at Ruby. "We have important news to share."

Wiping her hands, Carolina sat down, tugging her husband, Dante, into the chair beside her. "What is it, Niccolò?"

Ruby's pulse was pounding so hard she pressed a finger against her temple to hide the vein that throbbed whenever she was nervous. She was so anxious she could hardly breathe.

Niccolò squeezed her hand and faced his parents. "When

Ruby and I went to Lago di Como, we decided that we wanted to spend the rest of our lives together."

Carolina beamed at her son. "You want to get married?"

Ruby noticed that Dante looked less enthusiastic. She slid her free hand under the table and fidgeted with her cotton skirt.

A wondrous smile wreathed Niccolò's face. "We couldn't wait. The priest at the church in Varenna married us."

Carolina exclaimed. "Already?" She pressed a hand to her throat, clearly conflicted. "I'm happy for you, I am, but you could have had such a beautiful wedding here."

"It *was* beautiful, Mamma," Niccolò said, rising to hug his mother. "Think of how much money we saved, eh, Papà? For Valeria's wedding. You know she wants a big wedding."

Dante nodded reluctantly. "So, you did this without speaking to your family first." Gesturing with his hand, he shook his head. "Young people. I don't understand."

His wife jabbed him. "We are happy for them, Dante. We have a new daughter in our family." Carolina held out her arms to Ruby.

Ruby fell into Carolina's tearful embrace. Niccolò's father followed with a perfunctory hug. Ruby knew he was disappointed, but he seemed to accept their marriage. Would her parents feel the same way? Just thinking about them made her nervous.

"We will have a huge party," Carolina said, her eyes lighting with excitement. "And I know the perfect flat for you. A friend is moving soon. But of course, you'll stay here until then."

"Wait," Niccolò said, raising his hand. "There's more."

Ruby dreaded what he was about to say. Seated at the table again, she wound her hemline around her fingers and rocked slightly.

Niccolò beamed with excitement. "I'm going to Hollywood with Ruby. Her agent will represent me for movies." He swept his arm around Ruby. "This will be the beginning of our new life in America."

Carolina's face crumpled with sadness, and Dante took her hand. "That is a surprise," he said, stunned. In their eyes, their love and concern for Niccolò were evident. "We planned that you would come into the business with me. Finding new artists, building their careers with collectors. You will be very good at that."

A wave of disappointment washed over Niccolò's face. "Papà, I know this isn't what you'd planned, but I thought you'd be happy for us."

"Italy isn't good enough anymore?" Dante asked quietly, flexing the muscles in his jaw.

"Papà, please understand."

Dante rapped on the table. "Stay in Rome; have a good life. Raise your children with family they will know and trust. This is our way."

Carolina looked up at Ruby with sadness. "Niccolò is our eldest son. I would love your children and help you care for them. We are family now."

Hearing the pain in Carolina's voice, Ruby twisted her skirt tighter. This is what she'd feared. "I can't stay here. There's a drought in Texas, and if I don't return to work, my family will lose their ranch. I can't do that to them."

"See, Papà? We have to go."

"We know what happens," Dante said, his expression darkening. "People go to America, and they don't return. We will never see you again. Is that what you want? To bring your mother such misery?"

"I don't mean to hurt anyone." Niccolò's voice cracked. "But you have always encouraged me to follow my dreams."

"*Sì, a Roma*. In *Italia*," Dante said, shaking his finger. "Why do you want to live in America? It's so far, so big. It's not for you."

"I want to act. The art business is yours, and even Valeria would be a better choice than me."

"Valeria will have a family," Dante said, slapping his hand on the table. "Your grandfather started this business, passed it to me, and now it is your turn. You should be thinking of your responsibility." He swept his hand in a dismissive gesture. "But, if you must act, Cinecittà Studio is here in Rome. Why go to Hollywood?"

"But Ruby can't work in Italy," Niccolò said, grinding his

teeth. "She doesn't speak much Italian, and she must return to Hollywood. Besides, this is our dream."

Carolina dabbed her eyes with the edge of her apron. "If it's what he wants..." She shrugged, but her heart was obviously breaking.

"No, no, no." His father curled his hands, raising his voice as he spoke. "I know my son. This—" Dante paused, gesturing between Niccolò and Ruby. "This marriage was a mistake. You didn't even ask us first."

Ruby couldn't contain her heartbreak, and tears spilled onto her cheeks. His father's response was worse than they had imagined.

Niccolò turned to her to wipe her cheeks, but she pushed him away. In her heart, she knew they'd done the right thing by getting married, but in the process, they'd alienated his parents, who had valid points driven only by love. Seeing their reaction made her dread telling her parents even more. *What have we done?*

Niccolò spread his hands in an appeal. "Papà, I'm an adult. I can do what I want."

"I will not let you make another mistake," Dante said, jabbing the table. "How would you live in America? You don't even have enough money for your passage. No, you will stay here. You had your fun, and now I need your help in the business. That is final."

Niccolò jutted out his jaw and rose from his chair. "I will do what I want."

"You must get this marriage annulled," his father shot back. "That girl," he sputtered, pointing at Ruby. "If she takes you to America, then she is not the one for you. In Hollywood, you will forget your family. You will forget who you are."

"That's not true," Ruby cried out. As anger erupted in her chest, her head grew light, and her limbs tingled. She could hardly fathom what she'd heard. *Annul their marriage?*

"*No, no, non lo farò,*" Niccolò said, putting his arm protectively around Ruby. "We will not."

"*Mio Dio.*" His mother sucked in her breath and passed her hands over her face. "Ah, no, no, no..."

Niccolò smacked his forehead and muttered a few words in

Italian that Ruby didn't understand. But his father did. Within seconds, Niccolò and Dante were yelling at each other in Italian. Although Ruby didn't know what they were saying, she could guess. Guilt gathered in the pit of her stomach.

"*Quando è troppo è troppo,*" Carolina cried as she tried to calm her husband, but to no avail.

"*Finito,*" Dante yelled, gesturing toward Ruby. A dark shadow drew over his face, and he clenched Niccolò's shoulders. "If you disobey me, destroy your mother's heart, and turn your back on your responsibilities here, then you are finished. Board that ship if you want, but you will never return here."

As the argument escalated, Ruby's heart split. She'd caused this. If she'd been an Italian girl, none of this would have happened. She had ruined Niccolò's relationship with his parents.

With tears clouding her vision, Ruby pushed from the table and raced toward the front door. She grabbed her purse and flung open the door, desperate to get away from the anger and harm she'd inflicted on Niccolò and his family.

A taxi was dropping a passenger at the corner, and she ran toward it, stumbling on the cobblestones in the gathering twilight. When she reached the cab, she gave the driver her address and slid into the back seat, wiping tears from her cheeks. As the driver started, she heard a cry and turned around.

"Ruby! Stop!" Waving his arms, Niccolò raced toward the taxi.

"Don't stop," she said to the driver, motioning for him to keep going. "*Andiamo, per favore, andiamo.*"

Ashamed over leaving Niccolò, yet knowing it was the right thing to do, Ruby sank her face into her hands. Niccolò's father had rejected her, and he was forbidding Niccolò from leaving Italy. Even if Niccolò left with her, she'd destroyed his family. She couldn't bear that guilt.

Have I ruined Niccolò's life? As the taxi careened through the night, she moaned and clutched the silver half-heart around her neck, her heart breaking just as surely as the one she wore.

18

Lago di Como, 2010

"Here we are." Ruby paused in front of Lorenzo's café that overlooked the lake. Smiling at the young woman who stood at the reception desk, she said, "Please tell Lorenzo Pagani that Ruby Raines and her niece are here for lunch. He's expecting us."

The young woman's eyes widened. "Signora Raines, what a pleasure. I'll let him know right away." She hurried toward Lorenzo.

While they waited, Ruby glanced at Ariana. Yesterday her niece had gone out for coffee with Alessandro, and Ariana told her that they had gone to Villa d'Este in Lorenzo's yacht. Ruby studied the sparkle in Ariana's eyes and the spring in her step that she could attribute to only one thing.

Alessandro.

Ruby smiled. She liked him for her niece, but she wondered if they would have enough time to get to know one another. Yet, as she well knew, true love could move fast.

"Ariana, dear, have you heard from your mother lately?"

Mari hadn't responded to the letter Ruby had sent, but then, it hadn't been very long.

"She doesn't even know I called off the wedding," Ariana said softly.

Ruby felt sorry for Ariana that she wasn't close to her mother. Had history doomed their family to repetition? "I sure would like to see you two reconcile."

"It's not as if we argued," Ariana said. "Mom is so driven she doesn't have time for me. Or anyone else."

Ruby started to say that being driven had little to do with it, that one made time for those they loved. But that might make matters worse. Ruby wondered if Mari was capable of knowing how to love Ariana. Maybe she was missing the maternal instinct. Which was worse, Ruby wondered, to be shunned by your mother because she didn't have time for you or because she couldn't love you?

Perhaps Mari suffered from another, more deeply rooted cause. Fear of abandonment might be lodged deep in her psyche. But Ruby was not a therapist or a doctor.

Intruding into Ruby's thoughts, Ariana said, "The café looks full."

Across the way, Lorenzo motioned to a table with a white tablecloth and a reserved sign. The woman from the front desk quickly returned to Ruby and Ariana. "I'm so sorry to keep you waiting. This way, please. Lorenzo will be with you in a moment."

As they followed the woman to the table shaded with a red umbrella, Ariana asked, "How do you know Lorenzo?"

The woman pulled out her chair, and Ruby sat down. Lorenzo had reserved the best table for them.

"I came by here yesterday on the way to the post office," Ruby said. She didn't mention that she had been searching for this particular café. On her earlier visit to Bellagio with the tour group, Matteo had taken her to several restaurants, but none of them was the one that she and Niccolò had gone to after their wedding. She glanced around now, envisioning how the café had looked then and where they had sat. *What a wonderful evening that was.*

Ariana picked up a menu. "I've been famished lately."

"I'm not surprised." Ruby smiled and touched Ariana's hand. "I can't wait to spoil a little one."

"Like you spoiled me when I was young?"

"Like I still do, every chance I get." Ruby laughed. *Oh yes, this little one will have everything she wants. Or he.* Ruby wasn't picky. "If only you would let me spoil you more often."

Ariana twisted her lips to one side. "Guess Mom drilled a no-spoiling attitude into my head."

Across the café, Lorenzo made his way through the glamorous lunch crowd on the patio. He wore another expertly cut sport coat and an open-collared white shirt that showed off his trim, athletic figure. His sun-bleached hair was proof that Lorenzo spent a lot of his leisure time outdoors.

"Signora Raines," Lorenzo said with a broad smile. "This must be your lovely niece," he added, dipping his head in greeting.

"Why, yes, it is," Ruby said. "Allow me to present Ariana Ricci."

Lorenzo took Ariana's hand and executed a perfect air kiss a mere breath above her skin. To her credit, Ariana took this in stride, although Ruby doubted that anyone in Los Angeles had ever done that. Including, and especially, her thankfully ex-fiancé, Phillip.

Ruby closed the menu. "What is your specialty, Lorenzo? Food-wise," she added with a little smile. She noticed that Ariana was trying not to stare at Lorenzo, but her niece couldn't help enjoying the view.

While Lorenzo was reviewing the specialties, which included *trofie al pesto con gamberetti*—one of her favorite pasta with pesto and shrimp—Ruby glanced next door at the vacant shop. Years ago, Ariana had once talked about opening a studio. An idea formed in Ruby's mind. Perhaps her niece could be persuaded to stay.

After they ordered, Ruby rested her chin in her hand. "Why, look at that sweet little shop space. And with a beautiful view of the lake. Someone's going to be lucky to have that location."

Ariana turned toward the shop. "That is a wonderful

location."

"What kind of shop would be good there, I wonder."

"Are you thinking of opening a business, Aunt Ruby?"

Ruby laughed. "Not really, but I can see the potential. Look how busy this place is. Wouldn't that be an interesting location?" She glanced along the street. "Excellent foot traffic, too."

"You're too obvious."

Ruby pressed a hand to her chest. "About what?"

"An idea that would keep me here."

"Why, what a good thought." Ruby smiled. At least Ariana wasn't upset. In fact, she seemed to be considering it.

Ariana glanced around. "Yesterday, Alessandro brought me the most beautiful roll of silk fabric. It's a soft mint green, with a delicate print of ferns and flowers. He thought it would accent my eyes. I've been thinking about making a dress or a blouse with it. Of course, whatever I make, I wouldn't be able to wear long. For the obvious reason."

"You won't be pregnant forever," Ruby said. "Or make something you can wear for a few months, and then alter to fit you again afterward."

"I suppose I could."

Lorenzo returned to the table with two glasses of champagne. "Welcome to Bellagio, and I hope you enjoy Villa Fiori."

Ruby lifted the champagne in appreciation. "You must come and visit sometime."

Lorenzo's gaze lingered on Ariana. "I'd like that very much, *grazie*." He chatted for a few minutes before moving on to the next table.

When Lorenzo was out of earshot, Ruby leaned toward Ariana. "I think you have another admirer."

"Perhaps it's the hormones," Ariana said in a wry tone. "They're attracting men to me like sticky pollen."

"It's nice to have a choice, isn't it?"

"Auntie, I'm in no position to choose anyone. How would I explain my current predicament?"

Ruby shrugged. "If the man is truly in love, it wouldn't matter. Don't close yourself off to future possibilities."

"I have to return to Los Angeles. I have to go back to work."

Ruby tapped her fingers. "If only you had another option. It's not as if Kingsley would miss you."

Ariana glanced at the vacant space next door. "I couldn't possibly start a new project while I'm in this condition."

"Oh, to be young and full of energy," Ruby said.

"I can't imagine what I would do."

"You've always had the most wonderful imagination. I think you could manage it." Ruby gazed out at a ferry crossing the shimmering lake. "You'd be surprised what you can do while you're pregnant. You certainly have more motivation."

Ariana looked at her quizzically for a moment before returning her gaze to the vacant shop space. "Maybe some silk scarves with unique prints, a few simple designs. Casual wrap-around dresses made of beautiful silk." A smile curved on her lips. "Palazzo pants, halter tops, short shifts. Fun luxury."

Ruby smiled and nodded. "Intriguing thoughts."

"Oh, Aunt Ruby. Did you have this in mind all along?"

"Not at all," Ruby replied, laughing. "Perhaps it was destiny."

"And do you believe in destiny?"

Ruby gazed across the lake toward the bell tower in Varenna. "Crazy though it seems, I still do."

After they ate, and Ruby had finished both glasses of champagne that Lorenzo had brought to the table, she motioned for him. When he joined them, she asked, "Lorenzo, darling, do you know anything about that sweet little shop next door that's vacant?"

"You're lucky. The owner is at another table." Lorenzo gave a convincing act of surprise. "Shall I get him for you?"

"My goodness, imagine that," Ruby said. "We'd love to talk to him and see the space."

While Lorenzo hurried to another table, Ariana turned to Ruby. "Really? You're going to tell me this was a coincidence?"

Ruby winked. "Absolutely. I've long believed in synchronicity."

Lorenzo returned with a man he introduced as Cesare Gatti. Ruby invited him to join them and asked him to tell them about the shop space.

"Would you like to see it?" Cesare asked.

"Indeed, we would." Ruby beamed at Ariana. "What luck."

After they finished lunch, they walked next door to the vacant space. Cesare opened the door for them.

"This space was last used as a fashion boutique," Cesare said. "It was very successful until the owner sold it to another person." He shuddered. "The new owner had absolutely no sense of style, so the shop closed in six months."

"I don't think that would be a problem for Ariana," Ruby said with confidence. She watched as Ariana walked the length of the small shop, scrutinizing the dressing rooms, the mirrors and shelves, and the decor.

While Ariana paced off the space and reeled off questions for the property owner, Ruby gazed from the front windows. Ferries and boats crisscrossed the lake. It was a happy sight, and people were clearly enjoying themselves on this sunny day. As Ruby gazed across the lake, the distant bell tower that rose above the cathedral in Varenna drew her attention.

Ruby recalled the happiest day of her life. Whenever she closed her eyes, she could still see the look of love in Niccolò's eyes for her. She could smell the white roses that he had chosen from the garden for her bouquet, and she could feel the blush-pink silk dress on her skin.

Pressing her hand against her heart, Ruby relived the emotion of that day. The love they shared had never died. And no other man ever compared to Niccolò. Was that the perfection of young love, or had he become perfect in her memory with the passing years?

Her wedding had been like a sweet dream. Ruby might have been naïve, but she'd fallen in love. That entire summer in Italy existed in her memory as if captured in a crystal orb.

Ariana stopped beside Ruby, jolting her from her memories. "This could be such a charming shop," Ariana said. "And you couldn't ask for a better location. With the café next door, the foot traffic from other shops, and the fresh breeze off the lake with a view that just goes on and on." Ariana sighed. "If only my life was different."

Ruby put her arm around Ariana's shoulder. "What if it could be?" she asked, her words catching in her throat. If she couldn't rewind her life and run it in a different direction, at least she could help Ariana change her trajectory.

She had watched Ariana for years; she'd seen the joy sucked from her soul. No job was worth that. "My darling girl, you have the power to do whatever you want. All you have to do is believe that you can."

Ariana rested her head on Ruby's shoulder. "Is that what you did when you decided to buy the Villa Fiori?"

"That's what I've always done," Ruby said.

Or was it? How many times had Ruby replayed parts of her life, wondering if she had done everything in her power? Yet nothing good ever came of examining decisions already made. The only thing she could change was her future.

And now she was back on the shores of this beautiful lake where she had been united with the love of her life, if only for a brief time. She had never regretted the magic that she and Niccolò had shared here.

If Ruby were going to die, it would be with a view of the little church's bell tower outside of her window and Niccolò's name on her lips. She would end her life where it had really started.

Each of those days was suspended in her memory like a perfectly faceted prism that shimmered with the radiance of love. Ruby smiled. The love they had shared was her most precious possession; that which had flowed from their union she would cherish until her last breath.

Watching her, Ariana frowned. "Are you alright?"

Ruby blinked back tears forming on her lashes. "Of course, I am, my dear." She pressed her pinkie finger to the corner of her eyes. "I'm an actress; I'm dramatic by nature."

"Allow me," Cesare said, handing her a pressed handkerchief.

Ruby accepted it, and she noticed the look of surprise on Ariana's face. "Such a lovely gesture, isn't it?" Not many men carried handkerchiefs these days.

Glancing down at it, she saw the initial *N* embroidered on the fine cloth. Why would Cesare be carrying this? Ruby dabbed her eyes and handed it back to him.

Here on Lake Como, reminders of Niccolò were everywhere. Were they mere coincidences or perfect synchronicity?

19

Rome, 1952

*B*linded by tears, Ruby pawed through her purse to find the *lire* to pay the taxi driver. *"Grazie,"* she mumbled, fumbling at the door handle.

The driver hurried to open the door and help her, but she shrugged him off. She didn't want anyone's help; she only wanted to be left alone. Still in shock over the argument between Niccolò and his father just minutes ago, she staggered through the darkening night toward the small inn where she was staying. Hot tears trickled down her cheeks, and she angrily brushed them away.

The pensione owner, a kind middle-aged woman who'd helped her settle into Rome, looked up from her desk at her in alarm. *"Mio Dio. Signorina Raines, stai bene?"*

Searching for words, Ruby sliced her hands through the air. *"Niccolò, finito."*

The woman's face crumpled in sympathy, and she reached out to Ruby.

Anxious to shut out the world, Ruby shook her head and rushed toward the staircase. She stumbled up the dimly lit steps, her anguish escalating with each riser until she reached her room.

With her heart breaking over Niccolò and his father's rejection of their marriage, Ruby flung herself onto the bed in her room at the pensione. In the dark, she clutched the half of the silver heart she wore and sobbed into the pillow, her stomach twisting in on itself in agony.

She loved Niccolò with all her heart, but Niccolò was torn between her and his family. Unquestionably, his father would force him to annul their marriage. She couldn't rip Niccolò from the family he cherished.

These thoughts twisted in her heart like a knife, carving out all the happiness she'd found in Lake Como. She'd prayed that his father wouldn't react this way. As the moon outside her window rose in the sky, she cried herself to exhaustion.

Suddenly, she awoke to the sound of pounding on her door.

"Ruby, it's me." Niccolò's hoarse whisper echoed through the door.

Groaning, Ruby turned her back to the door. Unable to bear hearing words of finality from Niccolò, she pressed her hands against her ears. Yet she could still hear his muffled knocking, which grew more insistent.

Fearing he would wake neighboring guests, she pushed herself from the bed and dragged toward the door. Her blouse was damp with tears, and her hair was in disarray, but she didn't care.

Leaning against the door, she said, "If you've come to tell me it's over, just go away. Don't say it, don't apologize. I can't bear to hear it." She slid to the floor and hugged her knees.

Anywhere in the world was better than being here. As soon as the director released Ruby from the film, she would go home. *To the ranch.* Or maybe she could go early. Bending her head over her legs, she let tears trickle onto her bare knees. She couldn't manage here anymore. Not with a broken heart.

"I'll never let you go," Niccolò pleaded hoarsely, jiggling the knob. "Let me in. *Per favore, cuore mio.* We can't talk like this."

Ruby lifted her head, considering his words. *Never let you go.* Did he mean them? She scrubbed her hands over her face.

Grasping his lifeline, she rose on unsteady feet to open the door.

Niccolò swept her into his arms. "*Quanto ti amo,*" he murmured, crushing her to his chest.

"I love you, too," Ruby cried, throwing her arms around his neck.

In the next instant, Niccolò's mouth was on hers, and she hungrily returned his kiss, needing his touch, craving his reassurance.

They bumbled their way through the tiny, moonlit room, running their hands over each other's face, reassuring one another of their love until they reached the bed.

Ruby caught her breath. She had to know. "What happened after I left?"

"It was…terrible." Niccolò raked his hand through his thick hair, leaving it in disarray. "My father can't see that we are meant for each other. We are married, and that's forever."

Until death. Ruby would sooner die than live without Niccolò. "But, your family…"

Niccolò clasped her hands in his. "I will love you forever. My mother understands, and in time, my father will, too."

Although Carolina Mancini had welcomed her into the family, Dante had exploded. "What if he never does?"

Niccolò's grip on her hands intensified. "*Anima mia,* our love will last through this. You are my wife. Trust me," he said, his voice catching. "You *must* believe me."

The moonlight lit Niccolò's face, illuminating his earnest expression. Ruby chose to believe him, even though every nerve in her body twitched in warning.

"I do," she murmured. Closing her eyes, she met his lips, forcing the events of the evening from her mind. Together, like this, she could imagine that they were still in Lake Como. Without the burden of family disapproval. If only they could return to where they'd been so happy.

Wordlessly, they slipped from their clothes, finding their truth in the love they shared.

As the moon cast its glow upon them, Ruby rested in the protection of Niccolò's arms. This moment was all that mattered.

With her head nestled in the crook of his neck, she fixed this picture in her mind. Tomorrow, their world might splinter again, but she couldn't think of that. She drew her fingers across her husband's chest and watched his breath slow until, exhausted, they both fell into a deadened slumber.

In the morning, every muscle in Ruby's body ached from the stress of yesterday. When she tried to lift her head from Niccolò's chest, her forehead throbbed. She wasn't just tired; she was weary to the core of her being.

Only once before had Ruby felt such emotional destruction. In the spring of her twelfth year, a tornado had darkened the horizon near her parent's ranch in the midst of a thunderstorm. When her father spied it in the distance, he and Ruby drove the horses and livestock from the barn and away from their house. Animals had a natural instinct and would fare better outside of structures that could be demolished and cause injury.

Afterward, with the tornado upon them, they'd closed the barn door and hunkered down. Ruby saw a mixture of terror, sadness, and resolve in her father's lined face. He clutched her and shielded her body with his under a thick stack of horse blankets, and she could hear his fervent, whispered prayers in the dark as the tornado roared toward them.

Miraculously shifting at the last minute, the twister narrowly missed the barn and the house. When Ruby and her father emerged from the barn, they were stunned at the damage surrounding them. The tornado had ripped through a pasture, dismantling fences and lofting them like toothpicks, then scattering broken pieces across the land. Trees laden with fruit had been uprooted—even century-old live oaks. Mangled equipment lay twisted around them.

To this day, Ruby still remembered how drained and bone-tired she'd felt after the calamity.

She'd grown up that day, and the thought that her parents were in control of their world vanished. While she rebuilt the fence with her father, Ruby's childhood veneer was scraped away, nail by nail, board by board. As tall as her mother and on the brink of womanhood, Ruby faced the daily hardships of ranch life along with her parents. And on the adjoining property, her sister Patricia toiled long days beside her husband on their ranch.

Though several years had passed, Ruby still had moments of feeling like a scared child hiding under horse blankets. While she'd learned to hold her head up and get on with whatever task she had to do like an adult, that didn't mean that she wasn't impervious to anxiety and loss.

Ruby bit her lip as she thought of the events of last night. When Niccolò's father had lashed out at her and Niccolò, she worried that she should have stood up to him more. She had tried to, but she was an interloper in the family. Dante's anger was like that tornado, sucking the air from the room and leaving destruction in its wake.

Now tucked in Niccolò's safe embrace, Ruby listened to the early morning chatter of the pensione proprietor and vendors outside her window. The smell of fresh-baked bread wafted to her nose.

Niccolò stroked her hair, his touch as gentle as the breeze on Lake Como. "Are you awake?"

As long as Ruby kept her eyes closed, she wouldn't have to talk about last night or Niccolò's argument with his father. Or what their future might hold.

She sighed. But she'd also learned that when a storm approached, you fought for what was yours.

"I'm awake," she said, opening her eyes. His half of the silver heart gleamed against his sun-bronzed chest in the morning light.

"I'm not going home anymore," he said, kissing her forehead. "My home is with you now."

"When the film shoot is over, I have to return to the states." When Niccolò's smile drooped, she added, "Come with me. You can sign with my agent. He'll find work for you. I've been sleeping on my aunt's couch in Hollywood, but we can find a little place."

"I want to," he said. "But I need more money for my passage. I have to have the right papers to travel. And a passport."

"You don't have one?"

"Never needed one before."

Ruby ran her fingers across his brow. "How long do you think that will take?"

"The money or the passport?"

"Both, I guess." Ruby drew in her lower lip in thought. She had to help her husband, but she'd made a commitment to her family. She'd taken very little of her salary on the film for herself. "Once I return, I'll find work. I can help, too. Though I promised my family—"

Niccolò pressed a finger to her lips. "Keep your promise to them. I would have no pride if I accepted your money. I will do this."

She understood, but every day away from him would be agony. "I don't want to be apart from you," Ruby whispered.

Niccolò drew her closer. "It won't take long. That is my promise to you."

"We can write to each other," Ruby said, tracing his jawline. "Every day."

Niccolò laughed. "My English...I'm sorry, I don't write it very well. Many of your words have strange spellings, and I get them wrong. A lot, I'm told."

"I don't care. I want to hear from you." She threaded her fingers through his thick hair. "Write to me in Italian. I'm learning."

He shook his head in resignation. "I can't promise every day. I'll be working as much as I can."

"Acting, do you think?" Ruby asked.

"Doing anything I can as long as it gets me to you." Niccolò cupped her face in his hands. "*Cuore mio*, you are my only love, forever."

Ruby lifted her lips to his in a kiss that she never wanted to end. Until they parted, she would cherish every day as if it were a perfect pearl, stringing them together in a necklace of memories.

OVER THE NEXT TWO WEEKS, THE DIRECTOR COMPLETED FILMING most of the scenes in *Roman Holiday*. With every passing day,

Ruby felt her time with Niccolò growing more precious than ever.

Now, wearing a white lace dress with full sleeves and a tiny, belted waist, Ruby stood waiting in the Sala Grande Galleria of the Palazzo Colonna, one of Rome's grandest palaces. It was hundreds of years old, and the Colonna family still lived there. Ruby craned her head, never tiring of the Renaissance splendor, which was so unlike anything she'd ever seen.

Marble columns rose to the ceiling, and paintings in ornate gold frames stared down at them. Niccolò pointed out masterpieces by Caravaggio, Bronzino, Carrici, Locatelli.

Ruby gazed up. Overhead, frescoes swirled in brilliant detail and color. Sparkling Murano chandeliers lit the room. And underfoot, marble floors gleamed in richly veined onyx, ivory, and carnelian red. The majesty of the setting was utterly awe-inspiring. Even though Ruby was still only standing in for Audrey, she pulled back her shoulders, sensing the need to reach higher in the presence of such great artistry.

In the salon, Mr. Wyler's crew had set up additional lighting and equipment. The director and the lighting supervisor were conferring with other cast and crew members, while grips and gaffers made the necessary adjustments for the scene.

Niccolò would also be in the scene, posing as an extra reporter in the crowd behind Gregory Peck and Eddie Albert. He was already in costume, wearing a suit with his hair combed back.

Audrey sat beside her, her posture regal, studying the scene just as Ruby was. She glanced at Ruby. "Can you believe the filming is almost over? Being here has been such a dream. I never imagined that I would have such a break. Have you enjoyed Italy?"

"More than I can say." Instinctively, Ruby reached for the silver half-heart around her neck, but she'd removed it for this scene. Now she wore a double pearl choker with a jeweled centerpiece. She touched it instead with her white-gloved fingers.

"Where is your sweetheart?" Audrey asked, turning in her director's chair.

"Niccolò is running lines with the press extras." Mr. Wyler

had put out a casting call for real press professionals from foreign publications, and many had answered the call. Ruby smiled at Audrey and decided to confide in her—a little, anyway. "He's planning on coming to Hollywood as soon as he can."

As Audrey's dark, winged eyebrows shot up with glee, Ruby felt her cheeks color. No one on the set knew that she and Niccolò were married. For now, that was their delicious secret. They had agreed to wait until she told her parents, and, of course, she wanted Niccolò with her. Since Dante Mancini had exploded, Ruby was more nervous than ever about telling her parents, even though she knew she would disappoint her father. She glanced up at the ceiling again, mesmerized by the artistry. Ranch life simply wasn't for her anymore. Not with so many fascinating places in the world to explore—and Niccolò by her side.

"Where do you think you'll be married?" Audrey asked.

Ruby was bursting to tell her everything, but she'd promised Niccolò. "Somewhere beautiful and romantic," she said, recalling their holiday in Lake Como.

The only person Ruby and Niccolò confided in was the pensione owner, who became concerned about Ruby's reputation since Niccolò was staying over so much. When they told her, the woman had kissed them on the cheeks and wished them much happiness and many children. Ruby and Niccolò had laughed at that last part. They had plenty of time for a family. Many years, they assured her. First, they would become great actors and travel the world.

A smile danced on Audrey's lips. "You should marry in Italy. I'm going to return as soon as I can."

"I'd like that, too," Ruby said, continuing the ruse. But maybe she and Niccolò could return later. An idea struck her. "If I could live anywhere in Italy, I'd choose Lake Como."

Audrey looked at her with a knowing glance. "I think you fell in love in Lake Como."

"Irrevocably," Ruby said, trying out one of her new vocabulary words. She grinned, and the two women shared a laugh.

Mr. Wyler called for Ruby to stand in while they checked the lighting and camera angles.

They were reshooting the last scene, as the director hadn't been satisfied with previous takes. Mr. Wyler was a perfectionist, and Ruby felt fortunate to work with him. She'd learned so much on the set, listening to everything. She'd gained more insights as a stand-in than in her brief scene or as an extra.

Mr. Wyler made his way toward them. Speaking to Audrey, he said, "This will be a scene of great restraint. Here, you choose duty over love, a love that you cannot reveal, yet you try to convey to the one person who matters."

Listening to the directors, Ruby thought about how that might apply to her life. Would she ever choose duty over love? She couldn't imagine that. Her father couldn't force her into a future she didn't want. She was almost eighteen, an adult, really, and now, a married woman. She hugged her waist with happiness.

Mr. Wyler asked Ruby to stand in for a final check before filming began. Audrey winked at her before the two women parted.

"Good, now move a step toward stage left," Mr. Wyler said, checking her marks. "And would someone move that pot of red geraniums?"

When Ruby glanced back, she saw Niccolò. After a union crew member moved it, he plucked one of the red flowers and tucked it behind his ear.

She smothered a laugh, which earned a good-natured frown from Mr. Wyler.

Niccolò was impossible, and she loved him with all her heart.

At last, the film crew wrapped the primary filming and released most of the cast members, though the main stars—Audrey, Gregory, and Eddie—would stay a little longer. Ruby booked passage on a steamship to New York, where she would catch a train to Texas to see her family before continuing to Hollywood. Her agent sent her a telegram. *Lining up auditions for your return. Be ready to knock it out of the park.* Joseph was a big baseball fan. That always amused her.

Now in her room at the pensione, Ruby packed the last of

her few souvenirs into the suitcase.

"What about your clothes in the closet?" Niccolò asked.

"I'm leaving my old clothes here for the maid," Ruby said. "She wants them. I'm only taking what I bought here." She loved the vivid colors and had new dresses in sunny yellow, warm coral, and bright turquoise. She ran her hands over the patterned silk and lightweight wool scarves she could scarcely afford but couldn't bear to pass up.

"This is quite a lot," Niccolò said, struggling to close her suitcase.

"You should see what Audrey is taking home," Ruby said. The actress had fallen in love with her Edith Head-designed, *Roman Holiday* wardrobe. She'd asked if she could keep the clothes after filming. Paramount Studios agreed, and Audrey was thrilled. Someday, Ruby decided she would have such a wardrobe, too, complete with matching shoes and handbags and jewelry.

But more than the clothes or souvenirs, Ruby knew that she had won the ultimate prize in Italy.

Her Niccolò. She stole a kiss from him. "I'm luckier, though. I get to take you home."

Niccolò snapped the luggage clasp. "I wish I could sail with you." He swept her into his arms and buried his face in her hair. "I will miss all of you—the way your skin smells, your hair, your eyes, but most of all…" He slid his finger under her chin. "Your sweet, sweet kisses, *amore mio.*"

His kisses were another new language to her. At times, soft and gentle, then teasing, and later, ravishingly hungry. She'd never known there were so many different ways to kiss. But then, she'd never been kissed until Italy. Her parents shared quick smacks that were nothing like this.

Would they understand how much she loved him? Ruby prayed they would. Reluctantly, she pulled away from Niccolò's embrace. "We should go. I can't miss this ship."

"I wish you would," Niccolò said, teasing her again.

Or is he? The anguish in his eyes betrayed the lightness of his tone.

Blinking back tears that had threatened since she woke this

morning, Ruby picked up her purse and sighed heavily. "It's time."

"Chin up," Niccolò said, kissing her forehead. He lifted her suitcase from the bed. Instead of returning home, he'd told her that he would stay with a friend and gave her the address where she could write to him. In turn, she'd written down her Aunt Vivienne's address and telephone number in Hollywood.

Ruby looked back at the little room they'd shared, where'd they been so happy these last weeks. "I hate to leave our honeymoon haven."

"It's been sweet," Niccolò said. "And it will be even sweeter when I see you soon in Hollywood."

"You will come?" Ruby's voice hitched as she spoke. She needed his assurance, just once more.

Niccolò took her hand, kissed it, and pressed it against his chest. "You live in my heart. How could I stay away?"

Once they arrived at the crowded port of Civitavecchia near Rome, Ruby stared at the grand ocean liner that stretched before them, gleaming in the sunshine, its funnels painted in colors of the Italian flag—green, white, and red. Her chest tightened. The sight of the ship and the smell of the sea filled her with a frisson of foreboding. She worried that their separation might be longer than either of them realized.

Passengers who had already boarded were waving at loved ones from the ship. Those left behind were calling out and waving back. Ruby and Niccolò cut through the crowd. They didn't have much time left.

Ruby gripped her passport and the ticket she'd purchased. As they neared the check-in area, her pulse quickened. Throwing her arms around him, she swallowed hard to suppress the tears that threatened to overtake her. "I can't stand to be separated for very long."

"Neither can I, my love." Niccolò wrapped his arms around her. "Take care of your family. I will manage, and I will see you as soon as I can."

Ruby looked up at the immense ship. She had already crossed the Atlantic once. Instead of the excitement that had filled her, a sense of loss consumed her now. Despite their promises to one another, she couldn't help but wonder if this were all a lovely mirage, and soon she'd wake in Texas as before, like Dorothy from the *Wizard of Oz* in Kansas.

As a man's voice on a loudspeaker rang out, Niccolò lifted her hand to his lips and kissed it. "*Cuore mio*, they're calling for you."

Ruby and Niccolò had lingered all morning, putting off the inevitable. But now, people in uniforms were signaling for final passengers to board.

This is it. As her throat constricted, Ruby swung around to Niccolò. In desperation, she ran her hands over his hair and face, memorizing everything about him. *The high cut of his cheekbones, the full curve of his lips. Endless blue eyes that reflect the heavens. The angle of his shoulders, the touch of his skin. A lingering aroma of lemon-infused olive oil soap, mixing with his natural scent.* As he peppered her face with kisses, she rested her head against his chest, listening to a heart that pounded in sync with hers.

Tears slipped from her eyes. Ruby measured their last moments together as a goldsmith weighs precious gold shavings. She wished she could have stayed with Niccolò, but she had to return for work. Yet, her heart would remain in Rome in the care of her husband.

Niccolò crushed her to him, and Ruby gasped, finding his lips with hers for a kiss that would have to sustain them. His cheeks were damp with tears, too. They struggled to cry out the words they needed to say.

"*Cuore mio...anima mia. Quanto ti amo,*" Niccolò murmured.

"You are everything to me. *Cuore mio*, I love you, too," Ruby whispered, before dissolving with tears.

Niccolò stepped back from her and slid a finger under her chin to tilt it up. *Chin up.* Blinking hard, she turned away from him.

After boarding, Ruby wedged her way through the crushing crowd on the deck until she reached the railing. Tenting her hand above her eyes, she scanned the crowd.

There, below her, stood Niccolò, waving madly.

Waving back, she resolved that, no matter what, they would be together again.

20

Lago di Como, 2010

"*L*et's position the love seat between the two stone urns," Ariana said, directing Livia and Emilio. "Pink geraniums spilling from those urns would contrast well with blue cushions in the seating area." She put a finger to her chin, considering the patio furniture groupings on the terrace.

Ruby had given her carte blanche to design the exterior space, and Ariana was thoroughly enjoying herself. The blue lake beyond the terrace and the white-capped mountains as a majestic backdrop set a serene tableau.

She hadn't realized how much she needed this respite. Ariana's distress over Phillip was fading in the bright sunlight that beamed into her room every morning as if it were a serving of happiness to begin the day.

Ariana wished she could stay here with her aunt, yet the responsible action would be to return to Los Angeles; it was, after all, her home, and she needed to work as long as she could. Yet, the shop space next to the café intrigued her. Had Ruby filled her head with a fantasy, or could Ariana make a go of a design studio and boutique? That was what she'd studied, though she wondered if she could pull it off here. She didn't know many people, nor did she know the rules and regulations of the region.

As Ariana was thinking, her phone buzzed in her pocket, and she pulled it out. The name she'd been dreading appeared on the screen. *Kingsley*. Her boss.

She hesitated for a moment, calculating the time difference. It was awfully late in Los Angeles. Maybe it was an emergency.

"Hello?"

"There's the runaway bride," he said sarcastically. "Aren't you the clever one?"

Ariana gritted her teeth. "Hi, Kingsley. Guess you heard. Well, what can I help you with?"

"I'm wondering what's happened to one of my top costume designers."

Kingsley's words were slightly slurred. He'd been drinking. At the office, people feared his drunk calls. Signaling Livia, she stepped to the edge of the terrace. "Enjoying a much needed mental health trip."

"Ariana, don't be silly."

Biting her lip, Ariana braced herself against his condescending attitude.

"You've lied to me," Kingsley said. "You took time off for a honeymoon. Not a jaunt around the globe."

"How do you know where I am?" She pressed her lips together in consternation. Phillip must have spread the news.

"I know where you should be. And that's at your desk. I expect you here on Monday."

"That's impossible."

Kingsley's silence was fraught with threat. "Oh, is it?" he finally said.

"I'll check flights," Ariana said. He made her feel like a child playing hooky from school. But why? She was a grown woman. An experienced professional.

And Kingsley was a master manipulator and intimidator.

"I knew you'd come around," he said, sounding conciliatory. "I can always count on you. But don't ever test me again."

In a few months, she would have a baby. A child who would

depend on her protection against the Kingsleys and bullies of the world.

Kingsley wrapped up the conversation now, saying, "I'll see you on Mon—"

"No, you won't." Ariana sucked in a breath.

Silence.

"I'm taking the time I arranged," she said in a strong voice. "The time I've more than earned."

"You know I hate it when people renege on their promise."

Ariana squeezed her eyes. Did she dare jump from the professional ledge of safety? Or stay and take another heaping of boss abuse?

"I won't stand for this, Ariana."

She gulped a breath of courage. "Kingsley, consider this my notice of resignation."

A sneering chuckle erupted in Ariana's ear, followed by a few choice expletives. She held the phone away. But not far enough to hear Kingsley's parting shot.

"Good. Saved me the trouble of firing you."

Click.

Ariana stood in stunned silence.

"Darling?" Ruby's voice floated to her across the terrace. "Are you okay?"

Staring at the phone, Ariana turned around. "I just threw away my livelihood."

As Ruby crossed the terrace, her expression warmed with empathy and relief. "Thank goodness. Kingsley is a vile little man. Now you're free. You can start to have some fun." She wrapped her arms around Ariana.

Her heart hammering over what she'd just done, Ariana leaned her head against her aunt's shoulder. She was reeling in disbelief. "What's wrong with me? I'm acting crazy. Do pregnancy hormones do this?"

"You're waking up to life's possibilities." Ruby took her hand. "You have nothing to be afraid of. Come on, let's jump into the deep end of life."

"How?" Ariana asked, bewildered at the irresponsibility of

her action. She was the calm, orderly one who planned ahead. Panic swiftly set in, and she began to tremble.

"Lease that space before someone else gets it," Ruby said. "You have a lot of work to do now."

Ariana swept a hand across her face. "It's intriguing, but I don't know the first thing about starting a shop in Italy."

"If only you knew someone who had a business here," Ruby said pointedly.

"There's Lorenzo, I suppose," Ariana said. The café owner might be handsome and charming, but she wasn't attracted to him like she was to Alessandro. Lorenzo was the safe choice. After all, he was old enough to be her father.

Ruby arched an eyebrow.

Ariana couldn't fool Ruby. "Or maybe Alessandro." Even mentioning his name quickened her heartbeat. Why hadn't she ever felt this for Phillip? *Because he wasn't the one*, a little voice inside of her insisted. But her intense attraction to Alessandro wasn't normal either. Maybe it was merely raging hormones.

"Shall I call him for you?" Ruby asked.

"No, I will," Ariana replied, lifting her chin. This wasn't the time to let emotions get in the way. She had to take action, and at least explore the opportunity of a shop because she'd just lost her source of income. Ariana wouldn't ask her mother for help— Mari would have enough *I told you so's* as it was. Ruby would offer, but Ariana wanted to show that she could succeed on her terms. She had skills, and it was time to put them to use.

Ariana's head was whirling with what she needed to do. And fast.

"You've had a shock," Ruby said. "Let's sit down. Livia just made fresh juice from fruit harvested from our overgrown orchard. As it turns out, the oranges are naturally sweet. And good for you."

Ariana nodded. She knew she had to take better care of herself.

Ruby asked Livia to bring out a pitcher of juice and glasses. Ariana eased into one of the cushioned chairs they had just arranged.

"I like this furniture grouping," Ruby said. "We have a clear view of the lake, framed by pink bougainvillea."

"That was the idea," Ariana said. Her phone buzzed with a message, and she frowned at it.

Ruby sipped her juice. "Who is it, dear?"

"It's a message from Phillip. He says, 'Did you see Mom's email?'" She tapped a message. *I'm busy. Haven't checked.*

Another message appeared. *She wants an answer now. Like I told you before, I don't care what you decide.*

Ariana frowned and checked her email on her phone. "Listen to this. Phillip's mother says she is devastated that Phillip is already seeing someone else, but she still wants to be in her first grandchild's life." She looked up.

"Even though Phillip denies it's his child?" Ruby asked. "Interesting. And just what does she propose?"

"She's suggesting that she hire a nanny for me to take care of the baby."

"Generous," Ruby said cautiously.

"At her house while I work."

Ruby ran her fingers along the bright Venetian-glass necklace she wore. "Don't they live in Santa Barbara?"

Ariana read the rest of the email. "Seems I'd be welcome to pick the baby up on Friday night or Saturday morning for the weekends." She shook her head. "It's ironic. If I hadn't quit my job, I might have considered this."

Ruby's eyes flashed with sudden anger. "Absolutely not. That woman aims to take over your child. Before long, she'd file for custody."

"I don't think she would do that," Ariana said. *Or would she?*

"*Never* leave your child." Ruby's voice rang out like a command. She was visibly upset. "You don't know how easy it is to lose your baby."

"It's okay," Ariana said, smoothing a hand onto Ruby's trembling shoulder. It wasn't like her aunt to jump to such a conclusion. *Though, could she be right?* A chill coursed through Ariana. "I'll tell her I'm not interested, but I'll thank her."

"Just know this," Ruby said, jabbing her finger. "That woman is not acting magnanimously. I met her at the chapel, and I can smell a charade."

Ariana tapped a quick reply and turned off her phone. She wouldn't accept the offer, but she was puzzled by Ruby's intense reaction. *Anger, but also fear.* She'd never seen her aunt like this.

ARIANA WATCHED WHILE ALESSANDRO WALKED THE LENGTH OF the shop. Lorenzo and Cesare looked on. The shop space was perfect for what Ariana had in mind. She'd create an airy, welcoming ambiance filled with chic, casual clothing in luxurious fabrics. Thinking about it was exciting, and she couldn't wait to get started.

After she'd recovered from quitting her job, Ariana had taken Ruby's advice and plunged into the deep end. She'd called Alessandro, who'd sounded delighted to hear from her. She began sketching elements of a line to sew samples and take orders. The more she planned and thought, the more excited she grew. But first, she had to negotiate a fair price on the lease.

Alessandro spoke briefly to Cesare.

"The location is good," Alessandro said. "Although there is quite a lot of competition in the area."

Cesare spread his beefy, manicured hands. "There will always be competitors. You have to be better or different."

"The last shop here struggled because the rent was too high," Alessandro said, raising his hand to an imaginary bar for emphasis.

Ariana was surprised to hear that, but she didn't show it. When she'd called Alessandro and mentioned that she was considering leasing this space, he had offered to meet her here.

"No, no, no," Cesare said. "The failure was the shopkeeper's fault. Not enough money for marketing, not enough sales."

Alessandro shook his head. "You charged almost double what other landlords do. Who can afford a marketing campaign when the rent is so high? You promised sales from foot traffic would more than cover expenses and give the woman a nice profit."

"You don't know what you're talking about," Cesare said.

"Your last tenant was my friend's wife," Alessandro said. "I'm very well aware of what you did."

"Supply and demand," Cesare said, shrugging. "I had many people who wanted to rent this space."

Not to be outdone by Alessandro, Lorenzo turned to the landlord and began speaking rapidly in Italian. Ariana couldn't follow what he was saying, but Cesare's face was turning red.

Ariana withdrew a notebook from her purse and flipped it open. After making some calculations, she turned to Alessandro. "Here's what I was thinking," she said, tapping on the page. "What do you think?"

Alessandro considered her numbers. "That's a good figure. Maybe a little low, but then, he made a lot of money from the last tenant."

"That was terrible," Ariana said, keeping her voice low. "I hate to see people driven out of business by greed."

Alessandro leaned closer and whispered. "Between us, my friends can well afford it. I think it was more of a lark to her, and she grew tired of the responsibility. Still, the rent was far too high."

"I don't have that luxury." Ariana cleared her throat. "Excuse me. I have an offer to make."

Lorenzo and Cesare turned toward her, and Ariana named her figure, along with improvements she would need.

Cesare's face grew even redder. "At that price, you take food from my children's mouths."

Lorenzo chuckled. "Your children are grown and skiing at St. Mortiz, Cesare."

Ariana rolled her eyes. She'd also seen the landlord arrive in an expensive new car. "Or you can leave the shop vacant," she said straightforwardly. "But I won't risk my finances because my rent is too high relative to my revenue. Especially in the beginning, as I build my clientele. Like your previous tenant, I'll need a marketing budget, too."

Ariana could feel Alessandro's eyes on her. Glancing at him, she detected his approval. Ariana was good with budgets and projections because that had been part of her responsibility at the studio.

"Tough American woman," Cesare sputtered.

"I'm realistic," Ariana shot back. She rather enjoyed being called tough, because the alternative was to be taken advantage of. As a woman, she understood the coded meaning of the landlord's words all too well. With a man, it was a negotiation. With a woman, she was a—

"That's impossible," Cesare said with a huff.

"Then, I'm finished here." Ariana turned to leave. She was one step from the door when Cesare called her back.

Acting considerably less haughty, Cesare said, "If we keep this deal between us, you can have the space at that price."

Ariana named her move-in date. She'd need time to create her line and buy other inventory, as well as design the space.

Cesare agreed, and they shook hands. He promised to send the lease agreement for her to review.

After Ariana left with Alessandro, he suggested they walk along the water's edge by the mulberry trees. "I have a proposition for you," he said.

"And what might that be?"

"Will you come to supper at my home tonight?" Alessandro asked. "With the children and me," he quickly added. "Sometimes we play games after we eat or Sandro and Carmela play outside. Then I read to them and hope they go to sleep without too much fuss. After they go to sleep, we could have a glass of wine or limoncello."

This wasn't a date, Ariana noted. Just two people sharing an evening as friends. And why not? She enjoyed sharing ideas with Alessandro. She could ask him how he managed as a single parent, too—not that she was ready to confide in him.

"I'd like that," she said. And maybe if she spent more time around him, the strange, fluttery feeling in her chest would go away. That was it. She just needed to get used to him.

"I can hardly believe I made it." Ariana pulled into a cypress-lined drive that led to a home built of stone. As she turned off the ignition, she exhaled with relief.

Although she'd been studying street signs and was fairly

confident that she could navigate the roads, she hadn't been prepared for the narrow, twisty lanes that hugged the hillsides above the lake. The journey had proved harrowing, especially since residents whipped around curves with ease.

That evening, Ariana had dared to drive the car that Ruby had bought, even though Alessandro had offered to pick her up and have a ride-share service take her home. He couldn't leave the children, who had been staying with Paolina earlier. His sister and her husband had plans for the evening that they couldn't change. Ariana had assured him that she would be fine. She needed to learn her way around anyway.

Ariana looped a bag over her arm. She'd tucked a bottle of wine and a tin of chocolate chip cookies that she'd quickly baked into the bag. When Ariana told Ruby where she was going, she noted the quiet approval on Ruby's face, even though Ariana assured her they were only friends.

As she stepped from the car, Sandro and Carmela bolted from the house to greet her. They threw their arms around her.

Alessandro chuckled. "The children were so excited when I told them you were joining us for supper tonight."

As Alessandro leaned in and greeted Ariana with a pleasant kiss on each cheek, she detected a warm, slightly spicy scent he wore. His masculine aroma caught her off guard and drew her in. Quickly, she stepped back, feeling a little shaken.

"I brought a treat for the kids," Ariana said, holding up the bag with chocolate chip cookies. She opened it to let the children see inside, and then she lifted the lid of the cookie tin.

The children's eyes grew wide. "*Cioccolato*," they cried.

"Not before we eat," Alessandro said, laughing. "But this looks delicious," he added with surprise. "You bake?"

"A little, but I enjoy it."

When Ariana had stayed at Ruby's home in Palm Springs on school breaks, Stefano taught her how to make cookies and quick breads. That had been a long time ago, and the oven in the kitchen at Villa Fiori was different. The measuring cups were in metric measurements, too. Fortunately, she found a cups-to-milliliter conversion chart on a baking site, and Livia helped her watch the oven so the cookies weren't overdone.

"I'm thinking about taking a cooking class," Ariana said. "I'd like to learn some Italian specialties."

Alessandro's face lit with a smile. "If you don't mind, I could join you. I can share some recipes, too." Gesturing toward his children, he said, "I have to perform for this audience every evening."

Looking at the children's eager faces, she said, "I think that would be fun."

"Then you can be my sous chef tonight," he said. "I'm running late with supper because this one had a little accident." Alessandro scooped up Sandro with one arm and tucked the boy to his side. "He tumbled off his bicycle and scraped his knees."

Sandro giggled and kicked his legs. Little bandages covered both knees.

"I'm glad you're feeling better," Ariana said to Sandro, before realizing he probably couldn't understand her. She repeated herself in her basic Italian, and Sandro beamed at her.

Carmela tugged on Ariana's cotton turquoise sundress. Ariana knelt to the little five-year-old's height. "*Ciao, come stai?*"

The little girl beamed shyly at Ariana, hiding behind a wave of unruly curls that partly obscured her face. "*Bene.*"

Gently, Ariana lifted Carmela's tangled hair from her eyes. "*Bene.* Me, too."

"I'm afraid I'm not very good with girl's hair," Alessandro said. "I had it pulled back, but I don't know what happened to the clips. They are so tiny, and in my hands, they're hard to handle."

"I can help," Ariana said, smoothing her hand over Carmela's soft hair. She stood and took the little girl's small hand in hers.

Calmly, Carmela gazed up at her.

Alessandro stared at them for a moment. "I think she's in awe of you. I haven't seen her this quiet in a long time." Flipping Sandro onto the ground, he took the boy's hand, and they started toward the house.

Ariana stepped inside and looked around. It was a cozy family home, even though the rooms were quite large. The tiled floors and rugs and artwork in warm colors brought life to every room. In various patterns and vivid colors, sumptuous silk pillows brightened an over-stuffed sofa, and dolls and trucks had been pushed haphazardly into a corner.

"This way, Sandro." Alessandro took it all in stride, herding the rambunctious seven-year-old into the large kitchen, where a rustic table anchored the space that opened onto an airy, plant-filled terrace.

Immediately, Ariana felt at home. Surrounding a stove and a deep sink were tiles with hand-painted herbs sprinkled among the other ivory-colored tiles. Copper pots hung from a rack above, and children's artwork covered a large corkboard at one end of the kitchen.

Ariana dug into her purse and pulled out an elastic band. "Where's a brush for Carmela?"

"In her room. She'll show you." Alessandro said a few words to Carmela, and the little girl took Ariana's hand.

Ariana followed Carmela into a bedroom decorated in a rainbow of colors. A flurry of stuffed animals and baby dolls lined the bed. Ariana picked up a brush from a dresser and began to work it through Carmela's curls. The little girl stood very still, watching wide-eyed in the mirror. Ariana chatted while she smoothed Carmela's hair. Then she gathered it into a high, fluffy ponytail. Admiring her handiwork, Ariana couldn't help but wonder if she might soon have a little girl or boy.

"*Grazie*," Carmela said, grinning. She threw her arms around Ariana's neck and kissed her before racing back into the kitchen to show her father.

"Very pretty," Alessandro said, his gaze lingering on Ariana before he turned back to the refrigerator.

Giggling, the two children scrambled onto stools at a counter.

"They're not used to seeing anyone but my sister in the kitchen with me." Alessandro put out a bowl of marinated olives and a wedge of *Parmigiana-Reggiano* cheese with bread. "First, the *antipasti*. A little something to nibble on. Can you pour some of that olive oil into a little plate?"

Sandro pointed to a dishrack next to the sink. Ariana picked up a plate and poured the fragrant olive oil.

"That smells delicious," Ariana said.

Alessandro swirled in fresh rosemary, and then he tore off a small hunk of warm bread and dipped it into the oil. He lifted it to her mouth. "Taste it," he said, his eyes sparkling.

Ariana let him feed her, and the taste exploded in her mouth. "That's delicious," she said, swooning a little.

The children giggled, and Alessandro smiled. "We're just getting started. You must be food deprived."

"I'm extra hungry all of a sudden." Ariana thought of her new condition. Was this normal? Even though she hardly felt pregnant yet, she should make a doctor's appointment and start reading up on what to expect.

Alessandro grinned. "I like women who like to eat. Slice off some cheese to fortify yourself." He poured a glass of wine for her and slid it toward her.

"Oh, thanks," she said, inhaling the rich aroma of the red wine.

"It's a local wine," he said, pouring a small amount for himself. He touched her glass. "*Cincin.*"

Ariana lifted her glass, though she'd sworn off alcohol as soon as she'd discovered she was pregnant. Putting it down without drinking, she met Alessandro's gaze. "I'm so glad you invited me. This is a special treat."

Alessandro took a sip and smiled. Indicating a rack of knives, he said, "Choose your weapon."

From the refrigerator, he brought out broccoli, orange and yellow peppers, and an assortment of other vegetables and herbs for her to slice while he filled a large pot with water.

While they cooked together, they chatted, and the children joined in. Ariana asked what they were doing in school, and Sandro proudly showed off his writing and math. Carmelo brought out a picture of a cat that she had painted, and Ariana immediately saw her talent and praised her.

Soon supper was ready, and the four of them sat at the table. The pasta, vegetables, and sautéed lake fish were delicious— simply prepared and flavored to perfection.

After eating their chocolate chip cookies, the children played outside in a grassy area of the garden while Ariana and Alessandro sat and watched them.

As the sun was setting over the lake, casting brilliant colors on the water, Ariana turned to Alessandro. "This is so nice. You're lucky to have such a lovely family."

Alessandro inclined his head. "I'm grateful for my children, but luck was not with my wife, I'm afraid."

Ariana bit her lip. "I'm so sorry."

"It's all right," Alessandro said, resting his hand on hers. "We were lucky to have the time we did. I just miss her. She had breast cancer if you're wondering. Very aggressive. If it weren't for Paolina, I don't know how I would have managed the children. They were so sad; it was heartbreaking." He sipped the wine he'd brought out onto the terrace.

"I can't imagine how difficult it must have been."

"We're getting better," Alessandro said.

"I'm glad." Ariana asked a few questions about his wife, and Alessandro seemed to enjoy speaking about her.

"Not many people ask about her anymore," Alessandro said. "Thank you for letting me talk about her. And how about you?"

Ariana shook her head, and then, without really planning to, she told him about Phillip.

"It's better to know you're incompatible before the marriage than afterward," Alessandro said. "If you hadn't listened to your heart, you wouldn't be here now." He paused and touched her hand. "And I'm happy you're here."

"So am I," she said softly.

"I hate to break this up, but I have to put the children to bed," he said. "Will you stay longer?"

"I'd like that," Ariana said. "If you don't mind, I can help tuck them in."

Alessandro lifted a corner of his mouth. "They'd like that. So would I."

After reading to the children and putting them to bed, Ariana and Alessandro sat outside again, watching the lights of Lake Como glow in the night. Ariana cupped her hands around the bergamot-flavored tea that Alessandro had made for her.

"You don't drink wine?" Alessandro asked.

Ariana felt heat rise to her cheeks. "It's not that I don't drink wine, it's just that...I have to be careful about driving. I'm not used to such narrow, twisting roads."

Alessandro chuckled. "They take some getting used to."

As the night wore on, they talked for a long time. Ariana found it easy to share her thoughts on a range of topics that she hardly shared with anyone, from what she loved about designing to her relationship with her mother. And Alessandro told her what it was like growing up here and what he dreamed of for his children.

When it was time to leave, Alessandro walked her to her car.

"I had such a nice time," Ariana said. Her heart was thumping as he took a step closer and brushed a strand of hair from her face.

"It was more than nice," Alessandro said. "It's been so long since I could talk like we did tonight."

Ariana knew she should get in the car and drive away. But something inside of her welled up, and she acted on impulse. Raising her face to Alessandro's, she kissed him, not on the cheeks as he seemed to be expecting, but directly on those full lips that she couldn't resist.

Though clearly taken by surprise, Alessandro quickly responded, sliding his arm around her shoulders, tentatively at first, and then returning her kiss.

After a few moments, Ariana pulled away. Without a word, she slid into her car and turned the ignition. As she pulled from the driveway, she wondered where this friendship was going, and why she had taken such a chance.

21

Hollywood, 1952

*R*uby stepped off the bus in front of the studio lot, which loomed before her like a self-contained village. Clutching her purse, she stood in a line of people at the front gate. While she waited, she tamped down the churning feeling in her stomach. *Silly nerves,* she told herself. When it was her turn, she stepped up to the guard at the gatehouse.

"I'm Ruby Raines, and I'm here for an audition with Royce Blackstone." She relayed the details her agent had given her and waited while the guard found her name on his list. He handed her the lot address of the building, along with a map of the studio lot.

Ruby joined the flow of aspiring actors and crew members streaming onto the lot for auditions. She was thrilled to be among fellow artists, writers, and performers. Many people were bustling to the sets in makeup and costumes. Cowboys, dancers, an Egyptian queen. Some clutched scripts, while others waited in line at the commissary for breakfast. The smell of food made her stomach lurch.

This audition was critical. Ruby needed money to rent an

apartment for them when he arrived. She'd also have to wire funds to her parents for more food and supplies.

As Ruby crossed the studio lot, she imagined Niccolò whispering encouragement in her ear. *Chin up.* She wrote to him almost every day, although she'd only received a couple of brief letters in return.

Niccolò's spelling and grammar were indeed as poor as he'd described. She smiled as she thought of his embarrassment. He'd learned his English verbally, but she would help him with spelling and grammar.

Ruby and Niccolò had agreed to wait until he arrived in Hollywood to tell her parents about their wedding. Based on how his father had reacted, Niccolò insisted on being there to protect her in case her father was angry.

While her parents had been happy to see her sister Patricia marry, an Italian actor probably didn't meet their idea of a suitable son-in-law. Their parents were eagerly anticipating grandchildren, yet after eight years of marriage, Patricia and her husband had yet to have children. They were also struggling financially, as were all the local ranchers. Everyone was praying for an end to the drought.

Ruby hurried up the steps to a white building with tall columns and a wide front porch that looked more like a grand mansion in Pasadena. Drawing a deep breath, she opened the door.

"Good morning," Ruby said to the receptionist seated at a desk inside. "I'm here to see Royce Blackstone to audition for *Diary of a Pioneer Woman.*" She clutched her purse and tried to steady her breathing as an odd wave of nausea threatened to overtake her. Anxiety had never affected her quite like this. She swallowed hard against the tickling sensation.

"Please have a seat." The receptionist handed her a short script and motioned toward a row of chairs filled with other young women her age.

Ruby hadn't realized this would be such a large casting call. She took a seat and studied the script, trying to suppress her nausea.

After a few minutes, the uneasy feeling overtook her. She hurried to the reception desk. "Where's the ladies' room?"

"Down the hall." The receptionist pointed toward a door.

Ruby rushed toward it, her heels clicking on the hardwood floor like typewriter keys. She burst through the door and raced toward one of the stalls.

Just in time.

Thankfully, the ladies' room was empty. After being sick, she made her way to a couch in the mirrored makeup area. She was so dizzy. The room spun around her like a tilt-a-whirl at the county fair.

For the next hour, she alternated between the couch and the nearest bathroom stall. She couldn't remember when she had been so sick. She'd always had a hardy constitution.

Collapsed on the sofa again, she brushed tears from her cheeks. The worst of this was that she might miss the audition. She waited as other women cycled through the ladies' room. A few asked if she needed any help.

"I'll be okay soon," Ruby told them, but from the worried looks on the women's faces, she could tell they doubted her self-prognosis. She closed her eyes and tried to will away the feeling.

Ruby wasn't sure how much time had passed when the receptionist bustled into the ladies' room. "You're the last one on the list. They're waiting for you inside."

"I'm not sure I can do this," Ruby said.

The receptionist pressed her lips together. "You have to. Mr. Wyler sent a letter of recommendation for you. Mr. Blackstone is in there with the producer and the casting director. They're waiting for you, so pull yourself together."

Ruby groaned.

The woman turned on a faucet and dampened a paper towel. "Sit up and put this on your forehead. If you can't make the audition, they're going to give that part to another girl. And Mr. Blackstone and Mr. Wyler are friends, so you'd better get in there. I won't be blamed for not sending you in."

"I'm trying." Ruby pressed the cold towel to her face. With a couple of minutes, the spinning room slowed, and she pushed herself up from the couch.

Ruby forced herself to ignore the roiling in her stomach, fighting through it with every bit of grit she had. *Chin up.* "Tell them I'm on my way."

"I can get you five, maybe ten minutes, but that's it." The woman hurried out.

Ruby staggered to the sink to splash more cold water on her face. When she looked up into the mirror, she nearly gagged at her reflection. Her face was pale, and her carefully coiffed hair was in disarray. She thought about what David, the wardrobe assistant in Italy, would have said about her appearance. But there was nothing to be done about it. No makeup artist or hair-stylist could disguise the way she felt.

The only thing Ruby could rely on to get this part was her acting ability. She breathed in, summoning her strength. If she didn't get this part because of a silly stomach ailment and her parents lost their ranch, she would never forgive herself. Niccolò needed her, too.

And she needed him.

Ruby smoothed her hair and pushed her shoulders back. Walking out of the ladies' room, she called out, "I'm ready."

The receptionist pointed toward a closed door. "Go in, and good luck."

Ruby stepped inside the audition room. The room was bare except for a long table that anchored one side. Two men and a woman were seated at the table. Each had a stack of papers and a notepad in front of them.

"Come in," the woman said, consulting her notepad and a headshot that Ruby's agent must have sent. "You're Ruby Raines, correct?"

Ruby swallowed a wave of nausea. "Yes, I am. Very nice to meet you."

"I'm Meg Wallace, the casting director for *Diary of a Pioneer Woman*," the woman said. "We understand that you've been in Italy working with William Wyler."

"It was an excellent experience," Ruby managed to say.

Meg went on to introduce Mr. Blackstone and the producer. "We're also going to record this on film." She made a note on the pad in front of her.

Ruby wished she could protest. The thought of being immortalized on film when she looked like this was disturbing. She would have to make the best of it.

Just then, the lights snapped on, and a camera operator hurried in to take his position behind a large movie camera.

Ruby stood in the middle of the room, collecting her thoughts and breathing to quell the persistent sour feeling in her stomach. She couldn't think about what would happen if she became sick here. That wasn't an option. She *had* to get this part.

Ruby blinked, grounding herself in the scene.

Meg put down her pen. "State your name and begin when you're ready, please."

The director gave a signal to start.

Transforming herself into the character she was to play, Ruby rose and threw her head back as if she were looking at another actor. She gritted her teeth and cradled her arms in front of her as if she were clutching an infant.

"If you've come 'round these parts lookin' for a handout, you won't find it here," Ruby said, letting her Texan accent come out. "My baby's real sick, and with this drought, I'm nearly out of food."

Mr. Blackstone read the part of the other actor in a flat monotone voice. Other actors might have found it challenging to maintain a high emotional level against that kind of reading, but not Ruby. She drew on her anger and charged ahead with the scene, filling the room with her character's desperation. This character and situation she knew all too well.

With a burst of emotion, Ruby finished the scene and held it.

No one said anything for several seconds. Ruby could feel her stomach churning and prayed the growling wasn't loud enough to be caught on film.

At last, the director said, "That's enough."

"We have everything we need." Meg stood up. "You may go. We'll be in touch with your agent soon."

Ruby thanked them and walked out, waiting until she had shut the door to race down the hall to the ladies' room once more. As she passed the receptionist, the woman gave her a thumbs-up sign.

Ruby knew that that was merely a supportive sign that she had persevered, not that she had prevailed. That audition had been the worst of Ruby's life, and she hated that she had gone through with it. Even worse, it was on film. Had it not been for Mr. Wyler's letter and her family's desperate financial need, Ruby would have skipped the audition and gone straight home to bed.

The bus ride back to her aunt's rented bungalow in Hollywood was grueling. As soon as Ruby returned, she nibbled on saltine crackers to calm her stomach. It seemed to work, and as soon as she felt better, she decided to write a letter to Niccolò.

She hadn't received mail from him in a few weeks, though he'd written to say he was working in construction and making good money. He had applied for his passport and papers, and he was waiting for those to arrive. Niccolò said that he and his cousin had to move, but he would send the new address as soon as they had it.

Ruby sat at a small desk in her aunt's living room that looked out over a busy street in Hollywood. The sounds of cars honking and people chattering floated up to the second story apartment through the open window. Outside, pink petunias in window boxes opened to the sun.

Ruby couldn't wait to share a home with Niccolò, even if it were a one-room flat. With that thought in mind, she pulled out the pretty ivory paper she'd bought at Woolworth's five-and-dime store to write letters to him, and picked up her fountain pen.

My darling Niccolò. She told him about her audition and how sick she'd been. *But there will be other auditions. I keep hearing your words in my mind: Chin up. Even thousands of miles away, you help me get through each day, my love.*

Her aunt Vivienne had seen Niccolò's letters from Italy arrive, and she'd quizzed Ruby about who was writing to her. Ruby had told her a little about Niccolò—leaving out the part where they got married—and she begged her aunt not to tell her parents. Though Aunt Vivienne liked to gossip, Ruby hoped she could trust her.

Ruby continued writing, imagining that Niccolò was there beside her. *Have you spoken to your father yet? You might not want to hear this, but I think it's important that you see him before you leave. You might be gone a long time, darling. Don't leave with an argument still festering.*

As Ruby wrote, the thought of Dante Mancini forcing Niccolò to annul the marriage clawed at the edges of her mind. *But Niccolò would never do that.* She closed her eyes and recalled their last kiss before she boarded the ship, remembering every detail of his face and how he held her. She wrapped her arms around herself, imagining him enveloping her with love.

Just then, Ruby heard the front door open. She snapped open her eyes.

"Lawd, child, what're you doing mooning about like that?" Aunt Vivienne balanced several bags of groceries. With a drawn face and pinched, red-painted lips in a perpetual frown, she said, "Don't just sit there. Help me."

Ruby sprang from her chair to take the groceries from her aunt.

Vivienne pushed all the bags into Ruby's arms. "It's been a hard day, and I need a tonic. I'm not like your mama. I don't have a man supporting me." Vivienne worked in a beauty shop cutting and curling hair for wealthy women whose husbands, she told her, ran Hollywood. Her hair was bleached and bobbed in the latest style.

"Mama works as hard as Dad," Ruby said, even as Vivienne shot her a withering look.

"That's her fault." A faraway look came into Vivienne's eyes. "I could have been a lady of leisure. Almost made it, I did." She winked. "Maybe you'll be the one."

Ruby didn't push the issue. Once, when Ruby had asked her mother why Vivienne wasn't married, Mercy replied that it wasn't good manners to speak of the *tragedy* her poor sister had endured. However, her father referred to Vivienne as an old spinster, though as her mother's youngest sister, she wasn't much older than Patricia. Ruby knew better than to ask her aunt about any of this. Until Vivienne had her evening tonic, her words could be sharp.

Even though Vivienne was often irritable, Ruby was grateful to Vivienne for sharing her photographs with Joseph. Had it not been for Vivienne, Ruby would never have gone into acting.

Vivienne glanced at the letter on the desk. "Writing to that boyfriend again?" Her voice was strangely flat.

Ruby tried to step between her aunt and the letter, but Vivienne beat her to it.

"Well, ain't that sweet." Vivienne stared at the stationery.

"It's private," Ruby said firmly. "Do you mind?"

Vivienne shrugged as if it was of no importance to her. "Plenty of rich, eligible men here if you're young and pretty. But you know your daddy has a grand old plan for you."

Ruby bristled against her words. "That's his plan, not mine. Any mail today?"

Vivienne quickly shook her head. "When you stopped in Texas, did you talk to your father about this plan for your future?"

Ruby ignored the question. "With the drought on, I have to keep working." Ruby had hoped she'd receive a note from Niccolò today. She turned over the letter and took the groceries into the kitchen.

However, Ruby had a sinking feeling as she recalled her visit to the ranch on her way back to California. She'd given her mother and sister scarves and her father a brass letter opener. Not that he had much use for it, but she couldn't think of anything else.

"Looking awfully grown-up," her father had said when they picked her up from the train station.

Ruby walked through a cloud of hot, swirling dust that settled onto her skin, making her itch. Still no rain, she surmised.

"Real cosmopolitan," her mother cooed, giving her a big hug. "Wait until your Johnston boy sees you now."

"About that, Mama," Ruby began.

"Why, you look so different now." Her mother held her by the shoulders, admiring Ruby's new look. "Like a real movie star."

"I hope so," Ruby said. For starters, she wore red lipstick now. She'd learned how to set her hair when it was damp to make it wavy. For the train trip, she'd worn one of her new sundresses with a printed silk scarf tied at a jaunty angle around her neck. And dark sunglasses that David had insisted she take.

Ruby's father glared at her. "We have a deal, Ruby." Her father's voice was low and even. Not threatening, just reminding her of the promise she'd made. *A man is only as good as his word*, he always said.

Ruby assumed that went for women, too.

Her mother saw the tension between them. "Are you excited to see Granger while you're here?" she asked.

"I've only got a couple of days, Mama. I want to spend that with you and Dad and Patricia. I'll be back soon enough." *With Niccolò.* By Christmas, she hoped.

After supper, Ruby's father went to the barn to check on a horse. While Ruby and her mother sat in the parlor stitching flour-sack cotton for a quilt, Ruby said, "I grew up a lot in Italy. I need to talk to you about Granger."

"I'm on your side," her mother said. "But you'll have to talk to your father about that matter. You know what was discussed."

Ruby put her needle down. "Mama, I can't marry Granger." She wished she could confide in her mother, but it would be too much for her mother to bear. Mercy was worried enough about the ranch and stretching their budget as far as she could.

"I didn't want to marry your father either," Mercy said in a weary voice. "But then I wouldn't have had you or Patricia. It's women's lot, honey."

"Times are changing, Mama. Say, is Minnie Becker still hankering after Granger?" *That would solve the issue.* Then they'd all be happy—except for her father.

Her mother's thread snapped, and she looked up. "That boy's waiting for you. A deal's a deal."

"But I want to keep acting. And you need the money."

Measuring out a new length of thread, her mother furrowed her brow. "You'll have one more year. Surely we'll have rain by then, and you can come home. And then we'll all be together and happy again."

Her parents were still cleaving to prayers, while Ruby was facing reality.

Now, as Ruby set the grocery bags on the tiled counter in Vivienne's kitchen, the telephone rang.

Vivienne's heels clicked on the wooden floor. "I'll get it. Pour my tonic, would you?"

Ruby brought the icy tonic water from the icebox and poured some into a glass. She measured an amount of gin, which turned her stomach, and stirred. Vivienne had sworn her to secrecy about her tonics, saying that Mercy wouldn't understand, which was true.

Placing her hands on the tiny, white hexagonal tiles on the counter, Ruby waited. Would the studio have made a decision already?

"It's Joseph, calling for you," Vivienne called out.

"Your tonic is in the kitchen." Ruby hurried to the telephone stand in the hallway. She couldn't help feeling hopeful about the audition, even though her performance had been dreadful. Pressing the telephone receiver to her ear, she said, "Hello?"

Joseph charged right into the conversation, as was his style. "Hey, kid. Blackstone, the casting director, and the producer said they had never seen an audition like yours in all their years of screen tests." He chuckled. "They said you sure fit the part of a downtrodden woman on the prairie—ragged, pale, and disheveled. What the heck happened to you in Italy?"

"I was so terribly ill that day," Ruby said, her words tumbling out. "If they could give me another chance—"

"Absolutely not," Joseph yelled over the line. "You had one shot at that role."

"And I bombed."

Joseph chuckled. "You got the part, kid."

Ruby didn't know what to say. She thought her audition had been horrible. "How?"

"The casting director said that all the other women were too pretty. The scene was about a woman who'd lost everything, and not only did you act the part, but you became the character. They could see you in that role because you embodied it." The agent paused. "Have you been studying method acting?"

"No, I was sick as I could be," Ruby said. She could deal with a stomach virus, but she hoped this wasn't something worse, like influenza. She felt a little better today but not great.

"Well, get yourself together because filming starts in a couple of weeks. You were the last important role to be cast."

Relief flooded her, and Ruby leaned against the wall. "Where will it be filmed?"

"New Mexico. You'll be out of touch for a while, but it's a fairly short schedule. You'll leave the first week in October, and you'll be finished by Christmas."

"That's good," she said, doing the mental calculations in her head. The money would be enough to last her family through the winter, even if she didn't get another part right away. "Any more auditions I can go on?"

"Over these next two weeks, I'll send you on auditions for films that start shooting in January," Joseph said. "Now that you've landed this part, your star is rising."

After Ruby hung up the phone, she let out a whoop. Nothing could stop her now.

Vivienne raced into the hallway, her breath smelling of gin. "Did you get the part?"

"Sure did," Ruby said. Elated, she threw her arms around her aunt. Yet, a moment later, she clamped a hand to her mouth and stepped back.

"What's wrong?" Vivienne asked.

Feeling sick to her stomach again, Ruby rushed to the bathroom. As she lay on the cold tile floor, her aunt cracked open the door.

"Are you okay in there?" Vivienne frowned.

"I'll be fine," Ruby said. "Whatever this is, I have two weeks to get over it. The filming is in New Mexico." She prayed she'd be up for it.

22

HOLLYWOOD, 1952

*R*uby balanced on the edge of the examination table at the doctor's office. "Pregnant?" she repeated numbly. She'd pegged this as a stomach virus, but the nausea hadn't gone away.

In two days, she was leaving for New Mexico to begin filming *Diary of a Pioneer Woman*. Stroking the half-heart pendant that dangled around her slim neck, Ruby thought about how she and Niccolò had tried to be careful.

Evidently, not careful enough.

"Morning sickness is common at about six weeks," the kindly doctor said, making a note on her chart. "You're young, but as long as you get plenty of rest and good food, you should be fine." He glanced at her chart and frowned. "I don't see your husband's name here. Was that a mistake?"

Ruby shook her head. She hadn't filled out the *Husband* line on the medical questionnaire. And she hadn't told her aunt about Niccolò.

Vivienne spoke up. "She's fixin' to be married, I assure you." She pursed her red lips and shot an angry look toward Ruby.

"That's good," the doctor said. "My nurse will see you out."

And just like that, Ruby's world changed.

As they walked toward her aunt's old Ford pickup, Vivienne said, "It's that boy, isn't it? Niccolò."

Ruby nodded. "But it's not what you think."

"Oh, it's exactly what I think," Vivienne spat out, whirling to face her with narrowed eyes. "You went to Italy and got knocked up. Stupid, stupid girl. I promised your mama and daddy I'd look after you, but as soon as you were out of my sight, you went and did this." Vivienne gestured angrily toward Ruby's abdomen.

Ruby had promised Niccolò that they would face her parents together, but they hadn't planned on her getting pregnant. "It's not as bad as you think."

Vivienne jabbed her fists to her waist. "And why might that be, missy? If you don't get back to work, your parents will lose their home."

Ruby had no choice. "I'm married."

"Oh, that's swell." Vivienne crossed her arms. "And where is this Romeo?"

"Niccolò."

"Does he have money?"

Ruby shook her head.

"And he's still in Italy, right?" Vivienne pointed her finger in Ruby's face. "You'll never see him again, you know. He's a bum, just like the rest of them."

"You don't know that," Ruby said, slapping her aunt's hand away. *How dare Vivienne accuse Niccolò?*

"Oh, yes, I do." Vivienne glared at her. "Why the devil do you think I left Texas?"

While Ruby was gaping at her, Vivienne pinched her ear and dragged her toward the truck. "We're going to call your mama first. Poor Mercy will have to break it to your father. Though you ought to be the one."

Her anger flaring, Ruby twisted out of Vivienne's grip. "My husband is on his way here."

"And when was the last time you heard from him?"

"Not long ago."

"It's been more than a month."

Ruby bit back a cry. "Niccolò is earning money to come here."

"Oldest story around." Vivienne dug into her purse and pulled out a cigarette, which she stuck between her lips. "Time to grow up, kid. Those guys are all hat, no cattle. Bet he showed you a real good time."

The sweetest time ever, Ruby wanted to scream, but she was still in a daze. She ignored her aunt's last comment. "I didn't know you smoked."

"There's a lot you don't know, child." Vivienne fumbled for a match. After lighting the cigarette, she inhaled and blew out a thick plume of smoke. Leaning against the truck, she said, "This is going to break your mother's heart."

Wrinkling her nose from the smoke, Ruby pushed her hair back from her forehead, which was damp with perspiration. Maybe from nerves, maybe from her new condition.

Although Ruby wanted to believe her mother would be happy for her—and the grandchildren they'd been waiting for Patricia to have—she knew her father would explode. And her mother would bear the brunt of his temper.

Ruby hadn't thought about that.

"And your father will kill you," Vivienne went on. "Unless…"

"What?"

"You go back to Texas and marry Granger Johnston right away. I've heard he might do well for himself."

"But I'm already married."

"In Italy. Who knows about that here?"

"Never." Ruby spun around to walk away.

Vivienne latched onto her arm. "Don't be twice an idiot. Granger would never know." She huffed. "That's what I should have done."

So this was the tragedy her mother spoke of that Vivienne had suffered. Ruby slid a glance toward her aunt. "I will not. I'll keep working."

"Like that?" Vivienne sneered. "Not a chance."

"We need the money. And I won't show until…" Ruby pressed a hand against her still smooth belly. "When will I actually look…" She couldn't bring herself to say it. *Pregnant.* Ruby brushed an errant tear from her hot cheeks. If only she could reach Niccolò. Surely he'd come right away. And he'd be happy, so happy. She'd write to him tonight.

"Well, you're tall and thin, so…" Her aunt looked her over. "You're probably good for three more months. Maybe four. You could wear a girdle and keep your weight down. Lots of women do that to keep working."

Ruby's head was spinning, and her stomach was threatening to heave again, but if she didn't focus on something else, she feared she'd collapse. She breathed out slowly. *A baby. Niccolò.* What could she do? Ruby pressed her fingers to her temple. "I'll go to New Mexico and finish that film by Christmas."

"And that new part you just got for January?"

Ruby's heart dropped. Her agent had been sending her out on auditions at the studio, and she'd gotten another part. "I'll talk to Joseph."

"Whatever you do, don't tell him you're with child," Vivienne's voice dropped to a whisper on the last word, as if pregnancy were shameful. "Women in your condition get blackballed. And you have a good shot at a big career. Just tell Joseph you need a break after Christmas."

"But I'm married. It's not like I'm pregnant out of wedlock."

"You might as well be. Studios like their stars shapely."

"I'll get back in shape fast after the baby is born," Ruby said.

Her aunt threw up her hands. "You're still only seventeen. In Hollywood, that's a scandal. Might as well marry Granger, because your film career will be deader than dead when this gets out." Vivienne stubbed out her cigarette and hoisted herself into the truck. "And here I thought you'd be rich enough to support us all someday."

Her aunt's words sliced through Ruby, yet she clung to the thought of Niccolò. They drove in silence back to her aunt's apartment.

After they returned, Ruby immediately wrote another letter to Niccolò.

My darling Niccolò,

I have such wonderful news. You're going to be a father! Please plan to come for Christmas, and we'll celebrate and get ready for our sweet baby together. I'm starting work on the new film I told you about, so I'll have a little money for an apartment.

WHEN RUBY FINISHED WRITING, SHE BRUSHED AWAY THE TEARS that dotted the page and sealed the letter right away so that her aunt, who was lingering nearby, couldn't read it. She tucked it into her purse to mail tomorrow.

But the next morning, Ruby woke up to severe nausea again.

Hurriedly, Vivienne mixed baking soda into a glass of water and squeezed lemon juice into it. "Sip this," she said, putting it on the coffee table next to the blue couch where Ruby slept.

Ruby did, but moments later, feeling sick, she careened toward the bathroom, nearly knocking over Vivienne's prized porcelain rooster collection in the process. After vomiting until she had dry heaves, Ruby rinsed her mouth and splashed cold water onto her face. When she finally emerged, her aunt was gone.

Easing onto the couch, Ruby sipped the lemon juice and baking soda concoction, determined to keep it down.

An hour later, Vivienne returned with more lemons. "Eventually, this will take the edge off."

"I think your mixture might have already helped." Ruby sat up. She still felt queasy, but not urgently so. Mostly, she just felt tired. She closed her eyes. *The letter.* Ruby pushed herself up.

"Stay there," Vivienne said. "Let your stomach settle."

"But I have to mail my letter to Niccolò."

"I just did," Vivienne said, smiling. "I saw you writing it, and I knew it was important. With you feeling so poorly, I thought you'd appreciate it." She fluffed a pillow for Ruby and tucked it behind her. "Relax. I'll take good care of you until you leave."

Ruby eased herself back down, relieved that Vivienne was no longer yelling at her as she had yesterday. "I need to call Mama."

"Why worry her? You have plenty of time." Vivienne sat beside Ruby and took her hand. "I hate to say this, what with your condition, but sometimes a woman's first go at making babies doesn't take."

Alarmed, Ruby scrunched her brow. "What do you mean?"

"You could have a miscarriage. It's not uncommon. If that happened, you would have worried your mother for nothing."

"I guess that makes sense," Ruby said slowly. She longed to hear her mother's voice, though she didn't want to bring any more misery into the poor woman's life.

"I'm sure of it. This inconvenience might just work itself out. Now, how about some hot broth and crackers?"

"Guess so," Ruby said. She had to get over this sickness soon. The film in New Mexico wouldn't wait.

RUBY TOOK HER DESIGNATED PLACE ON SET, WHICH WAS AN OLD farmhouse in New Mexico with monument rock formations in the background. The days were dry but still blazing hot, even for early October.

"Places, everyone," the director called out.

Ruby wore a brown wool skirt that brushed the dusty, wooden floor. The wardrobe supervisor had carefully smudged Ruby's wrinkled cotton shirt with dirt. Her hair was swept haphazardly from her face. She would have looked even more haggard except for the time she spent in makeup every morning. The makeup artist had a knack for covering the hollows under her eyes and cheekbones.

Still, Ruby fit the part of a weary woman on an unknown frontier.

Due to nausea, Ruby could hardly eat. She nibbled little during the day, except for saltine crackers and Vivienne's lemon juice and baking soda concoction. In the evening, her nausea lessened, so she managed to keep down fresh vegetables and protein for the baby. Mostly, she stayed in her trailer out of the sun, resting with a cool cloth on her forehead to preserve her strength for filming. Never in her life had she felt so tired.

"Hey, Slim," the director said, using his nickname for her. He approached her on the set. "After seeing the rushes last night, I have a few pointers for you. Overall, excellent work. But today's scene will be highly emotional. Are you up for that?"

Ruby nodded. "You can count on me." Knowing she would soon have a baby depending on her deepened her commitment to work. Ruby conferred with him for a few minutes. In the evenings, the director reviewed the footage they'd shot so they could do retakes before moving on to another setting or location.

Today, retakes didn't seem likely. Summoning the warring thoughts that raced through her mind—the baby, Niccolò, her mother and father—Ruby hit every emotional high the scene required. After one particularly gut-wrenching break-down, when the director called *cut* the crew broke out in applause.

Her co-star, who'd earned many awards in his illustrious career, winked and shook her hand. "That was Oscar-worthy, my dear. Simply brilliant."

After the daily shoots, Ruby wrote to Niccolò. When she could, she went to the nearest small town to call her aunt. Yet every time Ruby called to inquire, Vivienne said she still hadn't received any more letters from Niccolò.

He'd simply stopped writing.

Ruby worried that something had happened to Niccolò. If only she'd stayed in Rome, she would have known. Maybe he was in the hospital. If he were ill, she hoped his mother was nursing him back to health. Ruby wished she could remember the address of his parents so she could write to Carolina Mancini. But at the time, she'd simply gone along with Niccolò, not bothering to note the address or even the street.

Maybe he'd even died. But Ruby couldn't bear to think about that.

Nor did she want to face what her aunt asserted—that Niccolò no longer loved her. How could that be? The love she had for him would never dim.

Filming seemed to drag on. By December, the film was nearly finished. One Saturday, Ruby got a ride into the nearby town, where she made a telephone call from a payphone at the local Rexall Drugstore.

Her agent had sent an urgent telegram to the set the day before. *Call as soon as you can. Have big offer for you.*

Ruby connected to the operator and gave her Joseph's telephone number in Hollywood.

The operator placed the call. When Joseph picked up, the operator said, "I have a collect call for Mr. Joseph Applebaum from Miss Ruby Raines. Will you accept the charges?"

"Absolutely." The operator clicked off, and Joseph went on. "You'll never believe who called back and is now offering you *three times* the original offer." He told her the part she'd declined for January was alive again. "Maxwell Banksy, and the film is called *Forever a Rebel*."

Ruby leaned against the wall. "Joseph, I need to take some time off."

"Sweetheart, you'll have two weeks at the end of December."

"I need more time."

"Come on, your part shoots in January and February. By Valentine's Day, you'll be free." He named a figure that was far more money than she'd ever made.

Ruby was tempted. Quickly, she calculated the weeks—and her bank balance. With the right costumes, she could pull it off. "Okay, I'll do it."

Properly concealed, she could work up to six months. And maybe Niccolò would surprise her.

Ruby gripped the phone. "But after that, I need a break."

"You don't take a vacation just when you're getting hot," Joseph said. "I can get you into Wyler's next film. He's already asking about you."

Ruby bit her lip. She'd love to work with Mr. Wyler again. "When will that be?"

"Filming is on schedule for April. Pretty short notice, but you can take a couple of weeks off in March. This is your moment. Don't let up now."

By her calculations, the baby was due in early May. "I'm sorry, I just can't."

"And I can't represent moody actresses who don't feel like working," Joseph said, clearly frustrated. "You don't work, I don't get paid. Come on, Ruby, don't pass up this golden opportunity. You told me you wanted to work and make money, so give me one good reason why you can't take this part."

And then, even though Vivienne had warned her, Ruby had to tell him. She cupped her hand around the receiver and turned to the wall. "I'm going to have a baby," she whispered.

Over the phone line, Joseph let out a string of curses. "Who knows about this?"

"Only my aunt. And my doctor."

"Don't ruin your career." Joseph's voice dropped. "I know someone who takes care of problems like this. It can all go away. I'll set up an appointment as soon as you get back."

Ruby knew what he meant, and she was horrified. Vivienne had suggested the same thing one day. "I'm married."

"Oh, jeez. Is your husband in Los Angeles?"

"He's in Italy." Tears pooled in her eyes as she thought of Niccolò.

"Why isn't he with you?"

Why indeed? Ruby couldn't get the words out.

Joseph cursed again. "You're far too young for this."

"Elizabeth Taylor was eighteen when she married Nicky Hilton."

"Yeah, eighteen," Joseph said. "And divorced eight months later. You're not eighteen."

"Almost," Ruby shot back. "My passport says otherwise."

"You're making a huge mistake," Joseph said. "The contracts you sign have a detailed morals clause, among others. You're in violation, so that's cause for termination."

Ruby bit her lip. She'd heard horror stories about actors fired for even minor infractions. But surely being married would make a difference. She could explain everything.

Joseph went on. "Once the press gets hold of this story—and believe me, they will—I won't be able to book you for dog food commercials, let alone with top directors. I beg you, Ruby, don't throw away your shot. It won't come again. Not in this town. I know you need the money, so I'm giving it to you straight now."

Tears slid down Ruby's cheeks, and she kept her face to the wall. Behind her, she could hear the soda jerk flirting with another pretty young cast member. Ruby lowered her voice.

"Tell Mr. Wyler I can't do it, but ask him to keep me in mind for the next one."

Joseph blew out a breath. "Please tell me you're not keeping this baby."

"I am. But I'm going to need to work after it's born."

A long pause stretched between them.

"Ruby, when this comes out, it's going to be uglier than you can imagine. Someone will give up your real age. A neighbor, a relative—a lot of people are thrilled to see their name in the paper, and they don't care if it destroys you. In fact, they feed on it. See, you can't keep this baby. If you were my daughter..." Joseph hesitated. "Before you make any decisions, talk to your parents. They'll know what to do. And forget that guy in Italy. You're young. You have time to start over. Come back in June if you can. September at the latest."

"I'll think about it." Ruby hung up and hurried from the drugstore, her mind churning with anguish.

Joseph had echoed what her aunt had warned her about—and then some. If she couldn't work in films, how could she possibly earn the amount of money her family needed? Or provide for her child?

This dilemma wore on her, and by the time filming wrapped, Ruby had a difficult decision to make. She was growing increasingly worried about Niccolò. This silence wasn't like him. Unless he planned to surprise her in a few days at Christmas, she had to tell her parents soon and make plans.

Her waistline was beginning to thicken. By spring, she would be a mother.

23

Lago di Como, 2010

*A*s soon as Ruby opened her eyes, she saw the bell tower in the distance across the lake and smiled. When she'd first seen the villa's interior, this view from her bedroom had been the deciding factor.

Time was a strange phenomenon; this view had not changed over the years. Yet, one glance in the mirror told her that although the love in her heart had not aged, its vessel certainly had.

Her phone buzzed on the nightstand. She reached for it, wincing as she stretched. Simple movements weren't as easy as they'd once been. "Hello?"

"Good morning. I hope you're up."

Ruby smiled at her houseman's voice.

"I am, and I'm enjoying the most spectacular view. You really must come for a visit. How are things in Palm Springs?" Still in bed and wearing a pink silk gown, Ruby stretched to relieve the nighttime soreness that had set into her muscles.

"The house and garden are fine," Stefano said. "How is your Italian adventure redux?"

"Marvelous, darling. Even better the second time. On today's agenda, I have a long walk by the lake, followed by a hot stone massage and a whirlpool bath. And after that, I'll have a fine dinner and an excellent bottle of wine with my favorite niece. That's the best prescription for a happy life."

"You're working terribly hard at enjoying yourself." Stefano paused. "I wish you would tell me what's wrong."

Stefano knew her too well. She'd never spent large sums of money on a whim. Ruby sat up in bed. Where would she begin with the events that had changed the trajectory of her life? Instead, she said, "At my age, what does it matter?"

Stefano wasn't giving up. "Didn't you tell me some of your ancestors lived to be more than a hundred? If that's true, you still have a long way to go. To live in style, you have to feel your best. Mentally and emotionally, as well as physically."

"Plenty of stars have managed otherwise." Ruby chuckled at her joke, but Stefano wasn't laughing. "This is what I want, Stefano. Don't deny me life's simple pleasures."

"That's never my intent."

Ruby rubbed her neck. "I promise I'll relish this beautiful day. Just as I hope you're enjoying the high season in the desert." The peak tourist season in Palm Springs was between January and April, which meant that the snowbirds would soon leave town for their primary residences. "Better yet, why don't you close the house for the summer and come to Lake Como? The weather is glorious. My travel agent can book a ticket for you."

"Can't do it," Stefano said. "My employer insists I look after her botanicals, and I don't trust the plant-sitting services."

Ruby huffed over the phone. "You just don't want to miss your Tuesday night poker games and Saturday morning tee-times."

"And you just want an escort to social events."

Laughing, Ruby said, "We know each other too well, Stefano." The truth was, she missed him. "By the way, has Mari called or sent anything to the house?"

"If she does, I'll let you know. Does she have your address in Bellagio?"

"She does." Ruby sighed. What was taking Mari so long to

address Ruby's letter? She had sent it by express mail so that Mari would know it was important. Ruby had received an email stating that it had been delivered. Who waits weeks to reply to a clearly urgent communication? But Ruby couldn't rush her or even question her. She had sworn as much to Patricia, and Ruby would not dishonor her in death.

After saying goodbye to Stefano, Ruby hung up the phone and rubbed her stiff neck.

As an actress, Ruby couldn't let feeling bad get in her way. Pushing through discomfort to perform was part of the job.

She recalled the audition she'd had for *Diary of a Pioneer Woman*. She'd struggled through that audition with sheer fortitude even though she was desperately sick. Not only had she landed the part, but she'd also won a prestigious acting award for it.

After that film, her career had ignited. Her agent had been right about that, but she regretted following Joseph's advice on personal matters.

A warm bath, a brisk walk, and a good massage followed by a glass of wine were all she needed. Ruby was sure that she could rise above any minor inconvenience. She had lived a long life— longer than many. Overall, it had been a good life, although she'd had her regrets.

Now, she had to tend to the family matters Patricia had left to her. Her sister had been the kind one, while the challenges fell to Ruby.

Patricia had always said that Ruby was more fit for the task. *You're the strongest of us all, Ruby.*

That wasn't quite true. Ruby's strength was that she took action, yet she still suffered the heartbreaking aftermath of difficult decisions.

As for Patricia, she was the steady one. Unflappable in the face of any adversity.

With another sigh, Ruby pushed through her stiffness to swing out of bed. She put on her silk robe and slippers and padded across the floor to the picture window that opened onto Lake Como. As if she could touch the bell tower in the distance, she traced it on the glass, recalling that day, and how Niccolò had kissed her at the altar. They hadn't let anything deter them from following their hearts.

In the garden below, Ruby saw Ariana seated at a bistro table in the gazebo, sketching on a tablet.

What was keeping Mari? Ruby needed her in Lake Como, but she knew better than to prod the stubborn woman too soon. Perhaps Ruby's express letter had been carelessly tossed into Mari's incoming mail stack. Or if she were lucky, the visit to the bank was scheduled on Mari's calendar.

For now, Ruby had to ensure that Ariana would keep her baby and be free to live the life she wanted. Ruby saw so much of herself in Ariana. Having enough money wasn't the issue, although Ariana would have that one day. Ruby had made sure of it—even if a stock market crash wiped out her mother's portfolio. Ruby wanted Ariana to have the freedom to follow her chosen path.

After having Livia's strong coffee and homemade yogurt with blueberries and honey, Ruby began her walk to the hotel for her spa appointment.

As Ruby passed the vacant space that Ariana has leased, she noticed a flyer in the window of Lorenzo's café next door. Ruby paused and stepped closer. Translating the text out loud, she read, "This summer, see *Roman Holiday* on stage. Coming soon to Teatro Della Vigna." *A theater in the vineyard. Enchanting*, she thought.

Lorenzo hurried toward her. "*Buongiorno*, Signora Raines," he said, kissing her cheeks. "Always lovely to see you. Would you like a table?"

"*Ciao*, Lorenzo," Ruby said. "I'm on my way to the spa, but this theater production caught my eye."

"Teatro Della Vigna is one of our finest theaters for live performances," Lorenzo said. "It's a natural amphitheater tucked among the vineyards on a hillside overlooking the lake. The owner serves wine from the surrounding vineyard, as well as from his vineyard in Valtellina, the wine region just north of the lake. Valtellina wines are the nectar of the gods," Lorenzo said, kissing his fingers for emphasis.

"Why is that?" Ruby asked pleasantly. After visiting the café several times, she'd found that Lorenzo loved talking about the wine and food of the region.

Lorenzo's face lit with enthusiasm. "The Chiavennasca grapes are grown on steep, terraced hillsides just north of here. Those grapes are the same as the Nebbiolo grapes used for the coveted Barolo and Barbaresco wines from Piemonte. I'll give you a good bottle next time you and Ariana come in. You will love it."

"That all sounds fascinating," Ruby said, her interest piqued by both the stage production and the wine. Italy was a country of endless, enchanting surprises. "Especially the theater performance."

"You've seen *Vacanze Romane?*"

"Of course." Ruby smiled and touched Lorenzo's arm. "We call it *Roman Holiday* in America. It's one of my favorite films."

"Then you must attend," Lorenzo said with a broad smile. He reached into the window and gave her the flyer. "Here, take this. We have several."

"I should bring Ariana," Ruby said.

As memories of filming *Roman Holiday* warmed her heart, Ruby rolled up the flyer and tucked it into her purse. What fun it would be to see this production in an outdoor amphitheater, sipping wine under the stars and reminiscing. This is why Ruby had returned to Italy and bought the house in Bellagio. It was her last chance to reconnect with the happiest time of her life, even in the smallest of ways.

After saying goodbye to Lorenzo, Ruby continued on her way to the spa.

Later that afternoon, when Ruby returned to Villa Fiori, she felt revitalized. Nothing was wrong with her that a talented massage therapist couldn't put right.

Ruby made her way to the kitchen for a glass of wine to cap off the day.

"Aunt Ruby," Ariana said, looking up from the lemonade she was preparing. "How was your massage?"

"Enchanting," Ruby said. The sound of children's laughter floated through the open doors from the terrace. "I hear the sounds of happiness out there."

"I invited Alessandro over to continue talking about what I should do with the shop." Ariana's eyes shone brightly. "He's so knowledgeable, and business is a little different here in Italy." She arranged a few chocolate chip cookies she'd made yesterday on a colorful plate. "Sandro and Carmela make me laugh, too. I just adore them."

Ruby hadn't seen Ariana so animated in a long time. Alessandro was clearly the reason. "I'm glad they're here. Shall I have Livia make dinner for all of us?"

Ariana gazed outside. "That's kind, but I think Alessandro and I will make supper tonight. He's an excellent cook, and we had so much fun in the kitchen at his home."

Ruby was glad to hear that. She opened her purse and pulled out the flyer from Teatro Della Vigna.

"What's that, Aunt Ruby?"

"This is for an amphitheater production of *Roman Holiday*—under the stars and amidst the vines. I'd love to see it. Do come with me." She glanced outside again. "You could bring Alessandro, too. The children are welcome, but they might grow bored and cranky. Perhaps Paolina and her husband would watch them."

"It's a date." A smile played on Ariana's lips. "*Roman Holiday* is your favorite movie, isn't it?"

Ruby arched a brow. "I don't think I've ever mentioned that to you."

"It wasn't hard to figure out," Ariana said, laughing. "When I was younger, you used to watch the film after I went to bed. I've only seen it once, but I've heard it so much I think I know it word for word."

"I didn't realize you could hear it in your room."

"Sound carries when it's quiet at night. And I'd crack open the door to listen. It made me feel...safe. Closer to you." Ariana angled her head. "Why is that film so special to you?"

Ruby smoothed out the flyer on an antique desk and placed a vivid, blue-and-green Murano paperweight on it in a place of prominence. A stack of old, leather-bound recipe books written in Italian sat next to the fanciful orb.

"*Roman Holiday* was my first film," Ruby said, smiling. "Oh, but we had such fun filming it in Rome."

Ariana drew up her brow. "I didn't know you appeared in that. Wasn't *Diary of a Pioneer Woman* your first film role?"

"That was my first credited role," Ruby said. "But the summer before that, I had a small part in *Roman Holiday*. Unfortunately, that scene was left on the cutting room floor." A small laugh bubbled through her. "Or perhaps it deserved to die there."

"What a shame." Ariana looked quizzically at her. "Is that where you met Audrey Hepburn?"

Ruby nodded. "I was also a stand-in for Audrey, and it was so exciting being on the set and meeting her and other members of the cast. The entire filming was like a vacation. That film changed my life." Ruby paused as her voice caught in her throat, and tears welled in her eyes. "And it was, without a doubt, the best time of my life."

"Aunt Ruby, are you all right?" With her brow drawn in concern, Ariana stepped forward. "Why haven't you ever told me this story?"

"Oh, my darling girl, I've lived such a long life," Ruby said, blinking away the sudden tears. "I've hardly had time to share everything I've ever done with you. But I promise we'll make up for it this summer."

Ruby hugged Ariana. "Now go back to Alessandro and the children," she said. "And if you don't mind, I'd like to relax and have a glass of wine in my room. Give my regards to Alessandro."

Ruby made her way upstairs to her bedroom. After opening the doors to her balcony, she sat outside in a chaise lounge that Ariana had positioned to catch the sun. She pulled a lightweight throw over her legs. Sipping her wine, she watched Alessandro's children play in the orchard and garden below. Carmela and Sandro were sweet children—and soon, Ariana would have one of her own.

Besides the children's laughter, Ruby could also hear the soft chatter of Ariana and Alessandro as they leaned toward each other across a table. They were talking about the shop and the new collection. Enthusiasm was evident in Ariana's voice as it rose in the air.

Ruby was pleased that Ariana had left the studio and was planning her future. She sipped her wine and smiled. That was one item Ruby could cross off her list. She leaned forward slightly so that she could see the pair.

As they talked, Alessandro reached across the table for Ariana's hand, which she slipped into his in a small, natural movement.

Ariana had told Ruby about the supper she'd had with Alessandro and the children at his home. Although her niece had tried to downplay the developing relationship with Alessandro, the look in Ariana's eyes gave her away.

Ruby sipped her wine in thought. Ariana had also told her that she had no intention of telling Alessandro about her pregnancy until later because they were only friends.

But what if Alessandro were the right man for Ariana? If she waited too long to tell him, he could be devastated by her lack of trust. Or he might be angered, feeling like he had been played. And if that happened, Ariana would be equally destroyed. Ruby couldn't help but fear for Ariana if she broke her heart over Alessandro.

For all Ruby knew, babies might feel their mother's grief. She wanted her niece to have a happy pregnancy. More than ever, Ariana needed people around her who loved her.

This much, Ruby knew for certain.

24

Texas Hill Country, 1953

*G*ale force winds rattled the windows in Ruby's bedroom at the ranch as a cold norther seeped through frosted glass panes, chilling the room. February in Texas was usually bitter cold. The wind whistled across the pastures, bending trees until their frigid limbs froze, forming awkward, akimbo skeletons listing to one side.

Footsteps sounded through the house. On the coldest of nights such as this in the higher elevation on the Edwards Plateau, Ruby's father woke long before sunrise to make sure the animals were moving so they wouldn't die from temperatures far below freezing. With less feed this year, the cattle had thin winter fur and less fat to insulate their bodies, so the risk was higher.

Even though Ruby had been sending funds to her parents and her sister, they were still suffering financial difficulties. Though her father had told her he was grateful to her, she could tell that Harrison Smith didn't like accepting money from his daughter. He'd been sullen and on edge since she'd arrived.

Unable to sleep, Ruby pulled a robe over her nightgown and rose to lay a fire in the kitchen hearth. She put the coffee pot on the stovetop and struck a match to light the gas, turning a knob just so. While the coffee simmered, she touched another match to the kindling in the fireplace and sat on a bench to warm her hands.

Ruby had remained in Los Angeles over Christmas, claiming that she had to go on auditions, but she wanted to be there in case Niccolò arrived. She hadn't heard from him and was growing increasingly worried. After her third film, *Forever a Rebel*, wrapped in mid-February, she'd decided it was time to go home.

As Ruby coaxed the flickering flames, she thought about how she would tell her parents about her pregnancy. She'd only been home a couple of days, and she'd managed to hide her expanding waistline beneath bulky sweaters. When she heard a noise, she looked up.

Her mother shuffled into the kitchen. "You're up mighty early."

"Couldn't sleep." Ruby glanced at her mother. Mercy's hair was considerably grayer than it had been last year, and she'd lost weight.

"Anything in particular on your mind?" Mercy asked.

Slowly, Ruby nodded. She thought of Joseph, and how he'd told her to tell her parents. *They'll know what to do.* She sucked in a breath and plunged in. "I've been keeping a secret. Several, in fact."

Sighing, her mother gave her a sad smile. "You're pregnant."

"Did Aunt Vivienne tell you?"

"Well, I wish one of you would have." Mercy poured two cups of coffee and handed one to her daughter. "To a mother, it's easy to see. As thin as your arms are, you've lost your waistline. Yet your face is radiant. It wasn't hard to guess."

"Think Dad knows?"

"Men rarely see the signs." Her mother frowned and sat beside her on the bench. Sipping her coffee, she asked quietly, "Want to tell me what happened?"

"His name is Niccolò, and we got married in Lake Como."

"Married?" Her mother breathed out a sigh of partial relief. "Well, where in heaven's name is he now?"

Ruby twisted her mouth to one side. "Still in Rome, I

suppose. Maybe dead, for all I know. He stopped writing to me in September." Since then, Ruby had gone through a range of emotions from devastation to worry to anger to dread.

Her mother rubbed Ruby's shoulder. "I'm sorry that happened."

"Me, too. I didn't want to worry you." She slid her hand into her mother's. "I had to keep working, and I can't very well marry Granger now."

"No." Her mother grew quiet. Finally, she asked, "Was he nice, or...?"

"Niccolò was wonderful, Mama. He was all I could have ever wished for in a husband. I only wish I could reach him. I'm afraid something might have happened to him."

Having shared her secret with her mother gave Ruby a measure of relief. She wished she could have told her sooner, but she hadn't wanted to burden her with more grief. The deep lines in her mother's face confirmed that Ruby had made the right decision.

Ruby shifted a log in the fireplace with a poker. "Dad's going to be furious, isn't he?"

"I'll talk to him first," Mercy said. "And I want you to know how much I appreciate what you're doing for us." She glanced around the modest kitchen. "This place might not be fancy enough for some people, but this land is our home. Because of your efforts, we've made it this far. If the rains come this spring, I pray we can catch up on our debt payments. Then you won't have to go back to Hollywood. Maybe that will help sway him."

"But I like working, Mama. I want to give my baby a chance at a good life."

Mercy sighed. "Have we lost you already?"

"I'll visit when I can." Ruby leaned her head on her mother's shoulder.

"Think about what's best for your child," Mercy said.

Even if Ruby wanted to quit Hollywood now, she couldn't. If the drought continued, her family would still need help. Even if they caught up, their debts were still more than they could pay. Now, more than ever, Ruby had to maintain her career. She would have to figure out a way to care for her child and work.

Ruby pulled her robe tighter and cupped the warm mug, yet the warmth did little to alleviate her trembling hands. "Are you going to tell Dad right away?"

"Might as well. You're pretty far along." Mercy patted Ruby's knee with a thin hand. "He might be madder than a wet cat at first, but we'll have a sweet grandbaby to celebrate soon."

During the filming in early February, Ruby had felt her baby's first movements, which made her feel closer to Niccolò.

Yet with every passing day, Ruby became more worried that something dreadful had happened to Niccolò. To suddenly cease communication was uncharacteristic of him. No one was that ashamed of their writing.

Ruby blinked back the tears that seemed to spring so quickly to her eyes now. Niccolò said he'd taken a job in construction to earn money for his passage. Maybe he'd been injured at work.

Perhaps he'd been so severely injured that he'd died.

As Ruby pondered this thought, it slowly came into horrifying focus. She could think of no other reason that he would stop writing. Even if his father had forced him to annul the marriage—which she doubted Niccolò would do—her husband would have written to her. Niccolò was forthright, and he lived by a code of honor.

Or would he have been so ashamed he couldn't tell her?

Blinking hard, Ruby bowed her head. It had been five-and-a-half months since he'd written his last letter. On the film set, she'd read in a magazine that if a spouse had gone missing, a person could annul a marriage by publishing it in the newspaper. A judge would have the final say. She wondered if that was the same in Italy. Did Niccolò think *she* was missing? Ruby sucked in a breath. She'd send another letter right away.

Her father walked in, banging the kitchen door behind him. "Morning," he said, his voice rough with cold.

"Coffee's ready, Harrison," Mercy said, rising to pour a cup for him. "I'll have your breakfast in a moment." She hurried to the stove.

"I'll do it, Mama." Ruby reached for a blackened cast-iron skillet.

"You're a movie star *and* you cook?" Her father shook his head. "How'd we get so lucky?" He chuckled at his joke.

Ruby shot her mother a look. Would he still think that after she told him? *Doubtful.* She and her mother quickly fell quiet. Ruby took bacon from the icebox and arranged strips in the cast-iron skillet. From a nearby basket, she scooped up several eggs— the production of their henhouse tenants.

While Ruby tended the bacon, Mercy opened the old Hoosier cabinet and reached for dry ingredients. She poured flour into a ceramic bowl, followed by baking soda and a dash of salt. Deftly, she cut cold butter into the mixture before adding buttermilk until it was just the right consistency for fluffy biscuits.

Harrison shivered. "Got more coffee?"

Ruby took the pot from the stove and refilled his cup.

Her father narrowed his eyes. "Why are you two so quiet? You're usually babbling on about something or other."

"Now, Harrison," Mercy said. "Don't start on Ruby. She's just arrived."

Her father shook his head. "If you two are keeping something from me, Mercy, I swear—"

"I'm going to have a baby," Ruby said, cutting him off. His eyes bulged, and she had to get out her words while she could. "I got married in Italy."

Harrison slammed his hand on the kitchen table, sending hot coffee splashing onto the wood and dripping over the edge. His face darkened with anger, and in a flash, he was towering over her.

Cornered in the kitchen, Ruby backed against the Hoosier cabinet. She was trembling, and every nerve in her body was on alert.

"I'll kill that son of a bitch," he yelled through gritted teeth, his fists raised above Ruby. "And you, you hussy. Just a cheap actress now, aren't you?"

Mercy slapped his arm. "Harrison, stop it. That's no way to handle this."

Ruby saw her father jerk his hand back, his palm open. Before he could strike her, she slid to her feet and ducked away, instinctively shielding her belly with one hand.

"Oh, no you don't." With his face contorted in anger, her father grabbed for her legs. Instead, he caught her robe and yanked it.

All Ruby could think to do was to run and protect her child.

She slipped from the robe. Breathing hard, Ruby scrambled toward the back door and thrust it open, tripping over the back steps. Glancing back, she saw her father right behind her, ranting about her lost virtue and calling her names she'd never heard him use.

In an instant, rage over his daughter's impurity blinded her father to reason. Harrison's eyes blazed with a red fury she'd never seen, and his insults burned in her ears, rendering her speechless.

Pressing her hands against her ears, Ruby raced toward the barn, ignoring the icy air and the rocks that cut her bare feet.

As her father gained on her, he stripped off his belt and gripped it in his hand. "I'll whip that devil child out of you," he screamed with a savagery she'd never heard from him.

Ruby cried out in disbelief at his insanity, his crazed actions terrifying her. Did he intend to whip her like a belligerent horse? *Her own father?* Even a horse didn't deserve such wrath.

Inside the barn, she flung open the stall gate to her quarter horse and swung herself onto Blaze's bare chestnut back in a swift motion. Ruby's breath formed clouds in the cold air as the horse trotted from the barn. Shivering, she clung to Blaze for warmth.

Still swearing, Harrison pounded toward her with his belt raised in his fist, cursing a blue streak. Her mother ran behind him, trying to stop him, but Mercy was no match for him. He flung her off his back and sent her tumbling to the ground.

"This is all your fault," he bellowed at Mercy. "You're the one who filled her mind with fancy Hollywood dreams." He raised his belt to her.

"Don't you dare touch her," Ruby screamed. "It's me you want to whip." She gestured to him. "Come on."

Ruby tilted her chin in defiance, goading him. Fearing her father would take out his wrath on her mother, she trotted past him, leading him away from Mercy. When Harrison was far enough away from her mother, Ruby turned her horse. Clicking her tongue, she rushed Blaze back to her mother. Reaching out for Mercy, she cried, "Grab my hand and get on."

Glancing back at her husband, Mercy hesitated. "I shouldn't leave him like this."

"If he can't get me, he's going to hurt you. We must get out of here." Tightening her legs around Blaze, Ruby clasped her mother's hand and pulled her up behind her, using every bit of strength she had. In the cold air, the muscles in her back and abdomen exploded from the sudden exertion.

"Hang on," Ruby called over her shoulder. When Mercy wrapped her arms around her, Ruby could feel her shivering. Whether it was fear or cold, she couldn't tell. Both, probably.

"Hut, hut," Ruby cried, squeezing her legs and lifting herself slightly on the horse. At her command, Blaze charged.

The frosty wind cut through Ruby's nightgown like a thousand pinpricks. Within moments Ruby couldn't feel her lips, yet she let her horse gallop.

Ruby didn't slow her mare until she reached her sister's house.

Patricia raced outside with her husband and held the horse while Michael helped Mercy down, then he reached for Ruby.

"Be careful with her," Mercy cried out.

"Are you hurt?" Michael asked, alarmed

"She's pregnant." A mixture of concern and fright filled Mercy's wide eyes. She glanced back the way they'd come. "Harrison is after her. He's plenty mad, and I'm scared."

Ruby slid her frozen limbs from the horse until Michael caught her and eased her down.

Though her father had essentially arranged Patricia's marriage, she'd been lucky. Michael was one of the sweetest guys Ruby knew. He was a gentle giant who always had a quick smile and a kind word for everyone.

"Aw, Harrison will settle down, don't you worry," Michael said. "Andrew stayed over last night. Harrison won't get past us. Let's get you ladies inside."

"Please put Blaze away," Ruby pleaded, fearing what her

father might do in his uncontrolled rage. She'd seen his anger before, but never, never like this.

"My brother will put her in the barn," Michael said.

Ruby tried to take a step, but her knees buckled. Michael caught her, then swept her into his arms as if she were a child.

Patricia helped Mercy up the steps, and once they were all inside the house, she brought out blankets and added another log onto the fire. Tucking a blanket around Ruby, Patricia drew back with a frown. "Poor child. Your nose is beet red, and your lips are blue with cold." She rubbed Ruby's arms vigorously. "I'll get a hot water bottle and put on a kettle for tea."

Huddled on the couch next to her mother, Ruby watched her sister hurry around. With dark blond curls that framed a delicate face, Patricia wasn't quite as tall or athletic as Ruby. Where Ruby was outspoken, Patricia was the sweet, long-suffering companion to her husband. They were well-suited for each other, and it was beyond anyone's understanding why they hadn't been blessed with a houseful of children yet. Michael had even built a home with plenty of bedrooms. Ruby had often wondered if those empty rooms were bitter reminders.

Michael locked the doors and drew the curtains. He woke his brother, who quickly pulled on overalls and ran to secure Blaze in the barn.

Ruby was still so cold she couldn't speak. Her teeth chattered, and she couldn't control her shivering. Her mother pulled her close, and as she did, a sharp pain erupted in Ruby's side. Something wasn't right. She smoothed a trembling hand around her softly rounded abdomen.

The child Ruby carried was a part of Niccolò. If she could never hold her beloved in her arms again, at least she could cradle their baby, created with the purity of their love. Such a child would be a wonder and a blessing—not the ugly word her father had hurled at her. If she lost this baby now, she would be devastated.

Outside, truck tires crunched on the gravel driveway, and an engine backfired. Sitting beside Ruby, Mercy yelped and clutched her closer. Ruby prayed her father would calm down, but then she heard him yelling outside the house, and a new fear seized her.

This madness was all her fault. She'd driven her father insane.

"Patricia, get them into a bedroom," Michael said grimly, letting his brother through the back door before locking it. "Andrew and I will handle your father."

25

Texas Hill Country, 1953

*R*uby stared at the barren, frostbitten hills from the bedroom window of her sister's home, where she'd been staying since seeking shelter from her father a week ago. Another round of coughing racked her body, and she fought to catch her breath.

Outside of her room, a door slammed, and she recoiled under the thick blanket. She could still hear the deafening argument between her father and brother-in-law that had shaken the walls. Pulling the quilt that Patricia had made up to her neck, she listened to voices in the hallway.

Her mother opened the door. "Ruby, Doc Schmidt is here." Mercy held the door for the old country doctor.

Doc Schmidt shuffled in. "Miss Ruby, I hear you have a bad cough."

"Among other conditions," Mercy said, throwing a pointed look at Ruby. "She says she was married in a church, though."

"Yes, I was, Mama, and I can speak for myself." Ruby turned to the gray-haired physician who'd delivered her in her parents' bed, but a coughing fit seized her before she could speak.

"There, there." The doctor latched on his stethoscope and began listening to her back and chest. While he continued checking her vitals, Ruby told him about her pregnancy.

Doc nodded. "Any problems so far?"

Ruby shook her head. "I was fine before I caught this cold."

"Don't forget to tell him about the blood," Mercy said softly.

Drawing his eyebrows together, Doc continued his exam. "Babies are always a blessing," he said in a pleasant tone that had likely comforted many mothers before her. "Who's the lucky father?"

Ruby told him about Niccolò and her marriage in Italy, while her mother sat in a chair and fretted with a cotton handkerchief. Her thin shoulders shivered.

"And will he be joining you soon?" Doc asked.

Ruby clenched her jaw, unsure of what to say. "He was delayed."

"Oh? I hope not too long."

Ruby pressed her fingers to the corners of her eyes to stem sudden tears. In the corner, her mother cleared her throat.

The doctor paused and looked between them. "Is there a problem?"

"Her husband suffered an accident," Mercy said softly. "Ruby is alone now."

"We're not sure," Ruby managed to say. "I haven't heard from him."

"It's been months," Mercy added.

If Niccolò were alive, Ruby believed he would have contacted her. But now, so much time had passed. There could be no other explanation.

Doc shook his head. "Such a young widow. I'm truly sorry. I'll do everything I can for you and your baby."

Widow. Ruby gagged at the label. *Is that what I am?* Her chest constricted in anguish, and she squeezed her eyes against this probable truth. Ruby covered her face, unable to process this likelihood as its gravity left her void of breath. Yet, with every passing day, the probability increased.

The doctor talked to Ruby about her lung condition, calling it pneumonia. "This is serious, but fortunately, you're young. Get plenty of rest and fluids, and call me if it worsens. As for your pregnancy, if you want a healthy baby, you'll need complete bed rest."

The doctor went on to say things that Ruby didn't understand, though her mother listened with a solemn expression.

"We'll make sure she stays in bed, Doc." Mercy stood to see him out.

Bed rest. As much as Ruby hated staying off her feet, she would do anything for this child.

Outside the door, Ruby could hear her mother and the doctor talking. She could only make out a few words Doc said. "Several years...presumption of death...in order to remarry...or adoption."

I will have none of that. Despair lodged in Ruby's chest, weighing on her like a massive anvil of iron. Her mother and father, the doctor, her agent, her aunt. So many people were against her decision to have and keep this baby. Ruby gulped and breathed, smoothing a hand over her belly to focus instead on the new life she carried.

That is what Niccolò would have wanted.

And Patricia, who was the only person who seemed as enthralled with the prospect of a new baby as Ruby. What would she have done without her sister?

After Doc Schmidt left, Mercy returned to Ruby's room a little while later. "I spoke to Patricia, and she insists that you stay here."

Ruby steeled herself against the torrent of emotions that threatened to overwhelm her. Her father had banned her from returning home, saying that she had brought shame to their family. But Ruby would be safe with Patricia and Michael. She had to be practical now.

"Ironic, isn't it?" Ruby croaked. She started to add that she should be welcome in the house she was paying for, but the worry in her mother's face silenced her. Ruby would continue paying the mortgage but only for her mother's sake and comfort.

"Shh, you need to rest," Mercy said. "You heard Doc."

Wheezing, Ruby shifted in bed. "I didn't understand a lot of it."

Mercy perched on the edge of the bed and ran her hand across Ruby's hair. "My poor, darling daughter. What a terrible year you've had, and now this."

"Mama, it wasn't all terrible." Ruby touched the silver half-heart she would never remove. Warm feelings flooded her as she thought of Niccolò and her summer in Italy. "It was...like living in a dream." *But then I woke up.* She drew a labored breath and asked, "What was all that Doc was talking about?"

"Shh, there will be time for that later," Mercy said, dabbing her eyes. "You have to be very careful. This baby needs to grow as strong as possible, and every week will improve its chances for survival."

Ruby struggled to sit up.

Mercy took her hand. "Don't be hasty about getting up."

A chill of terror raced through Ruby. Could she lose this baby? The world that had once seemed so glittery and full of possibilities was now a dark and somber place. Gritting her teeth, she rested her hands lightly on her curved belly, vowing to do whatever it took to protect Niccolò's sweet child.

"When the time comes, you'll have this baby in a proper hospital," Mercy said. "We won't take any chances with you."

As the days wore on, Ruby filled her time with reading, writing, and sewing. Her mother brought her school books, and the teacher from the small country school, Miss Naomi, agreed to test her knowledge. Ruby passed every subject exam with ease to earn her diploma.

Her teacher also brought her books about writing and composition, and Ruby devoured them. She recalled listening to Mr. Wyler on the set in Rome as he reviewed dialog with a writer, who often made changes to the script during filming.

As she lay in bed, she envisioned a story and began to write scenes that came to her. Soon, she strung her scenes together in a screenplay. Using her imagination made endless hours tolerable.

Missing the camaraderie on a film set, Ruby longed to go back to work. Despite her circumstance of birth, in her heart, Ruby knew she was born to act. As a child, she often crept into the hallway after bedtime and curled up to listen to her parents' radio dramas. The actors' voices were so rich with emotion they could make her cry or laugh or twist her favorite blanket in suspense. Those stories transported her to other worlds. Sometimes she fell asleep in the hallway, and her parents would carry her to bed.

What she saw in the movie house was a thousand times more exciting than radio. The costumes, the sets—all of it thrilled her. To grip emotions and transport people into another world—now, that was magic. It was all she'd ever wanted to do.

ONE DAY, RUBY WAS READING WHEN HER SISTER BROUGHT HER lunch on a tray.

"You're looking much better," Patricia said, placing the tray on the bed. She'd prepared fresh tomato-basil soup, garden greens, deviled eggs, and homemade bread. "Still writing?"

"I'm so excited. It's almost finished." Ruby carefully pushed aside her work. "I can't imagine what I would have done without you. I suppose I'd be back in Hollywood suffering Aunt Vivienne's wrath."

"That poor woman." Patricia shook her head.

"Are you kidding?" Ruby made a face. "She cussed me out for being pregnant. Called me a stupid girl. When I go back, I'm leasing an apartment. Nothing fancy, but it will be mine."

Patricia arched an eyebrow. "Do you know why Vivienne left Texas?"

"Mama only said she'd suffered a tragedy." Ruby tried to remember what Vivienne had said that awful day.

"She was pregnant by some guy who took off when she told him," Patricia said. "Our grandfather planned to send her away to a nun's maternity home, but Vivienne left the night before. She headed west and didn't stop until she hit the ocean. Supposedly, she had a miscarriage." Patricia raised her brow.

"Supposedly?"

"Mama said Vivienne can't have children now, and that's hurt her chances for marriage."

While Mercy was the oldest of all the children, Vivienne was the youngest, and not much older than Patricia.

Her sister lowered her voice. "I think Vivienne was so

desperate that she took a chance on a procedure that went horribly wrong. Mama says that even though Vivienne had almost died, she should pray for forgiveness."

Ruby was shocked at her sister's revelation. As she thought about Vivienne's dark recommendation in this new light, she was even more confused. Though her aunt could be crass, why had she suggested that Ruby take such a drastic measure and risk her life? Ruby shook her head. Was the shame of having a child out of wedlock greater than the possibility of death? There was still much she didn't understand.

"Why didn't anyone tell me this?" Ruby asked.

"You were too little to understand. It happened right before Michael and I married."

"That was a long time ago," Ruby said, feeling left out. "You could have said something before I left to live with her."

Patricia let out a long sigh. "There's a lot this family doesn't talk about. Like Daddy always says, if you can't say something in the good house of the Lord, then you shouldn't say it anywhere else."

"Then that makes him a hypocrite," Ruby said. "You heard him cussing a blue streak."

"That wasn't right," Patricia said. "I'm sure he asked for forgiveness."

"Not from me." Ruby folded her arms. Although the lunch beside her looked delicious, she'd lost her appetite.

Patricia fidgeted with the edge of her apron. "Are you sure you want to go back to Los Angeles? You could have a good life here."

"Barely scraping out a living like our folks?"

"I know, it's just that..." Patricia bit her lip.

Ruby reached for her sister's hand. "Don't worry. I'm not running away. I'll keep providing for Mama as long as she needs."

"It's not that," Patricia said. "Though I don't know what our folks—or us—would have done without your help. It's just that I can't imagine you on your own in that big city, raising a child in a little box of a place. And who'll look after your little one while you're away on sets in Italy or New Mexico?"

"I'll find someone I can trust. Or I'll take the baby with me." In truth, Ruby was worried about this.

"You could stay here," Patricia said. "I talked to Michael, and he says it's okay." Her face bloomed with a smile. "We'd love to have a little one around."

Ruby glanced at the stack of pages she'd been writing. "I know you mean well, but I'd feel like a bird with my wings clipped." She'd die a slow death under her father's constant disapproval. "Besides, what could I do here? You and Michael are having a tough time, too." She'd heard them discussing their family budget one night.

"There's the diner on the highway," Patricia said.

"I won't doom my child to that kind of life," Ruby said. "Or us. Would you want to see our mother working at that diner?" As soon as Ruby spoke, she regretted it, but it was true. They'd had a hardscrabble upbringing, and it wasn't getting any better.

Patricia bowed her head. "I pray it won't ever come to that."

"It's going to take more than prayers," Ruby said, a little more harshly than she'd intended. "My agent has a part lined up for me as soon as I return. I have to continue acting now more than ever. For my child, for our parents. Besides, my chance at Hollywood won't come around again." Joseph's warning still rang in her ears.

Patricia raised her eyes to Ruby. "You could leave your baby with us while you work. You know that no one would ever love that child as I would. You'd never have to worry about trusting a stranger. In between films, you would always have a home here."

"But I can't leave my child," Ruby said, shocked at Patricia's suggestion.

"Don't you want the best for it?" Patricia asked. "Maybe we weren't rich when we were kids, but we rode horses through wild-flowers, cooled off in the swimming hole, and learned to grow the best tomatoes in the county fair. Could your child do that in Hollywood?"

Ruby felt a nudge in her belly and smoothed her hand over it. "This little life is all I have left of Niccolò."

"We're not taking your baby away from you."

Ruby recalled growing up in the country. At seven years her

senior, Patricia had raised her in many ways. Patient beyond her years, Patricia had taught Ruby how to ride horses and coax vegetables from the soil. Their parents were always busy, working hard to scratch out a living and provide a home for them, even though Ruby and Patricia had their chores, too.

If Ruby had to leave her baby with anyone—and she would have to when she worked—it would comfort her to know that Patricia's loving arms would wrap her baby with all the genuine love and gentle care a child could want.

Patricia touched her hand. "We also have all the baby clothes and everything you'll need."

Ruby knew her sister had been preparing to care for children for years. With her neat stitching, Patricia had sewn and embroidered the most beautiful baby clothes—stacks and stacks of them —for the babies that she was sure would arrive. She had put forth so much trust and so many prayers that she'd be blessed with children. It was as if each tiny outfit was an act of faith, proof of the fine mother she could be if only she were given a chance.

A nursery was ready and waiting, and Patricia dusted it weekly. The wooden crib and dresser that Michael had painstakingly crafted were polished to a soft satin sheen.

Ruby leaned her head against the handmade, goose down pillows. Her child could grow and run free here, and Ruby could visit and stay as long as she wanted. She would always be her child's mother.

Patricia slid her arm around Ruby. "Will you think about it?"

"I will," Ruby replied.

In her heart, Ruby knew that what Patricia was proposing made sense. Ruby had to work, but being on her own in a big city with an infant would be difficult. Aunt Vivienne wouldn't be of much help—her mercurial personality didn't include maternal longings. But Patricia and Michael were responsible and kind; she'd never heard a foul word between them. And how happy a little one would make them; this big house needed a child's laughter.

Ruby could provide such a gift—a gift beyond value—to her sister. She rested her head on Patricia's shoulder. As Ruby thought about her dilemma, it seemed selfish not to share her good fortune of having a child with her sister. Were their roles reversed, Patricia wouldn't hesitate. With her generous nature, it wouldn't occur to her to be any other way. Ruby could play the part of a soft-spoken lady, but Patricia was the genuine article.

Yet, Ruby's arms ached to hold her baby. She hoped the child would have Niccolò's bright blue eyes and dark hair. She longed to see his beautiful features reflected in her baby's face. If he had to leave her alone in this life, instead of the one they'd once planned together, at least he'd given her a child that she could shower with love. To be separated from her child would be excruciating, but Ruby had few choices.

Niccolò would want the best for his child, too. Recalling the importance of family to him, she thought that he would agree.

Still, this wasn't a decision Ruby wanted to make.

In the thin light of dawn, Ruby woke from a fevered sleep and instantly knew that something was wrong. Her back had started aching yesterday, and she'd hardly slept. Now, her pillow was damp with perspiration, but more than that, she felt a downward pressure that scared her.

She tried to raise herself on the bed, but a pain shot through her. *No, no, no,* she thought. Calculating quickly, she realized it had been six weeks since Doc Schmidt's visit.

"Patricia, help!" She shifted and called out for her sister again.

Moments later, Patricia rushed in. "What's wrong?"

"I think it's the baby," Ruby said, panting against the growing pain. "I need Doc right away."

As Patricia hurried out, Ruby let out a long moan. With Niccolò's name on her lips, she gripped the sheet in her fist through searing pain.

Drifting through waves of agony that crested and barely subsided, Ruby didn't know how much time had passed before Doc arrived, but one thing was certain. It was too late to take Ruby to the nearest hospital, which was more than two hours away.

Her mother and Patricia worked to assist Doc, and Ruby could tell from their frowns and whispered prayers that something was dreadfully wrong.

"The baby is coming now," Doc said, rolling his sleeves up and issuing orders.

Patricia hurried in with a stack of towels, while Michael brought in hot water.

Doc leaned over her, and Ruby could see perspiration beading on his forehead. "Stay strong, Miss Ruby, and follow my instructions."

Ruby glanced at her mother, who nodded in agreement. Mercy's stoic expression struck terror in Ruby's heart. Gritting her teeth, she forced aside the feeling and clung to the image of Niccolò in her mind. She wrapped herself in the love they had shared.

Silent tears coursed down Patricia's cheeks, but she'd committed to assisting Doc, and that's what she did, swiping her cheeks every few minutes.

Niccolò, Niccolò. Ruby imagined him gripping her hand, willing her on, breathing his life force into their child.

"Baby's coming," Doc said. And then, "Hold up!" He barked his commands like a general. Ruby did her best to follow them, but she quickly grew tired and light-headed. Her limbs and muscles grew weaker with every effort.

Niccolò, be with me.

"Umbilical cord wrapped around," Doc muttered.

Ruby felt herself grow lighter, and she seemed to transcend her body. Floating above the scene below, she saw her wavy, dark red hair tangled across the damp pillows and her legs pale as toothpicks against blood-stained sheets. Doc gritted his teeth, working feverishly, while her mother and sister choked back sobs.

Sounds seemed muted, and the scene unfolded before her, as if in a movie. Ruby was wondering what would happen next when suddenly she felt jerked back into her body. Doc was checking her eyes, and then, as a torrent of pain ripped through her, she tilted her head back and screamed.

She didn't know how much time had passed before she heard Doc say, "Here she is."

Her mother rose anxiously from the bed. "Is she…breathing?"

She. A girl. Ruby twisted an edge of the sheet in her fist.

Doc looked grim as he held a thin, limp form in his hands.

Ruby panicked. "No, not my baby!" Blood roared through her head, and all she could think of was how she'd lost them both. Despair as dark as she'd ever known coursed through her, and she wished she could return to that strange, in-between place devoid of pain.

"Shh," Patricia said, gripping Ruby's hands as she flailed. "Let Doc work."

Tears wet her face as Ruby listened to the frantic prayer on her mother's lips. How could her baby have slipped away while she remained? She would have gladly changed places, giving her baby girl a chance to live.

Moments seemed like hours, but finally, a tiny cry erupted, followed by a thin wail that sent shivers through Ruby. "Is she okay?"

Doc gazed at her with sorrowful eyes. "She's premature, so her lungs might not be well-formed."

A chilling terror sliced through Ruby. "Will she…live?"

"If she can breathe on her own, she has a shot," Doc replied grimly, setting his jaw. "We'll do what we can."

26

Lago di Como, 2010

Tucking her sketches under her arm, Ariana hurried down the stairs at Villa Fiori, excited about her plans. Today Alessandro was picking her up, and they were going to the shop she'd leased to start work on the interior. But first, she wanted to show her aunt what she'd been working on for her debut signature collection.

Ruby was already outside on the terrace having breakfast.

"Good morning," Ariana sang out. She joined Ruby at the table, where Livia had set up a place for her and left a fresh pot of coffee. Pouring coffee, she said, "I brought some of my designs to show you what I have in mind for my collection."

"I'd love to see them." Ruby slid her grapefruit and granola to one side.

Ariana spread out a few sketches. "What I have in mind is a fusion of casual American and chic European style. Think Jacqueline Kennedy Onassis relaxing on a Greek island or Grace Kelly sailing to Monaco."

Perusing the sketches, Ruby smiled. "I see the mid-century

fashion influence, which looks very fresh in your hands." She tapped one of the drawings. "I'd certainly like this outfit. A swinging bodice with a boatneck top and three-quarter bell sleeves. Paired with a slim pant. Good lines. And I love it in this shade of coral."

"I thought you'd like that," Ariana said. "After all those years of playing in your closets, I know your style. Bold, dramatic, rich with flair."

"All the better to make an entrance, my dear." Ruby folded her hands. "So, how are you planning your production?"

"I have fabric from Alessandro," Ariana said. "And I'm having a dressmaker's form, a sewing machine, and other supplies delivered in a few days. I'll start by draping muslin on the form to create my designs. From that, a pattern maker can create patterns in a range of sizes. Customers can look at samples, order their size, and receive a custom fit."

Ruby nodded thoughtfully. "What about people who are here on holiday and need an outfit for dinner?"

Ariana had thought about that. "I'll also have some ready-to-wear in simple, luxurious resort-wear designs. Not quite one-size-fits-all, but close. Small, medium, and large. I'll start with just a few so I can see what delights my customers."

"Good idea," Ruby said, studying each design. "These are marvelous. But then, I have complete faith in you and your ability."

"There's just so much I need to do before…" Ariana chewed her lip. *Before I give birth,* she thought. The funny thing was that except for having a ravenous appetite, she hardly felt pregnant at all.

"That's wise," Ruby said solemnly. "You want to be prepared in the event of—well, anything. Have you checked with Vera for obstetrician recommendations yet? She has a list of medical providers."

Ariana sighed, pressing her fingers to her temple. "I will, but I feel fine. I have so much to do right now."

Ruby reached across the table and gripped her hand. "No, you must make arrangements now. If you want, I'll make an appointment for you."

Surprised at Ruby's urgency, Ariana pulled back. "I can do it, but I'd rather not broadcast my condition just yet."

"You must be under a doctor's care. Just in case." Worry lines creased Ruby's forehead. "Does this have something to do with Alessandro?"

Averting her eyes, Ariana blew on her hot coffee. She enjoyed spending time with Alessandro and the children and feared that if she told him she was pregnant, he would vanish. She wouldn't even blame him.

"I like Alessandro for you," Ruby said, tapping the table with her manicured nails. Her voice hardened with resolve. "But you must tell him soon. If you wait any longer, he'll be angry and upset that you didn't trust him enough to tell him."

"But I'm afraid," Ariana whispered, ashamed that she wasn't as strong as Ruby. Her aunt rarely found fault with her, and when she did, it hurt. "Maybe next week..."

Ruby raised her brow and shook her head. "Be honest with him." She stared across the water toward Varenna. "Otherwise, your life will become even more muddled and tangled than you think it is now. Sadly, I know this from experience."

Before Ariana could ask Ruby what she meant by that, her aunt dabbed her mouth with her napkin and rose, drawing her shoulders back imperiously. "Your designs are exquisite, my dear, but I hope you'll heed my warning about Alessandro."

After Ruby had gone, Ariana finished her breakfast. Her aunt was no longer coddling her, but nor did Ariana want her to. Ruby had a strong sense of right and wrong, as well as lofty expectations. Ariana often wondered how Ruby's will of iron had been forged.

As Alessandro drove Ariana the short distance to her nearby shop, Ariana turned over Ruby's advice in her mind. She gazed out the window at the lake, its surface broken by the occasional ferry or pleasure craft. *What lay beneath that surface?*

Glancing at Alessandro and catching his admiring smile, Ariana realized that she was not unlike that lake. He was unsuspecting, unaware of the secret she was concealing that could destroy their nascent relationship—the innocent party in her subterfuge. Guilt gathered in the pit of her stomach.

Since arriving in Bellagio, Ariana had been trying to partition the unpleasant thoughts in her mind and live in the moment. Isn't that what Ruby had always told her to do?

Yet, in a few short months, Ariana's dilemma would be evident for all to see. Was she crazy for quitting her job, turning down Phillip's mother's offer, and signing a lease on a shop in Italy that she could barely afford with the far-fetched dream of being a fashion designer? Maybe she'd been following Ruby and her exuberant way of living for so long that now she thought she could do it, too.

But there was only one Ruby Raines.

She, Ariana Ricci, had to make her own way. And she had to be smart about it. As she'd learned with Phillip, depending on a man was often fraught with complications. Or, Alessandro might have secrets of his own. She couldn't count on her mother, and she didn't want Ruby's handouts, even though her aunt always gave freely.

As much as Ariana loved her aunt, she could tell that something in Ruby's psyche had shifted. She was seizing opportunities —such as buying a villa that must have cost a fortune.

And then it hit Ariana. *Maybe Ruby is having one last fling.* Was her aunt ill? The thought troubled her, and she swallowed hard.

"You're awfully quiet," Alessandro said. "If there's anything you'd like to talk about, I'm here for you."

The opportunity was before her, and yet Ariana couldn't take that step. Instead, she turned to him and smiled. "I have so much running through my mind right now." That much was true. "From the shop renovation to the collection design to the thousand details about running a business here… It's a lot to think about."

"It will all fall into place," Alessandro said. "It won't always be this overwhelming."

Ariana reached into her purse for the key to the shop. "On top of that, my aunt wants me to 'be social,' as she puts it."

"You can't work all the time," Alessandro said. "Why would you want to anyway? Look around." He gestured toward the calm lake and the snow-capped mountains. "Here, enjoying life is a pleasure and a privilege. We cannot squander such riches of nature."

Realizing he had a point, Ariana smiled. "I suppose I should go out and meet people," she said, extracting the key. "Aunt Ruby found a local theater and wants me to attend an opening night performance. Would you like to go with us? She always gets the best seats."

"I'd like that very much," he said. "As long as Paolina can watch the children. What's the production?"

"*Roman Holiday*. Or, *Vacanze Romane*. She must've watched that movie a thousand times." Ariana slid the key in and tried to turn it.

"One of my favorites, too." Grinning, Alessandro said, "My uncle has underwritten that performance."

Alessandro started to say something, but Ariana cried out. "Ouch, something bit my hand."

"Here, let me help you. These old locks can be temperamental, and I see there's a jagged piece of metal that should be filed." Alessandro jiggled the key, and the door opened under his ministrations.

Once inside the shop, she gazed around. Overhead, a chandelier dimmed with dust hung from the coffered ceiling. "It's a beautiful starting place, but the floors are tragic." Layers of linoleum tile from different eras were curling at the edges.

Alessandro scraped his stubbled chin with his knuckles. "I know someone who could strip that floor for you."

"And then what would I do with it?"

"Looks like concrete under there."

Ariana had an idea. "I can paint and stencil the concrete, or even leave it as it is and put a high-gloss or satin finish over it. I could arrange some rugs to delineate different sections. And then, I can use drop lights to illuminate the collections. Wouldn't Murano glass flutes be amazing?"

Alessandro laughed. "I don't think you needed me here at all."

As her imagination came to life, Ariana felt better. Her doubt about her ability to pull this off dissipated. "In the car, I was fccling overwhelmed. But now that I'm here, I know exactly what needs to be done." She pulled a notepad from her bag and began sketching her vision.

"An entrepreneur's most important asset is her decision-making ability." Alessandro put his arm around her shoulders. "I think you're going to do just fine."

"I appreciate your confidence in me." The sureness of his grip filled her with sudden attraction. Alessandro was everything that Phillip wasn't. *Supportive, interested, mature, authentic.* How could she have thought Phillip was right for her? They'd started dating just after her graduation. Had she been so naïve that she accepted his actions as the norm?

Now that Alessandro had come into her life, she saw how different a genuine relationship could be.

Ariana raised her gaze to a pair of large, baroque framed-mirrors. The gold paint had faded and chipped, and dark spots peppered the beveled glass around the edges. Yet the old mirrors had a certain appeal. "What do you think about those?"

"Once they're cleaned, they'll be beautiful," Alessandro said. "They have history. That's important."

Ariana considered his words. "It is, isn't it?"

"We don't have to cover up history with a shiny new surface," Alessandro said. "Instead, we can expose imperfections and embrace them. Each scar is a triumph, each blemish unique. That's much more interesting."

"More philosophy?" Ariana asked, taking a step toward him. "You would have made a great professor."

"Maybe I'll write a book someday," he replied, his eyes twinkling. Drawing Ariana closer, he touched his forehead to hers.

Reaching up, she looped her arms around his neck and brushed her lips against his. Every nerve in her body seemed to crackle with an electrical charge. "Do you have any blemishes I should know about?"

"Plenty," he said. "Sometimes, I lose my patience with the children. It's hard to be a single parent. And my business occasionally demands more of my attention than I would like. Still, I tried to put life first and work second." A smile danced on his lips. "What about you? Any imperfections that you're hiding?"

"Definitely a few scars." Ariana stared into twin pools of gold-flecked, hazel eyes that sparkled with...was it a spark of love? And then she thought, *What does he see in mine?*

Alessandro raised his brow. "Are you going to make me guess?"

Ruby's admonitions rang in her mind, yet she dreaded breaking the spell. "There is something you should know, but I don't know how to tell you."

Alessandro brought her hand to his lips and kissed her palm. "Does this have anything to do with the fact that you're no longer drinking?"

When she nodded, he hesitated. "How long has it been?"

"A couple of months."

"One of my cousins is an alcoholic," he said, his expression softening with a mixture of empathy and encouragement. "It takes a lot of strength to do what you're doing. You can be proud of that."

"What?" She ran a hand over her face and shook her head. "You thought... Oh, no, that's not it. Not at all."

Alessandro frowned with confusion. "Then what is it?"

Unable to say the word, Ariana flung her hand out. "What's another reason a woman might not drink?"

"Interaction with a medication..."

Ariana shook her head.

"An alcohol allergy..."

"Really?" Ariana put a hand on her hip.

"Or she's pregnant..." Alessandro hesitated. "You're not..."

"I am."

"Ah, *mamma mia.*" He pushed a hand through his hair. "I don't know what to say. I mean, I'm very happy for you, but..." Alessandro tipped his head back as if searching for the right words to let her down gently. "I never imagined this. May I ask whose child it is? Besides, obviously, yours."

Ariana blinked back tears that rimmed her lashes. "Phillip's, although he wants no part of fatherhood."

Shaking his head, Alessandro made a clucking noise and turned away from her.

Seeing his shoulders droop, Ariana knew it was over. *Ruby was right.* Her heart lurched with despair; she should have told Alessandro earlier. *What was I thinking?*

Further, after all the years Ariana had spent with Phillip, she should have waited to let her heart mend before getting involved with someone again. This was a rebound relationship, and she couldn't expect Alessandro to take on another man's child. She was sure that, at best, this had been a lark on his part. *Nothing more.* But she didn't have the mental strength to do the same. She gave her heart too freely.

"Alessandro, I'm so sorry," she began.

He turned around and took her hand. "You don't have to apologize. You made the right decision. Children are a joy, a blessing."

"That test your patience," Ariana said. "Your words. I suppose I'll find out soon enough."

He chuckled. "My words, yes."

"This is why we are doomed," Ariana said, stepping into her courage. She had to let him know it was okay to leave, though she already felt her heart cracking. "I should have told you sooner, before…"

Alessandro slid a finger under her chin and raised her face to his. "Before we fell in love?"

We? Had she heard him correctly? Ariana's throat constricted as she realized she would break his heart, too. She could only nod.

Alessandro wrapped his arms around her and swayed as if to some music in his mind. "My dear Ariana. You have never been in love, not really. This Phillip—if what you say is true, and I'm sure it is—he didn't know how to love a woman. You would not have been happy. But I have known love—good, true love—and there is nothing like it in the world. I never thought I would know that again."

At his words, hope flared in Ariana. "And has that changed?"

Alessandro tapped her nose. "The moment you walked into the factory. And then when I saw my children race toward you with such joy in their hearts. You are the missing part of our family, Ariana. I'm sure of it." He framed her face with his hands. "Will you think about it?"

"But the baby…"

"I love children," he said quickly. "Two or three, or more, what does it matter? This baby is part of you, and I love all of you, Ariana."

Although Ariana longed for the happily-ever-after fairytale, that wasn't real life—as she had learned at the altar when faced with hard reality. And this time, children's tender hearts were also at stake.

Ariana gazed at him. "I am happy that you feel that way, and I want you to know that my feelings for you—and the children— are growing every day. You have captured my heart, Alessandro, but the next time I commit to someone, I must be sure."

27

Texas Hill Country, 1953

*𝒶*s Ruby sat in bed and smoothed her hand over her tiny baby's fine, light brown hair, her heart ached with love. And when her little one opened her eyes, Niccolò's vivid blue orbs stared back at Ruby. *Their child. Inquisitive, needy, and sweetly demanding.* Their baby had insisted on emerging early into the world, ready to take on nearly insurmountable challenges.

"Mariangela, my angel," Ruby murmured, thinking of Niccolò and his words on their first evening out at the opera.

Doc had stopped by to examine them both. It had been four weeks since the delivery.

"She'll need a lot of care," Doc said, removing his stethoscope and returning it to his bag. "Fortunately, she's a real fighter. Like her mother."

"We owe so much to Patricia, too." Ruby wasn't merely acknowledging her sister. She knew that if she had been in Los Angeles, she might have been alone, and Mariangela might well have died.

Patricia smiled. "I'd do anything for that little one."

"She's a lucky little girl to have you both." Doc Schmidt

picked up his hat and medical bag. "Remember to keep her warm at all times."

"I'll see you out," Patricia said, walking with him to the door.

After they'd left, Ruby slid a tiny pink cap that Mercy had knitted over Mariangela's head. "Hi, sweetie," Ruby cooed.

Since Mariangela was born about eight weeks premature, Doc's advice was critically important. Weak and scrawny-limbed, Mariangela had little fat on her body to maintain warmth. When she was born, Doc Schmidt suggested that they fashion a sling to nestle her against Ruby's chest. There the baby had stayed, skin-to-skin under one of Michael's voluminous flannel shirts. Doc Schmidt told them that this close contact would help Mariangela maintain her body temperature and gain weight.

Patricia and Michael moved Ruby's bed into the dining room to be close to the fireplace, which they kept burning around the clock, even as spring brought out bright bluebonnet flowers.

In the beginning, Mariangela couldn't latch onto Ruby's breast to feed, so Ruby filled a dropper with breast milk. She and Patricia took turns dribbling nourishment into Mariangela's mouth. The baby looked like a tiny kitten lapping the milk that landed in her mouth. Ruby was so exhausted that she often nodded off throughout the day. Half an hour here and there—though she was always alert to Mariangela's smallest quiver.

Now, Mariangela was growing stronger. She could nurse on her own, and her lungs had developed—along with more robust cries.

When Patricia returned, she held out her arms. "I'll take her if you'd like a break."

"I could use a few minutes outside." Ruby ducked her head to slide off the sling and transfer Mariangela to Patricia, who unbuttoned her shirt to snuggle her against her skin. The baby was just as comfortable with Patricia.

"Look at that," Ruby said. "It's as if she has two mothers."

"You're her only mother," Patricia said.

Yet a smile lit her face, and Ruby could tell Patricia was pleased. Her sister might never have children, and Ruby was genuinely happy that Patricia could share this experience of mothering. Sometimes Ruby felt a small twinge of jealousy when

Mariangela quieted as soon as she was in Patricia's arms. Being older, Patricia had held far more babies than she had, that was all.

Ruby stepped outside and walked toward the barn where her horse had been since she'd ridden here that frost-bitten morning more than two months ago. The spring sunshine warmed her face, and she breathed in the heady scents of honeysuckle and jasmine that rambled along the rear porch railing. A rocking chair sat ready for her—once the weather was warmer and Mariangela was strong enough to be outside.

Inside the barn, Ruby approached the mare with a lump of sugar she'd picked up in the kitchen.

"Hey, Blaze." Ruby opened the palm of her hand, and the mare picked up the sweet treat. Ruby let her outside for a short walk. She wished she could ride her and feel the wind in her hair, but Ruby was too weary.

Michael waved from the garden patch he'd been hoeing and ridding of weeds. Spring was short in these parts, with weather that could shift from frosty nights to hot, humid days in a flash. He put his tools aside and ambled toward her.

"Good to see you outside," Michael said, pushing his straw hat back from his forehead.

"Had to breathe in some fresh air. Gets hot inside." Ruby wasn't complaining, just stating a fact.

"What'd Doc have to say?"

"He seemed pleased with her progress," Ruby said, swinging her arms to regain circulation in her cramped arms. "She's gaining weight and shedding her wrinkled raisin look."

Michael chuckled. "Got to hand it to you and Patricia. Miracle workers, you are."

"Patricia always seems to know exactly what to do. She's a natural." Ruby laughed at herself. "I didn't know half of what she does."

"My wife was meant for this." Michael raked his knuckles against his scruffy beard. "Maybe we'll have one soon," he added with a rare glimmer of hope in his eyes.

Ruby nodded. During the long hours of caring for the baby together, Patricia had lamented to Ruby about her inability to conceive. "In the meantime, you'll have Mariangela," Ruby assured her. "You don't know how much I will appreciate your looking after her when I go back to work." Patricia's eyes gleamed with such brightness that Ruby's pain was eased, too.

Blaze trotted toward Ruby, nudging her to play, but Ruby didn't have the energy. She rubbed the mare's nose. "Soon, girl. Soon."

"I should be thanking you," Michael said, brushing his hand over the mare's coat. "Patricia hasn't been this happy in a long time."

Ruby thought of Michael as the brother she'd never have. "Mariangela will grow up thinking of you as her father." As she uttered the last word, her throat closed around it. Niccolò would have been such a good father. In her mind's eye, she could see them together. Niccolò would have cradled Mariangela in his strong arms against his chest, singing Italian lullabies to her.

"And I couldn't be prouder to fill that role for her," Michael said. "That's a big responsibility, but I want you to know that I will always look after her for you."

"I know you will." Ruby managed a smile before leading Blaze back to her stall. "We'll go for a ride soon," Ruby whispered, and the horse neighed in response. Ruby longed for respites, however brief. Five or ten minutes for a bath, a few minutes outside.

As she walked back to the house, Ruby heard the telephone trill through the open window. "I'll get it," she called out, racing through the door.

In the kitchen, she hurried to the telephone attached to the wall. "Hello?"

Her agent's voice crackled through the earpiece. "Ruby, it's Joseph. When will you be ready to audition for another part?"

Ruby grinned. Joseph Applebaum always got right down to business. "Not until July or August." Though she still wasn't talking to her father, her mother had indicated that supplies would be running low by then.

"You're going to be busy in the fall," Joseph said. "*Diary of a Pioneer Woman* will be released in September, followed by the film you just finished. The word on the street is that your performances are astounding."

"That's a relief," Ruby said.

Joseph's voice rose with excitement. "You might even be nominated for awards. I'm already working on that. Getting the right people at the premier."

"When is *Roman Holiday* coming out?" Ruby asked. She needed to see it. Already, last summer seemed like a dream. The thought of seeing Niccolò on the screen was sobering.

"September," Joseph said. "The premiere is in August, I believe."

"Could I go?" Ruby chewed on her lip.

"I'll get right on it," Joseph said. "You're about to be a star, Ruby. I hope you're ready."

The thought seemed so far away.

"Studio publicists are already releasing your photos to fan magazines. Building interest in our new star. I also got a contract to use your likeness for a nail polish endorsement."

Ruby looked at her short, bare nails and laughed. "I've only used nail varnish a couple of times," she said. Once in Rome for a party, and another time in Los Angeles for an important event at the Roosevelt Hotel. Ruby recalled the fancy evening. At the party around the pool, Ruby had spotted Marilyn Monroe, a blond actress the press often called a love goddess. When Joseph had told Ruby that Marilyn had posed sans coverage for a calendar, she'd assured him that she'd never do such a thing.

Her mother would die to see her with polish on her fingernails—except in films—let alone see her daughter's nude body welcoming in the month of May. And she couldn't even imagine the level of rage her father would have.

"I'll send you some fan mags with your photos," Joseph said. "Get used to seeing your picture because it's going to be plastered all over Sunset Boulevard when you return."

"Just make sure the checks don't bounce," Ruby told him before she hung up the telephone. She loved acting, and she sure liked being paid, but she didn't care much about fame.

Her privacy was much more important.

Still, Ruby was itching to go back to work. As much as she

loved Mariangela, she was secretly relieved that Patricia could care for her for a while. Though Ruby hated to admit it, she was exhausted. Not only from caring for her baby but also from the windswept monotony of the ranch. After spending the summer in Italy, she yearned to see more of the world. She had a life ahead of her, and she was eager to live it.

If only Niccolò were still by her side. These last few months, she had reeled through a gamut of emotions, from disbelief to anger to grief. The man she'd married would have contacted her if at all possible—and certainly if he planned to have their marriage annulled. That she was sure of. So far, none of the letters of inquiry she'd sent to Italy or people on the production had been fruitful.

Blinking through sudden tears, Ruby made her way back to Patricia. When she heard Mariangela cry, her breasts ached with the fullness of milk.

For now, her baby needed her. Of all her roles, Ruby relished this one the most, as exhausting as it was. Mariangela was a pure little soul, unfettered by the demands of mortgages and money that plagued her mother.

By mid-June, three months after birth, Mariangela had gained weight and taken on a healthy glow. Ruby had nursed Mariangela through the child's tenuous beginning to her life, and Patricia could now relieve her for longer periods.

Now, under sunny skies, Ruby pushed Blaze on, galloping through pastures on the first ride she'd had since Mariangela was born. After they returned, Blaze neighed and pranced, and Ruby fed her a treat of carrots. As glorious as the day was, Ruby was feeling anxious about returning to work. She hated to leave Mariangela, but it was necessary. Spring rains had been sparse, and the summer heat was settling in early.

After returning to the house, Ruby stopped in the kitchen to wash up before seeing her baby. Her brother-in-law walked into the kitchen.

"Have a good ride?" Michael asked.

As Ruby dried her hands on a cotton dish towel, she grinned.

"The best. When you haven't been able to do something you love, it's even sweeter when you finally can."

"If it weren't for you and Patricia, little Mari wouldn't have had a chance."

Mari. Michael had given the baby this nickname, saying that Mariangela was too long for him to pronounce, even though Ruby thought the name rolled beautifully off Patricia's tongue. Ruby wanted her baby to appreciate her Italian heritage as she grew older. If only Mariangela could have known Niccolò.

"Letter for you in here," Michael said, depositing the post on the kitchen table.

Ruby's heart fluttered with anticipation. Despite what she felt about Niccolò's possible demise, every time Michael brought the mail from the post office, she checked it, praying that Vivienne had received mail and forwarded it. But now, nine months since she'd heard from him, the chance was growing slimmer by the week.

"It's from my agent." Ruby slid open the envelope, postmarked *Hollywood.*

Scanning the letter, Ruby felt a surge of hope.

"What's good ol' Joseph have to say?" Michael asked.

"He's made arrangements for me to go to the premiere of *Roman Holiday* in New York. It's in August, and he's sending a train ticket." Ruby's pulse quickened. Perhaps it was too much to hope for, but she prayed that by some miracle, Niccolò—if he were alive—might find a way to attend the premiere. Or maybe someone among the cast or crew had seen him or heard from him.

Ruby pulled out a sheet of writing paper from a kitchen drawer. Taking a pen, she quickly composed a brief letter.

Send the ticket. I'll meet you there. And then she added, *Will be ready for auditions then. Must return to work.*

After tucking the letter into an envelope, she licked the flap and sealed it with the prayer that Niccolò might somehow be there. Or, at the very least, she might learn what had happened to him.

28

New York, 1953

*R*uby stood before a full-length mirror at the Plaza Hotel while the studio's costume supervisor tried to zip her into a strapless, lemon-yellow dress with a nipped waist.

"Will it close?" Ruby asked, sucking in her stomach.

"It's good until the bustline," David said. "And I had this made to your exact measurements from last summer." Looking askance at her fuller figure, he asked, "How did you blossom so in under a year?"

Ruby shrugged. "I've been doing a lot of special exercises." She'd tried to wean Mariangela before she left, but her décolletage was definitely more impressive than last year.

Arching an eyebrow, David eyed her with a measure of disbelief. "Must be quite the exercises. You were skinny as a whippet last year."

As he marked the dress with straight pins and dressmaker's chalk, Ruby summoned her courage. "Have you heard anything from Niccolò since last summer?" If a sliver of a chance remained that Niccolò was still alive, she might discover a clue here among those they had worked with on the set.

David removed a pin from his mouth. "Your sweetheart? Oh, gee, I'm sorry to say I haven't. I thought you two kids would stick."

Ruby blinked back tears that rushed to her eyes.

"Oh, come on now, sweetheart." He handed her a tissue. "In this business, it's hard to know anyone, especially actors. Then you get to know them—the real person—and the relationship is never the same. A lot of folks in this biz are just putting on an act."

"Not all of us," Ruby said, although she certainly was now. Perhaps more than anyone else.

"I don't know about that," David said. "You've sure changed from that naïve girl I met last summer. Is it an act, or is it for real?"

"Maybe I've just grown up," Ruby replied. *Was it that obvious?*

"Beautifully, too." David stepped back to appraise his work. "Word around town is that you're in the running for Charlie's next leading lady." At that, he frowned. "But watch out for him. Bad temper. He blows hot and cold."

Not unlike her father. "I can handle that."

David clapped his hands. "Give me fifteen or twenty minutes, and you'll be red-carpet-ready. Now, off with the dress."

Curving up a corner of her mouth, Ruby motioned for David to turn around while she slipped off her dress and put on a Plaza Hotel robe.

While she waited, Ruby put on the costume jewelry David had brought for her to wear, along with a special piece she'd brought with her. Soon, he returned with the dress. This time, it was a perfect fit.

Ruby made her way from the icy air conditioning of the Plaza outside into the muggy heat of New York. Cars were waiting to ferry them to the premiere. Ruby was so nervous she could hardly speak. What if Niccolò were there?

Their line of cars stopped, and Ruby stepped from the vehicle at the curb. The marquee above blazed the title, *Roman Holiday*. Ahead of her was Audrey Hepburn, who wore a strapless evening dress and opera-length white gloves. The actress's short, pixie haircut looked cool and chic, while Ruby's wavy locks were already sticky on her neck.

"This way, Miss Hepburn," a photographer called out.

Ruby watched as Audrey paused on the red carpet to flash her wide smile and wave. She admired how Audrey and the rest of the cast looked so effortlessly stylish and confident, despite the heatwave that gripped the city this late August day. Though Ruby was used to such temperatures, she wasn't accustomed to wearing evening wear in the heat.

While cameras flashed and popped, Ruby touched the silver half-heart pendant she wore and turned to scan the crowd, longing to see the one person she'd hoped would be here.

Niccolò. If only...

"Move along, miss." One of the organizers waved her onto the red carpet. "It's your turn."

Trying not to let her shoulders sag with disappointment, she straightened and tilted her chin.

Ruby stepped onto the red carpet for her turn with the photographers, who began to call out her name.

"Miss Raines! This way, turn right. Miss Raines, over here!"

The attention was startling, and her first thought was, *How do they know my name?* Recovering quickly, she smiled and twirled in her dress, looking coquettishly over her shoulder with a hand on her hip—a move that David had just taught her.

Following Audrey's lead, Ruby posed and focused on cool thoughts—like skinny-dipping in the swimming hole back home or braving the chilly Pacific waters at Venice Beach in Los Angeles.

Even though Ruby's scene was cut, Joseph got her on the invitation list. He'd insisted she go to New York, saying it was good exposure. Ruby glanced around at all the stars and fans that lined the street. She'd seen premieres on newsreels in theaters before the main film, but this event was more exciting than she could have imagined. Surprisingly, people were calling her name. Then she remembered the fan magazines that Joseph had mentioned.

As exhilarating as it all was, Ruby looked around, still harboring hope that Niccolò might appear. A lump formed in hcr throat. At thc vcry lcast, Ruby ycarncd to catch glimpscs of Niccolò in the film.

Just ahead, Ruby saw Joseph waiting for her. She wasn't his only client here today.

"Perfect timing, Ruby. Right behind Miss Hepburn." Joseph winked and offered her his arm. Her agent's sandy, sun-streaked hair made him appear even more youthful than his thirty years. Though he was young, Joseph had great knowledge of the industry. His mother and father had performed in Vaudeville and on radio, and one uncle was a screenwriter.

"Glad you came out for this," Joseph said. "Your career is about to explode. Ready to start auditions again?"

"Sure." Recalling what David had mentioned, she asked, "Who's Charlie? I heard I'm being considered for a part with someone named Charlie."

Joseph chuckled and named one of the biggest stars in Hollywood. "If you get the part, you can't take off again like you did. I'm going to need a commitment from you."

"You know why I had to take time off," Ruby said pointedly.

"And did you work out your problem?"

Ruby wanted to scream. "Mariangela is not a problem to be solved."

"Shh, not here." Joseph took her arm and pulled her aside from the crowd. "I'm going to forget you said that," he whispered. "You're too young to have had…that experience."

"I'm eighteen now."

Joseph drew a hand over his face. "Don't broadcast this issue to anyone, especially not the press."

Ruby loved Mariangela with all her heart. Why should she keep her hidden as if she'd done something wrong? After all, she had been married. "I love this child so much. She was premature, you know, and almost died."

Joseph heaved a sigh. "Okay, I get it. But I'm warning you, keep this quiet."

"I'm still going to need time between shoots to go home to Texas." Ruby planned to keep a small apartment in Hollywood to minimize her contact with Vivienne, who'd moved to another apartment.

Joseph sighed. "I'll try, but I don't control the filming schedule."

"I can't be gone too long at a stretch."

Ruby recalled the day she had left for New York. Leaving Mariangela with Patricia had been gut-wrenching. Though Patricia and Michael had repeatedly assured her, she'd been worried about everything, from how often her baby would eat to where she would now sleep. Ruby wanted Mariangela to stay in the bedroom with Patricia and Michael, so they'd hear her if she cried. At some point, they would move Mariangela into the nursery, but Ruby was anxious about her being lonely or left to cry if no one heard her.

Feeling anxious, Ruby turned to Joseph. "Did Niccolò from Italy ever contact you? I told you all about him."

"You've asked me this before," Joseph said quietly. "He never did, Ruby. And for the record, I'm genuinely sorry about what you went through. I want you to know that."

"Thanks." Ruby drew a full breath, and her dress felt even tighter. "If he contacted you, you'd tell me, right?"

"Of course, I would. But you must move on, Ruby. This business moves fast, and I don't want to see you left behind."

Joseph accompanied her into the theater, and they took their seats. When the lights went down, Ruby was alert, watching every frame to see if she could catch a glimpse of Niccolò.

"There," she cried out, pointing at the screen. People around her laughed, and Joseph sat up to pay attention. Ruby leaned forward, resting her elbows on her knees and warming her silver half-heart pendant in her palm.

On the screen, Ruby and Niccolò were seated at a table in front of a café. When Audrey and Gregory drove through the tables on a Vespa, Ruby leapt up in surprise, and Niccolò took her in his arms to protect her. The expression on his face was one of sweet adoration.

While others laughed at the scene, Ruby choked back a sob. Joseph quickly passed a monogrammed handkerchief to her. Dabbing her eyes, she continued watching the film, picking out Niccolò in different crowd scenes. Watching him was so painful, and yet, she loved reliving every moment. She remembered their conversations and how he'd held her and kissed her.

In the final scene, Niccolò played the part of a news reporter in the press crowd behind Gregory Peck and Eddie Albert while Audrey performed Princess Ann's heart-rending farewell. Niccolò was so handsome and convincing that Ruby could hardly control her flow of tears. It didn't seem possible that she might never see Niccolò again except on film.

At least she had that.

After the premiere was over, Ruby walked out with Joseph, though she still scanned the crowd for Niccolò. At the party after the film, when she saw other cast and crew members she knew, she asked them if they'd seen Niccolò. But no one had seen him since the final wrap party.

Niccolò had truly vanished. And Ruby feared the worst.

THE NEXT MORNING, RUBY REPORTED FOR A PHOTO-SHOOT AT an advertising agency on Madison Avenue, where Joseph had arranged an endorsement for a lipstick. Ravishing Red was a new color planned for holiday parties, so Ruby wore a red dress that showed off her new décolletage. As she posed for the photos, thoughts of Niccolò still filled her mind.

The wardrobe, hair, and makeup stylists made her look much older than her years. Her father would certainly disapprove. His hurtful words still rang in her ears, though she hardly cared anymore. She had to provide for her child.

The next month, Ruby's star shot through the heavens, just as Joseph had predicted. *Roman Holiday* was a huge success, bringing in millions at the box office. When *Diary of a Pioneer Woman*, the film that Ruby had starred in, came out the next week, publicists emphasized that Ruby had been in *Roman Holiday* as an extra, creating more press for the new movie. Ruby moved into a fully furnished studio apartment in Hollywood, where she could be available for auditions and seemingly endless interviews with the press.

By the time her next film, *Forever a Rebel*, came out, the attention intensified, and to Ruby's surprise, people on the street began to recognize her and ask for her autograph. She acted in film after film, sometimes managing only a week or two between jobs. Yet every time she had a break, she took a train to Texas to see Mariangela.

As much as Ruby enjoyed working, she lived for these breaks. Her baby was growing so quickly that Ruby didn't want to miss anything. And yet, she was. On Patricia's watch, Mariangela rolled over and sat up by herself for the first time.

At the end of a short break in December for Christmas, Ruby had to report to San Diego to start shooting a new film. Michael and Patricia drove Ruby to the train station, while she held Mariangela in her arms until they arrived. Reluctantly, Ruby surrendered the little one to Patricia and picked up her purse.

"You'll let me know if she gets sick?" Ruby asked as they walked toward the train platform. She was concerned about Mariangela, fearing she was still fragile. Yet, at eight months old, Mariangela was already developing a strong personality. She cried with gusto and immediately spat out anything she didn't like.

Patricia beamed as Mariangela flung her little arms around her neck. "Of course, I will. But Doc says she's strong now, so you needn't worry."

Ruby wrinkled her nose against the smell of engine grease and waited on the platform while travelers boarded. She held out her arms, saying, "I need one more cuddle from my baby before I go."

Patricia passed Mariangela to Ruby, but as the small child left the safety of Patricia's arms, she began to wail.

"Shh," Ruby said, clutching her. "Mommy loves you, always and forever." She nuzzled her face against Mariangela's neck, fixing the baby's sweet scent in her mind.

Patricia and Michael stood watching. "She'll settle down after you leave," Patricia said. "She's a little tired."

Ruby showered her baby with kisses, then reluctantly returned her to Patricia. Mariangela immediately ceased crying.

Patricia looked apologetic. "She's probably hungry. Don't you worry."

Ruby knew her sister was trying to make her feel less anxious, but she sensed her absences were impacting the bond she'd had with her baby. A wave of guilt crashed over her.

The final boarding call rang out.

Ruby boarded the train with other travelers hurrying on before departure and found the sleeper cabin that Joseph had arranged for her. The whistle screeched above the din, and as the long train began snaking from the station, Ruby struggled to open the window in her compartment. She waved a kid-gloved hand to her little girl, who turned away from her and into the safety of her sister's embrace.

"She's angry at me for leaving," Ruby muttered. She couldn't blame the child.

Still, Ruby had to report for work. She was under contract now and would suffer financial penalties if she didn't report on time. Her schedule was full for the year ahead, which was good because she now had to support her parents and contribute to Patricia and Michael for Mariangela's care. Formula, cloth diapers, glass bottles, and baby equipment. She hadn't thought about how much babies needed. From washing diapers to sterilizing bottles and caring for Mariangela, Ruby realized how much responsibility Patricia had taken on.

Amidst the clacking of its huge steel wheels, the train pulled away. Ruby saw Mariangela steal a glance at her, then turn away again. This little action broke Ruby's heart, and tears pooled in her eyes. Brushing them away, she continued to wave at her daughter until she disappeared from view.

Ruby leaned back against the seat, feeling very much alone. Without Niccolò and Mariangela, her success felt hollow.

Weeping softly, Ruby brought out a handkerchief from her purse. She yearned to spend more time with Mariangela. Compounding the issue, her father was hospitalized with pneumonia. While Harrison's health was improving, Doc Schmidt advised that he scale back his work, warning that if he didn't, his next hospitalization might be his last.

This next film, *Windswept Beach*, would cover the cost of her father's medical care, but she'd need to work all year to make up the shortfall for his inability to tend the ranch and their food production. Ruby would have to pay for help for them, too. With Harrison ill, Mercy couldn't do it all.

Ruby worried that the responsibility of providing for her family would interfere with her ability to see Mariangela. Leaving her baby left an open wound in her heart, and her only solace was that Patricia was there for her. She hated not being there for the milestones in her daughter's young life.

Ruby missed the early months she'd spent with Mariangela, nursing her every two hours, and keeping her baby warm against her body in the sling she tucked under flannel shirts. Now she worried that Mariangela might not even remember her the next time she saw her. Ruby was doing what she had to do, though she couldn't help wonder if Mariangela would forgive her if she ever discovered the truth.

29

Lago di Como, 2010

"$\mathcal{T}$he scenery is breathtaking," Ruby said, peering from the car she'd hired to take her, Ariana, and Alessandro to the *Roman Holiday* production at Teatro Della Vigna. She opened her window to breathe in the scents of the countryside.

As they drew close, the intimate, open-air theater came into view. It was situated on a plateau above the lake and surrounded by terraced vineyards that climbed the hillsides. Lights illuminated the vines, spotlighting burgeoning clusters of grapes. Their scent, warm from the afternoon sun, infused the night air. At one end of the plateau, a stage rose before rows of curved seats, stepped like a perfumer's organ. The effect was dramatic yet intimate.

"*Siamo arrivati,*" the driver said.

"This reminds me of the Hollywood Bowl," Ruby said to Ariana.

She extended her hand to Alessandro, who helped her from the car. She'd always loved attending outdoor concerts at the Hollywood Bowl. There was something magical about enjoying wine and a picnic supper with friends, feeling a soft summer breeze on your face, and sharing an artistic performance under the stars.

Ruby gathered the long skirt of her canary-yellow, bias-cut silk dress and slid from the car. This was one of Ariana's latest designs, and Ruby loved it. The golden hue accented her hair and glowed under the full moon that settled on her shoulders like a spotlight. She wore a long, opera-length strand of pearls with her silver half-heart on a platinum chain.

"We're going to have a grand time tonight," Ruby said, nodding graciously to a group of women who clearly recognized her. They poked each other and smiled knowingly as if they were in on a secret. "We'll enjoy a charming performance, and, I expect, magnificent wines." Alessandro had offered to drive, but Ruby wouldn't hear of it.

As Alessandro hurried to assist Ariana from the car, Ruby noticed the barely concealed passion that sparked between them. She smiled to herself. Besides Ariana's halo of infatuation, she also had a beautiful pregnancy glow that lit her face. And Alessandro could hardly tear his eyes from her. They seemed utterly, unequivocally in love.

Ruby knew that kind of love, and she had prayed Ariana would find it, too.

Ariana had confided in her that Alessandro had made his long-term intentions known. Ruby wasn't surprised because Ariana was such a talented, desirable young woman. And she adored Alessandro's children. Ariana had finally told Alessandro she was pregnant, and Ruby was proud of her for her courageous act.

If anything, Alessandro looked even more besotted with Ariana now.

Alessandro offered his arm to Ruby, and she slid her hand into the crook of his elbow.

"Why, thank you," Ruby said, inclining her head. "You have such impeccable manners." She turned to Ariana, who strolled beside her. "Isn't this lovely? The three of us gathered on such a marvelous night to see my favorite production."

Ariana kissed Ruby's cheek. "Thank you, Auntie. And that dress is magnificent on you. You bring it to life."

"With the right bearing and attitude, even a poor girl can be a queen," Ruby said. "Why, I remember Audrey on the set. Such magnificent posture, grace, and awareness. I learned so much from her. Only later did she tell me she was scared to death, too." She laughed and touched the half-heart pendant.

They made their way toward the front, where Ruby had reserved a box for them. A bottle of wine sat on the table. A card sat beside it with a note written in Italian. *Enjoy the show,* she translated.

"What a thoughtful gesture," Ruby said. A few moments later, a server delivered a tray of cheese and grapes and nuts to their table.

"*Molto benne,*" Alessandro said. "And sparkling water for the lady, *per favore.*"

Ariana slid her hand in his. "I appreciate that."

"I know how to take care of you," Alessandro replied, kissing Ariana's hand.

Ruby loved watching them. They reminded her of the love she had shared with Niccolò. Ruby couldn't follow everything that was said, though Alessandro seemed to know the young man. But then, Alessandro's family had lived here for generations.

"Everything is settled," Alessandro said, glancing at Ariana with a smile.

Ruby perused the program. Without her glasses, she couldn't make out the fine print in the waning light of dusk, and she didn't want to fumble through her purse. Handing the program to Ariana, she said, "Would you put this in your purse, dear? I'd like to look at it later."

Ruby lifted her glass. "To living your finest life," she said, touching their glasses. As she sipped the red wine that Alessandro told them was made from Nebbiolo grapes, she detected hints of cherry and toasted oak, with a honeyed, earthy finish that held the aroma of leather. "Bold, rich, and dry," she said. "Someone made an excellent choice."

"It's one of their finest wines," Alessandro said.

The house lights on the stage dimmed, and Ruby recalled a night, so long ago, when Niccolò held her in his arms. Resting her chin on her hand, she reminisced. "This reminds me of the first time I ever saw an opera. It was on a night such as this in Rome...*Aida* under the stars at Terme di Caracalla, the ancient Roman baths in Rome. Surrounded by beautiful, stylish people, fellow art lovers. It was one of the most magnificent evenings I've ever known."

"Teatro dell'Opera is incredible," Alessandro said. "We should go again. What year was that?"

Ruby smiled. Alessandro was cultured, and she liked that for Ariana. "It was 1952. A magical year for *Aida*." As Ruby glanced around, she had the satisfying sense that her history had come full circle. She was meant to be here now.

Soon, *Vacanze Romane* got underway, and Ruby watched the delightful trio of actors in the parts originated by Audrey Hepburn, Gregory Peck, and Eddie Albert. While the dialog was in Italian, Ruby followed with ease, as she knew the story by heart.

The scene at the café, where Princess Ann careened through the café tables, was delivered with humor and grace. Ruby smiled, recalling the feeling of Niccolò's protective arms around her, so many years ago. Here on the shore of Lake Como, she felt closer to him than she had in years. It was as if his presence lingered here, where they had been the happiest. She pressed her hand to her heart, caressing the simple pendant she wore that represented so much to her. Niccolò would always be the love of her life.

Over the years, she'd had a few romances, but now, looking back, her emotional life was so clear to her. She had only ever loved Niccolò, and she had saved her heart for him.

In the last scene in the palace, the actors were so close that Ruby could see the tears in the Princess Ann's eyes and hear the catch in her voice. Ruby was also impressed with the attention to detail by the costume and set designers. They had replicated even the smallest of details—such as the cut of Princess Ann's dress, and the pot of red geraniums that sat to one side, outside of the camera frame.

Those red flowers... Ruby blinked. Had she imagined that

recollection? Maybe the wine was creating pleasant false memories.

As Princess Ann was making her way down the line of foreign correspondents in the final scene, the spot where Niccolò had stood as an extra behind Gregory Peck drew Ruby's gaze.

She sucked in a breath. Surely her imagination was playing tricks on her. A handsome, older man stood in Niccolò's exact position. The shape of his head and the line of his profile were so familiar. And yet... Perhaps her mind's eye was superimposing her memories on the actor.

Ruby blinked away the sudden tears that rimmed her lashes. Her vision blurred, and by the time her eyes cleared, the actor was gone. In the final scene, the lead male actor playing Gregory's Peck role was alone on the stage.

How well Ruby understood the feelings in that last scene. Every time she watched the film, she felt the same sense of loss. For a brief time, two people had loved each other, even though they could never be together in their real lives.

All around her, cheers erupted, and the audience leapt to its feet. Ruby still felt stunned by her vision. One by one, the actors returned to the stage for a bow, and then, the entire troop assembled to thunderous applause. They acknowledged the musicians that had accompanied them. Next, with great fanfare, the director joined them on the stage. Finally, the applause intensified, and in response, a tall, elegant man with thick silver hair strode onto the stage, his face wreathed with joy.

Ruby blinked. *Is my mind playing tricks?* It was the same man who'd occupied Niccolò's spot in the last scene. If Niccolò had been older, he might have looked very much like this man. Rising unsteadily, she joined in the applause.

As the man turned toward her, his lips parted as if in shock, and he blinked. *Once, twice, three times.* The audience cheers stirred him again, and he pressed a hand to his heart as if registering disbelief. Then, bringing his hand to his lips, he kissed his palm and stretched his hand toward her. His graceful movement was so like one of Niccolò's etched in her memory.

"I think he recognizes you, Aunt Ruby," Ariana whispered. "He's quite handsome."

Ruby's pulse quickened. "Niccolò," she murmured. This man resembled her beloved husband of long ago.

Of course, that was an absurd thought.

And then the man smiled at her, his vivid blue eyes crinkling at the corners just so.

So much like Niccolò. Ruby's eyes blurred at this vision that appeared before her. Was she imagining this?

The actor smiled again, his expression conveying familiarity. Was he merely a fan, an admirer, a man who reminded her of Niccolò? Ruby blinked. But the line of his jaw, the shape of his lips, the angle of his head belied doubt

Her heart pounding, Ruby clutched Alessandro's arm for support. *Could it possibly be?*

Alessandro slid his arm around Ruby, supporting her as she weakened against him. "Are you well?" he asked.

"For a moment, I thought…" Or was she merely hallucinating what she yearned to see?

Ariana hurried to her. "Aunt Ruby," she cried, supporting her other arm.

Overwhelmed with shock at what couldn't possibly be, and yet, somehow, inexplicably was, Ruby teetered. Grasping ineffectively at the strong arms that held her, she felt herself slipping away into a void of muffled darkness.

30

Texas Hill Country, 1954

"That's a wrap for today," the director called out on the set of *Windswept Beach*.

Ruby swept up the edge of her cobalt-blue sarong costume and hurried across the sand toward her trailer. She had a private trailer to change in now—the result of a request in the latest contract Joseph had negotiated for her.

Even though filming had been extended on this current movie—a romantic comedy set at a hotel in Laguna Beach—she'd insisted that she needed to go to Texas. It was Mariangela's birthday, and she couldn't miss it. The director hadn't been happy, but it was in her contract. Her agent had also insisted on that contract clause for her, without revealing the reason.

"Ruby, wait up," another actress called out.

"Not now, Nancy." Ruby slipped through throngs of cast members, evading the other actress, who was obsessed about picking apart her performance, as well as Ruby's. Ever since Nancy had started taking the diet pills the set doctor had prescribed to reduce her weight, she'd been jittery and nervous. She exhausted Ruby with her incessant talking.

The morals clause was still intact in the contract, so Ruby had to be extra cautious about revealing anything about Mariangela. A weight clause was another humiliating addition to the agreement. Every week, a nurse conducted a weigh-in of the actresses on set. Their weight could not fluctuate more than five pounds up or down from their beginning weight. Ruby carefully managed her food intake, heaping her plate with vegetables and passing up bread. When she had the time, brisk walks on the beach helped, too.

However, Nancy had tipped the scales into the prohibited area. The doctor prescribed a medication that made Nancy even more nervous than before. The poor young woman barely slept, but Ruby had to focus on her job and not be swept into Nancy's drama.

After the success of her movies, Ruby was working nonstop now. She'd wrapped a film on location in San Diego, shot several commercials in Los Angeles, and was currently working on this movie in Laguna Beach. And the year was barely a quarter gone.

Ruby rushed into her trailer and fiddled with the lock on the door. It was temperamental; she'd even been locked in her trailer one day. She'd crawled out the window to make it to the set on time.

Safely inside, Ruby pulled out the shopping bags she'd hidden in the cupboards and behind the sofa. She'd been buying gifts for Mariangela and had to wrap them and pack before she left in the morning.

Ruby unfurled pink wrapping paper and placed a stuffed bear in the center. Just as she was cutting the paper, the door burst open. Ruby whirled around, trying to hide the gifts.

"Why didn't you stop when I called you?" Nancy said, stepping inside. "How do you think I did today? And I have to know why you chose to deliver that last monologue as you did." She tapped her fingers anxiously. The nails were bitten to the quick.

The director wouldn't be happy about that.

"Nancy, I told you I couldn't talk. I'm busy." Ruby was horrified. Of all the people to interrupt her. She'd heard that Nancy was jealous because she'd wanted Ruby's lead role but had been cast in a smaller supporting role.

Leaning around her, Nancy's eyes widened. "Baby gifts! Whose baby?"

"My sister's," Ruby said smoothly. "I'm catching the train tomorrow, and I have to wrap these for my niece." She wanted to make that point very clear.

"You're taking time off for your niece's birthday?"

"We're very close." Ruby turned around to hide her flushed face from Nancy. "Now, please go. You should catch up on your rest."

Nancy hesitated, her eyes roving over the toys Ruby had bought. "See you when you get back."

Ruby expelled a sigh of frustration.

EAGER TO SEE MARIANGELA, RUBY BURST THROUGH THE FRONT door of Patricia and Michael's home. "Where's my little sweetheart?" she called out.

"Patricia is probably in the nursery with Mary," Michael said, following her inside. "She was bathing her when I left for the train station."

"Mary?" Ruby hadn't heard her daughter called that name before, and she wasn't sure she liked it. A birthday cake on the kitchen table caught Ruby's eye. Patricia must have made it, which was thoughtful, except that Ruby had planned to make Mariangela's first cake. She hid her disappointment, but still, it was there.

Her high-heel pumps clicked across the pine floors as she hurried toward the nursery. Having just stepped off the train, Ruby still wore her light gray traveling suit with a burgundy silk blouse. Since she was becoming well-known, Joseph insisted she maintain her appearance wherever she went. Thankfully, that wasn't necessary on the ranch. When Ruby walked into the nursery filled with stuffed animals and toys that she'd sent to Mariangela, Patricia looked up.

"Aren't you fancy today?" Patricia said. She was holding Mariangela, who wore a soft pink sweater with a matching bow. Strands of reddish-brown hair framed her little face. "Mary is pretty fancy, too. I dressed her up for you."

"I heard you just had a bath," Ruby said, cooing to her daughter, whose bright blue eyes gleamed with life—just as her father's had. A lump formed in her throat at the memories.

"And lunch," Patricia said. "Be careful."

Ruby held out her arms, but her daughter began crying and turned back to Patricia, burying her face.

"There, there, it's your mommy," Patricia said, but the child wailed each time she tried to pass her to Ruby. "I guess she's just a little fussy now."

"How long has she been this way?" Ruby asked. Mariangela had grown so much since she'd seen her at Christmas.

"Well, she just started, but don't let that worry you."

It did, though. Ruby ached to hold her child, but the little girl simply refused to go to her, clutching at Patricia's blouse and wailing as if her mother didn't love her. But oh, she did, and so very, very much. Disappointment flooded Ruby. The train had taken three days' travel from Laguna Beach in California, and she'd spent that time anxiously waiting to hold Mariangela. She had a suitcase full of birthday presents, too.

Patricia tickled Mariangela's chin until the baby giggled. "That's better, Mary." To Ruby, she added, "We'll try again in a minute."

Ruby shrugged off her jacket and sat on a bench at the foot of the bed. "Why are you calling her 'Mary' now?"

"Michael was having a hard time saying Mariangela. It's so foreign-sounding. He thinks Mary with a 'y' is cute. It's more American, too."

Ruby was perturbed. "But that's exactly the point. Her name is Italian. It's to honor her father." She pressed her lips together in a thin line. "It's not that hard to say."

"I think it's a lovely name, but you know how people are in these parts. They like simple names. Joe, Bud, Jane. See?"

Crossing her arms, Ruby said, "If I'd wanted to name her Mary, I would have. Her name is Mariangela."

"Of course, it is," Patricia said in a soothing voice. "You've had a long trip, and I know you're tired. Please don't get upset over a silly nickname. Kids grow up with all sorts of nicknames. Like you did."

"Mari with an 'i,' then. But not Mary with a 'y.'" Ruby had to give in a little, but she still wanted her daughter to have a connection to her heritage. Yet, Michael meant no harm. Maybe his tongue did get twisted on Mariangela.

Finally, Mari settled down again, and Patricia sat beside Ruby, sliding the child into her arms. Mari seemed happy now, and Ruby sighed with relief.

"I'll get a clean towel for you to throw over that beautiful blouse." She stood to open a bureau draw. "Real silk, is it?"

"A gift from David, who supervised the wardrobe in my last film." Ruby nuzzled her face against Mariangela's face and hair, reveling in her sweet baby scent. Her hair had grown, and it was feather-soft.

"Is David someone special in your life?"

"He is, but not that way. I don't think he's available." Ruby didn't say exactly why, but she'd heard that David had a secret boyfriend. It didn't bother her, and maybe not Patricia, but their father would disapprove of such a friendship.

As Patricia opened a drawer, it fell forward, spilling its contents. She knelt to scoop up Mari's clothes and cloth diapers. "Maybe there's someone nice for you around here. As a matter of fact, I met a nice young man at church. He's the new assistant pastor."

"And poor as a church mouse, I'll bet." When Patricia nodded, Ruby added, "I couldn't afford him."

"I suppose you're right," Patricia said. "We've had so many expenses this past year. It's hard to get ahead, but we're so grateful to you and what you're doing. If it weren't for you, our parents would have surely lost the ranch. We would've had a hard time, too." Patricia tucked the clothing into the drawer and then handed a soft baby towel to her.

As Ruby reached for the towel, Mari spit up on her shoulder, a second before Ruby could drape the fabric over her blouse.

"Oh, dear," Patricia said. "That silk is a magnet for spit-up."

"I don't really care." Ruby dabbed her silk blouse. She just wanted to be with her baby.

"It happens." Patricia reached for Mari. "I'll take her while you clean up."

"It's okay," Ruby insisted. "I just want to hold her. I've been waiting so long to do this."

Patricia smiled. "I understand."

The two sisters chatted for a while, and Patricia told her all about Mari's progress. Mari seemed to grow used to Ruby again —almost as if she remembered the months spent cuddled next to her mother in a sling. After a while, the baby fell asleep, and Ruby put her down for a nap.

After tiptoeing from the nursery, Patricia said, "Mama and Daddy will be here soon. I told them you might want to freshen up first."

"I would like to change," Ruby said.

"Spring has come early this year, so we'll have the party on the back porch," Patricia said. "Michael screened in the downstairs porch and added electricity so that when Mari starts walking, she can play there. It'll keep the mosquitos away. Last year she got itchy red welts on her tender skin."

"Thanks," Ruby said. She hadn't heard about that. It must have happened when she'd been in New York.

"I hate to mention it, but the porch is for Mari," Patricia said. "Once we began building, it cost more than we thought it would." Patricia fidgeted with the edge of her collar. "Do you think—"

"I'll take care of it," Ruby said. "Let me know how much you'll need."

After Ruby changed into a blue-checked cotton dress, she set up Mari's birthday party on the new back porch. Ruby had brought a pink tablecloth and party napkins and a banner that read *Happy Birthday*. She piled wrapped toys beside the yellow, vinyl-covered high chair.

The rear screen-door banged. Mercy and Harrison arrived with their arms filled with packages.

"Oh, my Ruby," her mother cried. "Look at how you've changed." After placing her packages on the table, she held her arms open to Ruby.

"I've missed you, Mama," Ruby said, hugging her mother, who seemed thinner than she'd recalled.

"Welcome back," her father said, approaching her with awkward open arms under her mother's watchful eye.

As her parents exchanged a look, it was apparent to Ruby that her mother had engineered his forgiveness. She wondered what kind of force Mercy had exerted. Sometimes her mother stopped cooking for Harrison or sent him to sleep on the couch. Or worse. Had her mother threatened to leave him?

Ruby hadn't spoken to her father since before Mari was born. Mercy had been pleading with her to forgive her father for his anger. Ruby was trying, but she couldn't forget what he'd called her or how he'd threatened her mother. Although Ruby couldn't change the past, she hoped their future would be amicable, especially for Mari. She let her father give her a brief hug, and she played her part as well, stifling her anger and discomfort and trying to recall better times. Yet she would remain forever on guard.

A small sigh of relief escaped Mercy's lips.

Harrison shifted from one foot to another, his eyes downcast. "We sure appreciate what you're doing for us," he said, his ego deflated.

Mercy grasped her hands. "I don't know what we would've done, especially with your father so sick. Running a ranch is hard work at his age."

Her father frowned. "I'm not that old, Mercy. I'll be better soon."

Ruby squeezed her mother's hands. "Don't worry. I'm working a lot this year." Sensing the tension, Ruby said, "Can we wake Mari for her party yet?"

"Let's go get her," Patricia said.

Ruby propped up Mari in the high chair, and the little girl giggled and waved her arms. They sang to her, and Ruby helped her blow out a single candle. Patricia cut the cake and gave Mari a small piece, which the little girl smashed into her mouth, smearing frosting on her cheeks and laughing hysterically.

"Isn't she precious?" Mercy clapped her hands at Mari's antics. "It's so wonderful to have a little one around again."

Michael slid his arm around Patricia. They both looked so

proud of Mari. "It's hard to believe she's a year old already," he said. "She's made us so happy, especially my beautiful wife."

Ruby watched them, thinking how fulfilled her sister seemed. Patricia looked serene, and Michael doted on her. They tended to Mari together, and Ruby was so touched. Even though the separation from her daughter hurt, she'd made the right decision for them.

Ruby took photographs and then wiped Mari's face and hands. She helped her little girl unwrap her first present, a set of brightly colored wooden building blocks in red, blue, and green. "I hope she likes them," Ruby said.

"Oh, she does," Mercy said. "Michael just made some blocks for her."

Patricia quickly added, "They're perfect. A child can never have too many blocks."

Yet another thing I've missed, Ruby thought, feeling left out of Mari's young life. She reached for another gift.

While Ruby helped Mari unwrap her presents, the telephone rang. Michael went to answer it.

"That was your agent," Michael said when he returned. "He wants you to call him at once. An emergency of some sort. But I told him this was a special day, and you shouldn't be bothered."

"Is he still on the phone?"

"No, I hung up."

Though she was concerned about the call, Ruby appreciated her brother-in-law's thoughtfulness. "Thank you, Michael. But I'll need to telephone Joseph today. After the party."

An emergency. Ruby wondered what that could mean. As soon as she could slip away, she dialed the operator from the telephone she'd had installed in her bedroom.

Ruby heard several clicks on the line as the long-distance call went through. "Hello, Joseph?"

"Ruby! Thank heavens you called." Joseph's frantic words tumbled out. "A gossip magazine is running a story tomorrow about a teen star's illegitimate baby."

A chill coursed through Ruby. "Not about me?"

"Unfortunately, yes. We must respond to this story right away.

It's a publicity disaster. I told you not to let anything about your little issue get out. What the hell happened?"

"I don't know," Ruby cried. "I haven't said a word to anyone."

Suddenly, Ruby remembered. *Nancy.* Could the actress have betrayed her to the press?

Yes. Nancy must have called a tabloid right away. With a sinking feeling, Ruby remembered an interview she'd given last year. She had mentioned her sister and her husband. The reporter had asked if they had children. Ruby had told her they didn't. Could Nancy have remembered and leapt to a conclusion? Or maybe she was trying to steal Ruby's part.

Angry tears sprang to Ruby's eyes. "But it's not true."

"That doesn't matter," Joseph said. "It's going to hit the newsstands. And I got a call from the studio. They're threatening to invoke the morals clause of your contract."

Ruby flopped onto the bed. "What does that mean?"

"Essentially, you're fired."

Panic gripped Ruby. "They can't do that," she cried. "The film is almost finished."

"They'll hire another actress and reshoot your part," Joseph said. "Not the first time this has happened."

"And my next film?"

"Kiss your career good-bye. Unless you can disprove this, no one will touch you, even after the scandal dies."

Ruby shot up on the bed. "But there is no scandal! Niccolò and I were married in Italy. My baby has a father."

"Well, where is he?" Joseph asked. "Now would be a good time for him to make an entrance."

"I don't know. I think…he might have died," Ruby managed to say, her voice cracking with a gut-wrenching sob. Reflexively, she wrapped her fingers around her silver pendant.

"Great," Joseph said, huffing in exasperation. "The guy's dead. What about proof? Like a marriage certificate?"

"I don't know. Niccolò took care of all that."

"Was anyone else at your wedding? Were any pictures taken?"

Ruby had used up the film her mother had sent with her in Rome. "I'm sorry, no. It was just us."

"And a priest from Central Casting, no doubt." Joseph cursed on the line.

Ruby drew a hand over her face. And two elderly witnesses. She had no idea how to contact any of them. Her heart was pounding. *What will I do?*

Ruby gripped the telephone. "Joseph, please, I can't lose this contract. I have to keep working. For my family, please. I'll return to the set on the next train and go right to work." Her parents still needed help, as did Mari and Patricia and Michael. Feeling like her head was about to explode, Ruby pressed fingers to her throbbing temple. She had to keep working, now more than ever.

"Okay, okay, okay," Joseph said. "We need to explain this away. We need some kind of proof that the baby isn't yours."

"But she is!"

"You're not listening to me. There are two parts to this issue. First, an illegitimate baby. Second, your age. You're a teenager. You're barely eighteen years old now, and you were seventeen when this occurred."

"But my passport says—"

"Vivienne confirmed your real birth date to a *Modern Screen* gossip columnist. She'll probably cash a tidy check."

"My aunt did that?" Anger shot through Ruby, and she twisted the telephone cord in her fist.

Joseph sighed. "Don't act so shocked. Vivienne hears a lot at that beauty shop. She trades in gossip. So, who's taking care of the kid now?"

"My sister."

"Please tell me she's older."

"Patricia's twenty-five."

"Is she married?"

"To a sweet guy. A rancher." Ruby feared where this conversation was going.

"We have to save your reputation," Joseph said. "If they claim her, this might work. Don't go anywhere. I'll call you right back."

Ruby clutched the phone, yelling into it. "No, Joseph, no, no, no—"

"Don't be selfish. You'll thank me for this, Ruby."

Click.

Ruby's heart cracked at the thought of what Joseph was proposing. Torn between being a mother and needing to work to support her family, waves of anguish and fury crashed through her. Not yet nineteen, Ruby was carrying the weight of two families and ranches amid devastating drought conditions.

Sobbing, she let her tears fall, soaking her pillow. Joseph was sure Ruby would be fired and deemed untouchable by other studios. Or Ruby could quit acting and hide from the scandal.

But her family relied on her income now. Without it, her parents, along with Patricia and Michael, would lose their property and livelihoods. Farming and ranching were all they knew. Despite their prayers and grit, water was becoming scarce, and the price of feed had tripled. She shuddered to think what would become of her family.

Ruby had to keep working. She couldn't plunge her family into foreclosure and leave them homeless, adrift without skills.

But the cost of that decision was her beloved daughter.

Ruby cried out at the injustice. At the heavens stingy with rain. At a heartless system that valued the appearance of propriety over people's lives. At the talent she'd been given that would extract the ultimate price.

All she dreamed of was another chance at the life she'd glimpsed on the shores of Lake Como, nestled into the curve of Niccolò's arms and filled with love.

But her husband was gone. *Almost eighteen months.* To imagine that Niccolò had heartlessly left her to care for their child and struggle through the consequences was so devastating that if that were true, her anger and anguish would be so great that her heart would surely cease beating.

Niccolò *had* to be dead.

That was the only way Ruby could still love him—and not go insane.

She choked back a cry. Her only consolation was that her daughter would thrive in Patricia's embrace, in the boughs of a love so strong that Ruby knew, without a doubt, that her sister and her husband would claim Mariangela as their own and swear to it when necessary.

Patricia and Michael would salvage Ruby's career and reputation, though the heartrending loss of her precious, strong-willed daughter would be Ruby's to bear.

Her excruciatingly painful decision made, Ruby scrubbed her face and pushed herself from the bed, vowing that she would never succumb to injustice or heartbreak again.

31

Lago di Como, 2010

*M*uffled sounds reverberated in Ruby's ears as she fought her way to the surface of consciousness. The constellations seemed to spin above her. Her body felt so heavy she could hardly move.

Then, she realized she was flat on her back, staring at the stars above her.

"What happened?" Ruby struggled to sit up. "Ariana, are you here?"

A firm hand slid under her back, supporting her. "Try not to move," Alessandro said.

As Ruby's vision cleared, a woman she didn't know came into view.

"Relax, I'm a doctor," the woman said. "Don't try to get up. You fainted. You're at the amphitheater with your niece. Do you have any medical conditions I should know about?"

Ruby shook her head. That wasn't anybody's business but her own, and she was perfectly healthy. "I thought I saw someone I knew…long ago. But that's impossible."

Ariana knelt beside her. "Auntie, you weren't mistaken. I think you and Alessandro's uncle once knew each other."

But how can this be? Ruby saw a tall man—*Niccolò?*—come into view. Bright blue eyes, only slightly dimmed with age, held her in such a warm and loving gaze.

"I didn't mean to give you a fright," he said. The stage light behind him formed a halo around his thick silver hair. "Do you remember me?"

Ruby's heart ached with a torrent of emotion. With a wavering hand, she reached out to touch him. "How could I ever forget the man I married?" she murmured.

Niccolò clasped Ruby's hand in his and brought it to his lips, kissing her fingers as he had done so many years ago.

With her eyes welling with tears, she motioned him to come closer. "I thought you had died," she said, her voice catching on her words.

The doctor interjected, "*Scusi, Signora,* can you sit up now?"

With Niccolò's assistance, Ruby managed to sit upright. She glanced behind her, realizing that Alessandro had taken off his jacket to place under her head. "Oh, your lovely blazer is soiled, Alessandro." She shook her head. "How can Niccolò be your uncle?"

"My mother is his sister," Alessandro said.

Ruby turned to Niccolò, still feeling confused and overwhelmed.

"Valeria," Niccolò said. "Alessandro is her son. I believe you met her at our home in Rome. When we had dinner outside."

His voice was even more melodic than it had been when he was younger—and it still thrilled her. As Ruby took a deep breath, the fog in her mind lifted. "And you made *osso buco* and *risotto alla Milanese* with saffron. Showing off and proving that you could actually cook."

Ariana and the doctor exchanged looks of relief.

Niccolò laughed softly. "I'm flattered you remembered."

"I haven't forgotten a thing." The precious memories she'd strung like pearls to wear close to her heart sprang to life in the eyes of the man who held her hand.

With a questioning frown, Ariana leaned in. "Aunt Ruby, did you say you were married?"

Ruby sighed. "Did I say that?" She touched Ariana's hand. "Later, dear. I promise we'll talk."

Ariana pressed a cup of water to Ruby's lips while Alessandro said a few words to the doctor, who was still observing her.

Niccolò gazed at her. "Come into my home and relax. It's right here, and I have a golf cart that we can use. Unless the doctor thinks you should be examined right away."

"Maybe you should go to the hospital," Ariana said.

"Absolutely not," Ruby said, struggling to stand. "Niccolò just gave me a shock, that was all." She straightened and lifted her chin. "Although I would like to rest before we leave." She squeezed Niccolò's hand, and he helped her to her feet.

As Ruby stood, a small crowd of people who had gathered around broke out in polite applause.

Ruby glanced around and waved at them. "I didn't know I had an audience."

Niccolò chuckled. "You've always known how to steal a scene —even an opening night finale."

With a handsome man on either side, Ruby walked triumphantly to a golf cart parked by a row of vines. Ariana scooped up her purse and followed.

Niccolò helped her into his home, a renovated farmhouse situated on a small knoll amidst rows of grapevines. Once inside, they sat at a large wooden table, and he brought out a bottle of wine and a carafe of water. He also placed a loaf of bread with olive oil and a chunk of cheese on the table.

"Make yourself comfortable," Niccolò said. "Maybe you'd like something to nibble on. Have you eaten?"

"I'm not hungry," she said. "Although I could sure use a glass of wine. I'm still in shock that you're actually here with me." She turned to Ariana. "Are you sure I'm not dead?"

Ariana laughed nervously. "No, but I'm worried about you. Do you think it's a good idea to drink?"

"Wine calms the nerves," Ruby said, still trembling. "And if I'm not dead, I don't see why not."

Ruby glanced around the room while Niccolò poured the

wine. The ambiance of the old farmhouse had been preserved in the stone fireplace and rustic beams, while modern appliances filled the kitchen. Herbs grew in colorful, hand-painted pots in a bay window.

A thought gripped her. Had Niccolò married and had children? She shouldn't be surprised, though. So many years had passed.

"This wine is from the grapes we grow here," Niccolò said. "It's from my special reserve."

Ruby brought the glass to her nose, inhaling. "This is the wine we had earlier tonight. And it's utterly divine." She took a sip. "So, you've met Ariana, my beautiful niece."

A smile touched Niccolò's mouth. "Not formally, but yes, while you were languishing in the orchestra section."

"I see your sense of humor is still intact after all these years," Ruby said, arching an eyebrow. "Ariana, Alessandro, would you excuse us? Niccolò and I have some catching up to do."

"Let's go outside," Niccolò said. "I have a swing that overlooks the vineyards and the lake. We can sip our wine and talk." He held his hand out to Ruby, and they made their way outside, leaving Ariana and Alessandro gazing after them in surprise.

Niccolò helped Ruby ease onto a swing suspended from wooden beams above a tiled patio. Laughter floated through the air as the last of the theater guests and cast members left the amphitheater on the hillside beneath them. A soft breeze from the lake lifted strands of hair from her forehead. With it was the earthy aroma of rich soil and ripening grapes.

"This is a beautiful location," Ruby said as Niccolò sat beside her. "How did you come to find it?"

"It found me," he replied. "It was my grandfather's on my mother's side. When he passed away—far too young—he left it to me. Guiseppe Sala. Thus, Sala-Mancini wines." He showed her the label on the bottle. "He knew I would keep the property in the family, and he'd always dreamed of creating a theater among the vines. I don't know if you recall, but he was the one who encouraged me to follow my passion for acting."

Ruby lifted her glass. "And did you continue?"

"In Italy, yes," he said. "Some in England, too, while I

attended university. I discovered that I had more talent for producing films, so that's what I did for many years. Still do, sometimes. But mostly, I watch the vines grow and plan the summer theater season. I leave acting to the young and ambitious."

"That's a lie," Ruby said. "I saw you on stage."

Niccolò chuckled. "Ah, yes. I thought it would be fun to reprise my role in *Roman Holiday*."

Ruby swirled the wine in her glass. "I've watched it so many times that I know it by heart."

"I remember our scene at the café where I saved your life from a runaway Vespa." Niccolò touched her glass with his. "To those wonderful times. I wish they had never ended."

"They didn't have to." For a moment, she hesitated in anticipation of the topic they were both avoiding, but when she saw the frown on his face, she forged ahead.

"What I don't understand is why you never tried to reach me again," Ruby said. "Even years later, you could have found me through my agent or publicist or any studio I'd worked for." Hadn't he been a little curious when she'd written that she was pregnant?

Niccolò covered her hand with his, which still felt as it had years ago. Maybe a little rougher, but just as warm and loving.

"But I did come for you," he said. "Just as I'd promised."

Ruby doubted that. "When?"

"In December of 1952. My grandfather gave me the money to travel. I'd written to you, telling you that I would arrive in December, but I never heard from you. Your letters just stopped coming."

"So did yours," Ruby shot back. "I only received two from you." She still recalled every word of those letters—and how hurt she'd been when he didn't write again.

"But I wrote many more to you," he said, clearly confused.

Ruby had to ask. "Do you recall anything *special* in one of my letters?"

"I don't know what you mean," Niccolò said. "I still have both the ones you sent."

Ruby didn't understand what could have happened to their

correspondence. "In December, I was filming a western in New Mexico, *Diary of a Pioneer Woman.* After that, I went home to Texas."

Niccolò frowned. "On the first of December, I went to your apartment in Hollywood and talked to your aunt, Vivienne."

"Impossible." Ruby's pulse throbbed, and she took another sip of wine. *Why would he lie about this?* "Vivienne would have told me if you'd been there."

Niccolò pressed her hand to his chest. "I can tell you everything about your aunt and the apartment. That blue couch where you slept. The porcelain roosters she collected. The pink petunias in the window boxes."

"How...?" Ruby felt the blood draining from her face, and she searched for explanations. "Maybe you saw pictures in a fan magazine..."

"I went into the bathroom and saw a shampoo," he said. "White porcelain, blue lid. Lustre-Crème."

"That was a popular shampoo," Ruby said weakly. "I even did a print ad for the brand." Along with Lana Turner, Loretta Young, Maureen O'Hara, and so many other actresses.

Niccolò went on. "You'd left a yellow cotton scarf that you'd worn to Lake Como. I couldn't resist; I took it because I wanted something of yours." He sighed. "I know I shouldn't have, but I thought I'd see you again and give it back to you."

Ruby recalled asking her aunt for that scarf. Vivienne had hotly denied having it. "I thought I'd lost that scarf. It wasn't worth much to anyone but us."

Niccolò lifted a corner of his mouth. "If you want it back, it's inside."

Aunt Vivienne. Ruby felt her chest constrict with growing anger —though not at Niccolò.

"Vivienne told me you were filming out of town," Niccolò said. "And I told her how much in love we were, and that I would wait for you. That seemed to make her angry. She told me that you never wanted to see me again. Vivienne said you thought you'd made a mistake, and you wanted to forget me."

"Never," Ruby cried.

Gently, Niccolò brushed her hair over her shoulder. "I

refused to believe it, too. When I questioned Vivienne, she said she didn't know when you'd be back, so I stayed at a nearby motel. For a week, I walked to the apartment every day and knocked on the door to see if you'd returned. And then, on Saturday morning, she was gone. The apartment was empty."

Ruby drew her hands over her face. "By the time I finished filming, my aunt had moved. She'd told me that her landlord had kicked her out, and she needed more money for rent, so I gave it to her."

"Vivienne never told me she was moving," Niccolò said. "But I spoke to a neighbor who said she'd packed and left with no forwarding address. I even went to Paramount and talked someone into giving me your address, but it was the same one. I had no way of finding you." Niccolò's voice caught. "I was thoroughly devastated. I didn't want to accept that you'd changed your mind, that you didn't want to see me again, but finally, I had no choice."

Ruby gazed up at him. "But my agent…"

"I thought of that, too, but I only knew him as Joseph. I couldn't locate him," Niccolò said. "And you never gave me your address in Texas. Anyway, by then, my money had run out, and I had to ask my grandfather for a return ticket to Rome. I was completely humiliated." He leaned his head back. "For a long time, I didn't want to live without you."

His words struck Ruby's heart, and she could hardly speak.

Ruby recalled that after she'd become successful, Vivienne had often asked for money, citing how she'd given her a place to live when Ruby had first arrived in Hollywood. Though Ruby gave her money, she had never forgotten how her aunt had cussed her out over the baby. She could still hear her words. *Stupid girl!* And then there was the *Modern Screen* disaster. In the end, Vivienne had died a broken, bitter woman.

Ruby gazed over the vineyards. Considering that Vivienne had left for California—also pregnant—when her boyfriend spurned her, Ruby could understand why she'd done it. *Pure jealousy.*

"I never knew any of this," Ruby said. "My aunt had a lot of problems, and later I realized she was envious of me, even then.

Enough to thwart my chance for love and destroy our marriage."

And to deny a baby of her father, Ruby thought bitterly.

"I am so sorry I didn't try again," Niccolò said, smoothing his hand over hers. "Finally, I had to accept what I only knew as the truth. I became severely depressed, so my grandfather brought me here to recover. When I was feeling better, he sent me to England to study."

As tears filled her eyes, Ruby bowed her head. *Niccolò had suffered rejection, too.* She wiped her eyes and raised her face to his. "I should have tried to find you again, but when I didn't hear from you…" She dabbed her cheeks and went on. "In your letter, you said you were working in construction."

"I did," Niccolò said. "I left Rome to work on a new building in Milan with my friend. I sent the address to you, and I wrote many times, but I never received any more letters."

Ruby pressed a hand to her chest. "And I thought you'd had an accident and imagined you'd died. Because I couldn't face the alternative—that you didn't want to see me again."

Or our baby, she thought. How could she tell him this now? And yet, it was lies that had separated them, almost forever. She would not do that to him.

"That explains why you were so shocked when you saw me on stage," Niccolò said gently. "I was stunned, too. We have so much time to make up for."

Ruby nodded. "Did you reconcile with your father?" She recalled the argument that Niccolò and his father had about their marriage.

"Eventually," Niccolò said. "He'd been right, as far as I knew. I was so devastated that I think he finally felt sorry for me."

Ruby touched Niccolò's hand, recalling how he'd once caressed her youthful body with those hands. *And vice versa.* She swallowed hard. "Did you ever marry again?"

Niccolò raised his brow with surprise. "I've been married all these years."

Ruby's heart plummeted, though she tried not to show it. "To whom?"

Lifting her hand, he brushed his lips across her skin. "To you, my darling. Though I suppose I should ask if you'll have me again." His voice was older and deeper, but his words hadn't changed.

Niccolò was just as romantic as before. She lifted her lips to his in a soft, tentative kiss. At once, Ruby felt seventeen again, and so in love that the rest of the world ceased to exist. She recalled their idyllic days in Varenna and the feelings of love and exhilaration that had been her constant companions through the years.

Ruby pulled away. She wasn't seventeen anymore. It was one thing to have thoughts that brought comfort, but it was quite another to upheave her life at this late stage.

Of all the contingency planning Ruby had done over the years—life insurance, health insurance, pension funds, investments—never had she considered that Niccolò would rise from the grave and ask for her hand again.

Ruby smiled at him through misty eyes. "I think it's too late for us, my darling."

Niccolò shook his head. "Maybe too late to start that family we'd planned on, but not too late to grow old together. Unless, of course, you have someone else in your life."

"I've never loved anyone as I did you," Ruby said.

"I'm almost sorry to hear that," Niccolò said in a tender voice. "A woman like you should have married, had children."

His sweet comment sliced through Ruby. "How do you know I didn't?"

"I never received a request for a divorce. And, painful as it was for me, it wasn't too hard to follow the brilliant career and personal life of the world-famous Ruby Raines."

"The studio press department supplied most of that material, but you're right," she said. "I never married again."

Ruby lowered her eyes. She'd only half-addressed his comment. Her head was already spinning from seeing Niccolò and processing the details he'd shared—which were undoubtedly true.

Looking up, Ruby said, "I remember the night we told your parents we were married and how angry your father was. He advised you to annul the marriage. Why didn't you?"

Niccolò drew a deep breath. "My father insisted I fill out the paperwork, which I did. He thought an annulment would ease my mind and give me a fresh start." Reliving his memories, he wiped his eyes. "Except that I couldn't bring myself to sign the final documents. As long as you held my heart, it didn't matter what a piece of paper said. As you became more famous, I thought that someday you would call and ask for your freedom."

A wistful smile crossed his face, and Niccolò took her hand. "Or even ask to see me again. Until then, I still had a chance. My father never understood, but fortunately, my parents had many other grandchildren. The years passed, and the pain subsided. Finally, our love became a bittersweet memory. I still have the papers. If you want me to sign them, I will."

Listening to Niccolò, Ruby choked up. She couldn't answer him. He had suffered more than she'd ever imagined. How could she possibly tell him that she'd given away their precious child? Would this be too much for him now?

In the silence between them, Ruby thought about Niccolò's story of anguish. She shared his pain. She understood how devastating rejection was—she'd thought he had rejected her. In retrospect, Ruby wished that she had returned to Italy to search for him, but at the time, she didn't have the strength to return only to confirm his abandonment. The mind had a strange way of coping with what it couldn't handle to avoid a breakdown. Accepting his death was less painful than accepting his denial of her. Work kept her busy, and when she finally had time, too much time had passed.

Or so she'd thought.

Niccolò slid his arm over her shoulders, and she leaned into him, cherishing his presence. Still, he had a right to know that he had a daughter. Even if he never spoke to her again. Ruby cleared her throat.

"Would you like to retrace our steps in Varenna?" she asked.

"I'd like that very much," he replied, tilting his head to touch hers. "Those were the happiest days of my life."

"Mine, too," Ruby said. She hoped he'd still feel that way afterward.

32

Lago di Como, 2010

The sun hadn't been up long, and Ruby was having coffee on the terrace, enjoying the fresh morning *Tivano* breezes from Valtellina and the north. Her mind was full of Niccolò. She could scarcely believe he was alive and living on the shores of Lake Como. And that their love had endured the distance of time.

Sipping her coffee, she watched the early ferry cut through the water from Varenna to Bellagio. The morning bells of Chiesa di San Giorgio tolled in the distance, and the scent of honeysuckle drifted on the breeze, just as on the day they'd married.

Knowing that Niccolò was alive, Ruby had hardly slept. Adrenaline surged through her, and she felt the years melt away.

Watching the golden orioles flitting among the trees, Ruby smiled. Before they had parted last night, Niccolò promised to call her at noon today. *I don't think either of us will sleep much tonight,* he'd told her, as he held her in his arms on the swing at his farmhouse among the grapevines.

"*Scusi,* Signora Ruby," Livia said as she stepped onto the

terrace from the kitchen. "A woman is at the door. She says she is your niece. Mari?"

Ruby bolted upright. "Mari is here?" It wasn't like the perennially scheduled Mari to show up unannounced. "Don't wake Ariana, but when you hear her rustling in her room, warn her that her mother is here. I'll talk to Mari first. Let her know that." Ruby rushed from the terrace to the front door.

"My dear Mari," Ruby cried, swinging the door open. "Come in, come in."

Mari stood at the door dressed in black, looking worn and frazzled, no doubt from an overnight transatlantic flight.

"Hello, Aunt Ruby," Mari said. "Do you have any coffee? What I had on the flight was dreadful."

"Of course, put your things down there. Livia will see to them." Ruby noted how thin Mari was. She'd always worked out hard, but she looked haggard. "I wish I'd known you were coming."

"I booked the flight yesterday," Mari said, efficiently propping her designer purse and a laptop bag on top of her matching suitcase. "You said you wanted to see me. Sorry if I'm late, but I was having a tough time at work."

"I'm so glad you came." Ruby hugged Mari, and she was met with a limp embrace. "Let's get your coffee. We have breakfast, too, if you're hungry."

Mari followed her to the terrace and flopped sullenly onto a chair. Livia hurried out with a large cup of coffee and a pot for refills.

"Thank God," Mari said, cupping her hands around the earthenware mug.

"I'm glad you managed to take time from work," Ruby said, easing into the conversation she knew was coming.

Mari cringed. "I got fired two weeks ago, so I've had a lot of unexpected time to sort through my mess of a life."

"Oh, dear, I'm so sorry," Ruby said. "I know how much that job meant to you."

"It was my life. And it's sad to admit that." Mari pulled out a folded paper. "I didn't have time to read your letter until after I left the company."

Ruby recognized the stationery she'd bought for Patricia years ago. "You visited the bank?"

"Just recently. Do you know about this letter my mom left?"

Bracing herself, Ruby nodded. "I imagine she shared some information with you."

"I feel...manipulated," Mari said, angrily pushing her hand through her short brown hair. "Mom was always the softie, and then, well, you know how she deteriorated. But why didn't *you* tell me?"

"I couldn't come between you and Patricia," Ruby said as gently as she could. "I had promised her I'd honor her request."

Mari removed the letter from the envelope and handed it to Ruby. "You might as well read it. And then tell me if what I suspect is true."

MY DEAREST MARI,

I take no pleasure in writing this letter to you, but I cannot rest until I do. As you must know by now, I was diagnosed with Alzheimer's. My memory has been fading, and when I think of what lies ahead, it is quite humbling. I vacillate between sadness and fury at this dreadful disease that will rob me of the time I have left. However, if you're reading this, it means I am finally free of it and at peace in heaven.

It also means that Ruby has decided to share our story with you. I have given her this discretion.

You have been my most beloved child, dear Mari, and I cannot imagine what my life would have been like without you. While we haven't always agreed, I admire your drive and courage. After that husband of yours left you with little Ariana, you did what you had to do. Although you and I had our share of arguments, I hope you've never doubted the love I've had for you. From the first moment I saw your sweet little face, you were the child of my heart, loved even more because I could not have children.

Yes, you read that correctly.

You see, I could never carry a child of my own. And yet, I have loved you as if I had. Despite our disagreements, you have shown me your love in countless ways. I want you to know that I forgive every harsh word between us, and I hope you do the same. Let us only recall the good times; there have been so many.

Reading this, you might be angry with me that I have kept this secret for so long. Please forgive me, but it was not only mine to keep.

I am sure your next question will be about the circumstances of your birth. For this, you must speak to my sister. Ruby will answer all your questions because that is her story to tell. She became the star of our family, and I was determined to keep her starlight bright.

Thank you for caring for me all these years, as you must have. I can only imagine what you will have gone through by the time you read this letter. Please know that I am genuinely sorry for this disease that will rob me of precious moments with you. Undoubtedly, I will have been a burden on you, and for this, I ask for your understanding and forgiveness.

I love you always and forever, my darling daughter. And into eternity, I will remain your mother.

Love, Mom

RUBY LOWERED THE LETTER. MARI WAS EFFICIENT; SHE DEALT with facts. Ruby had to be direct with her. "You should get comfortable. It's a long story."

"Don't forget I've come a long way to find out," Mari said, crossing her arms.

"First of all, you are indeed my daughter," Ruby said. "I married when I was seventeen, and you were born when I was barely eighteen. By that time, I'd already worked on three films and had to support the family. Your parents included. There was a drought in Texas that left them penniless."

"And you've accused me of being all about the money," Mari said. "It's hard work supporting a family."

"Yes, it is," Ruby said, deflecting Mari's snide remark. "You've carried that burden a long time."

Mari frowned with annoyance. "So, who was my father?"

"Niccolò Mancini. I met him on a film set in Rome, where he lived. After I returned, a series of events occurred, contact ceased, and I could only assume he was dead. I gave birth to you at your parents' home."

"Prematurely," Mari interjected. "I knew that part. But did this Niccolò know you were pregnant?"

"Back then, times were different. Communication was difficult. I had his address in Rome, but that was all. We didn't think we would be separated very long."

"Why couldn't you keep me?" Mari narrowed her eyes. "Or were you too busy going to glitzy Hollywood parties? I've seen the photos."

"It was never like that." Ruby glared at Mari. "I didn't have a copy of my marriage certificate, so when someone tipped off the press that I had a child, word spread through the media that I had an illegitimate baby. The studio immediately invoked the morals clause in my contract to terminate me. I would have lost my career, but more than that, your parents—and mine—would have lost their homes and their livelihoods. They'd already been struggling. Those were lean drought years on the ranch."

"You just gave me up like that?" Mari snapped her fingers dismissively.

"Not at all," Ruby shot back, anxious to stifle Mari's attitude. "It nearly crushed me."

Mari twisted her lips to one side. "Sorry, it's been a tough week."

"We all have them." Though Ruby had expected Mari's insolence, she'd hoped her daughter would understand. "Everyone was older and more experienced than I was. What they said made a lot of sense. I didn't want to give you up, Mari. In the end, I did it so that you could have a real childhood."

"Still, you just left me on the ranch," Mari said, flinging her hand.

Ruby gripped Mari's hands. "I couldn't take you with me. I made one film after another and many on location. It wasn't as fun or as glamorous as it sounds. But on the ranch, you had a carefree childhood. Remember that horse you loved? Champ. How about the rodeos and your trips to Galveston at that beach house you adored? And your menagerie of pets. You couldn't have had them in an apartment in L.A. And more than that, you wouldn't have had the love of two solid parents."

Subdued, Mari glanced to one side. "I suppose you have a point."

Feeling her blood pressure rise, Ruby blew out a breath. "Patricia and Michael had already been looking after you whenever I had to work. After the studio took steps to terminate me, my agent came up with an idea to salvage my career. He had a vested interest, of course, but my parents quickly agreed and pressured me, too."

"Wait. There's one part I don't understand," Mari said. "I checked my birth certificate, which clearly states that my mom gave birth to me. She and my dad are listed on it."

"That's right," Ruby said. "The studios demanded legal proof that the child I'd been charged with having in the tabloids wasn't mine. Doc Schmidt, a country doctor, delivered you. So, my father and Michael approached him and arranged a deal. I paid the doctor and the local records office clerk to create and back-file a new birth certificate."

"Wow," Mari said. "Guess you could do that before computers?"

Ruby nodded. "When your parents produced that, the studio dropped its case against me, and my agent demanded an apology. Finally, the studio reinstated me, and the near-scandal faded away. But I was devastated. I loved you so much, and you were all I had left of my husband."

Mari stared into her coffee. "I suppose I can understand how you felt," she said quietly. "I couldn't imagine being forced to give up Ariana when she was a baby."

And yet, Mari had effectively given up Ariana to boarding schools. Ruby reined in her thoughts. Mari had been a single parent with a demanding position, reeling from a devastating divorce. She had done the best she could under trying circumstances. And Ruby had been thrilled to help.

"In retrospect, this plan was for the best," Ruby said. "Patricia and Michael loved you so much, and I was too young to be a proper mother. I was even a little jealous of Patricia for a long time. But I grew up and came to terms with it."

Mari bent her head, and Ruby heard a muffled sniffle.

"I understand your position," Mari said. "For years, I beat myself up about my failed marriage. I worked so hard to prove myself. I wasn't good at being a wife, or even a mother, but I could excel in business. And I did. Maybe I'm like you, after all."

Ruby smiled at her. "You and I, we've both made mistakes,

lived with our choices, and grew strong as a result. Ariana is one of us, too. She has the blood of strong women in her."

Mari drew her hands over her face. "These last few weeks, I've had time to think about my mistakes. I should've gone to Ariana's wedding. Worse, I didn't even call her to see how it went. I guess she went on her honeymoon. Of course, after the way I acted, I couldn't expect her to call me. So, how was the wedding?"

"Ariana changed her mind and left Phillip at the altar," Ruby said.

Mari sighed. "I should have been there. Was she shattered?"

"It wasn't easy," Ruby said. "But thankfully, she recognized that Phillip wasn't the one for her."

Mari tapped her fingers on the table. "Better than a divorce later. I should fly to L.A. after I leave here."

"You won't have to." Ruby touched Mari's hand, risking a connection. "Ariana is here. And she has a lot to share with you. All I ask is that you listen without judgment. She's smart, and she's changing her life for the better."

"I'll try," Mari said, her voice cracking. "This is a rough time for me, too."

Tentatively, Ruby put her arm around Mari's shoulders. She hadn't been able to get this close to Mari since she was a teenager. "Just when you think life is all set, it serves up surprises. We're all reimagining our lives right now."

Mari rested her head on Ruby's shoulder. "Change is scary at my age. A woman in her mid-fifties is ancient for Wall Street," she said with a bitter laugh. "Many burn out or become disillusioned, and I've lasted longer than most."

Ruby stroked Mari's short hair. "You probably have plenty of money to retire."

"I'm fortunate, but I'm not ready to retire," Mari said. "If you still want me to take over the management of your charitable foundation and portfolio, as you'd mentioned in your letter, I'd like that."

"I'm quite serious about that," Ruby said. "I'm going to be even busier than I realized now." She gazed at her daughter. For the first time in years, Mari seemed to be examining her life. A fresh surge of hope coursed through Ruby. There was still a chance to change their family dynamics.

Mari looked surprised. "Are you making more films?"

Ruby chuckled. "Oh, my dear, you have so much to catch up on. I know there will be a lot to take in, but I hope you'll allow me to make things up to you." She motioned to the Villa Fiori. "I have plenty of room, and I'd really like it if you could stay awhile. I know Ariana would like that, too."

Footsteps sounded behind them, and Ariana's voice rang out. "Mom? What are you doing here?" Ariana had pulled on a T-shirt and a pair of sweatpants, and her strawberry blond curls tumbled from a haphazard ponytail. Her mouth was set in a thin line—obviously prepared for the worst.

Ruby nodded to Mari. "Now is your chance," she whispered. A chance for Mari and Ariana to reconcile before Ruby shared the rest of her story—the ending of which not even she had dreamed possible.

Mari rose and rushed to meet her daughter. Embracing Ariana, Mari's words tumbled out. "I'm sorry I wasn't there for you at your wedding. That was wrong of me. But I'm so proud of you for knowing what you want—and what you don't."

Unprepared for her mother's uncharacteristic outpouring of support, Ariana's mouth fell open in disbelief. She returned her mother's hug with an awkward motion.

"Join us, Ariana," Ruby said. "We've been having a good talk, haven't we, Mari?"

Mari hooked her arm into Ariana's. "We'll have lots of time to talk. My job in New York is over, so I can stay for a while."

After they sat down, Ruby watched while Mari made an effort to show genuine interest in her daughter. Ariana told her mother about leaving her job at the studio and her plan to open a boutique and create a collection.

"You always wanted to do that," Mari said thoughtfully. "Since you're not a local, will that be difficult here?"

"Alessandro has been helping me with that." Ariana's face bloomed as she told her mother how they'd met and all about Sandro and Carmela.

Ruby could see Mari struggling to remain open-minded, but to her credit, she didn't offer her opinion. She listened, and that was all that Ariana had ever wanted. Ruby pressed her hand against her heart. Seeing them together here was all that she had longed for, but kismet was proving more generous that she'd imagined.

"Alessandro sounds like an interesting man," Mari said, smiling.

Ariana's eyes sparkled. "I'm so relieved that you think so because last night after the play, he asked me to marry him. And I said I would. But maybe not until after the—" Ariana cut herself off. When Ruby nodded for her to continue, Ariana said, "Mom, I'm pregnant. By Phillip, but he's not interested in being a father."

Ruby saw Mari bite back a comment, so she placed her hand on Mari's shoulder. "Alessandro is a fine man."

"And he's Niccolò's nephew," Ariana added, darting a glance at Ruby. "That's a huge coincidence." She turned to her mother. "Mom, did you know Aunt Ruby had been married a long time ago? And he's here."

Mari frowned, and then she swung around to face Ruby. "Niccolò. My birth father?"

"That's right," Ruby replied. "As it just turned out, he wasn't dead."

Ariana's mouth fell open. "Wait a minute. Aunt Ruby, your husband is Mom's dad?"

Ruby took each of them by the hand to fill in the missing parts of the story. After she had finished, both women stared at her in awe.

"I can't imagine what you went through," Mari said. Tears now filled Mari's eyes, and she hugged Ruby. "We've all been given a second chance." Clutching Ariana's hand, Mari added, "And now, I want to help my daughter with her baby, just as my mother—" She paused and smiled at Ruby. "As *both* my mothers did for me."

Ruby's eyes also brimmed with tears of happiness. "I'm happy for you, Mari, that you will have the chance to do that. At this stage in my life, I can tell you that nothing replaces family.

It's been my fervent desire to mend the rifts in this family and set the record straight before I pass on."

Ariana threw her arms around Ruby. "Don't be silly. You're not going anywhere for a long, long time. We need you, Auntie. Now, if you're my grandmother, I can't call you Aunt Ruby anymore, can I?"

Ruby kissed Ariana's cheek. "Why change now? We know who we are."

Clasping Ruby's and Ariana's hands, Mari said, "I want to be a better grandmother than I was a mother. It was tough for me to juggle being a single parent and working in a demanding job. That combination didn't bring out the best in me, and I know I was often insensitive, short-tempered, and distracted. Only when I lost the job I valued the most, did I realize what I should have valued all along."

Ruby's heart burst with love for Mari. She'd prayed that her daughter would realize the shortcomings of her lifestyle before it was too late. "I'm proud of you, Mari. I always have been, but even more right now."

Ruby had longed for this reunion, yet she had never dreamed that it might include Niccolò. Until yesterday, she couldn't have imagined that this revelation would have her introducing Mari to her natural father. With all her heart, Ruby prayed that Niccolò would understand why she had given away their child.

Her restless mind raced ahead, imagining different scenarios. Would Niccolò be angry or hurt and refuse to see her again? How would that impact Alessandro and Ariana? Though Mari and Ariana had accepted her explanation, Niccolò might not, for she had denied him the child and family life that should have been his.

With a prayer on her lips, Ruby squeezed her eyes shut. To lose Niccolò once was devastating; to lose him twice was unimaginable.

33

Lago di Como, 2010

*R*uby gazed at herself in the mirror, recalling how she'd looked the first time she'd met Niccolò. Did he still imagine that shapely, exuberant young woman in his mind's eye, or had she faded into the past? She pulled her shoulders back. Today was all that mattered any more.

"Aunt Ruby," Ariana called out, tapping on Ruby's bedroom door. "Niccolò just arrived for you."

"Thank you, darling. I'll be right down. But please, come in."

Ariana stepped inside Ruby's bedroom.

"What do you think of this outfit?" Ruby asked.

Ruby had changed clothes three times, trying to decide the right outfit to wear with Niccolò today. They were taking the ferry to Varenna. Looking at herself in the mirror, she decided the flowing silk blouse splashed with butterflies, along with a pink skirt, would set a happy tone for the day. And yet...

"It's lovely on you," Ariana said. "Are you nervous?"

Ruby smiled. "A little. It's been a long time."

When Niccolò had called at noon yesterday, she'd been with Mari and Ariana, so she suggested they meet today. Seeing Mari had been such a surprise. Though the reunion had exceeded her expectations, she could manage only one emotional upheaval per day at her age.

Besides that, Ruby needed to talk to Niccolò alone. Depending on how he received her news, this might be the last time she would ever see him.

Ruby sat at her vanity and opened a jewelry box. She held up two sets of earrings. "Pearls or rubies? Pearls light the face, but rubies…"

"Definitely the rubies. And don't worry. You look very nice." Ariana hesitated. "Were you and Niccolò very much in love?"

"Oh, yes. From the first moment we met. Like you and Alessandro." Ruby smiled as she recalled the day. With trembling fingers, she swept her hair back, and then clipped on the ruby earrings.

"And are you still in love with him?" Ariana asked.

Ruby frowned at the question. "It's complicated. I still love the memory of him." She glanced at her perfume bottles, trying to decide which one, if any, she should use.

Ariana perched on a brocade bench at the end of Ruby's bed. "Yesterday, you said you'd explain more. Tell me about when you and Niccolò met and married."

"We met when I was in Rome filming *Roman Holiday*," Ruby said, recalling the first time Niccolò had approached her on the Spanish Steps. "We married on holiday in Varenna, just across the lake. At that little church. You can see the bell tower from the window." Ruby chose a violet perfume made in Parma that she'd worn that summer in Rome. Niccolò had given it to her—not this bottle, of course—but one like it.

Ariana stood to look outside at the tower across the lake. "So, how long were you married?"

"We were only together in the summer of 1952."

Ariana's eyes widened. "If you thought he was dead, does that mean you're still married?"

"Yes, I believe that's how it works."

"Oh, wow." Ariana twisted her hair as she spoke. "But why did you separate?"

"Sadly, it wasn't by our choice," Ruby said. "I had an aunt,

Vivienne, who was my mother's sister. She was duplicitous, and she came between us."

"Why would she do that to you?"

Ruby sighed. "I suppose it was jealousy and just plain meanness. Unfortunately, Niccolò and I didn't know it at the time. We were so young that we believed what people we trusted told us. We just pieced together what happened."

"That's shocking," Ariana said, fussing with her curly hair.

"While I was waiting for him in Hollywood, we exchanged letters," Ruby said, dabbing perfume on her wrists. "But those were intercepted."

Ruby recalled how Vivienne would offer to mail her letters. The apartment building had locking mailboxes, and her aunt kept the only key. "When Niccolò came to Los Angeles, Aunt Vivienne told him I was no longer interested in him. Now we believe she stole our letters. I was shooting a film at the time, so I had no idea."

As she spoke, Ruby tried to clasp a necklace, but her fingers were trembling. "I must wear this today. Can you help me?"

Ariana crossed to the vanity and fastened the silver necklace with ease. She gazed at Ruby in the mirror. "This looks old. Did Niccolò give you this pendant?"

"No, but it has great meaning to me," Ruby said. "Audrey Hepburn gave it to me one day on the film set. A little while later, Niccolò and I were married with it." She nestled the cherished pendant in the neckline of her blouse. "We married on a whim. You see, it's half of a heart, and he kept the other half."

Ariana placed her hands over Ruby's shoulders. "Have you always loved him?"

Ruby touched Ariana's hand. "Yes, I have. Niccolò is a good man. And so is his nephew, I think."

"I can hardly believe Alessandro and Niccolò are related," Ariana said.

Ruby smiled. "That's some sort of divine destiny, I think. Would you bring me the taupe flats from my closet?"

"Sure." Ariana disappeared into the closet before returning with a pair of shoes. "What do you think you'll do about Niccolò now?"

Ruby slid her feet into the comfortable flats and stood. She had never imagined that Niccolò might reappear. When she was younger, she'd handled his absence by working incessantly and occupying her mind. And now, here he was. Yet how he would receive the news about Mari remained to be seen. "We'll wait and see. Now, I shouldn't keep Niccolò waiting any longer."

Niccolò greeted her with a bouquet of white roses that Livia put in a vase and promised to put in her bedroom. In the light of day, Ruby thought he looked even more handsome. After Niccolò and Ariana chatted for a few minutes, Niccolò suggested that he and Ruby catch the next ferry to Varenna, just as they had years ago. Ariana saw them off, and Ruby could tell that she was thrilled for her. Ruby kissed her on the cheeks as they left.

As they stepped onto the ferry boat, Niccolò grinned. "We did this on our wedding day. Do you recall?"

"I haven't forgotten a thing. Even that pot of red geraniums on the stage the other night. At the Palazzo Colonna, you plucked a flower and tucked it behind your ear."

He threw his head back and laughed. "Only you knew the story behind that."

Ruby leaned against the ferry railing next to Niccolò, enjoying the crisp lake breeze on her sun-warmed face. The past and present were fitting together like parts of a lost puzzle. They held hands, with Ruby's slender fingers resting in Niccolò's large, weathered hand that felt so secure, yet still sent thrills through her. More than anything, she'd missed having a deep connection with him.

As they drew closer to Varenna, the stone bell tower of Chiesa di San Giorgio came into view, and Niccolò kissed her forehead. Lightly, with respect.

"I remember that perfume you're wearing," he said. "It's Violetta di Parma."

Ruby smiled, touched that he'd recalled that small detail. "You gave me a little bottle in Rome." They made their way to the line of people queued to get off in Varenna.

"Do you remember walking this way?" Niccolò asked as they disembarked.

Ruby rested her hand on his proffered hand and stepped off

the boat, her white silk skirt printed with butterflies fluttering in the breeze. "I fixed every detail in my mind. I even found the café in Bellagio where we had our wedding dinner. It's still operating."

Niccolò's brow shot up. "Do you know Lorenzo Pagani?"

"Why, yes," Ruby said, surprised that Niccolò knew him, too. "I saw the flyer for your show in the window there. And Ariana just leased the space next door for a boutique."

"You see, we were destined to meet again," Niccolò said, placing a hand over his heart. "And Alessandro is very much in love with Ariana. While they haven't known each other very long, sometimes you just know it's right."

Ruby smiled up at him. "We were proof of that. If we'd remained together, do you think we would have lasted?"

"Let's say yes." Niccolò's eyes still twinkled with laughter, and his voice had aged to a golden baritone. "If I met you today for the first time, I'd still fall in love with you."

"I think I might, too," she said softly. She tucked her arm in the crook of his elbow, and they set off on cobblestone streets toward the church.

As they walked, the years fell away. Time had been kind to him. Sunshine glinted off his silver hair, and the lines in his face were products of happiness rather than worry. They wound slowly through the streets, bringing each other up to date on their lives. Niccolò congratulated her on her films and career, and she asked him about his family.

"My parents, of course, have long been gone." Niccolò shook his head. "I will never forget that night we told them we were married. How many times I have replayed that in mind, wishing we had never told them and fled for America instead."

"That wouldn't have been the right thing to do, either," Ruby said. As they talked about it, the distance of time blurred the hurtful edges, and Ruby understood his parents' fear of losing their eldest son.

"Have you lived a happy life?" she asked, wanting to know more about the man who walked beside her now.

"Not as happy as it would have been with you," Niccolò replied. "I feared you'd quickly outgrown me. I watched you from afar and wondered what I could offer you after you'd grown accustomed to meeting princes and dignitaries."

"I hope you grew out of that," Ruby said, reaching for his hand.

Niccolò nodded. "While that boy of eighteen is still within me, the wiser man now prevails. He knows that true love has no valuation, no measurement, no comparison. There is only love." He brought her hand to his and kissed it.

Niccolò told her more about what he had done with his life, from caring for the vineyards to nurturing young actors, writers, and directors in his theatre program. "My life is rich and rewarding, but there is still room for you."

Ruby squeezed his hand. The spirited, youthful man Ruby had known was still there, though now she appreciated his wisdom and maturity even more. While she listened to Niccolò speak, Ruby's heart grew with a new, more profound love.

They climbed the broad stone steps where moss and daisies had encroached, stopping in front of the old gray stone church's wooden door, which was open. The stone tower with a belfry and a clock marking time rose above them. Niccolò lifted a chain that he wore around his neck. "Remember this?"

"The other half of my heart," Ruby said, struck by the simple pendant.

"And you're still wearing yours, too." With glistening eyes, Niccolò kissed her softly. "Shall we go inside?"

Ruby slipped her hand into his, and they stepped inside the 14th-century basilica, blinking to adjust to the dimmer light. The sweet aroma of incense hung in the air, suffusing the atmosphere with the same scent Ruby recalled from years ago.

"It's just as I remember." Ruby admired the black marble underfoot and the rose stained-glass window high above that cast a kaleidoscope of colors into the church. The baroque altar and the polyptych of Saint George remained, as did other important frescoes. Above the nave and aisles rose circular bricked columns and high arches, which brought lightness to the dark interior.

"I appreciate this so much more now," Niccolò said. "Sometimes on summer evenings, orchestras play outside, and people sit under the stars to listen. I'd love to do that with you."

Ruby nodded. "Have you been back here since our wedding day?"

"Many times," Niccolò replied, his voice suddenly husky. "On our anniversary. Which is coming up soon, if you recall."

"How could I ever forget that day in August?" She'd had a ritual of her own over the years, but she'd love to come here on their anniversary. After that, they could go to Lorenzo's café, just as they had on that magical day. As long as Niccolò could understand her dilemma of all those years ago.

"Maybe this year we could renew our vows," Niccolò suggested with more than a hint of hope in his voice.

"Perhaps we will." Ruby looked up into his earnest eyes, and her heart quickened. This was the man she had pledged herself to so long ago. Though many years had passed and they'd both lived full lives in the interim, their spark of love had not dimmed. Ruby was as attracted to him as she had ever been. She prayed that he would still want her after what she had to tell him.

"Would you like to go back to the villa where we stayed?" Niccolò asked.

"You still have access to it?" Ruby was surprised that he would after all this time.

"One of my cousins lives in it now with her family. I rang her and asked if we could visit. She's going to be out, but she promised to leave the key for us."

"I'd love that."

Hand in hand, they walked along the same pink oleander-lined lane, albeit a little slower now. When they reached the stone villa on the hill, Ruby smiled. "They still have white roses."

"Those might even be the same bushes that I picked flowers from for your wedding bouquet."

"They're my favorites." Ruby paused to smell them while Niccolò opened the door. The old-fashioned, creamy white roses were just as heavenly as they had been on their wedding day.

Inside, Ruby saw the kitchen had been renovated. In the refrigerator, Niccolò's cousin had left a pitcher of lemonade for them, along with a bottle of chilled prosecco. She'd also left an assortment of nuts, olives, cheeses, and bread.

"Your choice," he said, opening the pantry for glassware.

Ruby touched his hand. "We're celebrating. I'll have the bubbles." She also needed to calm her jittery nerves.

"I'll join you." He poured two glasses for them. "To us, once again," he said, touching her glass.

As they sipped the sparkling wine, he took her on a tour of the house, pausing in the doorway of the bedroom where they had slept and made love so many years ago.

Leaning against the doorjamb, Ruby let out a sigh. Here is where their daughter was possibly conceived—and so beautifully. Tears misted her eyes, and she turned into Niccolò's waiting embrace.

"*Quanto ti amo*, my dear Ruby." Niccolò nuzzled her neck. "Ah, *cuore mio*. Such sweet hours we spent here. I remember it all."

Ruby held Niccolò so tightly, until finally, he said, "Shall we go outside and sit under the pergola?"

"I'd...like that," Ruby said, so overcome with emotion that she could hardly speak.

They stopped in the kitchen to refill their glasses. Niccolò brought the tray that his cousin had left for them.

As they wound their way outside, they walked under the purple wisteria-laden archway and passed the orchard that still bore figs, pomegranates, chestnuts, and olives. Other trees were heavy with lemons and grapefruit. On the way, Niccolò plucked a couple of ripe mandarin oranges.

Climbing roses still covered the pergola, shading the chairs under it from the midday sun and filling the air with their heady aroma. Orioles chirped nearby, and other birds joined in, serenading them with the sweetest of songs. Niccolò placed the *antipasti* assortment on a bistro table and pulled two chairs together to face the lake.

As Niccolò nibbled, Ruby sipped her prosecco. With the breeze in her hair, she regained her control. "This is even more romantic than I'd recalled."

"And you are even lovelier," Niccolò said, taking her hand. "After seeing you again the other night, I could hardly sleep. My deepest desire had come true, and you were once again in my arms, your kiss warm on my lips. Why then, *cuore mio*, are you sad? We should rejoice, for I am alive again," he said with a little laugh.

The time had come. Ruby put her glass down and turned to him, gripping his hands. "My dearest Niccolò, we were robbed of the life together that we deserved. Of the family we should have had and looked after—together."

"Since we cannot change the past, let's not regret what might have been," Niccolò said. "Our extended families make up for it. Our nieces and nephews are young and healthy. And who could have imagined that Alessandro and Ariana would have found each other? That makes my heart so glad."

Pausing, Ruby gathered every scrap of courage she possessed and steeled herself against his potential anger. She wouldn't blame him for turning away from her now. If only she had known he still lived.

Niccolò slid his arm around her. "Ruby, *amore mio*, please share what's on your mind."

There was simply no other way to tell him, except to be direct.

"You told me you stopped receiving my letters, which I believe," Ruby said. "But in one of those letters, I wrote to tell you that I was pregnant."

Niccolò's lips parted. "Did we have...a child?"

Ruby spoke as gently as she could. "We do, but she was unaware that we were her parents."

"You mean, you gave her away?" Niccolò's face contorted with confusion.

"I am so sorry, but I had to." Tears spilled onto Ruby's cheeks, but she pushed through her grief to tell Niccolò everything as he listened quietly. "My sister's only request was that our daughter not know anything about this."

As she finished, he lowered his head. "I hardly know what to say."

She clutched his hand.

Finally, Niccolò wiped tears from his eyes. "We have a daughter...imagine! Tell me all about her. Does she look like you?"

Ruby choked with relief at his reaction. "A little, but she has your bright blue eyes. Her name is Mariangela."

"I've always loved that name," he said, pressing a hand against his chest.

"You told me that when you took me to the opera. *Aida.* You said Maria Pedrini had the voice of an angel, and if you ever had a daughter—"

"I would name her Mariangela," he finished, clearly awestruck.

Ruby squeezed his hands. "She goes by Mari. And she just arrived here yesterday."

"She is here?" Niccolò's face clouded with concern. "Do you think she would like to meet me?"

"I know she would," Ruby said.

Niccolò exhaled, and a look of awe-filled gratitude filled his face.

Ruby stroked his hands. Every muscle in her body was sore from the tension she'd held, but now Niccolò's acceptance was sweeping away her pain.

"How I wish I had known," Niccolò said, his voice cracking with emotion.

"There's more," Ruby said. "And this is the part that will surprise you. Mari's daughter is Ariana, who is actually my granddaughter. And yours."

Tears sprang to Niccolò's eyes, and he wrapped her in an embrace. "You have made me the happiest man on earth, *amore mio.* Imagine, Alessandro and Ariana are destined to be together. Just like us."

"I stayed up late thinking about it," Ruby said, once again relieved at his reaction. "And worrying a little. Our relationship makes Ariana and Alessandro first cousins once-removed."

Niccolò kissed her on the cheek. "No need for concern. Valeria and her husband adopted Alessandro and his sister Paolina when they were very young. Their parents died in an accident. It was a double tragedy because they were distant cousins and close friends."

They sat and chatted about their family, with Ruby telling Niccolò all about Mari and Ariana, and Niccolò sharing more about Alessandro. By sunset, Ruby was even more convinced that Ariana and Alessandro were perfect for each other.

Ruby laughed. "You have no idea the effort it took to bring Mari and Ariana together. I thought, if that's my last act on earth, I wanted to make it count."

"*Ah, cuore mio, no, no, no.* The best time of our lives is just beginning." He smoothed his hand over her hers.

Smiling through her tears of joy, Ruby entwined her fingers with his. "I believe that, too. As it turns out, I'm healthy as a woman half my age, and just as ornery. So, yes, my love, the best is here now—with much more to come."

Niccolò swept a hand over her hair and touched his lips to hers. "We're back where we began, in the honeymoon of our marriage. That is, if you still want me."

"I've never stopped." Ruby framed Niccolò's face with her hands. This was the man she had loved all her life. The memories she'd cherished were coming to life again. And there would be so many more. "Here's to life—on our terms, this time."

EPILOGUE

Lago di Como, 2010

*R*uby held Niccolò's hand as they stood before the baroque altar. Next to them were Ariana and Alessandro, and in the audience were their family and friends. Stefano, who'd flown in from Palm Springs, Paolina and her husband and children, Niccolò's sister Valeria and his cousin and other family members. Lorenzo from the café, who was also catering the celebration party and dinner. Vera, the concierge, and her sister Gia who'd first introduced Ariana and Alessandro. Matteo, Livia, and Emilio. And so many others they'd befriended.

A priest stood before them. "I have performed double wedding ceremonies for twins, but I have never performed a marriage and a recommitment ceremony for grandparents and a granddaughter. This is truly a family event."

"Well, get on with it," Niccolò said. "Before Ruby disappears from my life again. I can't wait as long as I did before."

Laughing softly, Ruby nudged him. "I could say the same thing."

For the ceremony, Ariana had designed an aquamarine dress for her that was simple yet stunning. At Ruby's neck was the silver heart necklace that Audrey had given her, but now the two separate pieces were joined together, reunited with love.

Next to Ruby stood Niccolò, who looked so handsome in a white summer jacket with a creamy-white rose in his lapel. His cousin had also surprised Ruby with a bouquet of white roses and glossy, green ferns from the garden, just as she had carried on their wedding day.

On the other side of Ruby stood Mari, beaming at her birth parents. With her daughter and husband beside her, Ruby could easily see their remarkable resemblance. As soon as Mari and Niccolò met, they had bonded like two old friends. They had more in common than Ruby would have thought. As it turned out, Niccolò was a brilliant businessman, managing the vineyard and the theater. He and Mari connected quickly in the realm of finance.

Ruby felt so blessed to have her family reunited at last.

Also standing at the altar were Ariana and Alessandro. Their granddaughter wore a dress she had designed—a loosely flowing, pale-pink silk dress with a matching lace jacket. The soft colors accentuated her strawberry blond curls swept into a cascade down her back. At seven months, Ariana's baby bump was more pronounced, but she bore her pregnancy with grace, given her height and slender build.

"And now, Ruby Raines and Niccolò Mancini," the priest began. For their recommitment ceremony, he spoke of the durability of love, the resilience of the human spirit, and their love for their families.

Before the priest finished, Ruby was blinking back tears.

"*Amore mio*," Niccolò whispered, bringing a white cotton handkerchief from his pocket for her.

Ruby beamed at him. His brilliant blue eyes, brimming with love for her, overshadowed the years etched on his face.

Ruby and Niccolò committed to their vows once again, and then Niccolò slid onto her finger a slim, diamond-and-platinum band that cradled a blazing ruby stone. Ariana had helped them design the ring, along with a wide band for Niccolò that also held a single ruby stone. Sunlight from the rose window above glinted off the gemstones, casting a warm glow of color across their joined hands.

As they sealed their future with a kiss, a flurry of applause rose from the pews. With a heart full of love, Ruby laughed. "I'm glad our families approve this time."

"That only took a few decades," Niccolò said, squeezing her hand.

The priest turned to Ariana and Alessandro to perform the Sacrament of Matrimony. In the first pew, young Sandro and Carmela sat in rapt attention next to Paolina and her husband and children.

Before Ariana and Alessandro joined hands, she handed her bouquet of white roses and hydrangeas wrapped with trailing ivy to Carmela, who immediately stuck her nose deep into the flowers and said, "Che belli!"

Everyone chuckled, and the rest of the ceremony proceeded in such a lovely manner that Ruby continued dabbing her eyes with Niccolò's handkerchief.

Afterward, as they emerged from the church, the bells of Chiesa di San Giorgio clanged in honor of their joyful celebration. Niccolò kissed her cheek as Ariana and Alessandro walked ahead of them.

"What a beautiful couple," Ruby said, watching them, "Your nephew is so handsome."

"As good-looking as I was?" Niccolò asked.

Ruby nudged him. "Now you're just angling for compliments."

Ariana and Alessandro turned to embrace them. "Aunt Ruby, I can't thank you enough for insisting I come to Italy with you," Ariana said. "This trip changed my life."

Ruby pressed her cheek against Ariana's. "You were the one who took the chance, sweetheart. And now, just look at the life you've created."

Ariana smiled up at Alessandro before turning back to Ruby. "When I discovered you'd purchased an Italian villa on your holiday, I have to admit that I thought you'd been too extravagant."

"For some reason, I felt drawn here," Ruby said, squeezing Niccolò's hand. "Though we'll visit Palm Springs soon." Ruby and Niccolò had decided to spend a few winter months in Palm Springs before Teatro Della Vigna opened for the summer season. Although this year, they would wait until after Ariana had the baby. Ariana was having a girl, and she and Alessandro were still deciding on names.

Besides planning the wedding with Mari—whose organizational skills were put to good use—Ariana had been working hard on her first collection. The boutique would open after they returned from their honeymoon, which they planned to spend sailing along the Italian coast for two weeks, while Paolina and her husband looked after the children. Although Ariana's pregnancy seemed perfectly normal, she and Alessandro didn't want to venture too far, just in case. Mari seemed eager to help at the boutique, too.

Niccolò and Alessandro embraced as they congratulated one another, and then everyone made their way to the dock, where a fleet of boats waited to take everyone across the lake to Villa Fiori.

Ruby and Niccolò joined Ariana and Alessandro on his restored Riva yacht. They sped across the sun-dappled lake toward Bellagio and Villa Fiori with the breeze in their hair and the mist on their faces.

"What a grand day we're having," Ruby said, laughing and flinging her arms out. Inside, she still felt like that girl of seventeen, seeing the treasures of Lago di Como for the first time.

Chuckling, Niccolò wrapped his arms around her. "Won't let you escape this time."

"I hope we'll be just like you two someday," Alessandro said. "Full of life forever."

As they and their guests disembarked at Villa Fiori, the musicians that Ruby had hired began to play. Soon, music soared across the water, the champagne flowed, and everyone gathered to feast on the delicacies that Lorenzo had prepared for the wedding party. Tables filled the terrace on this autumn afternoon, although heat lamps were standing by to chase the evening chill. People began to fill the dance floor. Everyone was having a wonderful time.

Leaving Niccolò, Alessandro, and Ariana at a table, Ruby

strolled toward the kitchen with Mari to check on Lorenzo, who had a team of servers circulating with hors d'oeuvres. "I want you to know you're doing a fine job with the portfolio, Mari."

"With a calmer life, I have a clear mind for investing," Mari said. "I enjoyed overseeing the wedding arrangements for Ariana, too. I never thought I'd say that, but it's been fun. Lorenzo has been an enormous help, too. That man can certainly cook."

"And Ariana has loved having you here," Ruby said. Her daughter had gained a little weight and looked much happier, and she and Ariana were getting along very well.

As they walked into the kitchen, Lorenzo looked up from the stove, where he was preparing a sauce that smelled heavenly. Leaving the simmering concoction to an assistant, he hurried to them, holding his arms out wide. He looked handsome in a white chef's jacket, and he was clearly in his element.

"Congratulations," Lorenzo said, bestowing kisses on Ruby's cheeks. Turning to Mari, he did the same, although Ruby noticed that he held her gaze a little longer.

"Working on the planning with Lorenzo has been wonderful," Mari said, her eyes shining brightly.

"It was your suggestions that made all the difference," Lorenzo said. "I have a new salad that I made just the way you like. Maybe you could come by and try it before I add it to the menu?"

"I'd like that very much," Mari said, returning his smile. "How's tomorrow?"

"*Perfetto*," he said with a wide smile.

Ruby glanced from Mari to Lorenzo, suddenly realizing that a strong undercurrent of attraction hummed between them. *And why not?* Ruby thought. Lorenzo might be a few years younger than Mari, but she was quite youthful for her age.

Lorenzo was bursting with happiness. He turned back to Ruby. "I feel like I had a small, but important part in reuniting you with Niccolò," he said. "We have been great friends for many years. He was my first regular customer at the café, and brought so many of his friends."

Ruby smiled and took his hand. "If you hadn't posted that

flyer about the *Roman Holiday* production at Teatro Della Vigna, Niccolò and I might have never reconnected."

Just then, Ariana joined them. "I suddenly realized I'm famished. Guess that eating-for-two adage is true."

"Allow me," Lorenzo said, quickly compiling a special plate for her. "So many of my customers are waiting for you to open your boutique."

"I think we should have a grand opening party," Ariana said. "Lorenzo, would you cater the opening? It certainly wouldn't be far to walk."

"Of course," he said. "If you like, I can work on the details with your mother. She's very organized," he added. "Not like me."

Ariana turned to Mari. "Would you, Mom? That would be such a great help."

"I'd be happy to, honey." Mari hugged Ariana. "And I can't wait until your little one joins this crazy family."

Ariana reached out to Ruby. "Life is so strange. Remember that day that I found the envelopes postmarked Rome, Italy tucked in the box with your old photo albums?"

"Indeed, I do," Ruby said. The envelopes were still there, but the letters had fallen apart after years of re-reading them, even though she'd memorized every word.

"I couldn't have imagined that within the year, I would be married in Italy. That was more than coincidence." Ariana flung her arms around her grandmother. "You're like a fairy godmother, wielding a magical wand."

"Coincidence or kismet?" Ruby laughed. "Life is full of magic—if we only take time to see it."

Later that evening, after dinner and dancing had stretched beyond midnight, Ruby and Niccolò stood by the railing gazing over the lake. He wrapped his arms around her, just as he had so many years ago.

"Are you as happy as I am, *mio tesoro*?" Niccolò's rich, melodic voice was a soothing balm to her soul.

"Blissful." Ruby brushed her lips against his with a feathery touch that sent thrills of joy through her. While Ariana and Alessandro had a romantic suite reserved at Vera's lovely hotel tonight, Ruby and Niccolò would sleep at Villa Fiori. Ruby wanted to wake with Niccolò in her arms in their new home.

Niccolò returned her kiss, lingering on her lips. "Ready for our second honeymoon?"

As Niccolò's face glowed with anticipation, Ruby smiled. She had suggested that they tour the lake region. "Though I've treasured our first honeymoon, it's time to make new memories." She smoothed her hand over his crisp white dress shirt, feeling the warmth of his heart beating strong beneath it. "Yet, when I'm with you, those young lovers of long ago are still with us."

Niccolò covered her hand with his. "Inside, I'm a young man forever besotted with you. In my eyes, you will always be that enchanting young woman—who is even more beautiful today."

Ruby had asked Niccolò to show her the areas of Lago di Como that he loved. They planned to take his yacht around the lake in a leisurely fashion for a couple of weeks. Along the way, they would visit the quaint *comunes* from the southern branches of Como and Lecco to the lake's northern tip. They would call in to see friends and family, dine at his favorite restaurants, and explore historic villas.

"When we return, I'll move more of my belongings to Villa Fiori," Niccolò said. "And you may put as much as you want at the farmhouse."

"I'd like that," Ruby said. They'd decided to divide their time between their residences. Niccolò needed to be close enough to tend the vines, but they both loved the restaurants and social life in Bellagio. The coldest months they would spend in the sunshine of Palm Springs. It would be a perfect life for them, one they'd worked hard to achieve.

Humming softly, Niccolò swayed with the music. "I've been thinking about the farmhouse and theatre. It seems a shame for it to go to waste when we're not there. What do you think about using it for an artist-in-residence program for writers, actors, and directors to develop and stage new projects? Everyone would be excited to meet you, *mio tesoro.*"

Ruby smiled up at him. "Oh, darling, what a marvelous idea. We have so much experience to share." She imagined the fun they would have throwing their energy into new productions.

Upbeat music swept across the party, and Ruby glanced behind them as their family and friends filled the dance area, laughing and twirling to a popular tune. Seeing happiness on their faces was a gift beyond measure.

"Look at this miracle," she said, as deep joy bloomed within her. "It still amazes me that my path led back to you—and a second chance at life. If only I had come here sooner."

"Let's not think of what might have been, but what can be." Niccolò's eyes sparkled in the moonlight. "I've also been thinking about a new play. There's a part that's perfect for you—if you'd like to consider it."

"Always for you, *amore mio*," Ruby said happily. "Always and forever."

THE END

AUTHOR'S NOTE

Thank you for reading *Hepburn's Necklace*, and I hope you enjoyed the story of Ruby and Niccolò. You might also enjoy more of my 1950s historical sagas, such as *The Chocolatier*, which is set on the sunny coast of Amalfi, Italy. Or *The Winemakers*, which follows a winemaking family and will whisk you from Napa Valley vineyards to rolling Tuscan hillsides. And for a riveting WWII saga, look for *The Perfumer: Scent of Triumph*, a heartrending story of a French perfumer who seeks to reunite her family.

If you enjoy contemporary women's fiction, I invite you to the coast of Southern California to meet art teacher Ivy Bay and her sister Shelly as they renovate a historic beach house in *Seabreeze Inn*, the first in my Summer Beach series.

To keep up with new releases, please join my Reader's Club at www.JanMoran.com to receive news about special deals and other books. And as always, I wish you happy reading.

AFTERWORD

In *Hepburn's Necklace*, I sought to bring to life the summer of 1952 and the filming of *Roman Holiday* in Rome. Research on people involved in the filmmaking unearthed numerous written accounts and televised interviews, which provided many details incorporated into the story. It has been my privilege to imagine Ruby and Niccolò meeting and working on *Roman Holiday*.

As to scenes that included the film's stars—Audrey Hepburn, Gregory Peck, and Eddie Arnold, along with director William Wyler and costume designer Edith Head—the actions and conversations in these passages are fictional. The story is meant to celebrate collective efforts on a film loved by fans around the world.

On a personal note, I have long admired Audrey Hepburn for her grace, kindness, and strength of character. It is my pleasure to offer a heartfelt homage to a lovely woman who shall be long remembered by her devoted family, friends, and admirers.

To my readers, thank you for joining me on this fictional journey, and I hope you enjoyed it as I did.

DISCUSSION QUESTIONS

1. *Hepburn's Necklace* examines the theme of family secrets. Are you aware of any secrets in your family? If revealed, how did the new information affect family dynamics and relationships?

2. Although Ruby could afford far more expensive jewelry, she cherished the vintage necklace. Do you have any pieces of jewelry or other mementos that have significance to you?

3. Before the invention of email and mobile phones, the lack of instant communication often impeded relationships. In *Hepburn's Necklace*, Ruby treasured written communication and carefully composed a critical letter to her daughter Mari. Have you kept any old letters or cards? Do you write letters or send cards to friends and family? Why or why not?

4. While the deception of the birth certificate was to Ruby's initial benefit, do you think Ruby's sister Patricia was justified in concealing this information from Mari and Ariana in later years? Why or why not?

5. If Mari had been interested in researching her ancestors, a DNA test might have revealed that Patricia was indirectly related. Have you ever taken a DNA test to determine ancestral lineage,

or would you have trepidation? What would you do if results were not as expected?

6. Throughout history, pregnancy was often a cause for employment termination, but in Hollywood, it could potentially decimate a career, as Ruby experienced. Yet decades later, Ariana still encountered disparaging attitudes in the workplace regarding pregnancy. Despite protective employment laws in many countries, have you ever experienced or witnessed similar situations? What did you or would you do?

7. Ruby employed her acting skills and strong work ethic as defense mechanisms to overcome painful episodes and forge on with life. Yet she clung to cherished memories, reliving them as comfort. Ultimately, do you think her approach was beneficial or detrimental? In what way?

8. *Hepburn's Necklace* included many historical and industry details the author researched. Did you learn anything new about silk manufacturing, locales, Hollywood practices, or other interesting points?

9. Regarding the settings in the novel, what were your impressions about the chosen locations? Have you ever visited Rome, Lake Como, Hollywood, or Texas?

10. The inciting incident in *Hepburn's Necklace* is when Ruby and Niccolò meet at the *Roman Holiday* on-location filming. Have you seen the movie? If so, what are your favorite scenes?

ACKNOWLEDGMENTS

Bringing a novel to readers requires a dedicated behind-the-scenes team. My greatest appreciation goes to Kerstin Schaub, my extraordinarily talented editor at Goldmann Verlag, who not only guided *Hepburn's Necklace* but also *The Chocolatier (Die Chocolatière)* to publication. Special thanks to my literary agent Bastian Schlück in Germany, and heartfelt gratitude to my German translator, Stefanie Retterbush.

As always, heaps of gratitude to my family, Eric and Ginna Moran and young Zoë. To my friend Pamela Tinsley, who provided a beautiful, quiet writing refuge with a lovely pool and an expansive view. Staying in her home helped me complete *Hepburn's Necklace* during the chaotic months of the 2020 pandemic and quarantine.

And to my readers, with whom I love to share stories of challenges, hope, resilience, and triumph. Thank you for welcoming my characters into your heart. Readers and writers—how lucky we are to share our love of reading, especially during difficult times. I am grateful for such work and diversions, and I look forward to sharing many more stories with you.

Jan Moran
Los Angeles, California

ABOUT THE AUTHOR

Jan Moran is a *USA Today* bestselling author of stylish, uplifting, and emotionally rich contemporary and 20th-century historical women's fiction.

A few of her favorite things include a fine cup of coffee, dark chocolate, fresh flowers, laughter, and music that touches her soul. An avid traveler, Jan draws inspiration from locales steeped in history. She lives near the beach in southern California and is originally from Austin, Texas.

Most of her books are available as audiobooks, and her historical fiction is widely translated into German, Italian, Polish, Dutch, Turkish, Russian, Bulgarian, Romanian, Portuguese, and Lithuanian, among other languages.

If you enjoyed this book, please consider leaving a brief review online for your fellow readers where you purchased this book, or on Bookbub or Goodreads.

To read Jan's other historical and contemporary novels, visit www.JanMoran.com.

Made in the USA
Columbia, SC
09 February 2021